Praise for the novels of
#1 *New York Times* bestselling author

SUSAN WIGGS

"Wiggs is one of our best observers of stories
of the heart. Maybe that is because she knows how to
capture emotion on virtually every page of every book."
—*Salem Statesman-Journal*

"Susan Wiggs is a rare talent!
Boisterous, passionate, exciting! The characters
leap off the page and into your heart!"
—*Literary Times*

"[A] lovely, moving novel with
an engaging heroine… Readers who like Nora Roberts
and Susan Elizabeth Phillips will enjoy Wiggs's latest.
Highly recommended."
—*Library Journal* on *Just Breathe* [starred review]

"Tender and heartbreaking…a beautiful novel."
—Luanne Rice on *Just Breathe*

"Another excellent title [in]
her already outstanding body of work."
—*Booklist* on *Table for Five* [starred review]

"With the ease of a master, Wiggs introduces
complicated, flesh-and-blood characters into her idyllic
but identifiable small-town setting."
—*Publishers Weekly* on *The Winter Lodge*
[starred review, a *PW* Best Book of 2007]

SUSAN WIGGS

AT THE QUEEN'S SUMMONS
❀THE TUDOR ROSE TRILOGY❀

BOOK THREE

MIRA®

ISBN-13: 978-0-7783-2688-5

AT THE QUEEN'S SUMMONS

Copyright © 2009 by Susan Wiggs.

Updated from original publication DANCING ON AIR
Published by HarperCollins 1996.

www.MIRABooks.com

Printed in U.S.A.

Dedicated with love to my friend,
mentor and fellow writer,
Betty Traylor Gyenes.

ACKNOWLEDGMENTS

Special thanks to:

Barbara Dawson Smith, Betty Traylor Gyenes and Joyce Bell, for providing all the generous hours of critique and support

The many members of the GEnie® Romance Exchange, an electronic bulletin board of scholars, fools, dreamers and wisewomen

The Bord Failte of County Kerry, Ireland

And the sublime Trish Jensen for her eagle-eyed proofreading skills.

Now is this golden crown like a deep well
That owes two buckets filling one another;
The emptier ever dancing in the air,
The other down, unseen and full of water:
That bucket down and full of tears am I,
Drinking my griefs, whilst you mount up on high.

—William Shakespeare
King Richard II, Act IV, Scene i

Part One

Now is this golden crown like a deep well
That owes two buckets filling one another;
The emptier ever dancing in the air,
The other down, unseen and full of water;
That bucket down and full of tears am I,
Drinking my griefs, whilst you mount up on high.
—William Shakespeare
Richard II (IV, i, 184)

From the Annals of Innisfallen

In accordance with ancient and honorable tradition, I, Revelin of Innisfallen, take pen in hand to relate the noble and right valiant histories of the clan O Donoghue. This task has been done by my uncle and his uncle before him, since time no man can remember.

Canons we are, of the most holy Order of St. Augustine, and by the grace of God our home is the beech-wooded lake isle called Innisfallen.

Those before me filled these pages with tales of fabled heroes, mighty battles, cattle raids and perilous adventures. Now the role of the O Donoghue Mór has fallen to Aidan, and my work is to chronicle his exploits.

But—may the high King of Heaven forgive my clumsy pen—I know not where to begin. For Aidan O Donoghue is like no man I have ever known, and never has a chieftain been faced with such a challenge.

The O Donoghue Mór, known to the English as Lord of Castleross, has been summoned to London by the she-king who claims the right to rule us. I wonder, with shameful, un-Christian relish, after clapping eyes on Aidan O Donoghue and his entourage, if Her Sassenach Majesty will come to regret the summons.

—Revelin of Innisfallen

One

"How many noblemen does it take to light a candle?" asked a laughing voice.

Aidan O Donoghue lifted a hand to halt his escort. The English voice intrigued him. In the crowded London street behind him, his personal guard of a hundred gallowglass instantly stopped their purposeful march.

"How many?" someone yelled.

"Three!" came the shout from the center of St. Paul's churchyard.

Aidan nudged his horse forward into the area around the great church. A sea of booksellers, paupers, tricksters, merchants and rogues seethed around him. He could see the speaker now, just barely, a little lightning bolt of mad energy on the church steps.

"One to call a servant to pour the sack—" she reeled in mock drunkenness "—one to beat the servant senseless, one to botch the job and one to blame it on the French."

Her listeners hooted in derision. Then a man yelled, "That's four, wench!"

Aidan flexed his legs to stand in the stirrups. *Stirrups*.

Until a fortnight ago, he had never even used such a device, or a curbed bit, either. Perhaps, after all, there was some use in this visit to England. He could do without all the fancy draping Lord Lumley had insisted upon, though. Horses were horses in Ireland, not poppet dolls dressed in satin and plumes.

Elevated in the stirrups, he caught another glimpse of the girl: battered hat crammed down on matted hair, dirty, laughing face, ragged clothes.

"Well," she said to the heckler, "I never said I could count, unless it be the coppers you toss me."

A sly-looking man in tight hose joined her on the steps. "I saves me coppers for them what entertains me." Boldly he snaked an arm around the girl and drew her snugly against him.

She slapped her hands against her cheeks in mock surprise. "Sir! Your codpiece flatters my vanity!"

The clink of coins punctuated a spate of laughter. A fat man near the girl held three flaming torches aloft. "Sixpence says you can't juggle them."

"Ninepence says I can, sure as Queen Elizabeth's white arse sits upon the throne," hollered the girl, deftly catching the torches and tossing them into motion.

Aidan guided his horse closer still. The huge Florentine mare he'd christened Grania earned a few dirty looks and muttered curses from people she nudged out of the way, but none challenged Aidan. Although the Londoners could not know he was the O Donoghue Mór of Ross Castle, they seemed to sense that he and his horse were not a pair to be trifled with. Perhaps it was the prodigious size of the horse; perhaps it was the dangerous, wintry blue of the rider's eyes; but most likely it was the naked blade of the shortsword strapped to his thigh.

He left his massive escort milling outside the churchyard and passing the time by intimidating the Londoners. When he drew close to the street urchin, she was juggling the torches. The flaming brands formed a whirling frame for her grinning, sooty face.

She was an odd colleen, looking as if she had been stitched together from leftovers: wide eyes and wider mouth, button nose, and spiky hair better suited to a boy. She wore a chemise without a bodice, drooping canion trews and boots so old they might have been relics of the last century.

Yet her Maker had, by some foible, gifted her with the most dainty and deft pair of hands Aidan had ever seen. Round and round went the torches, and when she called for another, it joined the spinning circle with ease. Hand to hand she passed them, faster and faster. The big-bellied man then tossed her a shiny red apple.

She laughed and said, "Eh, Dove, you don't fear I'll tempt a man to sin?"

Her companion guffawed. "I like me wenches made of more than gristle and bad jests, Pippa girl."

She took no offense, and while Aidan silently mouthed the strange name, someone tossed a dead fish into the spinning mix.

Aidan cringed, but the girl called Pippa took the new challenge in stride. "Seems I've caught one of your relatives, Mort," she said to the man who had procured the fish.

The crowd roared its approval. A few red-heeled gentlemen dropped coins upon the steps. Even after a fortnight in London Aidan could ill understand the Sassenach. They would as lief toss coins to a street performer as see her hanged for vagrancy.

He felt something rub his leg and looked down. A sleepy-looking whore curved her hand around his thigh, fingers inching toward the horn-handled dagger tucked into the top of his boot.

With a dismissive smile, Aidan removed the whore's hand. "You'll find naught but ill fortune there, mistress."

She drew back her lips in a sneer. The French pox had begun to rot her gums. "Irish," she said, backing away. "Chaste as a priest, eh?"

Before he could respond, a high-pitched mew split the air, and the mare's ears pricked up. Aidan spied a half-grown cat flying through the air toward Pippa.

"Juggle *that*," a man shouted, howling with laughter.

"Jesu!" she said. Her hands seemed to be working of their own accord, keeping the objects spinning even as she tried to step out of range of the flying cat. But she caught it and managed to toss it from one hand to the next before the terrified creature leaped onto her head and clung there, claws sinking into the battered hat.

The hat slumped over the juggler's eyes, blinding her.

Torches, apple and fish all clattered to the ground. The skinny man called Mort stomped out the flames. The fat man called Dove tried to help but trod instead upon the slimy fish. He skated forward, sleeves ripping as his pudgy arms cartwheeled. Just as he lost his balance, his flailing fist slammed into a spectator, who immediately threw himself into the brawl. With shouts of glee, others joined the fisticuffs. It was all Aidan could do to keep the mare from rearing.

Still blinded by the cat, the girl stumbled forward, hands outstretched. She caught the end of a bookseller's cart. Cat and hat came off as one, and the crazed feline climbed a stack of tomes, toppling them into the mud of the churchyard.

"Imbecile!" the bookseller screeched, lunging at Pippa.

Dove had taken on several opponents by now. With a wet *thwap,* he slapped one across the face with the dead fish.

Pippa grasped the end of the cart and lifted. The remaining books slid down and slammed into the bookseller, knocking him backward to the ground.

"Where's my ninepence?" she demanded, surveying the steps. People were too busy brawling to respond. She snatched up a stray copper and shoved it into the voluminous sack tied to her waist with a frayed rope. Then she fled, darting toward St. Paul's Cross, a tall monument surrounded by an open rotunda. The bookseller followed, and now he had an ally—his wife, a formidable lady with arms like large hams.

"Come back here, you evil little monkey," the wife roared. "This day shall be your last!"

Dove was enjoying the fight by now. He had his opponent by the neck and was playing with the man's nose, slapping it back and forth and laughing.

Mort, his companion, was equally gleeful, squaring off with the whore who had approached Aidan earlier.

Pippa led a chase around the cross, the bookseller and his wife in hot pursuit.

More spectators joined in the fray. The horse backed up, eyes rolling in fear. Aidan made a crooning sound and stroked her neck, but he did not leave the square. He simply watched the fight and thought, for the hundredth time since his arrival, what a strange, foul and fascinating place London was. Just for a moment, he forgot the reason he had come. He turned spectator, giving his full attention to the antics of Pippa and her companions.

So this was St. Paul's, the throbbing heart of the city. It was more meeting place than house of worship to be sure, and this did not surprise Aidan. The Sassenach were a people who clung feebly to an anemic faith; all the passion and pageantry had been bled out of the church by the Rome-hating Reformers.

The steeple, long broken but never yet repaired, shadowed a collection of beggars and merchants, strolling players and thieves, whores and tricksters. At the opposite corner of the square stood a gentleman and a liveried constable. Prodded by the screeched urging of the bookseller's wife, they reluctantly moved in closer. The bookseller had cornered Pippa on the top step.

"Mort!" she cried. "Dove, help me!" Her companions promptly disappeared into the crowd. "Bastards!" she yelled after them. "Geld and splay you both!"

The bookseller barreled toward her. She stooped and picked up the dead fish, took keen aim at the bookseller and let fly.

The bookseller ducked. The fish struck the approaching gentleman in the face. Leaving slime and scales in its wake, the fish slid down the front of his silk brocade doublet and landed upon his slashed velvet court slippers.

Pippa froze and gawked in horror at the gentleman. "Oops," she said.

"Indeed." He fixed her with a fiery eye of accusation. Without even blinking, he motioned to the liveried constable.

"Sir," he said.

"Aye, my lord?"

"Arrest this, er, *rodent.*"

Pippa took a step back, praying the way was clear to make a run for it. Her backside collided with the solid bulk of the bookseller's wife.

"Oops," Pippa said again. Her hopes sank like a weighted corpse in the Thames.

"Let's see you worm your way out of *this* fix, missy," the woman hissed in her ear.

"Thank you," Pippa said cordially enough. "I intend to do just that." She put on her brightest I'm-an-urchin grin and tugged at a forelock. She had recently hacked off her hair to get rid of a particularly stubborn case of lice. "Good morrow, Your Worship."

The nobleman stroked his beard. "Not particularly good for you, scamp," he said. "Are you aware of the laws against strolling players?"

Her gaze burning with indignation, she looked right and left. "Strolling players?" she said with heated outrage. "Who? Where? To God, what is this city coming to that such vermin as strolling players would run loose in the streets?"

As she huffed up her chest, she furtively searched the crowd for Dove and Mortlock. Like the fearless gallants she knew them to be, her companions had vanished.

For a moment, her gaze settled on the man on the horse. She had noticed him earlier, richly garbed and well mounted, with a foreign air about him she could not readily place.

"You mean to say," the constable yelled at her, "that *you* are not a strolling player?"

"Sir, bite your tongue," she fired off. "I'm…I am…" She took a deep breath and plucked out a ready falsehood. "An evangelist, my lord. Come to preach the Good Word to the unconverted of St. Paul's."

The haughty gentleman lifted one eyebrow high. "The Good Word, eh? And what might that be?"

"You know," she said with an excess of patience. "The gospel according to Saint John." She paused, searching her memory for more tidbits gleaned from days she had spent huddled and hiding in church. An inveterate collector of colorful words and phrases, she took pride in using them. "The pistol of Saint Paul to the fossils."

"Ah." The constable's hands shot out. In a swift movement, he pinned her to the wall beside the *si quis* door. She twisted around to look longingly into the nave where the soaring stone pillars marched along Paul's Walk. Like a well-seasoned rat, she knew every cranny and cubbyhole of the church. If she could get inside, she could find another way out.

"You'd best do better than that," the constable said, "else I'll nail your foolish ears to the stocks."

She winced just thinking about it. "Very well, then." She heaved a dramatic sigh. "Here's the truth."

A small crowd had gathered, probably hoping to see nails driven through her ears. The stranger on horseback dismounted, passed his reins to a stirrup runner and drew closer.

The lust for blood was universal, Pippa decided. But perhaps not. Despite his savage-looking face and flowing black hair, the man had an air of reckless splendor that fascinated her. She took a deep breath. "Actually, sir, I *am* a strolling player. But I have a nobleman's warrant," she finished triumphantly.

"Have you, then?" His Lordship winked at the constable.

"Oh, aye, sir, upon my word." She hated it when gentlemen got into a playful mood. Their idea of play usually involved mutilating defenseless people or animals.

"And who might this patron be?"

"Why, Robert Dudley himself, the Earl of Leicester." Pippa threw back her shoulders proudly. How clever of her to think of the queen's perpetual favorite. She nudged the constable in the ribs, none too gently. "He's the queen's lover, you know, so you'd best not irritate me."

A few of her listeners' mouths dropped open. The nobleman's face drained to a sick gray hue; then hot color surged to his cheeks and jowls.

The constable gripped Pippa by the ear. "You lose, rodent." With a flourish, he indicated the haughty man. "*That* is the Earl of Leicester, and I don't believe he's ever seen you before."

"If I had, I would certainly remember," said Leicester.

She swallowed hard. "Can I change my mind?"

"Please do," Leicester invited.

"My patron is actually Lord Shelbourne." She eyed the men dubiously. "Er, he *is* still among the living, is he not?"

"Oh, indeed."

Pippa breathed a sigh of relief. "Well, then. He is my patron. Now I had best be go—"

"Not so fast." The grip on her ear tightened. Tears burned her nose and eyes. "He is locked up in the Tower, his lands forfeit and his title attainted."

Pippa gasped. Her mouth formed an O.

"I know," said Leicester. "Oops."

For the first time, her aplomb flagged. Usually she was nimble enough of wit and fleet enough of foot to get out of these scrapes. The thought of the stocks loomed large in her mind. This time, she was nailed indeed.

She decided to try a last ditch effort to gain a patron. Who? Lord Burghley? No, he was too old and humorless. Walsingham? No, not with his Puritan leanings. The queen herself, then. By the time Pippa's claim could be verified, she would be long gone.

Then she spied the tall stranger looming at the back of the throng. Though he was most certainly foreign, he watched her with an interest that might even be colored by sympathy. Perhaps he spoke no English.

"Actually," she said, "*he* is my patron." She pointed in the direction of the foreigner. Be Dutch, she prayed silently. Or Swiss. Or drunk. Or stupid. Just play along.

The earl and the constable swung around, craning their necks to see. They did not have far to crane. The stranger stood like an oak tree amid low weeds, head and shoulders taller, oddly placid as the usual St. Paul's crowd surged and seethed and whispered around him.

Pippa craned, too, getting her first close look at him. Their gazes locked. She, who had experienced practically everything in her uncounted years, felt a jolt of something so new and profound that she simply had no name for the feeling.

His eyes were a glittering, sapphire blue, but it was not the color or the startling face from which the eyes stared that mattered. A mysterious force dwelt behind the eyes, or in their depths. Awareness flew between Pippa and the stranger; she felt it enter her, dive into her depths like sunlight breaking through shadow.

Old Mab, the woman who had raised Pippa, would have called it magic.

Old Mab would have been right, for once.

The earl cupped his hands around his mouth. "You, sir!"

The foreigner pressed a very large hand to his much larger chest and raised a questioning black brow.

"Aye, sir," called the earl. "This elvish female claims she is performing under your warrant. Is that so, sir?"

The crowd waited. The earl and the constable waited. When they looked away from her, Pippa clasped her hands and looked pleadingly at the stranger. Her ear was going numb in the pinch of the constable.

Pleading looks were her specialty. She had practiced them for years, using her large, pale eyes to prize coppers and crusts from passing strangers.

The foreigner raised a hand. Into the alleyway behind him flooded a troop of—Pippa was not certain *what* they were.

They moved about in a great mob like soldiers, but instead of tunics these men wore horrible gray animal hides, wolfskins by the look of them. They carried battle-axes with long handles. Some had shaved heads; others wore their hair loose and wild, tumbling over their brows.

Everyone moved aside when they entered the yard. Pippa did not blame the Londoners for shrinking in fear. She would have shrunk herself, but for the iron grip of the constable.

"Is that what the colleen said, then?" He strode forward. He spoke English, damn him. He had a very strange accent, but it was English.

He was huge. As a rule, Pippa liked big men. Big men and big dogs. They seemed to have less need to swagger and boast and be cruel than small ones. This man actually had a slight swagger, but she realized it was his way of squeezing a path through the crowd.

His hair was black. It gleamed in the morning light with shards of indigo and violet, flowing over his shoulders. A slim ebony strand was ornamented with a strap of rawhide and beads.

Pippa chided herself for being fascinated by a tall man with sapphire eyes. She should be taking the opportunity to run for cover rather than gawking like a Bedlamite at the foreigner. At the very least, she should be cooking up a lie to explain how, without his knowledge, she had come to be under his protection.

He reached the steps in front of the door, where she stood between the constable and Leicester. His flame-blue eyes glared at the constable until the man relinquished his grasp on Pippa's ear.

Sighing with relief, she rubbed the abused, throbbing ear.

"I am Aidan," the stranger said, "the O Donoghue Mór."

A Moor! Immediately Pippa fell to her knees and snatched the hem of his deep blue mantle, bringing the dusty silk to her lips. The fabric felt heavy and rich, smooth as water and as exotic as the man himself.

"Do you not remember, Your Preeminence?" she cried, knowing important men adored honorary titles. "How you ever so tenderly extended your warrant of protection to my poor, downtrodden self so that I'd not starve?" As she rambled on, she found a most interesting bone-handled knife tucked into the cuff of his tall boot. Unable to resist, she stole it, her movements so fluid and furtive that no one saw her conceal it in her own boot.

Her gaze traveled upward over a strong leg. The sight set off a curious tingling. Strapped to his thigh was a shortsword as sharp and dangerous looking as the man himself.

"You said you did not wish me to suffer the tortures of Clink Prison, nor did you want my pitiful weight forever on your delicate conscience, making you terrified to burn in hell for eternity because you let a defenseless woman fall victim to—"

"Yes," said the Moor.

She dropped his hem and stared up at him. "What?" she asked stupidly.

"Yes indeed, I remember, Mistress…er—"

"Trueheart," she supplied helpfully, plucking a favorite name from the arsenal of her imagination. "Pippa Trueheart."

The Moor faced Leicester. The smaller man gaped up at him. "There you are, then," said the black-haired lord.

"Mistress Pippa Trueheart is performing under my warrant."

With a huge bear paw of a hand, he took her arm and brought her to her feet. "I do confess the little baggage is unmanageable at times and did slip away for today's performance. From now on I shall keep her in closer tow."

Leicester nodded and stroked his narrow beard. "That would be most appreciated, my lord of Castleross."

The constable looked at the Moor's huge escort. The members of the escort glared back, and the constable smiled nervously.

The Moor turned and addressed his fierce servants in a tongue so foreign, so unfamiliar, that Pippa did not recognize a single syllable of it. That was odd, for she had a keen and discerning ear for languages.

The skin-clad men marched out of the churchyard and clumped down Paternoster Row. The lad who served as stirrup runner led the big horse away. The Moor took hold of Pippa's arm.

"Let's go, *a storin*," he said.

"Why do you call me *a storin?*"

"It is an endearment meaning 'treasure.'"

"Oh. No one's ever called me a treasure before. A trial, perhaps."

His lilting accent and the scent of the wind that clung in his hair and mantle sent a thrill through her. She had never been rescued in her life, and certainly not by such a specimen as this black-haired lord.

As they walked toward the low gate linking St. Paul's with Cheapside, she looked sideways at him. "You seem rather nice for a Moor." She passed through the gate he held open for her.

"A Moor, you say? Mistress, sure and I am no Moor."

"But you said you were Aidan, the O Donoghue Moor."

He laughed. She stopped in her tracks. She earned her living by making people laugh, so she should be used to the sound of it, but this was different. His laughter was so deep and rich that she imagined she could actually *see* it, flowing like a banner of dark silk on the breeze.

He threw back his great, shaggy head. She saw that he had a full set of teeth. The eyes, blazing blue like the hearts of flames, drew her in with that same compelling magic she had felt earlier.

He was beginning to make her nervous.

"Why do you laugh?" she asked.

"Mór," he said. "I am the O Donoghue Mór. It means 'great.'"

"Ah." She nodded sagely, pretending she had known all along. "And are you?" She let her gaze travel the entire length of him, lingering on the more interesting parts.

God was a woman, Pippa thought with sudden certainty. Only a woman would create a man like the O Donoghue, forming such toothsome parts into an even more delectable whole. "Aside from the obvious, I mean."

Mirth still glowed about him, though his laughter had ceased. He touched her cheek, a surprisingly tender gesture, and said, "That, *a stor,* depends on whom you ask."

The light, brief touch shook Pippa to the core, though she refused to show it. When people touched her, it was to box her ears or send her packing, not to caress and comfort.

"And how does one address a man so great as yourself?" she asked in a teasing voice. "Your Worship? Your Excellency?" She winked. "Your Hugeness?"

He laughed again. "For a lowly player, you know some big words. Saucy ones, too."

"I collect them. I'm a very fast learner."

"Not fast enough to stay out of trouble today, it seems." He took her hand and continued walking eastward along Cheapside. They passed the pissing conduit and then the Eleanor Cross decked with gilded statues.

Pippa saw the foreigner frowning up at them. "The Puritans mutilate the figures," she explained, taking charge of his introduction to London. "They mislike graven images. At the Standard yonder, you might see *real* mutilated bodies. Dove said a murderer was executed Tuesday last."

When they reached the square pillar, they saw no corpse, but the usual motley assortment of students and 'prentices, convicts with branded faces, beggars, bawds, and a pair of soldiers tied to a cart and being flogged as they were conveyed to prison. Leavening all the grimness was the backdrop of Goldsmith Row, shiny white houses with black beams and gilt wooden statuary. The O Donoghue took it all in with quiet, thoughtful interest. He made no comment, though he discreetly passed coppers from his cupped hand to the beggars.

From the corner of her eye, Pippa saw Dove and Mortlock standing by an upended barrel near the Old 'Change. They were running a game with weighted dice and hollow coins. They smiled and waved as if nothing had happened, as if they had not just deserted her in a moment of dire peril.

She poked her nose in the air, haughty as any grande dame, and put her grubby hand on the arm of the great O Donoghue. Let Dove and Mort wonder and squirm with curiosity. *She* belonged to a lofty nobleman now. She belonged to the O Donoghue Mór.

* * *

Aidan was wondering how to get rid of the girl. She trotted at his side, chattering away about riots and rebels and boat races down the Thames. There was precious little for him to do in London while the queen left him cooling his heels, but that did not mean he needed to amuse himself with a pixielike female from St. Paul's.

Still, there was the matter of his knife, which she had stolen while groveling at his hem. Perhaps he ought to let her keep it, though, as the price of a morning's diversion. The lass was nothing if not wildly entertaining.

He shot a glance sideways, and the sight of her clutched unexpectedly at his heart. She bounced along with all the pride of a child wearing her first pair of shoes. Yet beneath the grime on her face, he could see the smudges of sleeplessness under her soft green eyes, the hollows of her cheekbones, the quiet resignation that bespoke a thousand days of tacit, unprotesting hunger.

By the staff of St. Brigid, he did not need this, any more than he had needed the furious royal summons to court in London.

Yet here she was. And his heart was moved by the look of want in her wide eyes.

"Have you eaten today?" he asked.

"Only if you count my own words."

He raised one eyebrow. "Is that so?"

"No food has passed these lips in a fortnight." She pretended to sway with weakness.

"That is a lie," Aidan said mildly.

"A week?"

"Also a lie."

"Since last night?" she said.

"That I am likely to believe. You do not need to lie to win my sympathy."

"It's a habit, like spitting. Sorry."

"Where can I get you a hearty meal, colleen?"

Her eyes danced with anticipation. "Oh, there, Your Greatness." She pointed across the way, past the 'Change, where armed guards flanked a chest of bullion. "The Nag's Head Inn has good pies and they don't water down their ale."

"Done." He strode into the middle of the road. A few market carts jostled past. A herd of laughing, filthy children charged past in pursuit of a runaway pig, and a noisome knacker's wagon, piled high with butchered horse parts, lumbered by. When at last the way seemed clear, Aidan grabbed Pippa's hand and hurried her across.

"Now," he said, ducking beneath the low lintel of the doorway and drawing her inside. "Here we are."

It took a moment for his eyes to adjust to the dimness. The tavern was nearly full despite the early hour. He took Pippa to a scarred table flanked by a pair of three-legged stools.

He called for food and drink. The alewife slumped lazily by the fire as if loath to bestir herself. In high dudgeon, Pippa marched over to her. "Did you not hear His Lordship? He desires to be served now." Puffed up with self-importance, she pointed out his rich mantle and the tunic beneath, decked in cut crystal points. The sight of a well-turned-out patron spurred the woman to bring the ale and pasties quickly.

Pippa picked up her wooden drinking mug and drained nearly half of it, until he rapped on the bottom. "Slowly now. It won't sit well on an empty stomach."

"If I drink enough, my stomach won't care." She set down the mug and dragged her sleeve across her mouth.

A certain glazed brightness came over her eyes, and he felt a welling of discomfort, for it had not been his purpose to make her stupid with drink.

"Eat something," he urged her. She gave him a vague smile and picked up one of the pies. She ate methodically and without savor. The Sassenach were terrible cooks, Aidan thought, not for the first time.

A hulking figure filled the doorway and plunged the tavern deeper into darkness. Aidan's hand went for his dagger; then he remembered the girl still had it.

As soon as the newcomer stepped inside, Aidan grinned and relaxed. He would need no weapon against this man.

"Come sit you down, Donal Og," he said in Gaelic, dragging a third stool to the table.

Aidan was known far and wide as a man of prodigious size, but his cousin dwarfed him. Donal Og had massive shoulders, legs like tree trunks and a broad, prominent brow that gave him the look of a simpleton. Nothing was farther from the truth. Donal Og was brilliant, wry and unfailingly loyal to Aidan.

Pippa stopped chewing to gape at him.

"This is Donal Og," said Aidan. "The captain of my guard."

"Donal Og," she repeated, her pronunciation perfect.

"It means Donal the Small," Donal Og explained.

Her gaze measured his height. "Where?"

"I was so dubbed at birth."

"Ah. That explains everything." She smiled broadly. "I am honored. My name is Pippa Trueblood."

"The honor is my own, surely," Donal Og said with faint irony in his voice.

Aidan frowned. "I thought you said Trueheart."

She laughed. "Silly me. Perhaps I did." She began licking grease and crumbs from her fingers.

"Where," Donal Og asked in Gaelic, "did you find *that?*"

"St. Paul's churchyard."

"The Sassenach will let *anyone* in their churches, even lunatics." Donal Og held out a hand, and the alewife served him a mug of ale. "Is she as crazy as she looks?"

Aidan kept a bland, pleasant smile on his face so the girl would not guess what they spoke of. "Probably."

"Are you Dutch?" she asked suddenly. "That language you're using to discuss me—is it Dutch? Or Norse, perhaps?"

Aidan laughed. "It is Gaelic. I thought you knew. We're Irish."

Her eyes widened. "*Irish.* I'm told the Irish are wild and fierce and more papist than the pope himself."

Donal Og chuckled. "You're right about the wild and fierce part."

She leaned forward with interest burning in her eyes. Aidan gamely ran a hand through his hair. "You'll see I have no antlers, so you can lay to rest that myth. If you like, I'll show you that I have no tail—"

"I believe you," she said quickly.

"Don't tell her about the blood sacrifices," Donal Og warned.

She gasped. "Blood sacrifices?"

"Not lately," Aidan concluded, his face deadly serious.

"Certainly not on a waning moon," Donal Og added.

But Pippa held herself a bit more stiffly and regarded them with wariness. She seemed to be measuring the distance from table to door with an expert eye. Aidan had the impression that she was quite accustomed to making swift escapes.

The alewife, no doubt drawn by the color of their money, sidled over with more brown ale. "Did ye know we're Irish, ma'am?" Pippa asked in a perfect imitation of Aidan's brogue.

The alewife's brow lifted. "Do tell!"

"I'm a nun, see," Pippa explained, "of the Order of Saint Dorcas of the Sisters of Virtue. We never forget a favor."

Suitably impressed, the alewife curtsied with new respect and withdrew.

"So," Aidan said, sipping his ale and hiding his amusement at her little performance. "We are Irish and you cannot decide on a family name for yourself. How is it that you came to be a strolling player in St. Paul's?"

Donal Og muttered in Gaelic, "Really, my lord, could we not just leave? Not only is she crazy, she's probably crawling with vermin. I'm sure I just saw a flea on her."

"Ah, that's a sad tale indeed," Pippa said. "My father was a great war hero."

"Which war?" Aidan asked.

"Which war do you suppose, my lord?"

"The Great Rebellion?" he guessed.

She nodded vigorously, her hacked-off hair bobbing. "The very one."

"Ah," said Aidan. "And your father was a hero, you say?"

"You're as giddy as she," grumbled Donal Og, still speaking Irish.

"Indeed he was," Pippa declared. "He saved a whole garrison from slaughter." A faraway look pervaded her eyes like morning mist. She looked past him, out the open door, at a patch of the sky visible between the gabled roofs of London. "He loved me more than life itself, and he wept when he had to leave me. Ah, that was a bleak day for the Truebeard family."

"True*heart*," Aidan corrected, curiously moved. The

story was as false as a strumpet's promise, yet the yearning he heard in the girl's voice rang true.

"Trueheart," she agreed easily. "I never saw my father again. My mother was carried off by pirates, and I was left quite alone to fend for myself."

"I've heard enough," said Donal Og. "Let's go."

Aidan ignored him. He found himself fascinated by the girl, watching as she helped herself to more ale and drank greedily, as if she would never get her fill.

Something about her touched him in a deep, hidden place he had long kept closed. It was in the very heart of him, embers of warmth that he guarded like a windbreak around a herdsman's fire. No one was allowed to share the inner life of Aidan O Donoghue. He had permitted that just once—and he had been so thoroughly doused that he had frozen himself to sentiment, to trust, to joy, to hope—to everything that made life worth living.

Now here was this strange woman, unwashed and underfed, with naught but her large soft eyes and her vivid imagination to shield her from the harshness of the world. True, she was strong and saucy as any rollicking street performer, but not too far beneath the gamine surface, he saw something that fanned at the banked embers inside him. She possessed a subtle, waiflike vulnerability that was, at least on the surface, at odds with her saucy mouth and nail-hard shell of insouciance.

And, though her hair and face and ill-fitting garments were smeared with grease and ashes, a charming, guileless appeal shone through.

"That is quite a tale of woe," Aidan commented.

Her smile favored them both like the sun bursting through stormclouds.

"Too bad it's a pack of lies," Donal Og said.

"I do wish you'd speak English," she said. "It's bad

manners to leave me out." She glared accusingly at him. "But I suppose, if you're going to say I'm crazy and a liar and things of that sort, it is probably best to speak Irish."

Seeing so huge a man squirm was an interesting spectacle. Donal Og shifted to and fro, causing the stool to creak. His hamlike face flushed to the ears. "Aye, well," he said in English, "you need not perform for Aidan and me. For us, the truth is good enough."

"I see." She elongated her words as the effects of the ale flowed through her. "Then I should indeed confess the truth and tell you exactly who I am."

Diary of a Lady

It is a mother's lot to rejoice and to grieve all at once. So it has always been, but knowing that has never eased my grief nor dimmed my joy.

In the early part of her reign, the queen gave our family a land grant in County Kerry, Munster, but until recently, we kept it in name only, content to leave Ireland to the Irish. Now, quite suddenly, we are expected to do something about it.

Today my son Richard received a royal commission. I wonder, when the queen's advisers empowered my son to lead an army, if they ever, even for an instant, imagined him as I knew him—a laughing small boy with grass stains on his elbows and the pure sweetness of an innocent heart shining from his eyes.

Ah, to me it seems only yesterday that I held that silky, golden head to my breast and scandalized all society by sending away the wet nurse.

Now they want him to lead men into battle for lands he never asked for, a cause he never embraced.

My heart sighs, and I tell myself to cling to the blessings that are mine: a loving husband, five grown children

and a shining faith in God that—only once, long ago—
went dim.

—Lark de Lacey,
Countess of Wimberleigh

Two

"**I** can't believe you brought her with us," said Donal Og the next day, pacing in the walled yard of the old Priory of the Crutched Friars.

As a visiting dignitary, Aidan had been given the house and adjacent priory by Lord Lumley, a staunch Catholic and unlikely but longtime royal favorite. The residence was in Aldgate, where all men of consequence lived while in London. The huge residence, once home to humble and devout clerks, comprised a veritable village, including a busy glassworks and a large yard and stables. It was oddly situated, bordered by broad Woodroffe Lane and crooked Hart Street and within shouting distance of a grim, skeletal scaffold and gallows.

Aidan had given Pippa a room of her own, one of the monks' cells facing a central arcade. The soldiers had strict orders to watch over her, but not to threaten or disturb her.

"I couldn't very well leave her at the Nag's Head." He glanced at the closed door of her cell. "She might've been accosted."

"She probably *has* been, probably makes her living at

it." Donal Og cut the air with an impatient gesture of his hand. "You take in strays, my lord, you always have—orphaned lambs, pups rejected by their dams, lame horses. Creatures better left—" He broke off, scowled and resumed pacing.

"To die," Aidan finished for him.

Donal Og swung around, his expression an odd mix of humanity and cold pragmatism. "It is the very rhythm of nature for some to struggle, some to survive, some to perish. We're Irish, man. Who knows that better than we? Neither you nor I can change the world. Nor were we meant to."

"But isn't that what we came to London to accomplish, cousin?" Aidan asked softly.

"We came because Queen Elizabeth summoned you," Donal Og snapped. "And now that we're here, she refuses to see you." He tilted his great blond head skyward and addressed the clouds. "Why?"

"It amuses her to keep foreign dignitaries cooling their heels, waiting for an audience."

"I think she's insulted because you go all about town with an army of one hundred. Mayhap a little more modesty would be in order."

Iago came out of the barracks, scratching his bare, ritually scarred chest and yawning. "Talk, talk, talk," he said in the lilting tones of his native island. "You never shut up."

Aidan said a perfunctory good morning to his marshal. Through an extraordinary chain of events, Iago had come ten years earlier from the West Indies of the New World. His mother was of mixed island native and African blood, his father a Spaniard.

Iago and Aidan had grown to full manhood together. Two years younger than Iago and in awe of the Caribbean man's strength and prowess, Aidan had insisted on emulating him. Gloriously drunk one day, he had endured the ritual scarring ceremony in secret, and in a great deal of pain. To the horror of his father, Aidan now bore, like Iago, a series of V-shaped scars down the center of his chest.

"I was just saying," Donal Og explained, "that Aidan is always taking in strays."

Iago laughed deeply, his mahogany face shining through the morning mist. "What a fool, eh?"

Chastened, Donal Og fell silent.

"So what did he drag home this time?" Iago asked.

Pippa lay perfectly still with her eyes closed, playing a familiar game. From earliest memory, she always awoke with the certain conviction that her life had been a nightmare and, upon awakening, she would find matters the way they should be, with her mother smiling like a Madonna while her father worshipped her on bended knee and both smiled upon their beloved daughter.

With a snort of self-derision, she beat back the fantasy. There was no place in her life for dreams. She opened her eyes and looked up to see a cracked, limewashed ceiling. Timber and wattled walls. The scent of slightly stale, crushed straw. The murmur of masculine voices outside a thick timber door.

It took a few moments to remember all that had happened the day before. While she reflected on the events, she found a crock of water and a basin and cupped her hands for a drink, finally plunging in her face to wash away the last cobwebby vestiges of her fantasies.

Yesterday had started out like any other day—a few antics in St. Paul's; then she and Mortlock and Dove would cut a purse or filch something to eat from a carter.

Like London smoke borne on a breeze, they would drift
aimlessly through the day, then return to the house on
Maiden Lane squished between two crumbling tene-
ments.

Pippa had the attic room all to herself. Almost. She
shared it with a rather aggressively inquisitive rat she
called, for no reason she could fathom, Pavlo. She also
shared quarters with all the private worries and dream-
like memories and unfocused sadness she refused to
confess to any other person.

Yesterday, the free-flowing course of her life had
altered. For better or worse, she knew not. She felt no ties
to Mort and Dove; the three of them used each other,
shared what they had to, and jealously guarded the rest.
If they missed her at all, it was because she had a knack
for drawing a crowd. If she missed them at all—she had
not decided whether or not she did—it was because they
were familiar, not necessarily beloved.

Pippa knew better than to love anyone.

She had come with the Irish nobleman simply because
she had nothing better to do. Perhaps fate had taken a
hand in her fortune at last. She had always wanted the
patronage of a rich man, but no one had ever taken notice
of her. In her more fanciful moments, she thought about
winning a place at court. For now, she would settle for
the Celtic lord.

After all, he was magnificently handsome, obviously
rich and surprisingly kind.

A girl could do far worse than that.

By the time he had brought her to this place, she had
been woozy with ale. She had a vague memory of riding
a large horse with the O Donoghue Mór seated in front
of her and all his strange, foreign warriors tramping
behind.

She made certain her shabby sack of belongings lay in a corner of the room, then dried her face. As she cleaned her teeth with the tail of her shift dipped in the water basin, she saw, wavering in the bottom of the bowl, a coat of arms.

Norman cross and hawk and arrows.

Lumley's device. She knew it well, because she had once stolen a silver badge from him as he had passed through St. Paul's.

She straightened up and combed her fingers through her hacked-off hair. She did not miss having long hair, but once in a while she thought about looking fashionable, like the glorious ladies who went about in barges on the Thames. In the past, when she bothered to wash her hair, it had hung in honey gold waves that glistened in the sun.

A definite liability. Men noticed glistening golden hair. And that was the last sort of attention she wanted.

She jammed on her hat—it was a slouch of brown wool that had seen better days—and wrenched open the door to greet the day.

Morning mist lay like a shroud over a rambling courtyard. Men and dogs and horses slipped in and out of view like wraiths. The fog insulated noise, and the arcade created soft, hollow echoes, so that the Irish voices of the men had an eerie intimacy.

She tucked her thumbs into her palms to ward off evil spirits—just in case.

Several yards from Pippa, three men stood talking in low tones. They made a most interesting picture—the O Donoghue with his blue mantle slung back over one shoulder, his booted foot propped on the tongue of a wagon, and his elbow braced upon his knee.

Donal Og, the rude cousin, leaned against the wagon

wheel, gesticulating like a man in the grips of St. Elmo's fire. The third man stood with his back turned, feet planted wide as if he were on the deck of a ship. He was tall—she wondered if prodigious height was a required quality of the Irish lord's retinue—and his long, soft tunic blazed with color in hues more vivid than April flowers.

She strolled out of her chamber to find that it was one of a long line of barracks or cells hunched against an ancient wall and shaded by the arcade. She walked over to the wagon, and in her usual forthright manner, she picked up the hem of the man's color-drenched garment and fingered the fabric.

"Now, colleen," Aidan O Donoghue said in a warning voice.

The man in the bright cloak turned.

Pippa's mouth dropped open. A squeak burst from her throat and she stumbled back. Her heel caught on a broken paving stone. She tripped and landed on her backside in a puddle of morning-chilled mud.

"Jesus Christ on a flaming crutch!" she said.

"Reverent, isn't she?" Donal Og asked wryly. "Faith, but she's a perfect little saint."

Pippa kept staring. *This* was a Moor. She had heard about them in story and song, but never had she seen one. His face was remarkable, a gleaming sculpture of high cheekbones, a bony jaw, beautiful mouth, eyes the color of the stoutest ale. He had a perfect black cloud of hair, and skin the color of antique, polished leather.

"My name is Iago," he said, stepping back and twitching the hem of his remarkable cloak out of the way of the mud.

"Pippa," she said breathlessly. "Pippa True—True—"

Aidan stuck out his hand and pulled her to her feet. She felt his smooth, easy strength as he did so, and his touch was a wonder to her, in its way, more of a wonder than the Moor's appearance.

Iago looked from Pippa to Aidan. "My lord, you have outdone yourself."

She felt the mud slide down her backside and legs, pooling in the tops of her ancient boots. Last winter, she had stolen them from a corpse lying frozen in an alley.

"Will you eat or bathe first?" the O Donoghue asked, not unkindly.

Her stomach cramped, but she was well used to hunger pangs. The chill mud made her shiver. "A bath, I suppose, Your Reverence."

Donal Og and Iago grinned at each other. "Your Reverence," Iago said in his deep, musical voice.

Donal Og pointed his toe and bowed. "Your Reverence."

Aidan ignored them. "A bath it is, then," he said.

"I've never had one before."

The O Donoghue looked at her for a long moment. His gaze burned over her, searing her face and form until she thought she might sizzle like a chicken on a spit.

"Why am I not surprised?" he asked.

She sang with a perfect, off-key joy. The room, adjoining the kitchen of Lumley House, was small and cramped and windowless, but the open door let in a flood of light. Aidan sat on the opposite side of the folding privy screen and put his hands over his ears, but her exuberant and bawdy song screeched through the barrier.

"At Steelyard store of wines there be
Your dulled minds to glad,
And handsome men that must not wed,
Except they leave their trade.

They oft shall seek for proper girls,
And some perhaps shall find—"

She broke off and called, "Do you like my song,
Your Worship?"

"It's grand," he forced himself to say. "Simply grand."

"I could sing you another if you wish," she said eagerly.

"Ah, that would be a high delight indeed, I'm sure,"
he said.

She took his patronage seriously. Too seriously.

"The bed it shook
As pleasure took
The carpet-knight for a ride…"

She belted the words out unblushingly. Aidan had never
seen a mere bath have this sort of effect on anyone. How a
wooden barrel half filled with lukewarm water could make
a woman positively drunk with elation was beyond him.

She splashed and sang and every once in a while he
could hear a scrubbing sound. He hoped she was availing
herself of the harsh wood-ash soap.

Pippa's singing had long since driven the Lumley
maids into the yard to gossip. When he had told them to
draw a bath, they had shaken their heads and muttered
about Lord Lumley's strange Irish guests.

But they had obeyed. Even in London, so many
leagues from his kingdom in Kerry, he was still the
O Donoghue Mór.

Except to Pippa. Despite her constant attempts to entertain him and seek his approval, she had no respect for
his status. She paused in her song to draw breath or perhaps—God forbid—think up another verse.

"Are you quite finished?" Aidan asked.

"Finished? Are we pressed for time?"

"You'll wind up pickled like a herring if you stew in there much longer."

"Oh, very well." He heard the slap of water sloshing against the sides of the barrel. "Where are my clothes?" she asked.

"In the kitchen. Iago will boil them. The maids found you a few things. I hung them on a peg—"

"Oooh." She managed to infuse the exclamation with a wealth of wonder and yearning. "These are truly a gift from heaven."

They were no gift, but the castoffs of a maid who had run off with a Venetian sailor the week before. He heard Pippa bumping around behind the screen. A few moments later, she emerged.

Haughty pride radiated from her small, straight figure. Aidan clamped his teeth down on his tongue to keep from laughing.

She had the skirt on backward and the buckram bodice upside down. Her damp hair stuck out in spikes like a crown of thorns. She was barefoot and cradling the leather slippers reverently in her hands.

Then she moved into the strands of sunlight streaming in through the kitchen door, and he saw her face for the first time devoid of soot and ashes.

It was like seeing the visage of a saint or an angel in one's dreams. Never, ever, had Aidan seen such a face. No single feature was remarkable in and of itself, but taken as a whole, the effect was staggering.

She had a wide, clear brow, her eyebrows bold above misty eyes. The sweet curves of nose and chin framed a soft mouth, which she held pursed as if expecting a kiss. Her cheekbones were highlighted by pink-scrubbed skin. Aidan thought of the angel carved in the plaster over the altar of the church at Innisfallen. Somehow, that same lofty, otherworldly magic touched Pippa.

"The clothes," she stated, "are magnificent."

He allowed himself a controlled smile designed to preserve her fervent pride. "And so they are. Let me help you with some of the fastenings."

"Ah, my silly lord, I've done them all up myself."

"Indeed you have. But since you lack a proper lady's maid to help you, I should take her part."

"You're very kind," she said.

"Not always," he replied, but she seemed oblivious of the warning edge in his voice. "Come here."

She crossed the room without hesitation. He could not decide whether that was healthy or not. Should a young woman alone be so trusting of a strange man? Her trust was no gift, but a burden.

"First the bodice," he said patiently, untying the haphazard knot she had made in the lacings. "I have never wondered why it mattered, but fashion demands that you wear it with the other end up."

"Truly?" She stared down at the stiff garment in dismay. "It covered more of me upside down. When you turn it the other way, I spill out like loaves from a pan."

His loins burned with the image, and he gritted his teeth. The last thing he had expected was that he might desire her. Pippa lifted her arms and held them steady while he unlaced the bodice.

It proved to be the most excruciating exercise in self-restraint he had ever endured. Somehow, the dust and ashes of her harsh life had masked an uncounted wealth of charms. He had the feeling that he was the first man to see beneath the grime and ill-fitting clothes.

As he pulled the laces through, his knuckles grazed her. The maids had provided neither shift nor corset. All that lay between Pippa's sweet flesh and his busy hands was a chemise of wispy lawn. He could feel the heat of her, could smell the clean, beeswaxy fragrance of her just washed skin and hair.

Setting his jaw with manly restraint, he turned the bodice right side up and brought it around her. As he slowly laced the garment, watching the stiff buckram close around a narrow waist and then widen over the subtle womanly flare of her hips, pushing up her breasts, he could not banish his insistent desire.

True to her earlier observation, her bosom swelled out over the top with frank appeal, barely contained by the sheer fabric of the chemise. He could see the high, rounded shapes, the rosy shadows of the tips, and for a long, agonizing moment all he could think of was touching her there, tenderly, learning the shape and weight of her breasts, burying his face in them, drowning in the essence of her.

A roaring, like the noise of the sea, started in his ears, swishing with the quickening rhythm of his blood. He bent his head closer, closer, his tongue already anticipating the flavor of her, his lips hungry for the budded texture. His mouth hovered so close that he could feel the warmth emanating from her.

She drew in a deep, shuddering breath, and the movement reminded him to think with his brain—even the small part of it that happened to be working at the moment—not with his loins.

He was the O Donoghue Mór, an Irish chieftain who, a year before, had given up all rights to touch another woman. He had no business dallying with—of all things—a Sassenach vagabond, probably a madwoman at that.

He forced himself to stare not at the bodice, but into

her eyes. And what he saw there was more dangerous than the lush curves of her body. What he saw there was not madness, but a painful eagerness.

It struck him like a slap, and he caught his breath, then hissed out air between his teeth.

He wanted to shake her. *Don't show me your yearning,* he wanted to say. *Don't expect me to do anything about it.*

What he said was, "I am in London on official business. I will return to Ireland as soon as I am able."

"I've never been to Ireland," she said, an ember of unbearable hope glowing in her eyes.

"These days, it is a sad country, especially for those who love it." Sad. What a small, inadequate word to describe the horror and desolation he had seen—burned-out peel towers, scorched fields, empty villages, packs of wolves feeding off the unburied dead.

She tilted her head to one side. Unlike Aidan, she seemed perfectly comfortable with their proximity. A suspicion stung him. Perhaps it was nothing out of the ordinary for her to have a man tugging at her clothing.

The idea stirred him from his lassitude and froze the sympathy he felt for her. He made short, neat work of trussing her up, helped her slide her feet into the little shoes, then stepped back.

She ruined his hard-won indifference when she pointed a slippered toe, curtsied as if to the manner born and asked, "How do I look?"

From neck to floor, Aidan thought, like his own private dream of paradise.

But her expression disturbed him; she had the face of a cherub, filled with a trust and innocence that seemed all the more miraculous because of the hardships she must have endured living the life of a strolling player.

He studied her hair, because it was safer than looking at her face and drowning in her eyes. She lifted a hand, made a fluttery motion in the honey gold spikes. "It's that awful?" she asked. "After I cut it all off, Mort and Dove said I could use my head to swab out wine casks or clean lamp chimneys."

A reluctant laugh broke from him. "It is not so bad. But tell me, *why* is your hair cropped short? Or do I want to know?"

"Lice," she said simply. "I had the devil of a time with them."

He scratched his head. "Aye, well. I hope you're no longer troubled by the little pests."

"Not lately. Who dresses your hair, my lord? It is most extraordinary." Brazen as an inquisitive child, she stood on tiptoe and lifted the single thread-woven braid that hung amid his black locks.

"That would be Iago. He does strange things on shipboard to avoid boredom." Like getting me drunk and carving up my chest, Aidan thought grumpily. "I'll ask him to do something about this mop of yours."

He meant to reach out and tousle her hair, a meaningless, playful gesture. Instead, as if with its own mind, his palm cradled her cheek, his thumb brushing up into her sawed-off hair. The soft texture startled him.

"Will that be agreeable to you?" he heard himself ask in a whisper.

"Yes, Your Immensity." Pulling away, she craned her neck to see over his shoulder. "There is something I need." She hurried into the kitchen, where her old, soiled clothes lay in a heap.

Aidan frowned. He had not noticed any buttons worth

keeping on her much worn garb. She snatched up the tunic and groped along one of the seams. An audible sigh of relief slipped from her. Aidan saw a flash of metal.

Probably a bauble or copper she had lifted from a passing merchant in St. Paul's. He shrugged and went to the kitchen garden door to call for Iago.

As he turned, he saw Pippa lift the piece and press it to her mouth, closing her eyes and looking for all the world as if the bauble were more precious than gold.

From the Annals
of Innisfallen

I am old enough now to forgive Aidan's father, yet young enough to remember what a scoundrel Ronan O Donoghue was. Ah, I could roast for eternity in the fires of my unkind thoughts, but there you are, I hated the old jackass and wept no tears at his wake.

He expected more of his only son than any man could possibly give—loyalty, honor, truth, but most of all blind, stupid obedience. It was the one quality Aidan lacked. It was the one thing that could have saved the father, niggardly lout that he was, from dying.

For certain, Aidan thinks on that often, and with a great, seizing pain in his heart.

A pitiful waste if you ask me, Revelin of Innisfallen. For until he lets go of his guilt about what happened that fateful night, Aidan O Donoghue will not truly live.

—Revelin of Innisfallen

Three

"So after my father's ship went down," Pippa explained blithely, "his enemies assumed he had perished." She sat very still on the stool in the kitchen garden. The smell of blooming herbs filled the spring air.

"Naturally," Iago said in his dark honey voice. "And of course, your papa did not die at all. Even as we speak, he is attending the council of Her Majesty the queen."

"How did you know?" Beaming, Pippa twisted around on her stool to look up at him.

Framed by the nodding boughs of the old elm tree that shaded the garden path, he regarded her with tolerant interest, a comb in his hand and a gentle compassion in his velvety black eyes. "I, too, like to invent answers to the questions that keep me awake at night," he said.

"I invent nothing," she snapped. "It all happened just as I described it."

"Except that the story changes each time you encounter someone new." He spoke with mild amusement, but no accusation. "Your father has been pirate, knight, foreign prince, soldier of fortune and ratcatcher. Oh. And did I not hear you tell O Mahoney you were sired by the pope?"

Pippa blew out a breath, and her shoulders sagged. A raven cackled raucously in the elm tree, then whirred off into the London sky. Of course she invented stories about who she was and where she had come from. To face the truth was unthinkable. And impossible.

Iago's touch was soothing as he combed through her matted hair. He tilted her chin up and stared at her face-on for a long moment, intent as a sculptor. She stared back, rapt as a dreamer. What a remarkable person he was, with his lovely ebony skin and bell-toned voice, the fierce, inborn pride he wore like a mantle of silk.

He closed one eye; then he began to snip with his little crane-handled scissors, the very ones she had been tempted to steal from a side table in the kitchen.

As Iago worked, he said, "You tell the tales so well, *pequeña,* but they are just that—tales. I know this because I used to do the same. Used to lie awake at night trying to put together the face of my mother from fragments of memory. She became every good thing I knew about a mother, and before long she was more real to me than an actual woman. Only bigger. Better. Sweeter, kinder."

"Yes," she whispered past a sudden, unwelcome thickness in her throat. "Yes, I understand."

He twisted a few curls into a soft fringe upon her brow. The breeze sifted lightly through them. "If you were an Englishman, you would be the very rage of fashion. They call these lovelocks. They look better on you." He winked. "A dream mother. It was something I needed at a very dark time of my life."

"Tell me about the dark time," she said, fascinated by the deftness of his hands and the way they were so brown on one side, while the palms were sensitive and pale.

"Slavery," he said. "Being made to work until I fell on

my face from exhaustion, and then being beaten until I dragged myself up to work some more. You have a dream mother, too, eh?"

She closed her eyes. A lovely face smiled at her. She had spent a thousand nights and more painting her parents in her mind until they were perfect. Beautiful. All wise. Flawless, save for one minor detail. They had somehow managed to misplace their daughter.

"I have a dream mother," she confessed. "A father, too. The stories might change, but that does not." She opened her eyes to find him studying her critically again. "What about the O Donoghue?" she asked, pretending only idle curiosity.

"His father is dead, which is why Aidan is the lord. His mother is dead also, but his—" He cut himself off. "I have said too much already."

"Why are you so loyal to the O Donoghue?"

"He gave me my freedom."

"How was it his to give in the first place?"

Iago grinned, his face blossoming like an exotic flower. "It was not. I was put on a ship for transport from San Juan—that is on an island far across the Ocean Sea— to England. I was to be a gift for a great noblewoman. My master wished to impress her."

"A gift?" Pippa was hard-pressed to sit still on her stool. "You mean like a drinking cup or a salt cellar or a pet ermine?"

"You have a blunt way of putting it, but yes. The ship wrecked off the coast of Ireland. I swam straightaway from my master even as he begged me to save him."

Pippa sat forward, amazed. "Did he die?"

Iago nodded. "Drowned. I watched him. Does that shock you?"

"Yes! Was the water very cold?"

His chest-deep chuckle filled the air. "Close to freezing. I dragged myself to an island—I later found out it is called Skellig Michael—and there I met a pilgrim in sackcloth and ashes, climbing the great stairs to the shrine."

"The O Donoghue Mór in sackcloth and ashes?" In Pippa's mind, Aidan would always be swathed in flashing jewel tones, his jet hair gleaming in the sun; he was no drab pilgrim, but a prince from a fairy story.

"He was not the O Donoghue Mór then. He helped me get dry and warm, and he became my first and only true friend." Black fury shadowed Iago's eyes. "When Aidan's father saw me, he declared himself my master, tried to make me a slave again. And Aidan *let* him."

Pippa clutched the sides of the stool. "The jackdog! The bootlicker, the skainsmate—"

"It was a ruse. He claimed me on the grounds that he had found me. His father agreed, thinking it would enhance Aidan's station to be the first Irishman to own a black slave."

"The scullywarden!" she persisted. "The horse's a—"

"And then he set me free," Iago said, laughing at her. "He had a priest called Revelin draw up a paper. That day Aidan promised to help me return to my home when we were both grown. In fact, he promised to come with me across the Ocean Sea."

"Why would you want to go back to a land where you were a slave? And why would Aidan want to go with you?"

"Because I love the islands, and I no longer have a master. There was a girl called Serafina...." His voice trailed off, and he shook his head as if to cast away the thought. "Aidan wanted to come because he loves Ireland too much to stay." Iago fussed with more curls that tickled the nape of her neck.

"If he loves Ireland, why would he want to leave it?"

"When you come to know him better, you will understand. Have you ever been forced to watch a loved one die?"

She swallowed and nodded starkly, thinking of Mab. "I never felt so helpless in all my life."

"So it is with Aidan and Ireland," said Iago.

"Why is he here, in London?"

"Because the queen summoned him. Officially, he is here to sign treaties of surrender and regrant. He is styled Lord of Castleross. Unofficially, she is curious, I think, about Ross Castle. She wants to know why, after her interdict forbidding the construction of fortresses, it was completed."

The idea that her patron had the power to decide the fate of nations was almost too large for Pippa to grasp. "Is she very angry with him?" It even felt odd referring to Queen Elizabeth as "she," for Her Majesty had always been, to Pippa and others like her, a remote idea, more of an institution like a cathedral than a flesh-and-blood woman.

"She has kept him waiting here for a fortnight." Iago lifted her from the stool to the ground. "You look as pretty as an okasa blossom."

She touched her hair. Its shape felt different—softer, balanced, light as the breeze. She would have to go out to Hart Street Well and look at her reflection.

"You said when you met Aidan, he was not the O Donoghue Mór," she said, thinking that the queen must enjoy having the power to summon handsome men to her side.

"His father, Ronan, was. Aidan became Lord Castleross after Ronan died."

"And how did his father die?"

Iago went to the half door of the kitchen and held the lower part open. "Ask Aidan. It is not my place to say."

"Iago said you killed your father."

Aidan shot to his feet as if Pippa had touched a brand to his backside. "He said *what?*"

Hiding her apprehension, she strolled into the great hall of Lumley House and moved through gloomy evening shadows on the flagged floor. An ominous rumbling of thunder sounded in the distance. Aidan's fists were clenched, his face stark and taut. Instinct told her to flee, but she forced herself to stay.

"You heard me, my lord. If you're going to keep me, I want to make sure. Is it true? *Did* you kill your father?"

He grabbed an iron poker. A single Gaelic word burst from him as he stabbed at the fat log smoldering in the grate.

Pippa took a deep breath for courage. "It was Iago who—"

"Iago said nothing of the sort."

She emerged from the shadows and joined him by the hearth, praying he would deny her suggestion. "Did you, my lord?" she whispered.

He moved so swiftly, it took her breath away. One moment the iron poker clattered to the floor; the next he had his great hands clamped around her shoulders, her back against a stone pillar and his furious face pushed close to hers. Though she still stood cloaked in shadow, she could see the flames from the hearth fire reflected in his eyes.

"*Yes,* damn your meddling self. I killed my father."

"*What?*" She trembled in his grip.

Aidan thrust away from her, turning back to face the fire.

"Isn't that what you expected to hear?" He clenched his eyes shut and pinched the bridge of his nose. Sharp fragments of that last, explosive argument came back to slice fresh wounds into his soul.

He spun around to face Pippa, intending to carry her bodily out of the hall, out of Lumley House, out of his life. She stepped from the gloom and into the light. Aidan stopped dead in his tracks.

"What in God's name did Iago do to you?" he asked. As if to echo his words, thunder muttered outside the hall.

Her hand wavered a little as she brought it up to touch her hair, which now curled softly around her glowing face. "The best he could?" she attempted. Then she dropped her air of trembling uncertainty. "You are trying to change the subject. Are you or are you not a father-murderer?"

He planted his hands on his hips. "That depends on whom you ask."

She mimicked his aggressive stance, looking for all the world like a fierce pixie. "I'm asking you."

"And I've answered you."

"But it was the wrong answer," she said, so vehemently that he expected her to stomp her foot. Something—the washing, the grooming—had made her glow as if a host of fairies had showered her with a magical mist. "I demand an explanation."

"I feel no need to explain myself to a stranger," he said, dismayed by the intensity of his attraction to her.

"We are not strangers, Your Loftiness," she said with heavy irony. "Wasn't it just this morning that you undressed me and then dressed me like the most intimate of handmaids?"

He winced at the reminder. Beneath her elfin daintiness lay a soft, womanly body that he craved with a power that was both undeniable and inappropriate. Shed of her beggar's garb, she had become the sort of woman for whom men swore to win honors, slay dragons, cheerfully lay down their lives. And he was in no position to do any of those things.

"Some would say," he admitted darkly, "that the death of Ronan O Donoghue was an accident." From the corner of his eye, he saw a flicker of lightning through the mullioned windows on the east side of the hall.

"What do *you* say?" Pippa asked.

"I say it is none of your affair. And if you persist in talking about it, I might have to do something permanent to you."

She sniffed, clearly recognizing the idleness of his threat. He was not accustomed to females who were unafraid of him. "If *I* had a father, I'd cherish him."

"You do have a father. The war hero, remember?"

She blinked. "Oh. Him. Yes, of course."

Aidan slammed a fist on the stone mantel and regarded the Lumley shield hanging above as if it were a higher authority. "What am I going to do with you?" The wind hurled gusts against the windows, and he swung around to glower at her.

"'Do' with me?" She glanced back over her shoulder at the door. He didn't blame her for not wanting to be alone with him. She wouldn't be the first.

"You can't stay here forever," he stated. "I didn't ask to be your protector." The twist of guilt in his gut startled him. He was not used to making cruel statements to defenseless women.

She did not look surprised. Instead, she dropped one shoulder and regarded him warily. She resembled a dog so used to being kicked that it came as a surprise when it was *not* kicked.

Her rounded chin came up. "I never asked to stay forever. I can go back to Dove and Mortlock. We have plans to gain the patronage of…of the Holy Roman Emperor."

He remembered her disreputable companions from St. Paul's—the portly and greasy Dove and the cadaverous Mortlock. "They must be mad with worry over you."

"Those two?" She snorted and idly picked up the iron poker, stabbing at the log in the hearth. Sparks flew upward on a sweep of air, then disappeared. "They only worry about losing me because they need me to cry up a crowd. Their specialty is cutting purses."

"I won't let you go back to them," Aidan heard himself say. "I'll find you a—" he thought for a moment "—a situation with a gentlewoman—"

That made her snort again, this time with bitter laughter. "Oh, for that I should be well and truly suited." She slammed the poker back into its stand. "It has long been my aim in life to empty some lady's slops and pour wine for her." The hem of her skirts twitched in agitation as she pantomimed the menial work.

"It's a damned sight better than wandering the streets." Irritated, he walked to the table and sloshed wine into a cup. The lightning flashed again, stark and cold in the April night.

"Oh, do tell, my lord." She stalked across the room, slapped her palms on the table, leaned over and glared into his face. "Listen. I am an entertainer. I am good at it."

So he had noticed. She could mimic any accent, highborn or low, copy any movement with fluid grace, change character from one moment to the next like an actor trying on different masks.

"I didn't ask you to drag me out of St. Paul's and into your life," she stated.

"I don't remember any objections from you when I saved you from having your ears nailed to the stocks." He tasted the wine, a sweet sack favored by the English nobility. He missed his nightly draft of poteen. Pippa was enough to make him crave *two* drafts of the powerful liquor.

"I was hungry. But that doesn't mean I've surrendered my life to you. I can get another position in a nobleman's household just like that." She snapped her fingers.

She was so close, he could see the dimple that winked in her left cheek. She smelled of soap and sun-dried laundry, and now that her hair was fixed, it shone like spun gold in the glow from the hearth.

He took another sip of wine. Then, very gently, he set down the cup and reached across to touch a wispy curl that drifted across her cheek. "How can it be enough to simply survive?" he asked softly. "Do you never dream of doing more than that?"

"Damn *you*," she said, echoing his words to her. She shoved away from the table and turned her back on him. There was a heartbreaking pride in the stiff way she held herself, the set of her shoulders and the haughty tilt of her head. "Goodbye, Your Worship. Thank you for our brief association. We shan't be seeing each other again."

"Pippa, wait—"

In a sweep of skirts and injured dignity, she strode out of the hall, disappearing into the gloom of the cloister that bordered the herbiary. Aidan could not explain it, but the sight of her walking away from him caused a painful squeeze of guilt and regret in his chest.

He swore under his breath and finished his wine, then paced the room. He had more pressing matters to ponder than the fate of a saucy street performer. Clan wars and English aggression were tearing his district apart. The settlement he had negotiated last year was shaky at best. A sad matter, that, since he had paid such a dear price for the settlement. He had bought peace at the cost of his heart.

The thought caused his mind to jolt back to Pippa. The ungrateful little female. Let her storm off to her chamber and sulk until she came to her senses.

It occurred to him then that she was the sort not to sulk, but to act. She had survived—and thrived—by doing just that.

A jagged spear of lightning split the sky just as a terrible thought occurred to him. Hurling the pewter wine cup to the floor, he dashed out of the house and into the cloister of Crutched Friars, running down the arcade to her door, jerking it open.

Empty. He passed through the refectory and emerged onto the street. He had been right. He saw Pippa in the distance, hurrying down the broad, tree-lined road leading to Woodroffe Lane and the eerie, lawless area around Tower Hill. A gathering wind stirred the bobbing heads of chestnut trees. Clouds rolled and tumbled, blackening the sky, and when he breathed in, he caught the heavy taste and scent of rain and the faint, sizzling tang of close lightning.

She walked faster still, half running.

Turn back, he called to her silently, trying to will her to do his bidding. *Turn back and look at me.*

Instead, she lifted her skirts and began to run. As she passed the communal well of Hart Street, lightning struck.

From where Aidan stood, it looked as if the very hand of God had cleaved the heavens and sent a bolt of fire down to bury itself in the breast of London. A crash of thunder seemed to shake the ground. The clouds burst open like a ripe fruit, and it began to rain.

For an Irishman, Aidan was not very superstitious, but thunder and lightning were a clear sign from a powerful source. He should not have let her go.

Without a second thought, he plunged into the howling storm, racing between the rows of wildly bending chestnut trees. The rain pelted him in huge, cold drops, and lightning speared down through the clouds once more.

He dragged a hand across his rain-stung eyes and squinted through the sodden twilight. Already the ditch down the middle of the street ran like a small, flooding river, carrying off the effluvia of London households.

People scurried for cover here and there, but the darkness had swallowed Pippa. He shouted her name. The storm drowned his voice. With a curse, he began a methodical search of each side alley and path he encountered, working south toward the river, turning westward toward St. Paul's each time he saw a way through.

The storm gathered force, belting him in the face, tearing at his clothes. Mud spattered him to the thighs, but he ignored it.

He went farther west, turning into each alley, calling her name. The rain blinded him, the wind buffeted him, the mud sucked at his feet.

At a particularly grim-looking street, the wind tore down a painted sign of a blue devil and hurled it to the ground. It struck a slanting cellar door, then fell sideways onto a pile of wood chippings.

He heard a faint, muffled cry. With a surge of hope, he flung away the sign and the sawdust.

There she sat, knees drawn up to her chest, face tucked into the hollow between her hugging arms. Thunder crashed again, and she flinched as if struck by a whip.

"Pippa!" He touched her quaking shoulder.

She screamed and looked up at him.

Aidan's heart lurched. Her face, battered by rain and tears, shone stark white in the storm-dulled twilight. The panic in her eyes blinded her; she showed no recognition of him. That look of mindless terror was one he had seen only once before—in the face of his father just before Ronan had died.

"Faith, Pippa, are you hurt?"

She did not respond to her name, but blurted out something he could not comprehend. A nonsense word or a phrase in a foreign tongue?

Shaken, he bent and scooped her up, holding her against his chest and bending his head to shield her from the rain as best he could. She did not resist, but clung to him as if he were a raft in a raging sea. He felt a surge of fierce protectiveness. Never had he felt so painfully alive, so determined to safeguard the small stranger in his arms.

Still she showed no sign of recognition, and did not do so while he dashed back to Lumley House. A host of demons haunted the girl who called herself Pippa Trueheart.

And Aidan O Donoghue was seized by the need to slay each and every one of them.

"Batten the hatches! Secure the helm! There's naught to do now but run before the wind!"

The man in the striped jacket had a funny, rusty voice. He sounded cross, or maybe afraid, like Papa had been when his forehead got hot and he had to go to bed and not have any visitors.

She clung to her dog's furry neck and looked across the smelly, dark enclosure at Nurse. But Nurse had her hands all twisted up in a string of rosy beads—the ones she hid from Mama, who was Reformed—and all Nurse could say was Hail Mary Hail Mary Hail Mary.

Something scooped the ship up and up and up. She could feel the lifting in her belly. And then, much faster, a stronger force slapped them down.

Nurse screamed Hail Mary Hail Mary Hail Mary…

The hound whined. His fur smelled of dog and ocean.

A cracking noise hurt her ears. She heard the whine of ropes running through pulleys and a shriek from the man in the funny coat, and suddenly she had to get out of there, out of that close, wet place where the water was filling up the floor, where her chest wouldn't let her breathe.

She pushed the door open. The dog scrambled out first. She followed him up a slanting wooden stair. Loose barrels skittered all through the passageways and decks. She heard a great roar of water. She looked back to find Nurse, but all she saw was a hand waving, the rosy beads braided through the pale fingers. Water covered Nurse all the way to the top of her head….

"*No!*" Pippa sat straight up in the bed. For a moment, the room was all a pulsating blur. Slowly, it came into focus. Low-burning hearth fire. Candle flickering on the table. High, thick testers holding up the draperies.

The O Donoghue Mór sitting at the end of the bed.

She pressed her hand to her chest, hating the twitchy, air-starved feeling that sometimes seized her lungs when she took fright or breathed noxious or frozen air. Her heart was racing. Sweat bathed her face and neck.

"Bad dream?" he asked.

She shut her eyes. Like a mist driven by the wind, the images flew away, unremembered, but her sense of terror lingered. "It happens. Where am I?"

"I've given you a private chamber in Lumley House."

Her eyes widened in amazement, then narrowed in suspicion. "Why?"

"I am your patron. You'll lodge where I put you."

She thrust up her chin. "And what do you require of me in exchange for living in the lap of luxury?"

"Why must I expect anything at all from you?"

She regarded him for a long, measuring moment. No, the O Donoghue Mór was certainly not the sort of man who had to keep unwilling females at his beck and call. Any woman in her right mind would want him. Except, of course, Pippa herself. But that did not stop her from enjoying his strikingly splendid face and form, nor did it keep her from craving—against all good sense—his warmth and closeness.

"I take it you don't like storms," he said.

"No, I…" It all seemed so silly now. London offered far greater perils than storms, and she had survived London for years. "Thank you, my lord. Thank you for coming after me. I should not have left in such haste."

"True," he said gently.

"It is not every day a man makes me question my very reason for existing."

"Pippa, I didn't mean it that way. I should not have questioned the choices you've made."

She nodded. "People love to *manage* other people." Frowning, she looked around the room, noting the wonderful bed, the crackling fire in the grate, the clear, rain-washed night air wafting through a small, open window. "I don't remember much about the storm. Was it very bad?"

He smiled. It was a soft, unguarded smile, as if he truly meant it. "You were in a bit of a state when I found you."

She blushed and dropped her gaze, then blushed even deeper when she discovered she wore only a shift. She clutched the bedclothes to her chest.

"I hung your things to dry by the fire," Aidan said. "I got the shift from Lady Lumley's clothes press."

Pippa touched the sheer fabric of the sleeve. "I'll hang for certain."

"Nay. Lord and Lady Lumley are at their country estate in Wycherly. I'm to have full use of the house and all its contents."

She sighed dreamily. "How wonderful to be treated like such an important guest."

"Often I find it a burden, not a wonder."

She began to remember snatches of the storm, the lightning and thunder chasing her through the streets, the rain lashing her face. And then Aidan's strong arms and broad chest, and the sensation of speed as he rushed her back to the house. His hands had tenderly divested her of clothes and placed her in the only real bed she had ever slept in.

She had tucked her face into his strong shoulder and sobbed. Hard. He had stroked her hair, kissed it, and finally she had slept.

She looked up at him. "You're awfully kind for a father-murderer."

His smile wavered. "Sometimes I surprise myself." Leaning across the bed, he touched her cheek, his fingers skimming over her blush-heated skin. "You make it easy, colleen. You make me better than I am."

She felt such a profusion of warmth that she wondered if she had a fever. "Now what?" she whispered.

"Now, for once in your life, you'll tell the truth, Pippa. Who are you, where did you come from and what in God's name am I going to do with you?"

Diary of a Lady

❧∽◦∽❧

My son Richard's namesake is coming to London! The Reverend Richard Speed, of famous reputation, now the Bishop of Bath, will attend his nephew's military commission. Naturally Speed will bring his wife, Natalya, who is Oliver's dear sister and as beloved to me as blood kin.

Oliver's other siblings will come with husbands and wives. Belinda and Kit, Simon and Rosamund, whom I have not seen in two winters. Sebastian will come with one special friend or other; these days it is a gifted but disreputable young poet called Marlowe.

Dear Belinda still clings to her scandalous pastime of incendiary displays. She has lit her fireworks for members of the noble houses of Hapsburg and Valois, and of course for Her Majesty the queen. She has promised a special program of Italian colored fire in honor of Richard.

But I wonder, amid all the revelry, if anyone save Oliver will mark the event that tonight's storm reminds me of so poignantly. For many years I have struggled to survive our loss, and daily I thank God for my family.

Still, the storm hurled me back to that dark, rain-drenched night.

It is a time that lives in my heart as its most piercing memory.

—Lark de Lacey,
Countess of Wimberleigh

Four

Aidan was watching her with those penetrating flame-blue eyes. Pippa could tell from his fierce chieftain's glare that he would tolerate no more jests or sidestepping.

She combed her hair with both hands, raking her fingers through the damp, yellow tangles. She felt shaky, much as she did after being stricken with a fever and then getting up for the first time in days. The storm had slammed through her with terrifying force, leaving her limp.

"The problem is," she said with bleak, quiet honesty, "I have the same answer to all of your questions."

"And what is that?"

"I don't know." She watched him closely for a reaction, but he merely sat there at the end of the bed, waiting and watching. Firelight flared behind him, outlining his massive shoulders and the gleaming fall of his black hair.

His eyes never left her, and she wondered just what he saw. Why in heaven's name would a grand Irish lord take an interest in her? What did he hope to gain by befriending her? She had so little to offer—a handful of tricks, a few sorry jests, a chuckle or two. Yet he seemed enraptured, infinitely patient, as he awaited her explanation.

The rush of tenderness she felt for him was frightening. Ah, she could love this man, she could draw him into her heart. But she would not. In his way, he was as remote as the moon, beautiful and unreachable. Before long he would go back to Ireland, and she would resume her existence in London.

"I don't know who I am," she explained, "nor where I come from, nor even where I am going. And I certainly don't know what you're going to do with me." With an effort, she squared her shoulders. "Not that it's any of your concern. I am mistress of my own fate. If and when I decide to delve into my past, it will be to find the answers for me, not you."

"Ah, Pippa." He got up, took a dipper of wine from a cauldron near the hearth and poured the steaming, spice-scented liquid in a cup. "Sip it slowly," he said, handing her the drink, "and we'll see if we can sort this out."

Feeling cosseted, she accepted the wine and let a soothing swallow slide down her throat. Mab had been her teacher, her adviser in herbal arts and foraging, but the old woman had seen only to her most basic needs, keeping her dry and fed as if she were livestock. From Mab, Pippa had learned how to survive. And how to protect herself from being hurt.

"You do not know who you are?" he inquired, sitting again at the foot of the bed.

She hesitated, caught her lower lip with her teeth. Turmoil boiled up inside her, and her immediate reaction was to erupt with laughter and make yet another joke about being a sultan's daughter or a Hapsburg orphan. Then, cradling the cup in her hands, she lifted her gaze to his.

She saw concern burning like a flame in his eyes, and its appeal had a magical effect on her, warming her like the wine, unfurling the secrets inside her, plunging down through her to find the words she had never before spoken to another living soul.

Slowly, she set the cup on a stool beside the bed and began to talk to him. "For as long as I can remember, I have been Pippa. Just Pippa." The admission caught unpleasantly in her throat. She cleared it with a merry, practiced laugh. "It is a very liberating thing, my lord. Not knowing who I am frees me to be whoever I want to be. One day my parents are a duke and duchess, the next they are poor but proud crofters, the next, heroes of the Dutch revolt."

"But all you really want," he said softly, "is to belong somewhere. To someone."

She blinked at him and could summon no tart remark or laughter to answer the charge. And for the first time in her life, she admitted the stark, painful truth. "Oh, God in heaven, yes. All I want to know is that someone once loved me."

He reached across the bed and covered her hands with his. A strange, comfortable feeling rolled over her like a great wave. This man, this foreign chieftain who had all but admitted he'd killed his father, somehow made her feel safe and protected and cared for.

"Let us work back over time." He rubbed his thumbs gently over her wrists. "Tell me how you came to be there on the steps of St. Paul's the first day I met you."

He spoke of their meeting as if it had been a momentous occasion. She pulled her hands away and set her jaw, stubbornly refusing to say more. The fright from the storm had lowered her defenses. She struggled to shore them up again. Why should she confess the secrets of her heart to a virtual stranger, a man she would never see again after he left London?

"Pippa," he said, "it's a simple enough question."

"Why do you care?" she shot back. "What possible interest could it be to you?"

"I care because you matter to me." He raked a hand through his hair. "Is that so hard to understand?"

"Yes," she said.

He reached for her and then froze, his hand hovering between them for a moment before he pulled it back. He cleared his throat. "I am your patron. You perform under my warrant. And these are simple questions."

He made her feel silly for guarding her thoughts as if they were dark secrets. She took a deep breath, trying to decide just where to begin. "Very well. Mort and Dove said eventually, all of London passes through St. Paul's. I suppose—quite foolishly, as it happens—I hoped that one day I would look up and see a man and woman who would say, 'You belong to us.'" She plucked at a loose thread in the counterpane. "Stupid, am I not? Of course, that never happened." She gave a short laugh, tamping back an errant feeling of wistful longing. "Even if they did recognize me, why would they claim me, unwashed and dishonest, thieving from people in the churchyard?"

"*I* claimed you," he reminded her.

His words lit a glow inside her that warmed her chest. She wanted to fling herself against him, to babble with gratitude, to vow to stay with him always. Only the blade-sharp memories of other moments, other partings, held her aloof and wary.

"For that I shall always thank you, my lord," she said cordially. "You won't be sorry. I'll keep you royally entertained."

"Never mind that. So you continued to perform as a strolling player, just wandering about, homeless as a Gypsy?" he asked.

A sting of memory touched her, and she caught her breath in startlement.

"What is it?" he asked.

"Something extraordinary just occurred to me. Years ago, when I first came to London town, I saw a tribe of Gypsies camped in Moor Fields outside the city. I thought they were a troupe of players, but these people dressed and spoke differently. They were like a—a family. I was drawn to them."

Warming to her tale, she shook off the last vestiges of terror from the storm. She sat forward on the bed, draping her arms around her drawn-up knees. "Aidan, it was so exciting. There was something familiar about those people. I could almost understand their language, not the actual words, mind, but the rhythms and nuances."

"And they welcomed you?"

She nodded. "That night, there was a dance around a great bonfire. I was taken to meet a woman called Zara— she was very old. Ancient. Some said more than four-score years old. Her pallet had been set out so that she could watch the dancing." Pippa closed her eyes, picturing the snowy tangle of hair, the wizened-apple face, the night-dark eyes so intense they seemed to see into tomorrow.

"They said she was ill, not expected to live, but she asked to see me. Fancy that." Opening her eyes again, she peered at Aidan to see if he believed her or thought she was spinning yarns once more. She could not tell, for he merely watched and waited with calm interest. No one had ever listened to her with such great attention before.

"Go on," he said.

"Do you know the first thing she said to me? She said I would meet a man who would change my life."

He muttered something Celtic and scowled at her.

"No, it's true, my lord, you must believe me."

"Why should I? You've lied about everything else."

His observation should not have hurt her, but it did. She pressed her knees even closer to her chest and tried to will away the ache in her heart. "Not *everything,* Your Loftiness."

"Continue, then. Tell me what the witch woman said."

"Her speech was slow, broken." In her mind's eye, Pippa saw it all as if it had happened yesterday—the leaping flames and the ancient face, the deep eyes and the Gypsies whispering among themselves and pointing at Pippa, who had knelt beside Zara's pallet.

"She was babbling, I suppose, and speaking in more than one language, but I remember she told me about the man. And she also spoke of blood and vows and honor."

"Blood, vows and honor?" he repeated.

"Yes. That part was very distinct. She spoke the three words, just like that. She was dying, my lord, but clutching my hand with a grip stronger than death itself. I hadn't the heart to question her or show any doubt. It's as if she thought she knew me and somehow needed me in those last moments."

He folded his arms against his massive chest and studied her. Pippa was terrified that he would accuse her again of lying, but he gave the barest of nods. "They say those in extremis often mistake strangers for people they have known. Did the old woman say more?"

"One more thing." Pippa hesitated. She felt it all again, the emotions that had roared through her while the stranger held her hand. A feeling of terrible hope had welled from somewhere deep inside her. "A statement I will never, ever forget. She lifted her head, using the very last of her strength to fix me with a stare. And she said, 'The circle is complete.' Then, within an hour, she was dead. A few of the young Gypsies seemed suspicious of me, so I thought it prudent to leave after that. Besides, the woman's wild talk…"

"Frightened you?" Aidan asked.

"Not frightened so much as touched something inside me. As if the words she spoke were words I should know. I tell you, it gave me much to think on."

"I imagine it did."

"Not that anything ever came of it," she said, then ducked her head and lowered her voice. "Until now."

She watched him, studied his face. Lord, but he was beautiful. Not pretty, but beautiful in the way of a crag overlooking the moors of the north, or in the majestic stance of a roebuck surveying its domain deep in a green velvet wood. It was the sort of beauty that caught at her chest and held fast, defying all efforts to dislodge a dangerous, glorious worship.

Then she noticed that one eyebrow and one corner of his mouth were tilted up in wry irony. She released her breath in an explosive sigh. "I suppose that is the price of being an outrageous and constant liar."

"What is that?" he asked.

"When I finally tell the truth, you don't believe me."

"And why would you be thinking I don't believe you?"

"That *look,* Your Worship. You seem torn between laughing at me and summoning the warden of Bedlam."

The eyebrow inched up even higher. "Actually, I am torn between laughing at you and kissing you."

"I choose the kissing," she blurted out all in a rush.

Both of his eyebrows shot up, then lowered slowly over eyes gone soft and smoky. He gripped her hands and drew her forward so that she came up on her knees. The bedclothes pooled around her, and the thin shift whispered over her burning skin.

"I choose the kissing, too." He lifted his hand to her face. The pad of his thumb moved slowly, tantalizingly, along the curve of her cheekbone and then downward, slipping like silk over marble, to touch her bottom lip, to rub over the fullness until she almost did not *need* the kiss in order to feel him.

Almost.

"Have you ever been kissed before, colleen?"

The old bluster rose up inside her. "Well, of c—"

"Pippa," he said, pressing his thumb gently on her lips. "This would be a very bad time to lie to me."

"Oh. Then, no, Your Immensity. I have never been kissed." The few who had tried had had their noses rearranged by her fist, but she thought it prudent not to mention that.

"Do you know how it's done?"

"Yes."

"Pippa, the truth. You were doing so well."

"I've seen it happen, but I don't know how it's done in actual practice."

"The first thing that has to happen—"

"Yes?" Unable to believe her good fortune, she bounced up and down on her knees, setting the bed to creaking on the rope latticework that supported the mattress. "This is really too exciting, my lord—"

His thumb stopped her mouth again. "—is that you have to stop talking. And for God's sake don't *narrate* everything. This is supposed to be a gesture of affection, but you're turning it into a farce."

"Oh. Well, of course I didn't mean—"

Again he hushed her, and at the same moment a log fell

in the grate. The brief flare of sparks found, just for an instant, a bright home in the centers of his eyes. She moaned in sheer wanting but remembered at last not to speak.

"Ah, well done," he whispered, and his thumb moved again, with subtle, devastating tenderness, slipping just inside her mouth and then emerging to spread moisture along her lip.

"If you like, you can close your eyes."

She mutely shook her head. It was not every day she got a kiss from an Irish chieftain, and she was not about to miss a single instant of giddy bliss.

"Then just look up at me," he said, surging closer to her on the bed. "Just look up, and I'll do the rest."

She tilted her chin up as he lowered his head. His thumb slid aside to make room for his lips, and his mouth brushed over hers, softly, sweetly, with a sensation that made raw wanting jolt to life inside her.

She made a sound, but he caught it with his mouth and pressed down gently, until their lips were truly joined. His deft fingers rubbed with tender insistence along her jawline, and his lips pushed against the seam of hers.

Open.

Here was something she had not learned from spying on couples pumping away in the alleys of Southwark or groping one another in the shadows of the pillars of St. Paul's.

His tongue came into her, and she made a squeak of surprise and delight. Her hands drifted upward, over his chest and around behind his neck. She wanted this closeness with a staggering, overwhelming need. His mouth and tongue went deeper, and his hands smoothed down her back, fingers splaying as he pressed her closer, closer.

The quickness of his breath startled her into the realization that he, too, was moved by the intimacy. He, too, had chosen the kiss.

All her life, Pippa had been curious about every bright, shiny thing she saw, and loveplay was no different, yet wholly different. It was not a case of simple *wanting,* but the experience of a sudden, devastating need she did not know she had.

Tightening her arms around his neck, she thrust against him, wanting the closeness to last forever. She could feel his heartbeat against her chest, feel the life force of another person beating against her and, in an odd, spiritual way, joining with her.

He lifted his mouth from hers. A stunned expression bloomed on his face. "Ah, colleen," he whispered urgently, "we must stop before I—"

"Before what?" She reveled in the feel of his wine-sweet breath next to her face.

"Before I want more than just a kiss."

"Then it's too late for me," she admitted, "for I already want more."

He chuckled, very low and very softly, and there was a subtle edge of anguish in his voice. "When you decide to be honest, you don't stint, do you?"

"I suppose not. Ah, I *do* want you, Aidan."

A sad-sweet smile curved his beautiful mouth. "And I want you, lass. But we must not let this go any further."

"Why not?"

He lifted her hands away from him and rose from the bed, moving slowly as if he were in pain. "Because it's not proper."

Stung, she scowled. "I have never been preoccupied with what is proper."

"I have," he muttered, and turned away. From the

cauldron, he ladled himself a cup of wine and drank it in one gulp. "I'm sorry, Pippa."

Already he had withdrawn from her, and she shivered with the chill of rejection. "Can't you look at me and say that?"

He turned, and still his movements seemed labored. "I said I was sorry. I took advantage of your innocence, and I should never have done that."

"I chose the kiss."

"So did I."

"Then why did you stop?"

"I want you to tell me about yourself. Kissing gets in the way of clearheaded thinking."

"So if I tell you about myself, we can go back to the kissing?"

An annoyed tic started in his jaw. "I never said that."

"Well, can we?"

With exaggerated care, he set down his cup and walked over to the bed. Cradling her face between his hands, he gazed at her with heartbreaking regret. "No, colleen."

"But—"

"Consider the consequences. Some of them are quite lasting."

She swallowed. "You mean a baby." A wistful longing rose in her. Would it be such a catastrophe, she wondered, if the O Donoghue Mór were to give her a child? A small, helpless being that belonged solely to her?

She felt his hands, so gentle upon her face, yet his expression was one of painful denial. "Why should I do as you say?" she asked, resisting the urge to hurl herself at him, to cling to him and not let go.

"Because I'm asking you to, *a gradh*. Please."

She blew out a weary sigh, aware without asking that

the Irish word was an endearment. "Do you know how impossible it is to say no to you?"

He smiled a little, bent and kissed the top of her head before letting her go. "Now. We were working backward from your move to London. You met a mysterious hag—"

"Gypsy woman."

"In Ireland we would call her a woman of the *sidhe*."

"She said I'd meet a man who would change my life." Pippa leaned back against the banked pillows. She wondered if he noticed her blush-stung cheeks. "I always thought it meant I'd find my father. But I've changed my mind. She meant you."

He lowered himself to the foot of the bed and sat very quietly and thoughtfully. How could he be so indifferent upon learning he was the answer to a magical prophecy? What a fool he must think her. Then he asked, "What changed your mind?"

"The kiss." Jesu, she had not been so truthful in one conversation since she had first come to London. Aidan O Donoghue coaxed honesty from her; it was some power he possessed, one that made it safe to speak her mind and even her heart, if she dared.

He seemed to go rigid, though he did not move.

Idiot, Pippa chided herself. By now he probably could not wait to get rid of her. Surely he would drag her to Bedlam, collecting his fee for turning in a madwoman. He would not be the first to rid himself of a smitten girl in such a manner. "I shouldn't have said that," she explained, forcing out a laugh. "It was just a kiss, not a blood oath or some such nonsense. Verily, Your Magnitude, we should forget all about this."

"I'm Irish," he cut in softly, his musical lilt more pronounced than ever. "An Irishman does not take a kiss lightly."

"Oh." She stared at his firelit, mystical face and held her breath. It took all her willpower not to fling herself at him, ask him to toss up her skirts and do whatever it was a man did beneath a woman's skirts.

"Pippa?"

"Yes?"

"The story. Before you came to London, where did you live? What did you do?"

The simple questions drew vivid images from the well of her memories. She closed her eyes and traced her way back over the long, oft interrupted journey to London. She lost count of the strolling troupes she had belonged to. Always she was greeted first with skepticism; then, after a display of jests and juggling, she was welcomed. She never stayed long. Usually she slipped away in the night, more often than not leaving a half-conscious man on the ground, clutching a shattered jaw or broken nose, cursing her to high heaven or the belly of hell.

"Pippa?" Aidan prompted again.

She opened her eyes. Each time she looked at him, he grew more beautiful. Perhaps she was under some enchantment. Simply looking at him increased his appeal and weakened her will to resist him.

Almost wistfully, she touched her bobbed hair. I want to be like you, she thought. Beautiful and beloved, the sort of person others wish to embrace, not put in the pillory. The yearning felt like an aching knot in her chest, stunning in its power. Against her will, Aidan O Donoghue was awakening her to feelings she had spent a lifetime running from.

"I traveled slowly to London," she said, "jesting and juggling along the way. There were times I went hungry, or slept in the cold, but I didn't really mind. You see, I had always wanted to go to London."

"To seek your family."

How had he guessed? It was part of the magic of him, she decided. "Yes. I knew it was next to impossible, but sometimes—" She broke off and looked away in embarrassment at her own candor.

"Go on," he whispered. "What were you going to say?"

"Just that, sometimes the heart asks for the impossible."

He reached across the bed, lifted her chin with a finger and winked at her. "And sometimes the heart gets it."

She sent him a bashful smile. "Mab would agree with you."

"Mab?"

"The woman who reared me. She lived in Humberside, along the Hornsy Strand. It was a land that belonged to no one, so she simply settled there. That's how she told it. Mab was simple, but she was all I had."

"How did you come to live with her?"

"She found me." A dull sense of resignation weighted Pippa, for she had always hated the truth about herself. "According to her, I lay upon the strand, clinging to a herring keg. A large lurcher or hound was with me. I was tiny, Mab said, two or three, no more." Like a lightning bolt, memory pierced her, and she winced with the force of it. *Remember.* The command shimmered through her mind.

"Colleen?" Aidan asked. "Are you all right?"

She clasped her hands over her ears, trying to shut out the insistent swish of panic.

"No!" she shouted. "Please! I don't remember anymore!"

With a furious Irish exclamation, Aidan O Donoghue, Lord of Castleross, took her in his arms and let her bathe his shoulder in bitter tears.

* * *

"Act as if nothing's amiss," Donal Og hissed. He, Iago and Aidan were in the stableyard of Crutched Friars the next day. Aidan had grooms to look after his horse, but currying the huge mare was a task he enjoyed, particularly in the early morning when no one was about.

Iago looked miserable in the bright chill of early morn. He detested cold weather. He made impossible claims about the climate of his homeland, insisting that it never snowed in the Caribbean, never froze, and that the sea was warm enough to swim in.

Absently patting Grania's strong neck, Aidan studied his cousin and Iago. What a formidable pair they made, one dark, one fair, both as large and imposing as cliff rocks.

"Nothing *is* amiss," Aidan said, leaning down to pick up a currying brush. Then he saw what Donal Og had clutched in his hand. "Is it?"

Donal Og glanced to and fro. The stableyard was empty. A brake of rangy bushes separated the area from the kitchen garden of the main house and the glassworks of Crutched Friars. Through gaps in the bushes, Lumley House and its gardens appeared serene, the well-sweep and stalks of herbs adorned with drops of last night's rain that sparkled in the rising sun.

"Read for yourself." Donal Og shoved a paper at Aidan. "But for God's sake, don't react too strongly. Walsingham's spies are everywhere."

Aidan glanced back over his shoulder at the house. "Faith, I hope not."

Donal Og and Iago exchanged a glance. Their faces split into huge grins. "It is about time, amigo," Iago said.

Aidan's ears felt hot with foolish defensiveness. "It's not what you think. Sure and I'd hoped for better understanding from the two of you."

The manly grins subsided. "As you wish, coz," Donal Og said. "Far be it from such as us to suspect yourself of swiving your wee guest."

"Ahhh." A sweet female voice trilled in the distance. All three of them peered through the tall hedge at the house. Slamming open the double doors to the upper hall, Pippa emerged into the sunlight.

The parchment crinkled in Aidan's clenched hand. Aside from that, no one made a sound. They stood still, as if a sudden frost had frozen them. She stood on the top step, clad only in her shift. Clearly she thought she'd find no one in the private garden so early. She inhaled deeply, as if tasting the crisp morning air, cleansed by the rain.

Her hair was sleep tousled, soft and golden in the early light. Although Aidan had kissed her only once, he remembered vividly the rose-petal softness of her lips. Her eyes were faintly bruised by shadows from last night's tears.

As spellbinding as her remarkable face was her body. The thin shift, with the sun shimmering through, revealed high, upturned breasts, womanly hips, a tiny waist and long legs, shaded at the top by dark mystery.

She held a basin in her arms and shifted the vessel to perch on her hip. She descended the steps while three pairs of awestruck eyes, peering avidly through the stableyard hedge, watched her.

At the bottom of the steps, she stopped to shake back a tumble of golden curls. Then she bent forward over the well to draw the water. The thin fabric of the shift whispered over a backside so lush and shapely that Aidan's mouth went dry.

"*Ay, mujer*," whispered Iago. "Would that I had such a bedmate."

"It's not what you think," Aidan managed to repeat in a low, strained voice.

"No," said Donal Og with rueful envy, his jaw unhinging as Pippa straightened. Some of the water dampened the front of her shift, so that her flesh shone pearly pink through the white lawn fabric. She paused to pluck the top of a daffodil and tuck it behind her ear. "No doubt," Donal Og continued, "it is a hundred times *better* than we think."

Aidan grabbed him by the front of his tunic. "I'll see you do penance for six weeks if you don't quit staring."

Oblivious, Pippa slipped back into the house. Iago made a great show of wiping his brow while Donal Og paced the yard, limping as if in discomfort. The horse made a loud, rude sound.

"The urchin turned out to be a beauty, Aidan," he said. "I would never have looked twice at her, but you looked once and found a true jewel."

"I wasn't looking for treasure, cousin," Aidan said. "The lass was caught up in a riot and in danger of being thrown into prison. I merely—"

"Hush." Donal Og held up a hand. "You needn't explain, coz. We're happy for you. Sure it wasn't healthy for you to be living like a monk, pretending you were not troubled by a man's needs. It is not as if you and Felicity ever—"

"Cease your infernal blather," Aidan snapped, pierced to the core by the merest thought of Felicity. His grip on the parchment tightened. Perhaps the letter from Revelin of Innisfallen contained good news. Perhaps the bishop had granted the annulment. *Oh, please God, yes.*

"Don't speak of Felicity again. And by God, if you so much as insinuate that Pippa and I are lovers, I'll turn blood ties into a blood bath."

"You *didn't* bed her?" Iago demanded, horrified.

"No. She ran off at the height of the storm and I brought her back here. She seems to have a particular fear of storms."

"You," said Iago, aiming a finger at Aidan's chest, "are either a sick man or a saint. She has the body of a goddess. She adores you. Take her, Aidan. I am certain she's had offers from lesser men than an Irish chieftain. She will thank you for it."

Aidan swore and stalked over to a stone hitch post. Propping his hip on it, he unfurled the parchment and began to read.

The letter from Revelin of Innisfallen was in Irish. Aye, there it was, news regarding the marriage Aidan had made in hell and desperation. But that hardly mattered, considering the rest. Each word stabbed into him like a shard of ice. When he finished reading, he looked up at Donal Og and Iago.

"Who brought this?"

"A sailor on a flax boat from Cork. He can't read."

"You're certain?"

"Aye."

Aidan tore the parchment into three equal portions. "Good appetite, my friends," he said wryly. "I pray the words do not poison you."

"Tell me what I am eating," said Iago, chewing on the paper with a pained expression.

Aidan grimaced as he swallowed his portion. "An insurrection," he said.

By the time Aidan went back to Pippa's chamber, she had dressed herself. Her skirt and bodice had been laced correctly this time.

She sat at the thick-legged oaken table in the center of the room, and she did not look up when he entered.

Several objects lay before her on the table. The morning sun streamed over her in great, slanting bars. The light glinted in her hair and gilded her smooth, pearly skin. The daffodil she had picked adorned her curls more perfectly than a comb of solid gold.

Aidan felt a twist of sentiment deep in his gut. Just when he had thought he'd conquered and killed all tenderness within himself, he found a girl who reawakened his heart.

Devil take her. She looked like the soul of virtue and innocence, an angel in an idealized portrait with her sun-drenched face and halo of hair, the lean purity of her profile, the fullness of her lips as she pursed them in concentration.

"Sit down, Your Serenity," she said softly, still not looking up. "I've decided to tell you more because…"

"Because why?" Willingly shoving aside the news from Ireland, he approached the table and lowered himself to the bench beside her.

"Because you care."

"I shouldn't—"

"Yet you do," she insisted. "You do in spite of yourself."

He did not deny it, but crossed his arms on the table and leaned forward. "What is all this?"

"My things." She patted the limp, dusty bag she had worn tied to her waist the first day they had met. "It is uncanny how little one actually *needs* in order to survive. All I ever had fits in this bag. Each object has a special meaning to me, a special significance. If it does not, I get rid of it."

She rummaged with her hand in the bag and drew out a seashell, placing it on the table between them. It was shiny from much handling, bleached white on the outside while the inner curve was tinted with pearly shades of pink in graduated intensity.

"I don't remember ever actually finding this. Mab always said I was a great one for discovering things washed up on shore, and from the time I was very small, I would bring her the most marvelous objects. Apples to juggle, a pessary of wild herbs. One time I found the skull of a deer."

She took out a twist of hair, sharply contrasting black and white secured with a bit of string.

"I hope that's not poor Mab," Aidan commented.

She laughed. "Ah, please, Your Magnificence. I am not so bloodthirsty as that." She stroked the lock. "This is from the dog I was with when Mab found me. Mab swore the beast saved me from drowning. He was half drowned himself, but he revived and lived with us. She said I told her his name was Paul."

She propped her chin in her cupped hand and gazed at the whitewashed wall by the window, where the morning sun created colored ribbons of light on the plastered surface. "The dog died four years after Mab found us. I barely remember him, except—" She stopped and frowned.

"Except what?" asked Aidan.

"During storms at night, I would creep over to his pallet and sleep." She showed him a few more of her treasures—a page from a book she could not read. He saw that it was from an illegal pamphlet criticizing the queen's plans to marry the Duke of Alençon. "I like the picture," Pippa said simply, and showed him a few other objects: a ball of sealing wax and a tiny brass bell—"I nicked it from the Gypsy wagon"—flint and steel, a spoon.

It was, Aidan realized with a twinge of pity, the flotsam and jetsam of a hard life lived on the run.

And then, almost timidly, she displayed things recently collected: his horn-handled knife, which he hadn't the heart to reclaim; an ale weight from Nag's Head Tavern.

She looked him straight in the eye with a devotion that bordered discomfitingly on worship. "I have saved a memento of each day with you," she told him.

A tightness banded across his chest. He cleared his throat. "Indeed. Have you naught else to show me?"

She took her time putting all her treasures back in the bag. She worked so slowly and so deliberately that he felt an urge to help her, to speed her up.

The message he had received still burned in his mind. He had a potential disaster awaiting him in Ireland, and here he sat, reminiscing with a confused, possibly deluded girl.

The letter had come all the way from Kerry, first by horseman to Cork and then by ship. Revelin, the gentle scholar of Innisfallen, had sounded the alarm about a band of outlaws roving across Kerry, pillaging at will, robbing even fellow Irish, inciting idle men to rise against their oppressors. Revelin reported that the band had reached Killarney town and gathered around the residence of Fortitude Browne, recently appointed constable of the district. And a hated Englishman.

Revelin was not certain, but he suggested the outlaws would try to take hostages, perhaps Fortitude's fat, sniveling nephew, Valentine.

Aidan crushed his hands together as a feeling of powerlessness swept over him. He could do nothing from here in London. Queen Elizabeth had summoned him to force him to submit to her and then to regrant his lands to him. Just to show her might, she had kept him waiting. He battled the urge to storm out of London without even a by-your-leave. But that would be suicide—both for him and for his people. Elizabeth's armies in Ireland were the instruments of her wrath.

Just as Felicity had been.

He would write back to Revelin, of course, but beyond that, he could only pray that cooler heads prevailed and the reckless brigands dispersed.

"I must show you one more thing," Pippa said, snapping him out of his reverie.

He looked into her soft eyes and for no particular reason felt a lifting sensation inside him.

Something about her touched him. She reminded him of the hardscrabbling people of his district and their stubborn struggle against English rule. Her determination was as stout as that of his father, who had died rather than submit to the English. And yes—Pippa reminded him of Felicity Browne—*before* the cold English beauty had shown her true colors.

"Very well," he said, trying to clear his mind of the potential disaster seething back in Ireland. "Show me one more thing."

She took a deep breath, then released it slowly as she placed her fisted hand on the table. With a deliberate movement she turned her hand over to reveal a sizable yet rather ugly object of gold.

"It's mine," she declared.

"I never said it wasn't."

"I was worried you might. See?" She set it down. "It looks odd now, but it wasn't always. It was pinned to my frock when Mab found me." She angled it toward him. "It's got a hollow interior, as if something once fit inside. The outside used to have twelve matched pearls around a huge ruby in the middle. Mab said this pin, and the finely made frock I wore, are proof that I came from the nobility. What think you, my lord? Am I of noble stock?"

He studied her, the elfin features, the wide, fragile eyes, the expressive mouth. "I think you were made by fairies."

She laughed and continued her tale. "Each year, Mab sold one of the pearls. After she died, I tried to sell the ruby, but I was accused of stealing it and I had to run for my life."

She spoke matter-of-factly, even with an edge of wry humor, but that did not banish the image in his mind of a hungry, frightened young girl escaping the law.

"So now all I have left is this." She turned it over and pointed to some etchings on the back beneath the pin. "I'm quite certain I know what these symbols mean."

"Oh?" He grinned at her earnest expression.

"They are Celtic runes proclaiming the wearer of this brooch to be the incarnation of Queen Maeve."

"Indeed."

She shrugged. "Have you a better idea?"

He angled the brooch so that the sunlight picked out every detail of the etching. He started to nod his head and gamely declare that Pippa was absolutely right, when a memory teased him.

These were no random designs, but writings in a different alphabet. Not Hebrew or Greek; he had studied those. Then why did it look so familiar?

Frowning, Aidan found parchment and stylus. While Pippa watched in fascination, he carefully copied down the symbols, then turned the page this way and that, frowning in concentration.

"Aidan?" Pippa spoke loudly. "You're staring as if it's the flaming bush of Moses."

He handed back the pin. "It's very nice, and I have no doubt you *are* Queen Maeve's descendant." Absently, he tucked away the copy he had made. "Tell me. You faced starvation many times rather than selling that piece of gold. Why did you never try to pawn or trade it?"

She clutched the pin to her chest. "I will never give this up. It is the only thing I belong to. The only thing that belongs to me. When I hold it in my hand, sometimes I can—" She bit her lip and squeezed her eyes shut.

"Can what?"

"Can see them." She whispered the words.

"See them?"

"Yes," she said, opening her eyes. "Aidan, I have never told this to another living soul."

Then don't tell me, he wanted to caution her. *Don't make me privy to your dreams, for I cannot make any of them come true.*

Instead he waited, and in a moment she spoke again. "This idea has consumed me ever since Mab died. I must find them, Aidan. I want to find my family. I want to know where I came from."

"That is only natural. But you have so few clues."

"I know," she admitted. "But sometimes, when I'm just waking up, lying halfway between waking and sleep, I hear voices. See people. It's very vague and jumbled up, but I know it's all connected."

She put away the broken gold pin and clutched at his hand. "I have to believe I'm someone, my lord. Can you understand?"

He brought her hands to his lips and kissed her fingers softly, all the while holding her gaze with his. She made him uncomfortable with her lost, needy look, because it reminded him of what he could never give her.

She needed the constant, unconditional love of a man to heal her and help her learn to love and value herself. He could not possibly be that man.

Ah, he could love her passionately and well.

But not forever.

From the Annals
of Innisfallen

Even now, weeks after sending my missive to London, I flay myself for heaping woe upon the right brave shoulders of the O Donoghue Mór. I had hoped to soften the blow with the news that the Harridan—that is to say, his lady wife—is gone from his life, but the bishop equivocates and wrings his fat hands and procrastinates. Sometimes I think he fears the Sassenach more than the O Donoghue Mór, which is a grave mistake.

Although I felt it was my duty to inform Aidan about the insurrection, I hope he will not stray from his course in London. An agreement with Elizabeth, she-king of the isles, is our last, best hope. Especially now, and may the dreadful Almighty bless and preserve us.

All his life, my lord of Castleross has been most cruelly buffeted between forces that claim his loyalty, his energy, his love. His father taught him naught but hatred and war, raiding and reiving. I think I am the only one who sees him for what he truly is—a man torn between desire and duty, a son bound to fulfill the dream of a despised father, a chieftain struggling to meet the needs of his people.

Sometimes, in those half-awake pagan dreams that get me in such trouble with the abbot, I see the O Donoghue Mór striking forth unfettered like Fionn Mac Cool along the Giants' Causeway, walking not into the nest of vipers his district has become, but away, far away, toward a freedom earned with the sweat of his brow and great blessed pieces of his too generous heart.

—Revelin of Innisfallen

Five

"**Y**our Vast Abundance," Pippa announced in the voice she affected to cry up a show, "fortune favors you today." She smiled eagerly as Aidan looked up from the table where he, Donal Og and Iago were deep in conversation.

Donal Og sent her his customary "go away" scowl. Unwilling to let him dampen her plans, Pippa stuck her tongue out at him. "I was going to invite you along as well, but I might not."

Iago shot up from the table. "Where are we going?"

She beamed at him. Unlike Donal Og, Iago was always game for an adventure.

With Aidan, she could never tell.

He rubbed the bridge of his nose in a way that spoke of a sleepless night. She wished she could alleviate his worries, but he would not even share the nature of his concerns. Didn't he realize how much she cared? How much she longed to take his beautiful, weary face between her hands and ease the frown from his brow with kisses?

"Come along, my lord Reluctance," she urged, embarrassing herself with her own thoughts. "Even Atlas had to let go with one hand to scratch his arse every once in a while."

Aidan rolled his eyes. "How can I refuse such a charming offer?"

"She bestows more titles than the queen herself," said Donal Og.

"Ah, but I give them much more cheaply, Sir Donal of the Small Wit."

"To what do we owe this honor, Mistress Trueheart?" Aidan asked.

She felt an itchy flush creep up her neck to stain her cheeks. Blushing. *She* was blushing. How ridiculous. She was becoming as soft as a wool merchant's wife.

"You seem to need a diversion, my lord. In the past two days you have done nothing but write letters and yell at your men and pace and swear. And drink sack like it was rainwater."

"The perils of being a chieftain, *pequeña,*" said Iago.

She dipped a brief curtsy in his direction. Wearing decent clothes suited her better than she ever would have thought. "I have decided to take you to the public theater."

Iago clapped his huge hands. "Capital!" Then his thick brows clashed in puzzlement. "What is the public theater?"

Pippa spread her arms, wanting to embrace all three of them. "It's anything you want it to be."

An hour later Pippa stood in the stableyard, staring at a saddled horse as if it were a fire-breathing dragon. "I don't see why we can't walk."

"Ah, it'll be quicker," Aidan said. "You're not afraid, are you?"

"Afraid?" Her voice squeaked up an octave. "I? Pippa Trueborn, afraid of a—a midge-witted beast of burden?"

Aidan regarded her with laughing blue eyes. "I thought your first ride might frighten you, and I was right. I suppose we could both mount Grania—"

"Ha!" She poked a finger at the front of his doublet. "Watch me." In a whirl of skirts and indignation, she seized the saddlebow and attempted to hoist herself on the back of the tall bay. The horse's nostrils flared, and it sidled. "Come here, you flap-eared pestilence." She grabbed the saddle and managed to shove her foot into a dangling loop. The midge-wit chose that moment to trot across the yard. Shrieking, Pippa hopped along with the horse. "Oh God, the evil carrion's going to kill me," she yelled. "By all that's holy, save me!"

She had just taken a huge breath, readying herself for another shriek, when a pair of strong arms grasped her around the waist. It was Donal Og, laughing so hard she could feel his vast bulk trembling against her. Iago caught the bay's reins and guffawed. She treated them to a prodigious stream of oaths, which only increased their mirth, while Aidan, equally amused, disengaged her foot from the stirrup.

She staggered against him, then pushed back from his chest to glare at them all. "Braying clog-brains," she said. "I will ride this horse, even though I have scambling clowns for teachers."

To her surprise, it was Donal Og who proved to be most helpful. Though the big man took pains to appear gruff, he failed to hide his air of good-humored patience. It was he who showed her the proper way to hold the reins. He helped her hook one leg over the sidesaddle to keep her balance. Iago calmed the horse with a steady patter of lilting nonsense. Before long she sat proud and beaming, certain she had mastered the art of riding.

As the four of them left the yard, she asked, "My lord, what is this horse's name?"

"Didn't I tell you?" The O Donoghue Mór winked. "He is called Midge."

They rode out into Woodroffe Lane, leaving the narrow byways behind and trotting across Finsbury Fields, scattered with windmills. They passed Holywell, teeming with holidaymakers and their picnics. In the distance, the playing flag of the theater fluttered on the wind, and she gave a whoop of gladness.

Making a loud, urgent noise proved to be a mistake. The gelding surged out of its bearable trot into a full gallop. Pippa hollered in terror and clung, her fingers twining in the horse's flying mane. She looked down to see the ground racing past at a furious rate. Aidan shouted something, but she could not understand.

The knowledge that she was about to die a violent death was unexpectedly and intensely liberating. Acceptance stripped away the terror, and she found that the emotion building inside her was no longer fear, but joy. Never had she moved so swiftly. It was like flying, she decided. She was a feather on the breeze, rising higher and higher, and nothing else mattered but the speed.

Twin shadows encroached upon her. Aidan and Donal Og. They came up on either side, forcing her horse to slow. Like the feather, she settled slowly back to earth, her white-knuckled hands relaxing, her mouth widening in a grin of pure delight.

"We made it, my lord," she said, her voice trembling. "Look." Ahead of them loomed a rambling barn and a horse pond, and beyond that, the theater rose like a citadel.

Still exhilarated from the thrill of the ride, she slid to the ground. With a shaking hand, she gave the reins to a waiting groom. Aidan and his companions did the same, tossing coppers to the grooms and admonishing them to look after the beasts.

"Mind his mouth, then," she called after the boy leading her gelding away. "And give him a good long drink." The very idea of someone actually doing her bidding was heady indeed.

Beneath the playing flag gathered an audience of all manner of persons—nobleman, merchant, beggar and bawd. She tugged at Aidan's sleeve and led them toward the penny gate. "If you don't wish to pay, we can go stand in the yard, but for a penny each, we can—"

"I want to watch from up there." He pointed to the stairway leading to the curving rows of seats.

"Ah, my lord, it's a higher fare, and besides, the seats are for gentry."

"And what are we?" Iago asked with a haughty sniff. "Groundlings?"

She laughed. "I've always been perfectly comfortable with the penny public. Actors love us, for we laugh and cheer in all the right places. The Puritans hate us."

"Speak to me not of Puritans," Aidan said. "I have had my fill of such people."

"Ah, have you encountered your share of black crows, Your Reverence?"

Donal Og's reply, in Irish, seemed to indicate concurrence, possibly empathy, but before she could demand a translation, Iago hastened them toward the stairs.

"Wait," she said, balking. "I haven't a mask."

"You have now." Aidan held out a black silk half mask. "It is a curious practice, but the English are a curious race."

As she tied on the mask, she wished he had not spoken like that, pointing out how very foreign he was in the only world she had ever known.

But as she climbed the steps with her remarkable escorts, a sense of wonder filled her. As many times as she had come to stand with the penny public, she had never bought a seat at the theater.

The magnificent building was designed in circular fashion like the bear garden in Southwark. The sloping stage jutted out into the center of the arena. Paint and paste brought to life a colorful world of the imagination.

As they emerged onto the seating tier, people stared at Aidan, Donal Og and Iago. Flushed behind her silken mask, Pippa tilted up her chin in self-importance, enjoying the slack-jawed looks of awe and admiration. Iago, with his dark skin and colorful garb, was the most striking of the three, but Donal Og and Aidan, towering head and shoulders above the prosperous merchants and gentlemen, also garnered their share of admiring looks.

"*Diablo!*" Iago exclaimed, jumping and turning. "Someone *pinched* me."

Pippa smothered a giggle. A plump woman in a cherry-colored gown winked from behind a feathered mask at Iago. But then another woman, whose bosom all but erupted from her bodice, turned her attention to Aidan, lowering her eyelids halfway and running her red tongue over her lips.

Pippa grabbed Aidan's sleeve and pulled him along the riser. "Stay away from such as that one," she warned.

His eyes danced with merriment. "And why should I be doing that?"

"She is a wanton pestilence. You mark my words."

"I mark them," he said, laughing.

Pippa took a deep breath. "She might give you something you can't wash off."

He made a choking sound. Then he put a gentle hand on her shoulder. "Painted cows have little appeal for me."

His voice was low and intimate. "I much prefer the charm of innocence."

She felt wingbeats of joy fluttering inside her. Then he winked. "Not to mention a talent for juggling."

A thrill of excitement chased up her spine. She clung to his arm, so proud to be the favored partner of the O Donoghue Mór that she did not even feel the floor beneath her feet. Like a dry sponge, she absorbed the ways of the nobility, learning to flutter a fan in front of her bosom, to crook her finger daintily as she sampled the fare, to cover her mouth as she laughed at some jest on the stage.

The play concerned a thrice cuckolded husband and his insatiable wife, and Pippa enjoyed it thoroughly, though the drama was not what she would remember that day. Nor would she recall sampling the pies and nuts and comfits Donal Og bought from the trays of the concession men.

What she would remember was being with Aidan. Hearing the rich music of his laughter. Stealing glances at his magnificent profile. Mimicking the manners and expressions of the noble ladies, even though he protested that such posturing moved him not.

Pippa forgot to perform the ritual she had always done in the past. Every time she found herself in a crowd of people, she searched each face for something vague yet familiar—a tilt of the head, a lift of the mouth, something to mark her connection with another human being; something that would make her a member of a family.

Yet today her usual obsession lay quiet inside her. She wondered why, and answered the question in her heart.

When she was with Aidan O Donoghue, she did not *need* a family, for she belonged, heart and soul, to him.

* * *

He wondered how old she was. Some women wore their age like a coat of arms, this or that detail announcing plainly, whether she liked it or not, that she was eighteen, or twenty-six, or thirty-two.

Not so Pippa, bouncing at his side, laughing and squealing in delight at the farce on the stage. One moment he was certain she was no more than sixteen, girlish and breathless and fresh as the dawn. Then the melancholy would sweep like a mist over her, and she would make some observation that was so wise and world-weary that he would swear she was as old as time.

A troupe of clowns scurried out on stage, conking each other on the heads with mallets. Pippa threw back her head and guffawed, slapping her knees and forgetting she was amid noble ladies.

"How old are you?" Aidan finally asked. In the same moment that he spoke, he cursed himself for an idiot. He should not care.

Still laughing, she turned to him, then slowly sobered to that piercing earnestness against which he had no defense.

"I don't know," she said.

"How can you not know?"

She ducked her head. Laughter and applause masked their conversation so that he had to put his head very close to hers in order to hear. "You forget, my lord," she said. "I was not born, I was *found*. Who can say what my age was then? Two? Three? Four?"

He guessed that she was born out of wedlock and abandoned by a mother who couldn't afford to keep her, or perhaps she was orphaned when the mother died. The golden brooch and the expensive frock in which she had been found were intriguing clues. Yet even if she did come from noble stock, that did not change her circumstances now. She was utterly alone in the world. All Aidan knew for certain was that she had been wounded by a horrible force—the wound of abandonment.

The pain in her eyes made him want to flinch. "My lord, I can never keep from wondering. Was I *meant* to be found, or to lie there and die?"

He cupped his hands around her shoulders. "Pippa—"

"It was sheer, blind luck that Mab happened upon me, so I can only think I was not meant to live." She stared down at the tumbling clowns on the stage but did not seem to see them. "Imagine that. I had lived only a short time, and then someone decided it should be over for me."

"You cannot know that," he said, covering his pity with gruffness.

She blinked, and a winsome smile erased her melancholy. "I stayed with Mab for twelve years. One year for each pearl she traded."

"You said she always sold one at Michaelmas." He relaxed his grip on her shoulders and turned to feign interest in the stage.

"And then I came to London. I've been here eleven years."

"That narrows it some. You're between twenty-five and twenty-seven years of age."

She bit her lip. "Old enough to be a spinster."

He brushed a bright lock of hair off her brow. "You don't look like any spinster I've ever seen."

With a soft cry of joy, she clung to his arm and pressed her cheek against him. "Ah, you are kind, my lord. Mort used to say all Irish were savages, but you belie that." She gazed up at him with shining eyes. "No one has ever troubled himself to speak kindly to me."

Aidan felt Donal Og's glare like a brand, and he looked over her head at his cousin. Donal Og had managed to find the second most beautiful woman in the place, and the two of them were sharing spiced wine.

"I worry about you, coz. I really do," Donal Og said in Gaelic. "If you were to simply toss up her skirts and play hide the sausage, I'd understand. That's certainly what *I* intend to do with my lovely friend here."

The "lovely friend" affected a pout. "What secrets do you tell in your savage tongue?"

"That thing he does with lamp oil," Pippa said helpfully, "and a wine bot—"

Aidan placed his fingers over her mouth.

"Pay no mind to this mistress of the gutter," Donal Og said to his lady friend. "She has a twisted sense of the absurd."

Aidan was burningly aware of Pippa's hand slipping down his arm slowly, caressingly. "Please yourself and I'll do the same," he said in Irish to Donal Og.

The crowd roared with laughter at the antics of the acting troupe.

"Faith, Aidan, you're the O Donoghue Mór. Think what you're doing," Donal Og said with a note of warning in his voice. "Whether you like it or not, your destiny was sealed long ago by forces beyond the control of any one man. Even the Earl of Desmond has taken to the hills like a common reiver. You're charged with keeping the peace for an entire district. Not acting nursemaid to Sassenach street rabble."

"Don't you think I know that?" Aidan said. Her hand slid lower, fingers stroking his wrist, lingering over his pulse. He thought he had found his answer with Felicity Browne, a perfect English rose of a woman, part of the settlement to keep the peace, and the biggest mistake he had ever made.

"It'll do you no good to fall in love with such as that."
Donal Og indicated Pippa with a jerk of his head.

"And why would you be thinking I'm falling in love?"
Aidan demanded, hot with irritation. "Sure, and that's the
stupidest thing a man ever heard."

Even as he spoke, her hand slid into his and stayed
there shyly, like a small wild bird huddling from a storm.

No affinity with this woman was possible, even if he
did want her. Yet she fascinated him. She gave his natural
sense of mastery an unexpected jolt, challenging and con-
tradicting him, making him laugh and breaking his heart
all at once. Every moment with her gleamed like a jewel,
but the moments were just as fleeting as the flash of the
sun on moving water: brilliant, intense and instantly gone.

Each minute with this woman, he thought with a tightening of his chest, was a glimpse of what could never be.

He forced himself to laugh at the antics on the sloping
stage to cover the anguish that twisted his heart. If he were
truly his father's son, he would simply bed the wench.
God knew, his body kept urging him to do just that. Never,
ever, had he so yearned to taste a woman's mouth, to take
her in his arms and bury himself in the warmth of her.

The unquestioning trust she placed in him was disconcerting, especially considering his thoughts. Didn't she
know the position of an Irish chieftain was tenuous, his
life likely to end in blood and fire?

Aidan made his decision. As the acting troupe came
out to claim their huzzahs and tossed coppers, he thought
of one way to make certain Pippa remained safe, long
after he was gone.

"Absolutely not," she said the next day, trying to look
outraged, when inside, her heart was breaking. "I'll never
do as you suggest, my lord of the stupid ideas."

She paced the garden walk, sharply aware of the beauty of the day, the foxglove and columbine making a riot of springtime color and scent, the glinting sunlight touching the tops of the yew and elm trees.

"It is a fine idea." Aidan leaned against the edge of the well and crossed his booted feet at the ankles. He looked so indolently handsome that she wanted to slap him. "I think you should consider it."

"Court!" she burst out, almost choking on the word. "I cannot believe you think I could go to court. As a jester, perhaps. But as a lady? Never."

"At least hear me out." He wore his tunic open at the throat, and try as she might, she could not stop from imagining what his chest looked like, broad and muscled, dark, silky hair in the center....

She was instantly impatient with herself. Reaching up, she plucked three small green pears from a tree and juggled them idly, round and round. "I'm listening. I'll try not to snort in disgust too loudly."

He shoved away from the well and clasped his hands behind his back, looking for all the world like a battle commander planning a strategy.

Ah, but he is planning a strategy, said an ugly little voice inside her. A campaign to drive her out of his life.

But I've only just found you, she wanted to say.

"I've not yet met your queen," he said, "but I'm told she values lively company." His gaze followed the whirling pears she juggled effortlessly.

"And I've heard she took away a man's knighthood for farting in her presence," Pippa retorted.

"She would like you."

"How, pray, did you make the leap from farting knights to me? And how do you know if the queen would like me or not?"

"Everyone likes you. Even Donal Og."

"He has such a charming way of showing it. What was it he called me this morning?"

"A nightmare in taffeta." He could not keep the mirth from his voice.

"See?" She kept the pears in motion and pretended nonchalance. "And you, Aidan O Donoghue? Do you like me?"

"I am responsible for you. I want to do what is best for you."

"Is that peculiar to the Irish?" she asked.

"What?"

"Pretending to answer a question when you've given me no answer at all." She caught the pears, then tossed him one without warning. He caught it deftly. She took a bite of hers, making a face at the unripe tartness. "And how have I managed to survive twenty-five to twenty-seven years without you?" she demanded acidly.

"You've *survived,* Pippa. But can you honestly say you have lived? You say you want to find your family. You have reason to believe they were of gentle birth. What better place to begin looking than at court? You can find people there who keep bloodlines, census rolls, registers stolen from churches. You can inquire about families that lost a child—presumably to drowning."

She braced herself against a tug of yearning. "I think we both know what my chances are," she said quietly. "I don't know my family name, so how can I find myself in record books?"

He touched her hand. Did the man always have to be so damned tender?

"Don't say no," he said. "At least not yet. There is a masque at Durham House tonight. I am expected to attend. Say you'll come with me. Give yourself a chance to be with men who might be able to help you. Meet Robert Dudley—properly—and Christopher Hatton and Evan Carew—"

The names jumbled up in her mind, strange and alluring. "No," she said, "I don't belong there. I could never—"

"Tell me my ears deceive me." He cocked his head. "I never thought I would see you shrink in fear from a challenge."

She turned her back on him. Damn him, damn him, damn him. How was it that he could see into her heart, even when she took pains to hide it?

"What do you fear?" he asked, taking her by the shoulders and turning her to face him. "That you'll never find out who you are—or that you will?"

"What if I turn out to be the by-blow of some gouty old duke?" she asked.

"Then we'll call you Lady Pippa." Idly he tossed the pear up and down. "Perhaps this will mean you'll have to stop thinking of your mother as a princess in a glass tower. You might learn that she is all too human, as imperfect as you or I."

She stood staring up at him for a long moment. How fine he looked, with the glory of springtime blooming all around him. He was taking away her long-held dream, aye, but he was offering another dream in its place—one that had a chance of coming true.

"All right," she said, "I'll go."

"Iago said you sent away the maids," Aidan called in annoyance through her chamber door.

"So I did, Your Splendidness," she called back in a cheerful voice. It was her best, brightest, fool-the-crowd voice, and she had worked for years to perfect it. No one would guess that inside she smarted with wounds that cut to the quick of her pride. "It is beneath me to consort with such a mean class of people."

"They were sent specially by Lady Lumley," Aidan said. "Did you let them stay long enough to dress you?"

She leaned her forehead on a lozenge-shaped pane of a mullioned window and drew a deep breath past the lump in her throat. *I only let them stay long enough to call me the O Donoghue's whore. The laced mutton. The primped poppet.*

"I've decided not to go after all," she called. Ah, damnation. Her voice cracked with emotion. It was too much to hope he would not notice.

He noticed. He pushed open the door and strode into the chamber. He looked magnificent in a dark wool tunic and leather leggings. Iago had added polished silver beads to the long, braided strand of his hair. He looked wild and brooding, faintly dangerous as he stopped stock-still when he caught sight of her.

She wanted to shrivel and die, for she was clad only in an undershift and chemise, stockings pooled around her ankles and the rest of the elaborate costume laid out in confusion across the bed.

But he was not looking at her state of dishabille. He was looking at her face. Into her eyes.

"You've been crying," he said.

"The scent ball makes me sneeze," she insisted, plucking up the pomander by its string and holding it at arm's length.

He took the ball from her and set it on a table. "Is that why you sent the maids away? I went to some trouble to bring them here, with the dressmaker and that frock." He gestured at the garment, a silken fantasy of ice blue and silver. When she had laid eyes on it she had gone weak in the knees, for she had never seen such a beautiful garment. But that was before the maids had started taunting her.

"They say it was originally made for a lady-in-waiting," Aidan said, "but she—" He broke off and lifted one of the sleeves, inspecting it.

"She what?" Pippa demanded.

"She was banished from court."

"Why?"

He dropped the open-worked sleeve and faced her with an honestly baffled expression. "According to Iago, the lady in question petitioned the queen for permission to marry, and the queen refused. A few months later, the lady was discovered to be with child, having secretly wed her lover. He was imprisoned in the Tower, and she was sent from court."

For a moment, Pippa forgot her own troubles. "Why?"

"I asked the same question. One person dared to answer, but only in a whisper. The queen cannot find anyone to marry, and she is past the age to bear children."

"Marrying and having children are not all they're reputed to be," she said.

For a moment, a cold shadow seemed to pass over him. Then, just as fleetingly, amusement danced in his eyes. "And you are an authority on such matters."

"Dove once told me that celibate priests advise people on marriage."

"Ah. Now. About the dress—"

"Surely a frock to bring me good luck," Pippa said sourly.

"It's not to your taste?"

"My lord, the gown is fine. The dressmaker and her assistants were not to my taste."

"Did they offend you?"

"I didn't take offense on my own behalf. I've been called far worse than whore, laced mutton, primped pigeon—or was it poppet…?" She sent him her most insouciant grin, then her most outraged scowl. "It's what they said about you, my lord, that enraged me."

He lifted one eyebrow. "Oh? And what might that be?"

"Well, I'm not certain. I've never heard such talk before. What does bedswerver mean?"

His face flushed scarlet, and he ducked his head. "I do not understand the Sassenach, letting their women talk like tavern doxies."

"And what do you 'let' your women in Ireland do?" she asked.

Icy fury replaced the sheepish humor in his face. Then he blinked, and the dark look passed. "We don't let them do anything. They do as they please." He stepped toward her. "I'm sorry you had to endure those harpies. Let me help you dress. I swear I'll not call you names, except, perhaps…" He cleared his throat, endearingly discomfited.

"Except what?"

"*A storin.* Or perhaps *a gradh.*" His eyes smiled into her soul, raising a shiver on her skin.

She could not have resisted if she wanted to. "I submit!" she cried out in a theatrical swoon, bringing her wrist to her brow and swaying perilously. "I am yours to do what you will with me!"

Chuckling, he surveyed the elements of the costume on the bed. "I'm not certain I know how all this goes together. Truly, I do not know how you have managed to make the O Donoghue Mór play the handmaid not once, but twice."

"You secretly love it. You know you do."

He picked up an evil, steel-spined object. "A corset?"

"No, thank you. I have never understood why people wish to rearrange the way the Lord made them."

"Let us do this underskirt, then. It is pretty enough."

It was nothing less than splendid, the fine blue fabric shot through with silver threads, the hem worked in the same scalloped design as the sleeves. He pulled it over her head and positioned it around her waist. With his hands around behind her, he began tying the laces.

She experienced an overwhelming urge to lay her cheek upon his chest, to close her eyes and revel in their closeness. What would he say? she wondered, if he knew he had given her the only tenderness she had ever known?

Before she found the courage to confess her thoughts, he added the overskirt of heavier fabric, parted in the front to reveal the dainty underskirt.

Then came the bodice. "This is all backward, my lord," Pippa declared when he stepped behind her to lace it. "What possible use is a garment that laces up the *back?*"

"'Tis of social value. It proves you're rich enough to have maids to dress you."

"Oh. And how rich need I be that I have an Irish chieftain to dress me?"

"For that," he said, his warm breath caressing the back of her neck, "you need only be Pippa." His knuckles grazed her as he worked, and she began to tingle all over.

He gave her a feeling of coming to a roaring fire from out of the bitter cold. If it were possible to actually float, she would have done so. He had a perfect sense of what to say, when to tease and when to be serious. He was magical, his charm so abundant that she paid no heed to the occasional shadow that fell over him.

She laughed at the extra sleeves he laced over her

blousy white chemise. Apparently the more sleeves one possessed, the better. She balked, at last, when he picked up the stiff ruff collar.

"You can send that back to the torture chamber it came from," she declared. "I've done time in stocks that are more comfortable than that. Why on earth would someone take forty spans of lace, then crumple it up and make it all stiff with—with—"

"Starch, they call it," he said. "Because someone terribly clever invented starch, I suppose. This is meant to be sewn on after you're dressed."

"Is *that* how the collar stays on? How perfectly ridiculous. No wonder the nobles look like stuffed puppets who spend four hours dressing each day."

He winked at her and set down the ruff. "If you don't wish to wear it, I have a better idea."

"What is that?"

From a pouch on his hip he took a glittering necklace. The stones were rounded and polished, aglow with violet fire. Strange and sinuous knotwork twisted through the silver setting.

"Holy mother of God," she whispered. "It is too precious for me to wear."

"Believe me, you have more worth than a bauble. I had meant this as a gift for another lady, but she's being recalcitrant."

A chill touched her heart. She should hardly be surprised by his preference for another, but that did not dull the hurt. "Surely, Your Serenity, you should save it for that lady."

He paused with the necklace dangling elegantly from his fingers. "Glory be," he said softly, his eyes crinkling at the corners. "I believe you are jealous."

"Ha!" she burst out, her face flaming. "That is but a

fond dream of yours, my lord Peacock. Flatter yourself not at my expense."

He laughed softly. "Your protests flatter me."

"Conceit," she said, "thy name is O Donoghue."

When he stopped laughing, he said, "This was not a gift of the heart, but one of diplomacy. It was meant for the queen."

It was the last answer she had expected. "You want me to wear a necklace you brought for the queen?"

"For Gloriana herself." His tone mocked the name. "You would improve on the beauty of the jewel. It's amethyst," he said, "mined from the hills of the Burren." He stepped behind her and fastened the clasp. "The design is Celtic. Very ancient."

And lovely, its facets flashing as she moved this way and that. She whirled around to face him. "Are you magic?" she demanded.

He frowned, his black brows knitting in bemusement. "Magic?"

"You know. Under an enchantment. Mab once told me a story about a fairy prince who comes to life and grants a woman's every wish."

"I'm a chieftain, not a prince," he said, "and I'm certainly no fairy."

She almost laughed at his wry indignation. Then he bent and brushed his lips over her brow. The fluttering wingbeat of his caressing mouth echoed deep inside her.

"But I do confess," he whispered, "the idea of granting your every wish does have a certain appeal."

Diary of a Lady

There is a masque tonight at Durham House, but we have declined the invitation. Richard will go, for Richard is too young to be burdened with my pain. Ah, how hard we labor to protect our children. Richard has never known of our loss; since it occurred before he was born, we saw no point in telling him.

Only my dear husband understands the private ritual I perform each year on this day, the anniversary of the tragedy. At sunset, I shall take a bit of wood and a candle down the watersteps, just there, at the spot where I kissed my tiny daughter goodbye so long ago. I shall remember looking into her wide, trusting eyes and pressing an extra kiss "for later" into the palm of her chubby hand.

Then I'll set the little boat adrift with the candle burning, and I'll stand on the bank and watch it while the tears come, and I shall pray for the strength to bear the unbearable.

—Lark de Lacey,
Countess of Wimberleigh

Six

"I'll not be carried in a box like a corpse," Pippa declared.

Annoyed by her mutiny, Aidan took a deep breath. Donal Og and Iago exchanged looks of pure exasperation. Summoning an excess of patience, Aidan said, "Coaches seem strange to me as well. But Lord Lumley assured me that people of fashion ride in them."

Like a wispy blue fairy with a sour disposition, she peered suspiciously into the dark interior of the boxy wooden Mecklenburg coach. "*Dead* people of fashion," she groused. "This is a hearse."

"It is like a pageant-wagon," Iago said.

Aidan scowled at him. "What's a pageant-wagon?"

"They park them on street corners and act out plays on them." Iago folded his arms across his chest. "Right, *pequeña?*"

"This is nothing like a pageant-wagon. It's all enclosed and dark within," she said. "It must be for people who have something to hide."

Which makes me the perfect passenger, thought Aidan.

"Or people who do not care where they are going." She glared up at the driver, who perched on a narrow railed bench in front of the box. He glared back.

"I'll look after you," Aidan promised. With both large hands fitted snugly around her waist, he lifted her up and in. Then he took a seat on the lumpy horsehair bench opposite her. The interior of the coach was dim and close, smelling of leather and horse. The intimacy seized him, and his breath caught with an excruciating feeling of warmth for the recalcitrant woman scowling at him.

"You *still* haven't bedded the wench," Donal Og remarked in Irish as he and Iago clambered into the coach. "That much I can tell from your pained expression."

"Donal Og," Aidan said with surprising calm, "you are my blood kin, the closest thing I have to a brother. But if you make one more remark like that, I will cheerfully change your religion."

The driver cracked his whip and whistled. The coach surged forward. Pippa swore, nearly lurching out of her seat.

Donal Og slapped his hands on his knees. "What, the ice-eyed O Donoghue Mór is falling in love with a common doxy?"

"I won't hear her insulted, even in Gaelic."

"It is love," said Iago, nodding and rubbing his chin.

Setting his jaw, Aidan stole a surreptitious glance at Pippa. The glow of the sunset gilded her as she sat across from him, her cheek against the side of the unglazed window and her daintily gloved hands clenched in her lap. Moist-lipped, wide-eyed, her curls a halo, she had never looked more enchanting.

"I can't love her," Aidan muttered, stung by a feeling of futility.

"What makes you think you have a choice?" asked Donal Og.

"Speak English," Pippa said, "else I'll think you're talking about me. But of course you are." She shook an accusing finger. "Aren't you?"

"Yes," Iago admitted before Aidan could stop him. "We are explaining to the O Donoghue Mór that he has fallen in love with you."

"I am blessed by the most loyal of friends," said Aidan, his ears burning.

And after all, it was Pippa who rescued him, laughing. "Don't be ridiculous, Iago. Are such romantic illusions peculiar to the Irish, or to men in general? Now, cease your gossip and pay attention. I shall tell you about this part of London."

"As you wish." Iago put out a strong arm to steady her as the coach swayed around a corner and started down Ivy Bridge Lane.

As she chattered on about famous houses and shops, Aidan wished he could feel for Pippa a simple, healthy, red-blooded lust. Instead, he looked at her and was seized by an emotion so piercing he felt actual pain.

She touched people. Affected them. Iago was her devoted slave. Even Donal Og, as hard and rugged as the Cliffs of Moher, admired her. And when he thought no one noticed, he was patient and kind. She brought out a man's urge to protect, perhaps because she insisted on not being protected at all.

As if she felt him looking at her, she met his gaze. A fleeting, almost shy smile curved her lips. "This is not so bad after all, Your Abundance," she said. "I rather like riding in a coach."

He answered her with a smile, taking pleasure in her enjoyment. *Who are you?* he wondered. The sad truth was, she had probably been born to a trull who could not afford to keep her, didn't want her. The words she had spoken came back to haunt him: *Was I meant to be found, or to lie there and die?*

He wanted to hold her close, to stroke her hair and reassure her, to promise her she had not been abandoned but was simply lost. What sort of creature would leave a child like Pippa? He could almost believe she had no mother at all, but was made by the *sidhe*.

After passing under the gatehouse archway and into an inner courtyard, the coach lumbered and creaked to a halt. Liveried footmen swarmed forth to help the passengers out. Durham House was lofty and stately, with marble pillars and two great turrets. The grace-and-favor residence embodied the very essence of English wealth and privilege. Yet rather than holding it in awe, Aidan felt contempt. The Sassenach labored hard to set himself above his people. Not so Aidan, and his blood was the blood of kings. He held his banquets and councils in broad, open fields, welcoming all rather than walling himself off from the common folk.

He glanced at Pippa and saw that she was impressed indeed, pausing at the main door to finger a silk tassel hanging from a bellpull. But when she began to untie the prize, he realized her intent and chuckled. "I think it would be bad form to be caught nicking the furnishings."

In the anteroom of the gallery, servants gaped in open admiration at Pippa, and Aidan felt a swell of pride. Not so long ago, these awestruck retainers would not have found her good enough to spit upon; now they bowed and stooped, convinced she was a highborn lady.

Bug-eyed stares greeted Iago; there was the usual amount of surreptitious brushing against him to see if his coloring was real or just painted on. He bore it all with his usual charm and aplomb.

At the arched entranceway to the gallery, they could

see a whirling sea of merrymakers. Pippa hesitated, her color fading to a chalky pallor. To Aidan's surprise, she looked terrified. But then, before he could reassure her, she threw back her shoulders, lifted her chin and swept forward proudly, trailed by Iago and a dozen slack-jawed stares.

Donal Og nudged Aidan hard in the ribs. "We have not even been announced yet. What will happen when the guests see them?"

People were staring. Pippa noticed that right away as she walked between Iago and Donal Og, all three of them preceding Aidan, the ranking lord. The first person they encountered was a man in a red silk doublet. His splendid mustache flew outward as he greeted them. Pippa pointed her toe, about to launch into a curtsy.

Donal Og put his hand discreetly on her arm. "That's the majordomo, lass. He'll announce us."

The very idea of being announced was as heady as a cup of fine wine.

The majordomo shouted out their names to the other guests in the crowded room. A mass of people, easily as many as she had seen gathered at St. Paul's, turned inquisitive looks on the Irish party.

Iago, of course, was the most striking, with his dark skin and bright cloak, his ready smile. Like a seasoned performer, he played to the curiosity seekers, flaring his nostrils and pressing his palms together as if performing some exotic, foreign greeting.

Pippa earned her living by making a spectacle of herself, so she found the attention gratifying. Introduced as the mistress of revels of the O Donoghue Mór, she beamed at the watching throng, singling out a few for a special nod or wave—a fat man encased like sausage in an overstuffed doublet and scarlet hose, a lady holding a spangled half mask to her face, a pageboy who nearly choked on a grape when she winked at him.

"So this is our Irish chieftain," a man exclaimed, smiling with ill-concealed fury at Aidan. "You look quite as savage as your father." The smile hardened. "He murdered my own father, you know. I am Arthur, Lord Grey de Wilton."

Pippa stared in astonishment as hatred crackled between the two—the slim, elegant Englishman and the magnificent, black-haired Irish chieftain.

"I am sorry for your loss," Aidan said, his voice toneless, almost bland. "It is a pity your father attempted to drive off a herd of my father's cattle without paying for them." He walked away.

Pippa started after him, but Iago held her back. "Give him time to simmer down. He is not fond of defending his father."

Donal Og joined his cousin, bent his fair head to Aidan's dark one and whispered something in Gaelic. Aidan gave him a curt reply, then turned and took Pippa's hand, leading her down three steps into the crowd.

A blur of London's elite followed on a whirlwind of introductions: the Lord Keeper and Lord Chancellor, a Swedish princess, three knights from Saxony, an admiral and a bishop, and dozens of grande dames and ladies of rank. Lady Helmsley dropped her feathered mask, raised a pair of spectacles to her eyes and peered at Pippa.

Pippa, who had never seen spectacles before, leaned forward and peered back.

"Is it customary for an Irish lord to go about with his mummer?" the lady asked. "And a bodyguard of one hundred savages?"

Pippa sent her a dazzling smile. "Madam, do you have

a point to make or are you simply trying to convince me you are a horse's backside?"

"Well!" The lady fanned herself in agitation. "In sooth you must be his lightskirt."

"Only in my dreams, Your Ladyship. Only in my dreams."

Iago led her off before she did damage to the woman. The next people she encountered were far more pleasant—a merry poet named Sharpe, a pair of identical twins called Lucy and Letty, a fat woman with a goiter, and the queen's dwarf, Ann. The tiny, stocky lady fascinated Pippa, and they chatted happily for a few moments.

"Get yourself to court," Ann advised her. "It's the only place for the likes of us."

"You are likely correct," Pippa admitted.

High in a railed gallery above the throng, musicians played a dance tune. After an hour of smiling and nodding, Pippa wanted desperately to dance. But Aidan's grim expression and stormy eyes warned her that now was not the time to ask him. Instead, she looked for a way to extract him from the press of admirers and curiosity seekers.

She gripped his arm. "Here comes that foul Lady Helmsley again. Shall I tell her she has a spider crawling up her back?"

The haughty grande dame glared at them and swept past. Pippa looked down into her hand at the diamond bracelet she held.

"Where did you get that?" Aidan asked in an undertone. "Ah, faith, mind your manners." He snatched the pilfered bracelet from her and dropped it on the floor. "My lady," he called after her, "you dropped this." With an exaggerated courtly flourish, he restored it to her.

If Pippa had not known better, she would have

believed the sincerity of his glittering smile and gallant pose. In the blink of an eye, Lady Helmsley's disdain thawed. She thanked him with a disgusting simper before moving off.

"I genuflect to your Irish charm," Pippa whispered.

"No more thievery," Aidan muttered. "I mean it."

She lifted her hand to her heart. "Word of honor."

He glanced down at her, and his expression softened. "Are you hungry?"

"Always."

And then he laughed. It was the most beautiful sound she knew. He led her through the crowd, and she could not help but notice how different he was from the English nobles.

The men in the room wore silken hose and kid slippers. The blousy canion trousers bulged obscenely, as if the wearer had done something disgraceful in them. The formfitting peascod doublets, all crusted with baubles, added a haughty puffiness to chests too skinny to impress on their own. Just as Iago had said, the English gentlemen had lovelocks bobbing beneath their velvet toques.

In contrast, Aidan wore leather leggings and boots cuffed at the knee, a tunic cinched at the waist by a wide belt decked with polished stones, and the dramatic blue mantle that swirled around him like a king's raiments.

"Colleen." His soft voice near her ear startled her.

"What!"

"You're staring at me rather than feasting your eyes on the cream of English nobility." Bemused, he placed a silver cup in her hand and coaxed her to drink.

She tasted the musky sweet wine and smiled. "In sooth, my lord, you are much more agreeable to look upon than the others."

He muttered something Celtic and dark.

"What?" she demanded.

"Sometimes you are too frank for your own good." He held her by the shoulders and turned her around to face the crowd.

"Now, pay attention," he said sternly. "Look at those I point out. There are those who hold sway over the queen's favor, and their friendship would not come amiss."

Flagrantly disobeying him, she shut her eyes and leaned back against his endless hard length. How good it felt to be held, to have his warmth so close to her, to inhale his scent of leather and man.

"Pippa!" His fingers pressed into her shoulders.

Her eyes drifted open. "I'm listening."

"All right. See that man standing in front of the tapestry?"

Her gaze swept a floral hanging and came to rest upon a man all in black. His thin mustache twitched like tiny whiplashes.

"Yes?"

"Watch him closely. I assure you, his spies are watching us."

"Spies?" she hissed, fascinated.

"That's Francis Walsingham. Hates Catholics with a vengeance and would cheerfully see me roasted alive if he could get away with it. He is the queen's spymaster. Everyone despises him, the queen included, but they have a healthy respect for his abilities. With him are Lords Norfolk and Arundel, both pleasant, neither particularly dangerous."

His hand found the nape of her neck and cradled it gently. She felt giddy from the caress, but he seemed determined to educate her at the moment. He turned her toward a white-haired little man and a tall, fair-haired lady.

"That is the Venetian ambassador. He is shrewd, fair and knows everyone's business. The woman with him is his widowed daughter Rosaria, the Contessa Cerniglia. She is even more shrewd than her father, but I have heard she does *not* play fair."

"How do you know all this?" she asked, her head swimming with titles.

"The queen has her spies and I have mine. I cannot afford to ignore Sassenach matters of state," he said. "Well? What think you of this esteemed company?"

She sighed. The splendid revelers shimmered in the setting of gilded halls and endless glass-windowed galleries, the torchlit rambling gardens and fountains outside, the priceless art treasures and tapestries. She studied faces—shining eyes behind masks, smiling mouths—and wondered if one of these ladies had lost a child long ago, and if she had, would she have put it out of her mind, or did she think of it constantly?

"I don't know," she said at last. "In my dreams, I grew up in a place like this, surrounded by cheerful, wealthy people. Yet I don't feel as if I belong here."

"In most of these people, the cheerfulness and sometimes even the wealth are an illusion."

"What about my parents?" she wondered, feeling an anxious tightening of her stomach. The very idea that she could belong to such company seemed ludicrous. "Shall I just go and tap someone on the shoulder and say, 'Pardon me, but did you happen to misplace a daughter once upon a time?'"

He rubbed the nape of her neck. "Don't be hasty, else you go against the wrong person. We should find William Cecil and begin our inquiries with him, for he is one of the few ministers I trust. I'd surely hate to see you accused of being a fraud."

She turned in his arms so fast that for a moment he truly was embracing her. He dropped his hands. She muttered, "I would die if they accused me of being a fraud."

His blue eyes scanned the crowd, lingering on the balding head of Cecil, Lord Burghley. "No one had a particular reaction to hearing your name spoken. Of course, we don't know for certain what your name is."

She sighed again. "Do you know what I would really like?"

"What?"

"For you to dance with me."

She braced herself for ridicule or a rejection. Instead he smiled and bowed from the waist.

"In sooth the Sassenach way of dancing is rather sedate compared to the Irish way. But I'll try to please you," he said.

She could not feel the floor beneath her feet as she followed him to the dancing quadrangle. Couples moved in a circle, their slow, measured steps reminiscent of the pace of a funeral cortege.

Aidan and Pippa fell in, hands clasped and raised, his arm circling her waist.

"Who died?" she asked from the corner of her mouth.

He gave a stifled laugh. "The musicians?"

As they passed Donal Og and Iago, Aidan mouthed a few silent words, then jerked his head toward the railed gallery.

"What are they doing?" she asked.

"Trying to bring the dead to life?" he teased.

Iago and Donal Og disappeared behind a paneled wall. A few seconds later, they emerged into the high gallery.

Donal Og took up a skin drum while Iago helped himself
to a long flute.

A loud trill from the flute halted the dancers in their
path. The master of revels, looking white-faced and
harassed, went to the rail and gave a forced smile.

"My lords and ladies," he called, "in honor of our
noble guest from Ireland, we shall give a musical salute."

Full of a young man's swaggering confidence, the
Earl of Essex sidled up to Aidan. "That was ill-
mannered," he said, "but I suppose all Irish are rude,
judging by those I have met."

Pippa gave him her biggest smile. "Why, my lord! Did
you practice for years to become insufferable or does the
talent come naturally?"

He stared at her as if she were a worm floating in his
cup. "I beg your pardon?"

She sent him a broad wink. "I suppose, lacking a prick,
you endeavor to become one, is that it?"

Essex's eyes flared. "O Donoghue, take your doxy
from my sight or I'll—"

Aidan moved one step forward. He stood so close to
the earl that no one but Pippa saw him take a fistful of
Essex's padded doublet and twist until the starched ruff
nearly engulfed his face.

"One more word about her," Aidan said with icy calm,
"and I'll wipe the floor with you, my lord."

The music exploded into a lively, almost frenzied reel.
Aidan turned his back on Essex, gave a loud Gaelic howl,
and started to dance.

His wild spirit engulfed Pippa like a wave. In his aggressive, overbearing presence, she felt swept along on
a raft of excitement.

It was easy to dance with him. She simply had to
submit. He held her by the waist, lifting her so her feet

didn't touch the floor. She spun and laughed; people began clapping and stamping their feet to the rapid rhythm. Round and round they whirled, and the glittering hall turned in a blur. Before she knew what was happening, he smoothly broke away from the crowd and danced her out through a set of tall doors to a dimly lit loggia adjacent to the hall.

The music subsided and they came to a halt. Pippa collapsed, breathless and laughing, against his chest. "That was splendid," she declared. "A good dance is very much like I imagine flying would be."

A high-pitched giggle came from the shadows of the loggia. She turned in time to see a beautiful lady rush up through the darkened garden.

Like Pippa, the lady was breathless and flushed. Unlike Pippa, this one smiled with lips that were full and bruised by kisses. Her ruff hung askew; grass stains smeared the hem of her gown. Her eyes sparkled with the secret joy of having been loved well and recently.

"Aidan," Pippa whispered, "who—"

"Cordelia, there you are." A man dashed in and snatched her around her wasp-thin waist. "My beloved rodent of virtue has scuttled away!" They both laughed, the lady unoffended, and he led her into the circle of torchlight from the hall.

Pippa froze. For a moment, she thought her heart had stopped beating, but the next instant it lurched into a rapid, nervous tattoo. As from a distance, she heard Aidan speak her name questioningly, but she could not answer him.

She could only stare at the fair-haired stranger.

To call him handsome would be laughable, for so banal a term could not begin to describe the lavish male beauty with which he had been gifted.

Hair the color of the sun crowned a face that would
not have been out of place amid a host of angels. Full,
bowed lips. A glorious symmetry of high cheekbones
and sweeping brown lashes around eyes the color of
morning glory. Just to make certain this man would never,
ever, find his equal in looks, his Maker in all Her wisdom
had added a perfect cleft in his chin, an incomparable set
of white teeth and a look of irreverent humor that made
the corners of his mouth turn up.

"Colleen." Aidan spoke with amused tolerance. "If
you stare at him any harder, he'll think you're putting him
under the evil eye."

She blinked. The image of the stranger shimmered like
new-minted gold. He was laughing now, leading his lady
into the gallery, head bent toward her as they shared a
private jest.

His appearance garnered many stares. Women young
and old contrived to pass by him; one dropped a fan and
tittered when he picked it up. Another managed to lose
her garter. As the golden Adonis replaced it, he murmured
the age-old disclaimer: *"Honi soit qui mal y pense."*

"She looks ill," Aidan said with laughter in his voice.
"Do you think she'll swoon?"

All at once Pippa, too, was struck by the ridiculous-
ness of it, and she giggled. "Who *is* that man?" she said.

"I don't know. My question is, how can he bear all the
simpering?"

She leaned against the door frame and watched the
young man, a glowing star surrounded by basking lesser
beauties. Not just the women, but the men too seemed
drawn to him. He had an air of easy grace; he was comfortable with himself and others. He seemed to have no particular problem with being the most beautiful man in the
world.

"Such attention," she said to herself, "cannot be so hard to bear."

Unexpectedly, she felt Aidan's hand at the back of her waist. The gesture was subtle yet full of tenderness.

For a moment she was staggered by an idea so outrageous that she caught her breath in surprise. This man, this Irish stranger, understood her. He knew her need for attention, for approval, for a gentle touch.

"Aidan," she said, emotion welling in her throat, "I must tell you—"

"—the honor of this dance?" asked a golden voice.

Her mouth dropped open. With infinite patience, Aidan placed his finger under her chin and closed her mouth.

The golden man bowed before her, then held out his hand.

"I daresay my lovely guest would like to dance with you," Aidan said. "Perhaps you would do her the honor of introducing yourself."

The god took her hand. As he led her to the dance floor, he inclined his shining head in Aidan's direction. "My name is Richard, my lord. Richard de Lacey."

A curious change came over Aidan. Until now, he had shown tolerance and bemused patience. Upon hearing the man's name, the O Donoghue Mór all but turned to stone.

Richard de Lacey drew her into a pavane, tilting his head to whisper into her ear, "You are quite the most dazzling creature in here. But clearly, the O Donoghue claims you for his own."

She glanced over her shoulder at Aidan. He had not moved. "You know who he is."

"My little sugared quince, everyone has heard of the Lord of Castleross. Under different circumstances, I would endeavor to be his friend. But as things stand, he is bound to despise me." He nodded regally to passing couples. "And not just because I find you dazzling."

"Why, then?" she asked, intrigued by him but missing Aidan's nearness.

"Because I have been granted a commission in Ireland, in the district of the O Donoghue Mór."

By the next morning, Pippa was sick and tired of hearing about Richard de Lacey. The chamber she shared with several other ladies rang with passionate recitations of his charms, both physical and social.

"I couldn't believe it. He *touched* me. He actually *touched* me." Lady Barbara Throckmorton Smythe held out a limp, pale hand.

"Ooh!" Three others gathered around to inspect the favored appendage.

Finally, after hearing Richard de Lacey compared to every mythical and astrological figure the ladies could imagine, Pippa gave an exasperated snort.

Lady Barbara glared at her. "Well, mistress of revels, I did not see you sniffing at his invitation to dance."

"True." Pippa winced; the handmaid who was combing her short hair caught a snag. "I reserve my sniffing for less desirable invitations."

"What was it like?" Bessie Josephine Traylor demanded. "You *must* tell us, for you're the only one he danced with other than that painted tart, Cordelia Carruthers."

"Yes, tell us," urged Lady Jocelyn Bellmore. She studied Pippa's short golden curls, then ran a hand through her own long red hair. "I've been thinking I'd have this cropped short. Richard adores short hair."

Pippa rolled her eyes. What silly gamehens they were, pecking and squawking after the cock of the walk. But they were looking at her so expectantly that the natural performer in her came out.

"Well, I am far too much the lady to go into detail," she said in a conspiratorial whisper. "But if I were to give Richard de Lacey a nickname, it would surely be the Blond Stallion."

The women collapsed in helpless giggles and the maid dropped her comb. Pippa picked it up, chuckling at her companions, and grew thoughtful as they chattered on.

As beautiful as he was, Richard de Lacey had a different sort of appeal for her. She felt drawn to him, but in a mysterious way that had nothing to do with the wanting she felt for Aidan O Donoghue.

There was something in the way Richard cocked his head, a certain crooked slant to his smile, and a gentle quality in his touch that tugged at her heart. It was not recognition she felt; it could not be. She had never seen him before in her life.

"What sort of boat race?" Pippa demanded, striding down through the gardens at Aidan's side.

"I'm not quite certain." He watched her from the corner of his eye. "I believe it is a sculling race down the Thames." She looked as fresh as a newly opened rose with the dew still clinging to its petals. How naturally she fit into this rarefied setting of aristocrats with their elaborate manners and games. The girl's gift for imitation served her well here. Her courtly graces seemed as seasoned as those of a woman trained from the cradle.

Today she wore a gown of lilac with all the sleeves and furnishings properly attached and fastened. Her hair was caught back in a coif beaded with gleaming onyx.

"I believe," he explained, "that the race is held for a

winner's cup. You and the other ladies will watch at the finish line—that would be the watersteps."

"I see." She squinted at the beribboned string that stretched clear across the river.

"Did you get on with them?" he asked, then scowled. He was not supposed to care one way or the other.

"The other ladies?" She looked up, gave him a false smile and fluttered a pretend fan in her face. "Oh, la, sir, surely you know what deep joy I take in discussing fashion and rose breeding."

He laughed. "They know no better. The Sassenach keep their women on a short leash."

"A charming image. And are Irishwomen kept on a *long* leash?"

"Some would say, in Ireland, the woman wields the leash herself."

She beamed. "That sounds much more sensible."

"I take it they're all deeply smitten with Richard de Lacey."

"Of course. We discussed him in exhaustive detail." She pantomimed a fluttering fan. "The cleft in his chin, his perfectly turned calf, the tenor of his voice, the charm of his manners, all kept us in gossip fodder for half the night."

A stab of feeling he refused to name invaded Aidan. "So you're smitten with him, too."

She blew upward at a curl that had escaped her coif to dangle upon her brow. "I should be. It seems almost a sacrilege not to be."

"But?" Undeniable hope kindled inside him.

"But…" A teasing light glinted in her eye. "I don't know, Your Potency. I'm not certain how to put this. I prefer my men to be tall, dark and Irish." She laughed at his thunderstruck expression. "Richard de Lacey is too perfect to render me smitten and swooning. Does that make sense to you?"

He held a smile in check. "Perfect sense. Being smitten is a serious and sometimes painful business."

She caught her lip in her teeth and gazed at him with eyes so luminescent that he could see his own reflection.

"Aidan!" Donal Og called from the end of the garden. "Reel in your tongue and get down here." His broad Gaelic rang like pagan music through the fussy arbors and knot gardens of Durham House. "The Sassenach sheep-swivers want a lesson in rowing."

"My lord," Pippa called as he turned to leave, "Richard said you would hate him because of his commission in Ireland. Is that true?"

Aidan paused, startled both by her question and by how much she pleased him. He was not accustomed to a woman's empathy, her understanding. "I do not hate him," Aidan said, turning toward Donal Og. "Yet."

He left her seated amid a few dozen spectators at the river landing, then went to hear the particulars of the race.

He was fast learning that the social games of the English had subtle and serious purposes. A man's status among his peers rose or fell with his prowess at sport. Most important of all, the queen herself was given a full report of each man's performance.

They rode a mile upriver to the contestants' boats. Donal Og settled eagerly into one. "It is like a curragh!" he declared, referring to the seagoing rowboats of the Irish.

"They will all drown like dogs in our wake," Iago said with complete certainty.

As he saw the other teams settle into the boats, Aidan felt no need to disagree. Not one of these Sassenach looked as if he had ever exerted himself into an actual sweat. They wore precious clothes and precious, smug expressions on their faces.

Strutting in front of their ranks, Iago put on his scariest I'm-a-savage look, with glowering eyes and protruding lips, muscles flexed until they bulged. The air of English superiority dissipated.

"I think they get the point," Aidan said, smothering a laugh. Already he had decided what to do with the winner's cup. He would give it to the queen as a gift with all the others he had brought for her.

The hoary old bitch. She was beginning to try his patience.

Then the gorgeous Richard de Lacey appeared and Aidan felt his first stab of doubt. The charming young man had two extraordinary retainers in tow. They looked almost as exotic as Donal Og and Iago. Though not as tall as Aidan's companions, they were broad and powerfully built. One had cropped black hair, a black mustache and black eyes. He wore black boots, old-fashioned trews and a richly embroidered tunic with a sleeveless red jacket over it.

The other man had a mustache so wide that its stiffened tips extended past the width of his face in the shape of a stout set of bull's horns.

As these formidable challengers scrambled into their boat, Richard smiled and greeted all his rivals. He was a merry fellow indeed, and clearly it was not just the ladies who thought so.

Richard would need to bring more than charm to Ireland, Aidan thought. He had seen young men, Irish and English alike, made old in mere months by the rigors of privation during the endless, pointless campaigns.

Then Richard spoke to his companions, and an odd chill shot down Aidan's spine. It was a strange language they spoke, guttural and nasal, so wholly foreign he could not pick out a single word of it.

"What are they?" Iago asked. "Demon men?"

"Prussian or Turkish?" Donal Og guessed.

"No matter." Aidan clamped his hands around the oars. "As far as *we* are concerned, they are defeated."

A whistle pierced the air, and they were off. As Aidan had predicted, the Sassenach fell behind immediately. The only serious challenge was from Richard and his cohorts.

Setting his jaw, Aidan threw all of his strength into the race. He rowed with a vigor and rhythm that caused the sweat to pour down his face and arms. His hands blistered and the blisters burst, yet he did not slacken his pace.

He held one clear thought in his mind. Pippa watched from the finish line. He would be less than the O Donoghue Mór if he let her see him lose.

Yet some equally powerful thought was driving Richard de Lacey and his crew, for they too rowed at a furious rate; they were as grim and focused as Aidan and his companions.

Before long, he could hear the low roar of cheering. He blocked it out. He listened only to the thump and splash of the oars, the pounding of his heart, his own steady breathing.

From the corner of his eye, he saw Richard's boat draw even with his. Then, whipping his head around for a split second, he saw the banner of ribbons stretched across the finish line.

The strength that surged through him had deep roots. It was the stubborn ferocity of the ancient Celt that gripped and held him, then shot energy like fire through his limbs.

The last oar stroke flowed from his shoulders to the

tips of the oars, and on a surge of speed that drew gasps from the crowd, the boat shot forward. Aidan snatched down the banner. To loud huzzahs and a few anti-Irish boos, he held it aloft.

Richard's boat ran alongside his, and Richard inclined his head. "Well done, my lord of Castleross. I only regret I was not a more worthy opponent."

"You were not so bad for a Sassenach," said Donal Og, examining the raw blisters on his hands.

De Lacey's companions exchanged words in their incomprehensible tongue.

"By my soul, but I've worked up a sweat." Aidan sluiced water over his neck and shoulders. Iago and Donal Og did the same.

The spectators were oddly quiet as the Irishmen drifted toward the river landing. Aidan did not realize why until he set aside his oars and looked up to see the crowd drawn to the very edge of the landing, the women pushing past the men to gape at the drenched savages. Even Pippa went to the brink, her soft eyes wide with interest.

It was more than any man's pride could resist. Aidan exchanged a sly glance with his cousin and then with Iago. All three of them managed to row with the maximum display of flexed muscles that drew murmurs from the ladies.

Unnoticed by Pippa, a grossly overdressed man— Lord Temple Newsome, Aidan recalled—came up behind her.

From a distance, Aidan could not see exactly where Newsome put his hand, but the outraged expression on Pippa's face gave him a good idea. She straightened up and, in the same motion, seized the gentleman by his left arm. In a move that would have done a seasoned wrestler credit, she bent forward, jerking Temple Newsome up and over her head. Screaming, he flopped head over heels into the water.

"So *that* is how she kept her virtue all these years," Donal Og said thoughtfully.

"I wondered that as well," said Iago.

A barked oath burst from the back of the crowd. While Temple Newsome gasped and flailed, his manservant grabbed Pippa by the arm. She pulled away from him. The movement was too abrupt. Her arms made wide circles in the air as she toppled into the river.

For a moment, the skirts spread around her like a bell. "You bean-fed, braying ass," she yelled in a coarse accent, then sank out of sight.

In a heartbeat of time, Aidan experienced a raw sense of panic and loss unlike anything he had ever felt. Neither losing his father in such a horrible manner nor Felicity's betrayal could even approach this sense of dread. He had not realized what having Pippa in his life had given him—until now, when he was in danger of losing her.

In one swift motion, he stood and dove cleanly into the water. He swam straight past the drowning Newsome, who grasped at him, and when he reached the spot where Pippa had gone under, he dove deep.

Sunlight shone through a blurry filter of silt and river weeds. He saw the vague outline of a waving arm. He grabbed at it; missed. *Hurry!* his mind screamed. *Hurry!* Not until this moment had the survival of another person mattered so much to him. With a strong, scissorslike kick, he surged to the surface, taking mere seconds to gulp air before diving again. A flow of skirts caught his eye. Knowing now the full meaning of wordless, heartfelt prayer, he reached for her. His hand closed around fabric. He tugged, the fabric rent, and she slipped away. He surged toward her, and when he touched her hand—the hand of an Englishwoman, a stranger, a commoner, his heart nearly burst with gladness. He hauled her to the surface.

Pippa gagged and then coughed, spewing river water and vile oaths. He hooked his arm around her and took her to the watersteps. When he reached the shallows, he caught her around the waist and under her knees, sweeping her up into his arms. She clung to his neck and swallowed great gulps of air. He climbed the watersteps with care, for they were green and slimy.

"You're carrying me," said Pippa.

"Aye."

"I can't believe I needed saving."

"Again," he reminded her.

"Well, at least I am consistent."

He reached the landing. The crowd moved back to give them a wide berth, and he set Pippa on her feet. He tried to pretend it was not happening, but he could not hide the truth from himself. He was trembling.

"Utterly hopeless," she said.

He looked into her eyes, seeing anguish and hope and the thing he dreaded most—a love so sweet and clear that it pierced him like a sword thrust.

"We're both hopeless," he said huskily, thinking of Ireland, of Felicity, of all the countless reasons he could not return her love.

Richard de Lacey stood in his boat. Aidan expected derision, but Richard began to clap his hands slowly. Others joined in, and applause rang across the river.

Shaking off her brush with disaster along with bits of river weed, Pippa immediately pulled away from him. She adopted her showman's stance, plucking her sodden, torn skirts and dipping in an elaborate curtsy. Lord

Temple Newsome struggled on hands and knees up the slippery watersteps.

"Next time you decide to pinch a lady's arse," she called, "be sure your victim is either too helpless to resist or too stupid to mind."

"You are a common trollop."

"Thank you, my lord *Noisome,*" she shot back with a false obeisance.

"Charming," he said, spitting on the ground.

"*You* have the charm of a closestool," she retorted.

Newsome glared at Aidan. "Where did you find this—this piecemeal maid?"

"Did the first dunking fail to clean up your mouth, Newsome?" Aidan asked, advancing on him.

He said nothing, but squished along a garden path toward the house.

Aidan bent forward and peeled off his tunic and shirt. He straightened, shaking back his wet hair, to find everyone staring at him. Again.

Female whispers swept the goggling throng. Pippa wore an expression that raised his vanity to new heights. Her eyes were misty, her mouth slightly open; her tongue slipped out to moisten her lips. He held the tunic lower to conceal his body's reaction.

"What are those scars?" she asked with quiet awe.

"That," he said, feeling a flush creep up his neck, "is a long story. We had best get ourselves dry."

"And so you had," said a laughing, friendly voice. Richard de Lacey clambered up to the river landing. "Come with me to Wimberleigh House. It's just there, at the top of the garden." He pointed at a beautiful, turreted mansion bristling with finials, with great bays of oriel windows facing the river. "It would be an honor to play host to such singular company."

* * *

Two hours later, Pippa stood at the top of the grand staircase of Wimberleigh House and frowned down the length of steps. The residence was not as big and rambling as Lumley House and Crutched Friars, nor was it as opulent as Durham House.

Yet she felt immediately comfortable here. They had given her clean clothes, and a bashful maid had helped her dress. She inhaled the aroma of beeswax and verbena polish, alien scents to her, so why did they seem so familiar and evocative? She studied the paneled walls and painted cloth hangings. She could imagine Richard de Lacey growing up in this place, a lovely golden child racing through the galleries and halls or cavorting in the garden.

As she leaned on the top newel post, the wooden orb bent to one side. Pippa gasped and jumped back.

"Don't mind that," said a cheery voice.

She spun around to see a smiling maid bustling toward her, holding a lit candle in her hand. "I be Tess Harbutt, come to light the chandelier." She bobbed her coiffed head at the newel post. "There used to be a series of pulleys here to help my own dear grandmum up and down the stairs when she were getting on in years."

Tess clumped down the stairs and slid back a wooden panel to reveal a system of ropes and hooks. While Pippa watched with keen interest, the maid paid out the rope, which caused the chandelier to lower slowly.

"The old Lord Wimberleigh—he be the Earl of Lynley now, Master Richard's grandsire—was quite the inventor," Tess explained. "Always dreaming up this or that convenience."

Pippa hurried down the stairs to get a closer look. The chandelier hung at eye level now, a great, heavy wheel of candles, each with a chimney of cut glass.

"May I?" She took Tess's candle and touched its burning head to each candle in the fixture. They were thick and white, not all smelly with tallow like the ones she was used to.

"That's him there." Tess pointed to a portrait on the wall along the stairway. "His name is Stephen de Lacey."

She looked up. Ah, there was where Richard got his golden good looks, she noted.

"That next one is Stephen de Lacey's second wife, the Lady Juliana." The matronly dark-haired lady held a fan to her bosom and was surrounded by children. An unusual, long-haired dog lay curled at their feet.

"Juliana," Pippa said. "Pretty name." She was almost to the last candle.

"Some as say she is Russian royalty," Tess explained, warming to her tale. Dropping her voice to a gossipy whisper, she added, "Others as say she was a Gypsy."

Pippa jerked her hand in startlement, oversetting the last candle. The glass chimney fell, but she caught it before it shattered. "What did you say?" She put the glass back.

Tess's face flushed. "Idle gossip, is all. I misspoke, ma'am."

Yet as she lit the last candle and Tess used a crank to raise the chandelier, Pippa frowned up at the portrait.

Juliana. A Gypsy. Some elusive thought hovered at the edge of her awareness, then flitted away. It must be her own encounter with the old Gypsy that jogged her memory, she decided. She pointed to two rectangular shadows on the paneling. "What portraits were removed?"

"Those would be Master Richard's parents, Lord and Lady Wimberleigh. They was taken down for packing. Master Richard's got himself a military commission, he does. He has some miniature limnings of his brothers and sister—Masters Lucas, Leighton and Michael, and of course Mistress Caroline, the family favorite."

Pippa stared a moment longer at the portraits. A family. How alien the notion was to her. Discomfited by both longing and a sense of awkwardness, she plucked at her skirts. She was ever the misfit, ever the odd man out. "Do I look all right?"

"Oh, aye, ma'am. That's one of Mistress Caroline's old ones. Perfect for you." The maid eyed Pippa's cropped hair, started to say something, then looked away politely. "You'd best be off to the dining hall. I think they're waiting for you."

Pippa crossed the antechamber, flanked by grand archways, and went through the doors on her right.

"Sorry, ma'am. I didn't realize you'd been here before," said Tess.

"I haven't."

"Then how do you know the way to the dining hall?"

Pippa stood still in her tracks. Again she felt that prickle, that chill. Thoughts teased at her and disappeared, unformed. She looked helplessly at the friendly maid. "A lucky guess, I suppose."

From the Annals of Innisfallen

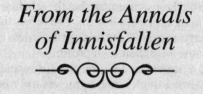

I am a Christian as well as a Celt, which makes for some awkward moments in the confessional. I am not supposed to feel the dark prescience of disaster deep in my bones, for that smacks of paganism and is an affront to He who made us all.

Still, there are times when I am forced to admit that the ancients do whisper secrets in my unsuspecting ear, and of late the secrets disturb me.

There is mischief afoot in Killarney town and at Ross Castle. I have no reason to know this except that the chill in my brittle old bones tells me so. That, and the shifty way the bride of the O Donoghue refused to look at me when I went up to the keep to lead the rogation processional. Our "pagan" ceremonies do offend her Puritan sensibilities, but she displayed more than her usual hatred and distrust.

The bishop has promised, at last, to help. It was a marriage that never should have been. In point of fact, it is no marriage at all. I shall send good news to Aidan regarding the annulment.

Meanwhile, the rebellion of which I wrote so urgently to the O Donoghue Mór has been suppressed by Lord Constable Browne; I shudder to think how ruthlessly. A few stray rebels managed to take hostages, including that fat warthog Valentine Browne, nephew of the Constable. It is an unfortunate situation that reeks of deception. I think it is a little too convenient that the rebels seized only men unfit to fight or even govern. The rebels themselves are not Kerry men, but outsiders, masterless men who serve no cause save their own profit.

A dark, dastardly and entirely awful suspicion overtakes me when I think about who was truly behind the hostage-taking, and whom the English will blame when they hear of it.

If the she-king in London finds out about the mischief, she will lock up the O Donoghue Mór and throw away the key.

—Revelin of Innisfallen

Seven

~~~~~∞∞∞~~~~~

They dined in a lofty hall with a hammer beam roof. A small army of servitors conveyed sumptuous dishes to a table that was so long, Pippa could hardly see Donal Og and Iago. Those two were engaged in an animated, if halting, conversation with Richard's foreign companions.

She discovered two things immediately. She hated eels in mustard, and she adored being waited on. More gradually, she discovered the delights of blancmange and dried figs, the feel of a real silver wine chalice against her bottom lip. Having dining companions who spoke to her politely, in complete sentences, was an unforeseen boon.

"I am expecting my parents from Hertfordshire," Richard explained, "and my aunts and uncles and cousins. I've a large family and they're all quite endearingly mad. We've had wild times together, always have."

Aidan watched him with a charming smile. Pippa suspected she was the only one who knew the meaning of the flinty look in his eyes. He said, "And will you and your family have wild times in Ireland, my good friend? You'd not be the first English family to do so."

"I assure you, my lord, if any of my family were to come to Ireland, it would not be to lay waste to the land," Richard said soberly.

A wave of wistful longing came over Pippa. The very idea of a family filled her with a bittersweet yearning for that warm, unknowable sense of belonging. "Hold fast to them," she murmured. "A family is a blessing some fail to appreciate until they lack one." She blushed and ducked her head. "I reveal too much of myself," she said.

A servant placed a platter of salad greens before her. She stared at them blankly, uncertain how to eat them.

"Use a fork," said Richard.

"Don't speak to a lady like that," Aidan snapped.

"Fork, I said. Use your fork." Richard held up a three-pronged device that resembled a tiny pikestaff.

"Oh." Aidan relaxed against the back of his carved chair. "Sure and I thought you were being impertinent."

Richard threw back his head and laughed, and then he demonstrated the use of a fork.

"Stirrups and forks," said Aidan with his customary rich chuckle. "I have found two useful things among the Sassenachs."

Pippa experimented with her fork and found it much to her liking. In spite of the tension between Aidan and Richard, she found the company much to her liking, too. At the far end of the table, Donal Og and Iago continued to regale their uncomprehending listeners with tales recounted in English, Spanish and Gaelic. There was an undeniable appeal in watching a group of men in high spirits. The sight of all that lavish handsomeness struck her silent with wonder. She felt as if she had dropped into the very lap of heaven, where God in Her infinite wisdom made every man perfect to behold.

One among them was *too* flawless. Here she sat in the house of the most beautiful man in England, yet she felt no breathless attraction to him. Instead, her gaze kept wandering to Aidan, with his long hair, his craggy features, his piercing eyes and the mouth that made her shiver when she remembered touching it with her own. She pictured him just out of the river, his hair streaming like black ribbons over his shoulders, his shirt peeled off to reveal his magnificent chest. She pictured the mat of inky hair arrowing down over a ridged stomach. The scars, fanning outward, must have been inflicted long ago and caused him untold agony.

Was it a Catholic matter? she wondered. She would ask him about them soon.

"I think she is smitten with you," Richard remarked laughingly to Aidan.

She sniffed, hoping she would not blush. "Are you unhappy that I'm not smitten with you?"

"No." Richard grinned. "Just surprised."

Her jaw and her fork dropped. "I gather self-love is another of your myriad virtues."

He roared with laughter. "You are a breath of fresh air, is she not, my lord of Castleross?"

Aidan regarded her with such warmth and tenderness that she wanted to weep. "It is," he said, "a privilege to know her. And sadly, I doubt any of us fully appreciate the gift of her."

She tried to counter with some bawdy comment, but for the life of her, she could not. Saucy words had never before failed her, but they did now. It was as if her tongue would not allow her to pour acid on the sweetness of his comment, to destroy the moment with a flippant remark, to render meaningless his gentle regard.

Just those few words, spoken in Aidan's deep, melodious voice, fired her skin with a blush that blotched her cheeks, her neck, even her bosom. She wished she had worn the ruff the maid had brought with her borrowed gown.

She felt a prickling in her throat, a hot dewiness in her eyes, and at last she realized what had come over her. Somehow these two men, Richard with his humor and godlike good looks, and Aidan with his majestic and mystical Celtic spirit, gave her a sense of belonging.

As soon as the thought struck her, she recoiled from it as if she had been singed. She knew well the price of affection, and it was a price she was not willing to pay. Drawing a deep breath, she became again Pippa the wandering juggler, a clown hiding the tears in her eyes.

"A privilege indeed," she blurted out, jumping to her feet, snatching up three forks and tossing them in the air. "It is not every table that boasts a resident juggler."

Richard leaned forward with his elbows on the table and his ruff mingling with his salad.

"Are you all right?" Aidan asked.

Richard stared at Pippa until she caught the forks and sat down, certain he had examined her to the last eyelash.

Then he blinked. "My apologies. I am not usually so gauche." He flashed his world-brightening smile. "Just for a moment there, you reminded me of someone. But I cannot think whom it could be. Now, never let it be said that at Wimberleigh House we make the guests provide the entertainment." He clapped his hands, and three musicians appeared, one with a gittern, one with a reed pipe, and a singer. "Perhaps this will be more to your taste than the noise at Durham House," he said.

The singer, an effete young man who wore a look of artistic intensity, pinched out most of the candles on the table, plunging the room into moody half-light. A subtle chord rippled from the gittern, and the singer closed his eyes and swayed slightly, then began to sing in a perfect tenor. The reed pipe played a haunting countermelody, and the two blended with a plaintive splendor that was piercing in its beauty. The mingling of tones made Pippa feel raw and vulnerable, as if some part of her had been bared against her will.

She sneaked a glance at Aidan. He was watching her, not the musicians, and not with the mild, polite interest with which one listened to a performance. Despite the dimness she could see him clearly, for the single candle left burning in the middle of the table threw a gleam of antique gold across his face. He sat forward, his face expressionless and his mouth set, yet the frank passion in his regard was unmistakable. Despite his unmoving pose, there was a turbulence deep in his eyes that enraptured her. She was his spellbound victim, open to him and helpless to resist, every inch of her flesh burning with the need to touch him. While she looked across the table, she remembered every moment they had shared, from the day she had knelt at his feet and stolen his knife to this afternoon when his strong arms had yanked her from the river. Her thoughts lingered on the night he had kissed her, a night of candleglow and drumming rain when she could hold none of her secret dreams inside her. It was as if they had lived a lifetime together rather than mere weeks.

Only when the song ended did Aidan relinquish her from his stare, leaving her as weak and shaken as if he had actually caressed her.

"God's light," Richard drawled in heavy amusement, "I have heard talk of making love with one's eyes, but until now I have not actually seen it done."

Pippa forced a light laugh. "Your musicians have uncommon talent. You ought to bottle it like wine."

The delighted performers bowed with a flourish and struck up another tune.

Richard drained his wine goblet, waved away a servant who came to refill it and stood. "Do forgive me. I have many preparations to make before my family comes to see me off. I do hope you'll have a chance to meet them."

She had, just for a second, tasted the sweetness of belonging, but now it was gone. Richard de Lacey and Aidan O Donoghue were virtual strangers. She almost hated them for giving her a glimpse of another world beyond her dreams.

The entire company left the dining hall. Richard's retainers followed and stood in a formal row before the grand staircase. He turned to his guests. "I'll bid you good-night, then." He and Aidan exchanged manly nods; then he took Pippa's hand and pressed it to his lips. The candlelight from the lofty chandelier flickered in his golden hair.

"Good night, my lord." She turned to Aidan, unable to suppress a smile. "Good night."

He took her hand, too, but his manner was completely different from Richard's. Very lightly, perhaps by accident only, his finger skimmed along her palm. His eyes held hers as he slowly brought her hand to his mouth. First she felt the warm flutter of his breath, and that was enough to raise goose bumps along her arms. Then he pressed his lips to her skin. Secretly, his tongue flicked out and touched her.

She gasped.

Richard laughed. "Aidan, I could take lessons from you."

She snatched back her hand. "Please don't. The man is obnoxious." *And I am completely mad about him,* her errant heart added.

He laughed. "Perhaps it is my Irish blood. There is more than one way to make war on the Sassenach."

Aidan and Richard stepped aside and let her precede them to the stairs. Just before she set foot on the bottom step, she heard a slight, curious sound.

One of Richard's footmen called a guttural warning.

Without thinking, she ducked out of the way. In the same instant, a glass chimney toppled from the chandelier and landed with a clatter on the spot where she had been standing.

"Are you all right?" Richard asked the question, but it was Aidan's arms that went around her.

"Of course." She swished back the hem of her skirt to make certain no shards of glass hid in the folds, then smiled at the footman. "Thank you for warning me."

Richard scratched his head and frowned.

"Is something amiss?" She leaned back against Aidan, liking the solid feel of him behind her.

"Not really, but… This is an odd question. Do you speak Russian?"

She laughed. "I barely speak English, my lord. Why do you ask?"

"Because Yuri—" he indicated the footman with a nod "—speaks only Russian. How could you possibly have understood his warning?"

A chill slid through her. There was something strange about this house, something strange about the portraits of the beautiful de Lacey family, something strange about the things she felt when she looked at Richard.

She glanced back at Aidan. He watched her with as much curiosity as Richard.

She shrugged. "I suppose his urgent tone caught me. I have always lived by my wits, Richard."

The broken glass was cleared away, and the entire party climbed the stairs to the upper chambers. In the dimly lit hall, Pippa bade a final good-night to Richard and Aidan.

There was no more hand kissing, but what Aidan did was worse, in a way. His searing gaze caressed her like a lover's hands, and he whispered, "Sweet dreams, *a gradh*," in her ear, flooding her with forbidden sensation.

Just as she nearly dropped to her knees in weak wanting, Aidan left to seek his own bed.

Hours later, surrounded by fussy, majestic luxury, Pippa still could not fall asleep. She wore her borrowed shift and a loose robe over that as she paced in the watery moonlight glimmering across the floor of her chamber. She should be reveling in every moment spent here. She should explore every stick of furniture, every pane of glass, every tapestry that graced the walls. This was luxury such as she used to dream of. Now that she was in its lush lap, she could not seem to enjoy it.

Instead, she tormented herself with thoughts of Aidan. Why did she let herself be drawn to him when she knew it could lead only to heartbreak? Why couldn't she keep him at a distance as she did all others?

A shadow flickered in the moonwashed garden below. Drawn by the movement, she went to the window and looked down through the leaded-glass panes.

What she saw gave her a dark surge of satisfaction. Aidan O Donoghue could not sleep, either.

Like a great, hulking ghost, he paced up and down a garden path, pausing now and then to brood at the slick ribbon of river visible at the end of the lawn.

A fever built in the pit of her belly and spread over her

skin. She clenched her fists and pressed her burning brow to the glass.

What *was* it about the man?

His aura of masculinity overwhelmed her; of that she had no doubt. He was not as flawlessly handsome as Richard, nor as witty as Sir Christopher Hatton, nor as merry as Iago, yet he drew her. She wanted to be with him, touch him, talk to him, feel his mouth on hers as she had the night of the storm.

"No," she said through her teeth. "I won't care about you. I cannot." She sucked in a breath and held it, willing herself to keep control. Every time she let herself dream of belonging to someone—her unremembered family, Mab, members of troupes she had joined—she had been abandoned.

"You'll abandon me, too," she whispered, her breath fogging the glass. "But I don't care." Aye, there was her answer. Surely there was a way to steal a few moments of splendor with him yet come away with her heart still intact. "It can be done," she said aloud, tugging the robe securely around herself and hurrying out the door. "I shall prove it this very night."

London was never truly silent, Aidan thought, staring out at the Thames. Here it was the very dead of night, and he could still hear voices and horses and the occasional hush of oars—smugglers or clandestine lovers or a party of revelers returning home late.

Sounds of merriment, sounds of suffering, sounds of business being done, crimes being committed. They all surrounded him in a great, discordant chorus that was as strange to him as forks and Protestants.

He had told no one of the summons he had received after the boating race today. A special messenger had delivered it to him at Wimberleigh House. Apparently, news of his performance had reached the queen, and she had decided to favor him with a royal audience.

He was ready for her. Past ready. He both longed and dreaded to leave London. As soon as he had heard from Revelin of Innisfallen, he'd wanted to sail for home. Donal Og and Iago had convinced him to stay, for if he left London in defiance of the queen, matters would only grow worse. She would tell her military strategists to deploy more troops to Kerry, to evict more Irish people, to burn more Irish fields and raze more Irish forests. That was exactly what he had hoped to prevent by coming here.

Yet a fortnight had come and gone, and what had he to show for his efforts? A few trinkets, a good horse, a meeting with the de Lacey heir, a fork, for chrissake—

"Your Worship, I must speak to you," piped a clear voice in the night.

And Pippa, he thought, turning away from the river. How could he possibly forget Pippa? His burden. His treasure.

"Yes?" he called, searching the shadows. He saw her small shape coming down the path toward him. She disappeared beneath the darkness of an arbor and then reemerged like a wraith.

A feeling coursed through him, a sort of terrible ecstasy and a sudden bright surge of hope. It was as if she were a princess of the *sidhe*, moving from her fairy kingdom into the real world.

Aye, there was something magic and fey about the girl, of that he had no doubt. Still, his ill-governed body reminded him painfully that she was a flesh-and-blood woman. He wanted her with a powerful need he felt in every bone and fiber and nerve. But he could not have her. Not ever. He had not made love to a woman since he had married, and he couldn't, not as long as Felicity drew breath.

"Aidan?" she called softly. "Are you there?"

"Here." Taking a few steps forward, he touched her arm.

She gasped and stiffened. He braced himself. "There now, I'd not want to end up like poor Temple Newsome."

"He deserved worse than the dunking I gave him."

He chuckled. "So he did. Come here. I vow I will not grab you in an inappropriate spot."

"That is exactly what I came to talk to you about."

Ah, God. The words alone shot a jolt of desire through him. "You *want* me to grab you?"

He heard her breath catch. It was too dark to see her face.

"Don't you dare," she said, her voice curiously tremulous. "What I want you to know is that I am exceedingly grateful for all the kindness you have shown me. I don't even know why you decided to take me in."

Wry amusement curved his mouth. "You gave me little choice. How could I resist the sight of you groveling at my hem?"

"I am an excellent groveler," she said.

Though her voice was full of humor, he did not want to hear any more. He simply could not bear knowing what she had endured in order to hone such a skill.

"The fact is," he said gently, "you are well worth saving, and I have no idea why some worthy patron did not see that long ago."

"Stop it!" She made a jerky movement; he realized she was clapping her hands over her ears. "You are making this harder than it has to be."

"Making what harder?"

She lowered her hands and blew out an exasperated breath. "What I came to tell you." She spoke slowly, as if to a man of limited mental capacity.

"And what is that?" he asked.

"That I won't love you. Never. Ever."

He took a moment to absorb the words. He wanted to laugh at her vehemence. He wanted to rage at her and weep for her. But most of all, he wanted to gather her into his arms and never let go. More fool he.

"Ah, colleen," he said on a sigh. "What was it that hurt you so badly that you'd feel the need to say such a thing? It was losing your family, wasn't it?"

She was silent and still for a long time. Finally she said, "All you need to know is that I don't love you and I never will."

He told himself he should feel relieved. He forced out a brief, quiet laugh. "Your love is the last thing I need."

She tilted up her chin. "Fine. I thought as much. It makes things so much simpler."

"So much simpler." He felt hollow and raw. "Now that means we must be friends. The Irish have a saying, 'If you be not mine enemy, then I count you for a friend.'"

"That is lovely." Her voice sounded curiously thick. She sidled away from him and sat down on a marble bench overlooking the river walk. "Would you tell me about Ireland? Is it true there are wee folk in the woods there?"

He closed his eyes briefly, and a sharp yearning gripped his heart. "There are many magical and wonderful things in Ireland. Many dangerous things, too."

Her hands covered his in a gentle caress. He was grateful for the darkness. He could reveal more of himself than he did by light of day, for the night was a great leveler, hiding flaws as well as virtues.

He thought of his homeland with both bittersweet affection and a desperate resignation. Ireland was a place of harsh splendor and alluring danger. It was a place where a man could live close to the land—or so it had been until the English had come.

"Well, then," he said, gazing off into the shifting shadows of the garden. "On a sunny day, Lough Leane looks like a blue mirror reflecting the endless sky. The forests are emerald green. There are mountains with raging torrents, rivers teeming with salmon and trout, and in the middle of the lake, there is a place called Innisfallen."

"Innisfallen." She tasted the word. "An island?"

"Aye. The island is home to canons of the order of St. Augustine. My boyhood tutor, Revelin, lives there." Aidan had spent hours on the isle, sitting against the cool stone wall of the abbey and letting the holy silence of the place surround him and cushion his dreams. Revelin was as vast and imposing as the Almighty Himself.

"And Ross Castle?" she asked. "Iago said you displeased the queen by completing the building."

A ghost of the old pain wafted over him. "Ross Castle was my father's dream. But *my* penance."

The words were out before he could stop himself. Curse the darkness and the false sense of security it gave him. When would he learn that no place was safe to bare his soul? Was this strange Sassenach woman enchanted, then, able to draw confessions from a reluctant heart?

He snatched his hands away and drove deep furrows into his hair with his fingers.

"Don't stop talking to me," she said. "Please. I want to know. What do you mean, penance?"

She must be under an enchantment, he decided. For he heard himself say, "After my father died, I felt duty bound to complete the castle even in defiance of English law. My father refused to see that our people were losing the fight to stay free of the Sassenach. Year after year I watched him raise armies and lead them off to die. Year after year I listened to the keening of widows and orphans left to starve because my father refused to compromise with the English."

"Aidan," she said, "I'm so sorry."

"Don't sorrow for me, but for those who fought and died, those they left behind." He dropped his head into his hands and thought of the awesome price he had paid to stanch the bleeding wounds of his people. "Their strength has reached its limit. The English Lord Constable is in place in Killarney town, and so long as we rebel, he'll deal with us harshly. For myself, I would fight to my death, but I cannot ask that sacrifice of my people."

"Your father did," she stated.

"Aye." The flood of memories washed over him: the shouting, the pleading…the violence. God in heaven, they had been like mortal enemies rather than blood kin.

"What will you ask of the queen?" she asked.

"Mercy, and some measure of self-rule. If I can negotiate a lasting peace, there will be less bloodshed."

"So you are willing to pay the price of your pride."

"To save lives." He shot up and started to pace. "Damn it, I have no choice."

"My lord, what know you of Elizabeth the queen?"

"That she is intelligent, manipulative and vain. That she is capricious in her decisions. That she is the most cunning and powerful monarch in Christendom."

"She has a famous temper, I can tell you that. One time, Tom Canty went to beg a favor on behalf of the brewers' guild, and she ended up fining the guild."

"Why?"

"Because Tom went to her with his hat in his hand. My lord, if you humble yourself before the queen, she will scorn you."

"Would you have me declare war?" he asked, giving a harsh laugh.

"No." With a quiet swish of her robe, she got up out of the shadows and came to stand before him. The moonlight limned a strange, pale beauty in her face. By night, her appeal had a wistful quality too subtle to be seen by light of day.

"Aidan," she said, "I know I make sport of you with my lofty titles, but here is the truth. You are descended of ancient kings, a ruler in your own right, the O Donoghue Mór, a chieftain."

He felt a curious melting of emotion in his chest. Words, he told himself. She spoke mere words, yet they affected him profoundly. He told himself she was a homeless waif, her opinions did not matter, but her statement made a splendid sense, and his soul thirsted for the faith she had in him. God knew, he had never gotten it from Felicity.

"I am," he said with his old assurance, "the O Donoghue Mór." He swept her up into his arms and whirled her around. Her laughter floated on the night wind and echoed across the river. Like leaves on a breeze, they subsided and settled to the ground, where the soft, damp grass cushioned them. He propped himself on one elbow and gazed down at her laughing face. Then, casting off the last of his hesitation, he kissed her hard and thirstily, drinking courage and wisdom from her startled lips.

She lifted herself into his kiss, arching her pale throat, winding her arms around his neck. Her loose robe fell open, and he was lost in a world of thoughtless sensation.

His hand slipped in between her robe and shift, finding the sweet curves of her body. She had a slim waist and gently flaring hips, strong smooth legs that moved restively when he caressed her thighs.

Yet somewhere, buried deep beneath his passion for her, was a spark of honor that told him to stop. *No.* He squeezed his eyes shut, plunging the spark back into darkness. He would have these moments with her, even if he had to steal them.

She was an innocent in many ways, so open to his caresses, so needful of his affection. And he was a life-scarred warrior, hungry for the trust she gave him, for her complete, unquestioning certainty that there was goodness in him—even though he knew better.

She touched his hard, scarred chest with one finger and drew back to whisper, "I did not come here for this."

"But I'll not let you leave without it." And with that, the last spark of his conscience died utterly. He brushed his hand up over her midsection and cupped one of her breasts. She made a whimpering sound in the back of her throat and raised herself higher so that her breast fit into the palm of his hand. Desire scalded him.

"God, Pippa," he said in a choked voice. He had not anticipated the force of his passion. He shared the same terrible wanting he sensed in her. Suddenly his own desire, his own pleasure, became that which pleasured her. He kissed the side of her throat, lingering over her gently fluttering pulse, tasting the faint spice of sandalwood on her soft, creamy skin.

He moved lower still, using one hand to brush aside the laces of her shift. The garment gaped wide, baring her breasts to the night air. She caught her breath, then whispered, "It's cold."

"I'll warm you, love." He lowered his head to one

breast and his hand to the other. She made no sound, but her flesh seemed to sing to him as she arched into his embrace. He wanted to cover her like a stallion, to lose control and draw cries of ecstasy from her. God, it had been so long…too long… And then the spark of honor flared back to life, as he had known it would. No matter what the reason, he had made a vow to Felicity, and his insidious correctness reared its self-righteous head.

As gently as he could, he stopped kissing Pippa and pulled the robe back around her. In the shadows and moonlight, her eyes looked huge, bewildered.

He sat up. For a moment, he could not speak. It hurt too much, and not just in his aching loins. In his heart. For that was where he wanted to bring Pippa, and—God help him—he could not.

He touched her cheek. "Colleen?"

"What?" She sounded wary, like a child who knew she was about to be punished.

"I want to make love to you," he said. "You know that, don't you?"

"I sensed it as soon as you threw me on the ground and started ravishing me."

He tried to smile at her cocky words.

She sat up and hugged her knees to her chest. "I have one question, Your Excellency."

"Aye?"

"Why did you stop?"

Tell her, he urged himself. *Tell her the truth.*

Instead, he brushed a curly lock of hair from her forehead. "I don't want to hurt you. Can you believe that?"

"Of course," she said, and faith shone in her eyes. She looked away. "But it hurts when you stop."

"God!" His chest felt ripped in two by a devastating

struggle. Before he could talk himself out of it, he grabbed her by the shoulders. "I do want you."

He fumbled for words. Other men made adultery look so easy, and in his case it was justifiable, some would say. Donal Og and Iago had been urging him for months to indulge himself. "I want you for my mistress."

She clutched his arms with her hands. "Mistress!"

"You'll wake the household." He dragged himself to his feet and pulled her up with him. "I desire you, Pippa. You desire me. I'll be good to you. I swear it. You'll want for nothing."

"Except for my pride. But of course, someone of my station should be honored by your offer. In fact, I *am* honored. Look at me. I'm all choked up." A humorless laugh burst from her, and he heard her desperation. She laughed to keep from weeping. That was how she had survived this long.

"I'm sorry," he said in a low voice. "I should have thought—I'm sorry."

"You need not apologize," she said, "for you see, you can't hurt me, Aidan. Don't you remember why I came out here to find you?"

"To tell me you don't love me."

"Exactly so. I do not love you. I will not. Ever."

He took a step toward her, cradled her face between his hands, and glided his thumbs gently over her warm, damp cheeks. "Then why the tears, *a gradh?*" he asked quietly.

"I'm just…just…"

"Just what?"

"Trying to get used to not loving you. And you're not helping one bit."

She was so revealing, so honest with him. "Colleen—"

"This is going to sound insane to you, but I do not feel

honored after all. I feel insulted, Your Stupidity. Let go of me. Don't hold me like this."

He wanted never to let her go. It felt so good, so right, to hold her.

"Aidan, if I have to do serious damage to your codpiece, I will. *Let go.*"

He dropped his hands to his sides. It was the hardest thing he had ever done.

The second hardest thing was to let her walk away.

After a week passed, Pippa realized that she was not going to die of a broken heart.

She was going to live with it.

And what was more, she was going to ignore it, try to find her family, and meet the queen of England.

She meant to use the opportunity to find herself another rich patron. One who appreciated her. One who didn't insult her. One who didn't break her heart.

Standing at her chamber window, she looked down into the central cloister of Crutched Friars. It resembled an innyard just before a play, with men running to and fro, fussing with their hair and weapons.

Only this time the hair was long and wild, and the weapons were real. Aidan had certainly taken her advice to heart. All one hundred of his kerns or gallowglass or whatever he called them were girding themselves for battle.

Shortly they would march on Whitehall Palace into the presence of Queen Elizabeth. Then what? What if the plan went awry? The queen would have them all put to death.

Pippa forced herself to calm down and moved away from the window. She stopped to study her reflection in the sheet of polished brass that served as a mirror.

"A face not even a mother could love," she said,

poking sullenly at her hair. "I look like a mop standing on end."

"I would not say that." Resplendent as a Turkish sultan, Iago sauntered into the room. "You have more curves than a mop."

For a moment, she could do no more than stare at him. He wore loose trousers of blue silk and knee boots that laced up the sides. His chemise gaped open to reveal a broad, hard-muscled chest bearing scars similar to those she had seen on Aidan. Rather than a doublet, Iago wore a short, sleeveless coat and a brilliant sash around his waist. A long, thin rapier traced the length of his thigh.

She could not help smiling. "Truly, Iago, you should have been a showman. The women will be on you like flies on honey."

He grinned back at her. "Is there a court lady in my future, I wonder?"

"If you smile at everyone like that, there might be more than one. Perhaps the queen herself."

He shivered. "No, thank you. Her admirers do not always fare so well."

She scowled back into the mirror. "At least I won't have to worry about being plagued by pernicious admirers."

He stood behind her and rested his hands on her shoulders. "*Pequeña,* why do you not let the maids help you dress? Are you modest? Hiding some secret deformity?"

She leaned against his chest and tilted her head back to look at him. "I do not like the maids of Lumley House. They're not like the ones at Durham or Wimberleigh. They say ugly things about me."

He made a hissing sound of anger and squeezed her shoulders tight. "*Putas.* Why didn't you say something?"

She lowered her head. "They were right. Except for

the part about me being the lover of the O Donoghue Mór." The only part I wish could be true, she thought, cursing her wayward heart.

Iago said something else in Spanish, then turned her to face him. With hands as deft and gentle as any skilled costumer's, he began to dress her, layering garments over her shift and chemise. First came the backlaced corset, then the belled petticoat and underskirt.

As he worked, he spoke in the low, melodic patois she found so fascinating. "I do not understand you," he muttered. "You have everything—charm, youth, beauty, humor—and yet all I see when I look into your eyes is sorrow."

She bit her lip as he made her hold out one arm for a sleeve. "Then you have a wild imagination. What have I to grieve about? I've had you and Aidan both for my hand-maids. Can any other woman in London make that claim?"

"I know what sorrow looks like. You cannot hide it from me."

She studied his face, sculpted and grave, the eyes snapping with lively intelligence, and yes, there it was. A pervasive, soul-haunting melancholy that burdened him even when he smiled.

"Save your pity for homeless beggars. *I* have a plan for my life."

"Fine," he said. "But tell me. As long as I am playing lady's maid, I should play the confidante as well."

He finished with her sleeves and started on her hair with a wooden comb. She took a deep breath. "Iago, it is this. I don't know who or what I am. One day I convince myself I am a princess lost by mistake. The next I am certain a fishwife spawned me and left me to die or to be succored by strangers. I could accept either explanation, as long as I knew it was true. I think what hurts is not knowing."

He took out a net coif decked with seed pearls. It had been in the chest with the other things, but she had not known what to do with it. He scooped up the loose curls at the back of her neck and fitted on the coif. Its draping folds gave the illusion of length. She was heartened by the improvement.

"Listen, *pequeña*," he said, "I am hardly the one to complain to about that. Look at me."

She looked. "You are an uncommonly beautiful man."

He shook his head, beaded braids clicking. "My father was a rapist, and my mother a murderer."

She blinked. "Your stories are almost as outrageous as mine."

"No, I tell you the truth. My father was a Spanish hidalgo who owned a huge hacienda in the islands. My mother was a mestiza house servant."

"Mes—what?"

"Mestiza. Of mixed blood—island native and African slave."

She saw it all in his face, then, a magnificent blending of haughty Spanish nobility, rich African coloring, and the exotic native bone structure.

He finished pinning on her coif. "My father raped my mother, and she killed him. So you see, *pequeña,* there are worse things than not knowing who you are."

"Ah, Iago. I am so sorry."

He kissed her brow, and she marveled at his gentleness. He had been born of sin and rage, had been beaten and enslaved, and yet here he was, bathing her in the radiance of friendship and understanding.

"Aidan was my salvation," he said suddenly.

"What?" Just the sound of his name raised prickles on her skin.

Iago smiled. "There is such goodness in him as the angels would envy. But—" He looked away and distractedly plucked at her hem.

"But what?"

"Too many depend on him. He is like the poui tree of legend. It is a tree so large that its top branches brush the clouds. It supports everything that comes to it—monkeys and parrots, lizards and snakes, beetles and bees. The natives use its branches and leaves for shelter, its bark and sap for building *canoas*. But finally, the poui cannot support all who demand life from it, and the tree dies."

He turned her to face the brass mirror. "Now, look at yourself. The fishwife's daughter is a princess, no?"

"No," she said, yet a thrill chased up her spine. "But let's see if we can fool the royal court."

Diary of a Lady

Sometimes at night, when he thinks I am asleep, my husband arises and paces the floor. Oliver does not want me to see his worry; ever has he been protective of me.

It is concern for our son Richard that stirs my beloved husband from his slumber. Richard is as young and golden as the morning—and in many ways as innocent. He does not know what it means to go to war. He thinks only of flying pennons and blares from trumpets, thundering hoofbeats and grand, dramatic gestures.

Oliver knows better. He has seen the face of war; he has looked death in the face, and it is not a thing he wants his son to encounter.

But this is a matter of state, and women are not supposed to concern themselves with such things.

That I find to be a grand fallacy. For the person most concerned of all is a woman—Elizabeth of England.

—Lark de Lacey,
Countess of Wimberleigh

Eight

The queen had finally summoned the Lord of Castleross to court. All the way to Whitehall Palace, Pippa had not been able to catch a glimpse of him, for Iago insisted on keeping her at his side, ahead of the bodyguard. Like a king from a mythical realm, Aidan remained invisible, remote, holding himself back, waiting to appear suddenly with dramatic impact.

As his escort of one hundred armed Irishmen tramped along the Strand, she understood the full impact of marching. The sound of feet pounding on the road had a profoundly visceral effect, like a sinister heartbeat.

The citizens of London and Westminster seemed to share her opinion. People tripped over each other to move out of the way. Men plastered themselves against walls or slipped into side alleys. Women gathered children into the shelter of their skirts and retreated into doorways. Pale young students of Westminster School clutched their scholars' scrips and stared with wild eyes.

Iago had been sent ahead to act as herald, and he arrived early with Pippa in tow. The entrance to the palace was an arched portal overburdened by a forbidding gate-

house. Iago and Pippa waited in an open court called the
Preaching Place. She felt the pricking eyes of guards and
pensioners and palace officials, but like Iago, she held her
chin aloft and ignored them.

Iago stood in the middle of the Preaching Place,
staring the onlookers into silence. "Aidan, the
O Donoghue Mór," he shouted after a long pause.
"Chieftain of the sept O Donoghue, and known in these
parts as the Lord of Castleross."

After some minutes, she heard again the pulsebeat of
marching. The iron portico of the court gate gaped open
to admit the Irish chieftain. So that his escort would not
be shut out, he came in last, mounted on his fully capari-
soned mare.

Grooms and ministers and lesser folk of the palace
rushed out to look. The crowd jostled Pippa back against
a thick wall. She craned her neck but lost sight of Aidan.

"Never mind," whispered Iago. "You'll see him when
he greets the queen. If he gets his way, the whole world
will see him."

From a distance, she watched him dismount with a
blue flutter of his mantle. Then Donal Og called something in Irish and the troops formed two lines. A piper
and drummer began to play a strange, minor-toned
march, and the entire assembly crossed the court to the
Privy Gallery.

"This is an outrage," blustered a liveried, soldierly
looking man stationed at the entrance. "The O Donoghue
might as well fling down a gauntlet and declare war."

"May his cursed Irish head roll," said another guardsman.

"It may indeed. Watch him dig his own grave."

Iago and Pippa exchanged dubious glances. Then they,
too, hurried into the long, elegant building.

The main gallery seemed endless, with stone walls and stone floors that made the marching footfalls reverberate like thunder. At the end, a soaring doorway opened to the Presence Chamber.

Pippa entered with Iago. He led her along the side of the chamber where it was less crowded. They continued toward the light-flooded end of the room where there was a dais with a canopy so high that it resembled a great tent.

"Where are we going?" Pippa demanded.

"This will do." Iago stepped to the middle of the gallery, bowed low, and repeated his announcement. Then he returned to Pippa's side and escorted her to the end of the room. "Can you see now?"

She peered past a thick stone column and felt as if the very hand of God had frozen her in place, stricken her so that she could not move.

It was her first glimpse of Queen Elizabeth, and Pippa was awestruck. Here, she thought, was majesty. It was a quality far more rare and fearsome than mere beauty, noble grace or lively intelligence, although the queen possessed all three in abundance.

Elizabeth sat on her throne of state, a huge box chair carven and canopied and draped with hangings. An array of shields were hung along the wall behind her.

Wearing the most elaborate costume Pippa had ever seen, the queen appeared tiny, yet her diminutive size was like the very heart of a flower, the nectar surrounded by lavish petals.

A starched white collar framed her face, and braids of pearls and jewels adorned her cloud of fading reddish hair. From where Pippa stood, the queen's face looked stark white, her eyes a shining, canny black.

Fascinated, Pippa moved away from the pillar and

began edging closer to the dais. Iago hissed something at her, but she ignored him. She found a spot in the shadows where she could observe the queen in profile as well as the grand aisle leading to the dais.

The thump of drums and the scree of pipes sounded from the antechamber. The deadly tramp of marching feet never faltered.

Elizabeth's black eyes flashed like moonlight on water. She leaned over to the man standing at her side. "Robbie, what *is* the meaning of this?"

"The Earl of Leicester," Iago whispered to Pippa. "Her lord chancellor."

"I know. He tried to have me arrested the day I met Aidan."

Essex, the preening lord she recalled unpleasantly from the masque at Durham House, bent to whisper to the queen. The feather in his ridiculous velvet hat brushed the queen's cheek. "Out of my sight," she barked. "I have not forgiven you for winning at mumchance." Flushing, Essex stepped back a safe distance.

The heavy doors parted. Even Pippa, who had expected the ploy, caught her breath and gaped in amazement. The unsuspecting courtiers simply froze and stared.

In came Aidan's escort of one hundred gallowglass, looking more savage than a pack of wolves. They wore their rough beards and wolfskins like trophies of conquest, and each man bore full arms. She doubted the Presence Chamber had ever seen such an array of battle-axes and broadswords, maces and pikes and clubs.

The queen's guards bared their own swords, but the Irish made them look like toy soldiers, dressed for show rather than action.

The sound of the pipes shrilled and expanded, rolling out to each corner of the room before falling silent. The gallowglass formed two long lines, the sheer numbers of their bodies sweeping aside the palace guards.

Then a shadow loomed in the arched portal. Backlit by a blaze of sunlight from the antechamber, Aidan appeared massive and godlike, his gleaming cloak rustling and belling out like a huge set of wings.

His mane of hair flowed with his movements, the single decked strand looking defiantly pagan. His face wore an arrogance and pride Pippa had never seen before.

Somehow, the light managed to pick out every angle and plane of his remarkable face: the broad, intelligent brow. The high cheekbones and square jaw. The sensual lips and fierce eyes. He radiated authority and majesty.

He was the O Donoghue Mór.

No one who saw him today would fail to know that. No one would ever forget him. Not even the queen of England.

He stood there long enough for the impact of his appearance to peak. Then he strode into the room, past frozen sentries and the Irish escort, directly to the base of the dais.

To her credit, the queen did none of the gasping and whispering and bosom fanning that erupted among her ladies, who stood in a group near Pippa. Elizabeth merely sat still, pale as ivory, unsmiling, her eyebrows barely lifted.

Aidan flung his cloak back over one shoulder. His silver rowan brooch flashed. Then, with a movement so abrupt Pippa feared he had been shot, he prostrated himself on the floor before the dais.

He lay facedown with his arms spread wide, looking like a fallen angel.

Clearly the queen had not anticipated this show of submission. No doubt, like everyone else, she was wondering just what it meant.

Submission? Even in this prone pose, the O Donoghue Mór radiated power. Fealty? That was doubtful indeed, given his distrust of things English.

"Rise, my lord of Castleross," the queen said at last. She had a rich, loud voice, the vowels round as cultured pearls.

Aidan stood before her. Sunlight streamed down through the high, arched windows, cloaking him in translucent gold. He could not have arranged for a more dramatic setting.

Pippa felt a tightness in her throat. She had never seen such a man, and she had sneaked her way into dozens of plays and revels in which men transformed themselves into birds and angels and Greek gods. But this was no playacting, no illusion of costume and character. There was something intensely moving about such a princely man confronting the queen in this manner.

He broke the silence then—with a howl so loud it caused people to jump in startlement. With savage fury he flung back his head and bellowed an ancient war cry— at least it sounded so to Pippa.

Then he began to pace, his hands clasped behind his back, his boots and spurs ringing on the flagstones. His speech was in Gaelic, delivered with such passion and conviction that the foreign words did not matter. His tone said it all. He was an Irish chieftain, a ruler in his own right.

Beside Pippa, someone stifled a chuckle. She glanced over to see Iago nearby, cloaked in shadow.

"What is he saying?" she whispered out of the corner of her mouth.

Aidan ranted on, sometimes pausing in his pacing to gesticulate while the tirade never ceased.

"You do not want to know," Iago whispered. "But the

least of what he is saying could earn him a penalty of death."

"God have mercy," murmured Pippa, thinking of the comments she had overheard in the antechamber. Chills swept over her skin.

As Aidan paused to draw breath, the gentleman pensioner on the queen's right thumped his halberd on the floor.

"My lord," said Sir Christopher Hatton, "Her Majesty desires for you to address her in English."

Pippa held her breath to see how Aidan would respond.

He faced her directly and bowed his head. "Madam," he said, "it is an honor to address you in your native tongue."

"Ooh," whispered a lady-in-waiting. "He has the most gorgeous Irish brogue!"

Pippa rolled her eyes. Clearly, Aidan O Donoghue had the desired effect on these ninnies. The question was, did his powers affect the queen?

"I wonder if he is in need of company," the lady's companion said. "Surely he is lonely, so far from home."

"He has plenty of company," Pippa hissed at them. "So back off!"

The ladies gasped and fell silent.

Iago chuckled softly. "You are always so discreet, *pequeña.*"

"...my absolute authority as Lord of Castleross," Aidan was saying. "And furthermore, whilst I am in London, I shall attend mass at the Spanish embassy. These matters are required of my station as the O Donoghue Mór, good madam, a station that must carry equal respect, as your own."

"I see," Elizabeth said in a loud, unpleasant voice.

"But I have not challenged you in matters of faith, my lord, have I?"

He sent her a grin that started the ladies' fans fluttering again. "Nay, in this you are the soul of tolerance. I come to you on far more immediate matters, madam."

She tilted her head, clearly intrigued. "Go on."

"My people are suffering. Their crops have been burned. The women raped. Men hanged for made-up offenses."

"Your people have defied their English ruler," she countered.

"We would rule ourselves and send a tithe to Your Majesty," he shot back. "Under present conditions, you will receive nothing, for our lands are in ruin, thanks to Lord Constable Browne and other greedy opportunists. Keep on your present course, and there will be nothing left to claim."

The queen seemed, uncannily, to swell and grow in size. Pippa knew it was impossible, yet as Elizabeth's temper flared, so did her presence.

She was like a thin flame goaded to brightness by a blast of wind. In her intense, diminutive way, she matched the powerful presence of the Irish chieftain.

But she did not exceed it.

"Are you quite finished, my lord of Castleross?" she asked at last.

"Madam," he replied, "I have barely begun."

Her nostrils flared. "If you seek to impress us with your defiance, you have succeeded."

Pippa cocked her head to one side. She heard a quavering thrum in the queen's voice. "Oh, no," she whispered to Iago. "She is absolutely furious."

"Therefore, my lord," Elizabeth said, "we would ask one thing of you. It is a small matter, but one you might be hard-pressed to give."

"And what is that, Your Majesty?" asked Aidan.

"We should like you to give us one reason why we should not have you clapped in irons."

Aidan O Donoghue did the unthinkable. He threw back his head and laughed. It was that banner of dark mirth Pippa had heard the first day she had met him, and the rich, sultry sound of it echoed through the chamber.

The queen's eyes flared brighter. Leicester bent and said something to her in a pleading tone, but she waved him away.

At last Aidan's mirth subsided. "Madam, to answer your question."

Pippa wondered if the queen could detect the steel beneath the smooth silk of his tone.

He swept his arm back to gesture at the Irish soldiers. "When you mow down one blade of Irish grass, two more sprout in its place. And there are men far less cooperative than I. They would not hesitate to take my place if you remove me."

Silence fell, and within that silence thrummed a strain so taut that Pippa lifted her shoulders, ready to flinch when the tension snapped. Aidan was a dead man. She could read his fate in the eyes of the queen, in the grim whispers of her courtiers, on the outraged faces of her guards.

Then, like an arrow out of the blue, came an idea. Before she could talk herself out of it, she charged forward, breaking through the ranks of courtiers and gallowglass.

"Make way," she called, mimicking the majordomo's bell-like tones. "Make way!"

All were too startled to stop her. After stepping in front of Aidan, she curtsied deeply before the dais.

"Your Majesty, I must *insist* that you let this man go.

You see, he has promised to do something for me, and he has not yet delivered."

Deliberately, she stumbled back against MacHurley, one of Aidan's troop leaders. "Ye gods!" she shrieked, clapping her hands to her cheeks and springing back to stare at him. "It is a lamb in wolf's clothing!"

Nervous titters drifted from the ladies, followed by a subtle murmur of male laughter from the group of courtiers beside the dais. Aidan scowled and hissed a warning under his breath, but she ignored him.

She stroked MacHurley's war tunic. "I do like a man in fur," she announced, and looked pointedly at Essex's foppish hat. Aye, the lordling was in trouble with the queen, so it was safe to torment him. "It's so much preferable to feathers."

"See here now," Essex burst out, red-faced with rage.

Pippa sidled up to him. He was so overdressed with trusses and shirt stuffing that he never felt her relieve him of his purse. With a flourish, she dangled it in front of his horrified face.

"Ah, see *here*," she said in a teasing voice. "What is it, my lord, that purples your complexion? A lock of hair from your lady love?"

The other courtiers burst into guffaws.

"What," the queen said, silencing the laughter, "is the meaning of this?"

Pippa turned back to the queen, to that pale, unreadable face, those snapping black eyes. "Your Majesty, I am but a humble strolling player in the employ of Lord Castleross. If he is clapped in irons, I shall be idle." She gave the queen a broad wink. "You know the perils of a woman in idleness, surely. I might actually have an intelligent thought. And *then* where would mankind be?"

The queen's mouth tightened. For a moment Pippa

thought she might smile. "I take great pains to avoid idle thoughts," she said.

Pippa laughed, but no one else did.

"Guards! Remove her at once," said Leicester.

Two guards came toward her.

"Wait!" called the queen. Everyone froze. She looked from Aidan to Pippa and back again. "My lord of Castleross," she said.

"Madam."

"Get you gone from my sight, and take this—this *player* with you. On the morrow shall you return, and *then* I will render my decision regarding your defiance and the people of your district. Is that clear?"

"Abundantly." He did not wait for her to dismiss him. He swung around, bellowing a command in Gaelic. The pipes and drums started up. Grabbing Pippa by the arm to pull her along, he led his entourage out of the Presence Chamber.

Once he had reached the great quadrangle outside, he paused. "Well," he said, "I presume you have an explanation for your little performance."

"My performance was nothing compared to yours," she retorted. "You could have had yourself arrested for treason. I owe no explanation to you."

He caught her other arm and brought her around to face him. She could feel the heat emanating from him, could see the flecks of silver in his blue eyes.

"Ah, but you will talk to me, *a stor*. Tonight, I will have what I want from you."

She was late. The contrary female was deliberately making him sweat and pace and fret.

He went to the hearth in the great hall of Lumley House and savagely poked at a flame-eaten log. Sparks flew up the chimney. The infernal woman consumed him. He could think of naught but her, with her impish smile and lush body. His passion for her was like a fever for which he knew no cure save one—to have her on *his* terms, in his own manner, and damn the consequences.

Unfortunately, Pippa had a mind of her own and no fear of asserting her strong will. It was a quality that both drew and repelled him. Why couldn't she be more tractable? He answered his own question: because weak, compliant females held no appeal for him.

A terrible thought occurred to him. What if she had run off?

Ah, but she would be better off if she did leave. He could bring her only heartache.

A sense of loss clogged his throat. He slammed home the iron poker and strode for the door, flinging it wide open and pounding up the steps to her chamber. Without pausing to knock, he jerked the door open.

Empty. No trace of Pippa lingered save a light, elusive floral scent. He should feel relieved, he thought, closing the door with exaggerated control. She took the decision away from him. It was wrong to desire a woman who could never be his. Wrong to avoid telling her about Felicity. But then, what could he say to anyone about Felicity? He never spoke of her. There was simply no explaining about her, especially to Pippa, who had grown to trust him implicitly.

He stalked back to his chambers. He almost smacked into Pippa, who was on her way out. She gazed up at him, an ironic smile quirking her mouth. "There you are, Your Worship. You were late, and I came looking for you."

"I was late!" he yelled. With a curse to cover his relief, he drew her into the room and kicked the door shut. He had told himself to be stern with her. To censure her for interfering with his audience with the queen.

Instead, unable to stop himself, he gave a great whoop of triumph, lifted her up and swung her around gleefully.

"By the blessed heart of Saint Brigid," he declared, setting her on her feet and giving her a great smacking kiss on each cheek. Though he wanted to let his lips linger over the smoothness of her skin, he pulled back and said, "We were *good* today. We walked into the lion's den and lived to tell the tale."

She took a moment to recover herself. Then she grinned. "I told you so. Admit you were afraid, just for half a second. Admit you feared she would have you arrested and locked up."

"I was *not* afraid for half a second," he said in a blustering tone. "I was pissing scared the entire time, you saucy baggage."

She laughed. "You forced the queen to see you as a man, a worthy rival, rather than a beggar seeking favors. It was better that you risked all."

"Including my people. That was stupid of me."

"Nay, it was bold. Your people would think so."

"Perhaps. Now what, pray, was the meaning of your little performance?"

She gave an elaborate shrug. Feigned innocence, but ah, faith, she was wondrous. Her spilling curls looked as if they had been gilt by the fairies. She still wore her court gown, though without the coif and extra set of sleeves.

"Someone had to divert the queen's attention so she'd forget about punishing you." She went to the sideboard and poured herself a goblet of wine from a stoneware decanter. She turned around and took a bracing gulp. "Not that I give a rat's furry arse," she amended.

"Ah." He stared at her, remembering what she had said. *I don't love you*.... The memory wrenched at his heart and tweaked his conscience, too. What a fool he had been to ask her to become his mistress. What made him think he could possess any part of her without giving all of himself?

"Pippa, about what I said yesterday…" he began, desperate to ease the hurt that knit her brow.

She tossed her head. "Badger me no more about it, my answer is still the same. You are an overwhelming male specimen. Your touch is magic. When you kiss me, the world seems to melt around the edges. But I don't love you, and I won't be your mistress. You'd not want me, anyway. I would spend all your money, drive you mad with all my chatter and bad singing. So it is best for us to—"

He strode across the room, stopped her with a hard, lingering kiss and did not let up until he felt her all but collapse in surrender against him.

"I meant to say I'm sorry," he whispered into her ear. Then he let her go and moved away, out of her reach. "That's all I wanted to say. And you sing beautifully."

"S-sorry?" she said in a dazed voice.

"To dishonor you with my request."

She stared at him until he grew uncomfortable under her stern regard. She continued to stare even as she lifted the wine goblet to her lips and drank. She did not flinch as the strong draft went down.

Finally she said in all solemnity. "Dishonor me?"

"I spoke without thinking, in the heat of the moment."

With exaggerated care, she set down the goblet. "You're not listening, my lord. I refuse to be your mistress. I do not want to be your arm ornament at revels. I do not want you to dedicate songs and poems and—God forbid—jousts and tourneys to me."

She paused, took a deep breath and said, "But I do want you…I invite you…I *implore* you to dishonor me."

Her intensity, her candor, tore at his heart. "Colleen," he said, "you don't know what you're asking."

She pushed away from the sideboard and crossed the room toward him, her brilliant skirts and petticoats whispering on the flagstoned floor. She stood before him, close enough for him to feel the warmth of her, to catch her scent of silk and fresh air.

"I know exactly what I'm asking." She spoke softly but with conviction and an edge of defiance. "I want the whirlwinds and bonfires they sing about in ballads. I want the feeling I get when you touch me."

It took much strength to keep his hands fisted at his sides when all he wanted to do was take her in his arms. "You've been saying you don't love me—"

"And pray you, remember that," she snapped. "This has naught to do with love."

"Then what has it to do with?"

She swallowed. Though it seemed to require some effort, she kept her gaze steadily on his. "It has to do with need, my lord. The need of a young girl on the road, making her way to London with nothing but a dream to sustain her. The need of a strolling player in St. Paul's, making strangers laugh at her and pretending to laugh with them, when sometimes all she wants to do is cry."

Her desperation seemed to reach down inside him and clasp his heart until he could no longer separate her pain from his own. "Pippa—"

"No, let me finish. I'm not asking for your pity. I'm simply telling you these things so you'll understand. Please, may I continue?"

He did not want to hear any more, for he already understood all too well the source of her heartache. In one way or another, she had been deserted all her life. Now she had some notion that he could heal her, and in that, she was dead wrong. But he nodded, almost against his will, and said, "I'm listening."

"By now you know everything there is to know about me, except for one thing."

"And what is that?" he asked. It took all of his resolve not to touch her, to feel her softness, to inhale her scent.

"It's this." She took a deep breath. "I have never been touched in the way you touch me."

"In what way is that?" he asked, dry-mouthed.

"You touch me as if you care."

He could not help himself then. He did not even try to stop his hands as they came up, slowly, brushing over her wrists and traveling up her arms, finally cresting at her shoulders and, so gently, as if she were as fragile as the spun glass of Crutched Friars, cradling her soft, flushed cheeks.

"I do care," he confessed. "That is why I must ask you not to tempt me. Cling to your honor, Pippa. It is the only thing a person has that cannot be taken away."

She smiled grimly. "You think I care about honor? I?" She closed her eyes, and for a moment her mouth thinned as if she were in agony. Then she looked up at him. "I have lied, cheated and stolen in order to survive. For the right price, I would have sold my body." She took his hands away from her face and clung to them. A bitter, mirthless laugh escaped her. "The funny thing is, no man ever considered me worth paying for. A few tried to simply help themselves, but even I had the sense to rebuff them."

She paused, and silence hung in the room. Evening was deepening to twilight. Soon it would be time for them to go to the hall for supper, but neither moved.

Finally she spoke again. "So you see, I have no honor.

You cannot take from me something I never possessed in the first place."

"Faith, Pippa, you have more honor than a legion of Sassenach nobles."

"Don't ply that Irish charm on me. Words just get in the way. I want you, Aidan. All of you. Everything. But if I can have you for tonight only, then that is what I will settle for."

He pulled his hands out of her grip. "You're asking me to hurt you."

She caught the front of his tunic, twisting her fingers into the heavy silk. "Have you not heard a word I've said? I hurt *now,* Aidan! How much worse can it be?"

A curse of frustration erupted from him. He grabbed her and hauled her close, crushing her against him. He slid one hand down to cup her backside; the other hand he buried in her hair, tilting her head back until his mouth was a mere whisper away from hers.

"Is this what you want, then? Is this no worse than the pain you already feel?" Before she could answer, he plunged his mouth down on hers, tasting the wine she had drunk, violating her with his tongue, hearing her whimper and forcing himself to ignore the sound of her distress.

Her hands slid up over his chest. He expected her to try to push him away. Instead, she clung to him, pressed herself against him, mad with wanting, driving *him* mad. Somehow she had sensed that his rough embrace was only an act designed to discourage her. He had not fooled her in the least.

Somewhere, buried deep in a corner of his mind, was a reason he should not let this continue, should not build this emotional bond with her.

Deliberately he closed his mind to it.

And when she made a yearning, straining movement

with her hips against him, he could not even remember his own name.

Still kissing, still embracing, they moved like a pair of dancers toward the chamber door. It opened with a push of his foot, and they entered the bedchamber.

No candles had been lit. The twilight gleamed dully through the wavy panes of the mullioned windows. A few coals breathed faintly in a brazier.

He guided her backward until, with a sweet, surrendering sigh, she sank onto the bed. He leaned over her, watching the way the curls spilled around her face like the gilded petals of a flower.

The stark need in her eyes reached for him, caught at him. Ah, that need. It was the one thing he could not resist about her.

"Turn over," he whispered.

She obeyed unquestioningly. He took hold of her bodice laces and tugged, then peeled away the stiff garment. Beneath, she wore only a chemise of fabric so thin that even in the dull purple light he could see the shape of her breasts, the darkness of the areolae.

He leaned down, brushed his mouth over her lips, and then leaned lower to nuzzle aside the chemise and kiss each breast lingeringly, trying to hold his own sharp need at bay while giving her the sweetest pleasure he could impart.

He lifted his head and looked at her. The sight of her bare breasts, moist and budded from his kisses, nearly made him come out of his skin with wanting her.

She shifted restlessly, and he caught the hem of her skirt, drawing the garment up and over her knees to reveal knitted stockings, hugging her shapely legs. These he peeled away slowly, with relish, kissing and tasting each bit of flesh he revealed. His hands blazed a tantalizing path up her bare thighs, finding at last the treasure at their crest. Ah, she was ready for him, warm and moist and pulsing already, offering no resistance, only welcome. He bent his head and kissed her there, and grew drunk on the heady essence of her.

She lay as if frozen by shock, but then her hands clutched at his shoulders, and her breath came in thin, shallow gasps. She gave a startled cry and grasped at him, pulling him up and kissing him almost frantically.

He felt her tongue enter his mouth, and without volition, his hand went to unlace his codpiece, his only goal to bury himself in her, to ease the intolerable ache she created in him. He had never known a desire as piercing, as all-consuming, as this. She had lit a wildfire in his blood, and the heat surged through him until he lost all sense of who he was. Then her hand crept down to help with his codpiece, and against his mouth, she whispered, "If this be dishonor, then what is the point of honor?" She kissed him again, her mouth soft and moist, her body arching toward his.

What is the point of honor?

In the dimmest reaches of his conscience, a sense of guilt flickered dully. He forced himself to remember who he was. What he was. A chieftain. A foreigner. A husband.

Stopping himself from making love to Pippa was like keeping the waves from pounding at the shore. His passion flooded in all directions, exploding through him until he nearly surrendered. What stopped him was no loyalty to his married state, but a thought of Pippa. She trusted him, admired him, even. He could not bring himself to shatter her image of him, to disappoint her as she had been disappointed all her life.

He forced himself to lighten their kiss, all the while cursing inwardly. Very gently, he lifted his mouth from hers.

Her eyes fluttered open. "Oh, Aidan, Jesu, that was… we…you…"

He smiled, touched her cheek, tried to ignore the ravaged state of his body. "I know, lass. I know."

A tiny frown puckered her brow. "How can you know? *I* had all the pleasure."

His smile broadened. It was amazing that she could make him smile when an inferno burned inside him. "There you are wrong."

"You mean you…we…"

He brushed a tendril of hair off her temple. "For someone who talks so much, you seem to be at a loss for words. There is more than a little enjoyment in this for me as well." With hands both discreet and tender, he drew her bodice up and her skirts down.

Her eyes narrowed. "I think you're lying."

"And I think," he said, "that you have failed to understand something. You matter to me. Your pleasure matters to me. Giving you pleasure is my reward."

"Well, then, what about *my* reward?" She reached for him.

He laughed softly and stopped her. Before tonight, he had no idea it was possible to be as hard as bog oak and still be able to laugh. "Don't get greedy on me."

"I said I wanted you to dishonor me," she said. "I don't feel dishonored yet."

Her words froze his blood. Suddenly the whole world rushed back at him. He was no longer detached, remote, free. For he remembered it all now, remembered why he had no right to be here, with Pippa, taking joy in her joy.

With stiff movements, aching as he did on the day after a battle, he pulled away from her and stood.

"You're wrong," he said, passing a weary hand through his hair. "We are both dishonored."

She lay awake that night, trying as hard as she could to die of a broken heart. It wasn't working. She was beginning to think these things happened only in tawdry love ballads.

Even when she pictured Aidan, glorious and mysterious as a dark angel, turning from her and leaving her cold, she could not will her heart to stop or to shatter or to do whatever it was hearts did when someone broke them.

When she thought of the way he had held her and whispered in her ear, when she remembered his intimate kisses and caresses, she wept, but she did not die.

She took out her brooch, fingering the warm gold as she thought about her plan to find her family. What a foolish notion, to fancy she could accomplish such a feat. Even her own mother had abandoned her. Why should Aidan be any different? And how could she have thought an Irish chieftain could love a girl off the streets?

By dawn she had decided that she was going to survive after all. The question was, what was she going to do with herself?

She got up and stepped over the clothes she had left in a heap on the floor. After Aidan had— What had he done? Made love to her? No, it was something more controlled and cold-blooded than that, for he had refused to give her the one thing she needed—his heart.

Just for a moment, he had opened a window into his heart. But before she could truly peer inside, he had closed back up, shunted her away.

"Damn your Irish eyes, Aidan O Donoghue," she muttered, stepping into her petticoat and skirts. She could not avoid remembering the way he had helped her dress, laughing at the absurd complexities of Sassenach clothing. She tugged on her bodice, defiantly lacing it in front, and then she went to the basin and bathed her face in cool water.

In the stableyard, she found Iago. Just the sight of him, putting a horse through its paces, was a balm to her heart. He had become that rarest of treasures, a true friend.

He tugged at the lunge rein to stop the horse. "What happened to you?" he demanded. "You look terrible."

"Thank you," she said mockingly. "How very kind of you to point that out."

He led the palfrey over to a drystone wall and tethered it. "You were with Aidan last night."

"Yes." To Iago, she could deny nothing. "But he…didn't stay."

The mare sidled restively. He patted her neck with a soothing hand. "Ah. I feared—" He suddenly seemed very interested in inspecting the horse's bit.

"What?" She leaned her elbows on the rough wall and scowled down at him. "What do you fear?"

He took his time adjusting the bit. Then he regarded her with placid melancholy. "That Aidan's conscience and his sense of duty would get the best of him. He ignores the call of his heart."

"I don't understand."

"It is not my place to explain. Soon, we will all go back to Ireland. None of this will matter."

In the back of her mind, Pippa had always known Aidan O Donoghue did not belong here in London amid the littered streets and wreaths of smoke and pervasive sewage smell. She envisioned him in his native Ireland, a place as dramatic and wild as the O Donoghue Mór himself.

Ireland was his home. He was never meant to be here, never meant to pick up a penny player from St. Paul's and steal her heart. It should not have happened, but it had.

The mare nickered and stamped the ground.

"In all my wandering years," she told Iago in a surprisingly steady voice, "I have learned one important thing."

"What is that, little one?"

"To leave first. So I am not the one being left."

He touched her hand, ever so gently, and his tenderness made her weep inside. "That is not such a bad plan."

She gave him a tremulous smile. "You're supposed to talk me out of it."

"That would only postpone the inevitable."

She dragged in a shaking breath and patted his hand. "I suppose so. But now the question is, where do I go next?"

His smile flashed like silver in sunlight. "*Pequeña,* I thought you would never ask."

From the Annals
of Innisfallen

───⋙⋘───

I worry that the nine-fingered courier seen taking ship out of Dingle Bay is up to some mischief.

At least, though, I have a smidgen of happy news to record. By now, the O Donoghue should have received my letter about the marriage, saying he is a free man, and a high praise be to all the saints and angels for that blessing.

The question that plagues my poor soul now is, can the damage wrought to his heart ever be mended?

—Revelin of Innisfallen

Nine

"She left?" Aidan stood with Iago outside the Crutched Friars glassworks, where they had gone to fetch a gift for the queen. He had commissioned it from the glassblowers, but Iago's news made him forget his purpose.

Pretending only idle curiosity, he had asked after the whereabouts of Pippa, who had been conspicuously absent last night at supper and this morning at breakfast.

"Yes, my lord," Iago said evenly, "she has departed."

Aidan stopped next to a hive-shaped glass forge and tried to absorb the shock of losing her. It was not supposed to matter to him, but somehow she had embedded herself in his heart, and her absence left a gaping void.

Especially now. A message had come from Revelin, claiming the ordeal with Felicity was over. Aidan felt cautious, though, and would not believe the truth until he was certain.

In a brusque voice he said, "I should have known Pippa would leave, inconstant female." A fiery ache started in his heart and then rolled outward along his limbs to his hands and feet and head. If he did not know himself to be in good health, he would have thought the sweat was coming over him.

He choked out a curse and turned away from Iago, clenching his teeth and pressing his palms together on the plaster outer wall of the hut. The forge heated the wall, but not enough, not nearly enough to warm the cold empty place carved out by Pippa's departure.

When had he begun to love her, he wondered, and how had he managed to deny it for so long?

Images of her shone like sunlight in his mind. He remembered his first glimpse of her, insolent and exuberant upon the steps of St. Paul's. He remembered her belting out a bawdy song as she took her first bath, banishing the maids with heartbreaking pride, diverting the queen's wrath with reckless courage. And finally, begging him to make love to her—begging him and then recoiling in the face of his rejection.

"She went to court," Iago said quietly.

Aidan stopped breathing for a moment, then started again with a great heave. "To court."

"That is best for her, no? She will live in decent quarters, will be safer than she was scrounging about St. Paul's."

He closed his eyes and pictured her at court, moving with perfect ease amid nobles and diplomats and jurists. Perhaps she would find another man to charm, a protector who could give her his heart as Aidan never could. He pushed away the intolerable thought. "If anyone can succeed at court," he said, "Pippa can."

"Indeed. And of course, she might actually find her family, just as you suggested."

Aidan gave a bark of humorless laughter. "I merely suggested it to dissuade her from risky living among thieves and pimps."

"I think she believed you, my lord. I think, in her

heart, she dreams she will find her family. She needs to know she is loved."

A shiver passed like the winter wind over Aidan. "She needs me," he said, half to himself.

Iago made a *tsk*ing sound with his tongue. "But what of the future? Can you give her the constancy she needs?"

Futile rage boiled up in Aidan, and he pushed away from the hut to glare at Iago. "I cannot. You know that." In the wake of the rage came a gray tide of bleakness. "Do you ever just want to turn your back on it all? To simply let go of everything and walk away?"

"I have done that." Mischief gleamed in his eyes. "Only in my case, I swam."

Aidan forced a smile. At the same time, his errant heart led him to a decision. "Go and fetch the queen's gift. I must get myself dressed."

"Diablo!" Iago said. "Do not tell me—"

"Yes." Aidan started back toward the house. "I am taking the gift to court myself."

"…and so," Pippa said with a confidential wink at the queen, "the brewer's daughter could only make one choice. To poison the keg!"

Queen Elizabeth's smile was slow and filled with pleasure. Other listeners took their cue from the queen and chuckled.

Pippa curtsied and surreptitiously released her breath. Her Majesty's moods were capricious. Stories she found amusing one moment might land the teller in the stocks the next. So far, Pippa had been lucky.

Of course, it was only her second day as the royal fool. Thus far, the queen had made no decision regarding the O Donoghue Mór, but Pippa kept an ear cocked for any whisper of his fate.

"Well told," the queen said. "In sooth, virtue and innocence do not always triumph, do they?"

"Not nearly so often, ma'am, as old age and cunning," Pippa blurted out, then froze.

The queen stared at her for a long moment. Her face, already smooth and pale with its coating of ceruse and powder, seemed to whiten even more. Then she let out a hoot of laughter, and the courtiers joined in.

"You are a tonic, my poppet," she said. "I am pleased indeed that you petitioned me for a player's warrant. I do like to nurture talent. And you are well rid of that foreign chieftain."

"Ma'am." Hiding her regret, Pippa sank to one knee and snatched up the hem of the queen's gown. "I am so humbly grateful."

"Yes, yes." Faint impatience underscored the queen's words. "Do stand up and let me look at you."

Pippa stood. The queen's bird-black eyes flicked over her, and she said, "That gown is familiar to mine eyes."

"I am told it belonged to Lady Cheyney," Pippa said baldly, knowing the truth was safer than lying and then being found out. "But here's the fact, ma'am. The gown does not a fool make. I have worn this for two days and have not felt the slightest urge to invite a gentleman to my chambers."

The queen tapped a long finger on the arm of her chair. "You are a fool in name only." Her smile tightened. "Still, you should consult the master of revels for the proper mode of dress. My sister Mary, of honored memory, did make her fool shave her head and wear striped garb."

Pippa lifted a hand to the curls escaping her coif. "There are worse things, madam, than shaving one's head," she said bravely. Still, she felt a heavy disappointment. Her hair was finally beginning to grow out to a more becoming length.

"Fear not, for I—" The queen glanced at the distant doorway of the Presence Chamber. "Yes?" she called.

"The O Donoghue Mór, Lord of Castleross," intoned the majordomo.

Elizabeth waved away the other courtiers clustered round the canopied throne. Pippa found herself standing next to the Contessa Cerniglia. Of the many people Pippa had met at court, Rosaria was her favorite. Fair and tall, she had a pleasantly cynical view of life and a keen ear for gossip.

With her heart pounding wildly, Pippa trained her gaze on the door. Aidan!

Why had he returned? Part of her prayed he had come for her, while another part dreaded seeing him again, feeling that twist of raw wanting and the sting of his indifference.

She stood as still as a marble pillar and waited.

With the dramatic suddenness of a darkening storm, he filled the doorway, flanked by Donal Og and Iago. Looking like mythical giants, they made their unhurried way down the center of the room.

He wore his princely garb, the stone-bedecked tunic and rich blue mantle. He knelt before the queen. Iago and Donal Og did likewise; then simultaneously the three of them stood.

"We bring gifts, my queen," Aidan said formally. He kept his gaze straight ahead, but Pippa had an uncanny sense that he was aware of her in the room.

"Ah, and he speaks English today," Elizabeth said with wry humor. "We are making progress."

Iago and Donal Og placed the gifts at her feet. One was the most elaborate salt cellar Pippa had ever seen, a tall fantasy of spun glass. It resembled a stylized castle, its slender turrets reaching upward, the tiny chamber where the salt was held surrounded by thin threads and coils of glass.

The other gift was a bracelet of cut amethyst that caught the light and seemed to shine from within. Pippa remembered wearing the matching necklace, remembered the magic of that night, and she blinked back tears.

"That is lovely." The queen held out her hand for the bauble and lifted it to spin on its gold chain in the light.

"The jewels were mined by Irish hands in the Burren," Aidan said.

"Indeed. For that honor, I thank you, my lord." She spoke pleasantly and smiled, yet at the same time her small, slippered foot pushed at the base of the salt cellar.

Pippa gaped in horror as the perfect glass tower shattered on the flagstone floor. Tiny shards and needles of glass scattered every which way.

The O Donoghue Mór did not flinch. The bright, wasted glitter covered the floor all around his feet.

"Such a pity." The queen fixed her black-eyed stare on Aidan. "You see, my lord, when a man builds a castle without proper consent, accidents are bound to happen."

The Contessa Cerniglia gave a soft murmur of dismay. Delicately she plucked at her skirt. A small cut marred her ankle. Instantly Donal Og knelt at her feet and touched the tiny bright bead of blood that seeped through her stocking. The lady's dismay changed quickly to romantic interest as she gazed down at Donal Og. She had large bosoms, which she displayed proudly with a low-cut, jeweled bodice. The effect was not lost on Donal Og.

"It is also a pity," Aidan said, "that accidents are capricious by nature. Sadly, it is often the innocent who suffer." He directed a meaningful look at the blond contessa.

"Sometimes the strong suffer, too." The queen rose from her throne. Leicester and Hatton moved in fast to escort her out of the Presence Chamber. Before she left, she said, "My lord of Castleross, I trust you'll join us at supper and revels tonight."

No. Pippa tried to will him to refuse. It was dangerous for him here. The queen was playing some cruel game with him. He ought to leave while he had the chance.

The O Donoghue Mór bowed from the waist. "Madam, I am most humbly honored."

The revels that night consisted of wild, skirling music and a troupe of Italian acrobats. Donal Og and Iago watched with rapt attention.

Aidan watched Pippa. She sat at one of the lower tables amid minor officials and the queen's lesser ladies. Court, he noted with a pang, agreed with Pippa.

She laughed with practiced charm and wielded her fork and knife as if she had dined at table for years. Though he could not hear what she said, he guessed that she was in rare form. She looked animated and flushed. Everyone nearby listened to her and laughed.

Yet he began to notice an almost feverish desperation beneath her chatter. Her gaze darted about the hall and searched every noble face.

He knew what she was looking for. The mother and father whose image she had tended so lovingly in her imagination. When, he wondered, would she realize the futility of her dream? Not only had he hurt her, but she was bound to suffer when her impossible quest failed.

As soon as the dancing began, he sought her out. She

was standing beneath the musicians' gallery with Donal Og and the Venetian contessa, urging them to dance the volta.

Aidan could not help smiling at the picture they made, giant Donal Og gazing in helpless adoration at the blond beauty.

Pippa shooed them out onto the dance floor, then watched them with a satisfied air.

"In Ireland," Aidan said softly, coming up behind her, "we do leave matchmaking to crones and tanists."

She turned and caught her breath. He stopped walking toward her, wanting to freeze the moment, to hold this image of her forever in his heart. She had that look of timeless beauty, her face smooth, eyes wide with a startled look, a crown of curls gleaming in the rushlight.

How had she done it? he wondered. How had she managed to stay so winsome and innocent when every day of her life had been a struggle to survive?

Finally she spoke. "I'm sorry about the salt cellar."

He smiled. "Revelin used to say 'When you sup with the devil, you need a long spoon.'"

She laughed and said something, but her words were drowned by a brassy blare of trumpets from the gallery above.

"Come with me." He steered her by the elbow toward a side exit. Within moments they had gone through a low-ceilinged passageway and emerged into a garden. At the end of the sloping yard, the river gleamed with starlight. Aidan took a deep breath of the cool night air. "That is better," he said.

"No one is supposed to depart until the queen gives leave," said Pippa.

"Is that so? I wonder how I dared."

"Must be your long spoon. Aidan—"

"Pippa—"

They both spoke at once, both laughed awkwardly.

"Go on," he said. "What were you going to say?"

She strolled down a walkway, her slippered feet silent on the path. Then she stopped and turned to him, leaning back against the rail of the knot garden. "I wanted to explain why I left."

"Without a word," he reminded her, staring at the slim, pale column of her throat, the tops of her breasts where they pushed up from her bodice.

"This was all your idea," she said. "You said I might find a way to discover who I am, where I came from." Her eyes narrowed. "Or was that another of your lies?"

Her distrust cut at him like a blade. "I never—"

"You did," she shot back before he could finish. "You asked me to be your mistress. You had me begging to be your lover, and then you denied me." She fixed him with an insolent stare. "I tell you, my lord, I have had better days. *Much* better days. Such as the time I was set upon by dogs at the bear-baiting ring."

"You were attacked by dogs at the bear-baiting ring?" He felt sick. He had seen the curs kenneled outside the ring at Southwark. Slavering, vicious beasts, they were.

"No," she snapped, "but if I had been, it would have made for a better day than being cast off by you."

Aidan swore in Gaelic. She had managed to singe his temper, and he was glad. It was the only way to keep his desire in check. "You're a fine performer indeed. Tell me, was the queen as gullible as I was when you came to beg a place in her household? If you had said your loyalty was for sale, I would not have worried so much."

"The queen's offer tempts me far greater than yours," she retorted. "I would have paid for yours in heartbreak."

If her voice had stayed firm, he could have stood it. But it did not. Instead, her speech quavered with a bitter hurt that seared his soul. "Ah, Pippa. You were right to leave me. I can't give you what you need."

She squeezed her eyes shut. He had a powerful urge to kiss her, to use mouth and tongue to change her expression from pain to pleasure. But he resisted.

"We should not quarrel. It serves nothing." She drew away from him. He folded his arms to keep from pulling her back into his embrace.

"There is a dream I used to have of a dark-haired woman bending to kiss me," Pippa said. "'Mind Mama's brooch, darling,' she would say. 'Don't prick your finger on it.'" Pippa plucked at the head of a rose. "I don't know if it's a flight of fancy or a true memory, but I do know that last night I dreamt it again. And I dreamt of a man's merry laughter, and a grandmother singing to me in a strange language."

"Singing what?" he asked. "Do you recall the tune?"

"The song lingers still." She sang, the words so unfamiliar they sounded like gibberish, but she seemed quite sure of herself. "I feel close to them here, Aidan. As if I might spy a face in the crowd and recognize it. Recognize *myself*."

For a long moment, he did not—could not—speak. What must it be like, not to know one's family? Aidan O Donoghue had known from the cradle who he was. It had brought him little pleasure and much pain, but at least he had known. Again he ached for her. The chance of finding her family was too painfully slim. She could walk right past her mother and not know it.

"I think I understand your hunger," he said at last. "And I am Irish. I would never be so foolish as to underestimate the power of a dream."

"Thank you for saying that," she said. "All I want to know is that someone once loved me. And perhaps then I can believe someone could love me once again."

Someone wants to love you, *a gradh,* Aidan thought, biting his tongue to keep from blurting out the words. The problem is, the wrong man wants to love you.

Wimberleigh House, the soaring Strand residence of Richard de Lacey, teemed with activity. The garden doors of the house had been flung wide open, and servants paraded down a path to the river, carrying parcels of all shapes and sizes to a commodious river barge.

And there was the low-bellied bastard Aidan was looking for.

"Lord Castleross!" From the river landing Richard waved in greeting.

Feeling grim as winter, Aidan stalked down to the landing where Richard stood amid parcels and barrels.

"You just missed making the acquaintance of my parents, the Earl and Countess of Wimberleigh," Richard said. "They've taken themselves off to Hertfordshire. We did celebrate a grand farewell. My aunt Belinda set off colored fire and rockets, ah, that was a sight to see, and—"

"I'm certain it was." Aidan wasted no time in idle talk. "Why didn't you tell me your commission was a post in Kerry?"

Richard's ears reddened. "In sooth, my lord, I did not know. I expected a post in Ireland, but my assignment to your domain came as a surprise to me."

"But you accepted it," Aidan said tautly. All during his wild ride through the streets of London, he had hoped the gossip he'd heard the night before was wrong.

Richard made no attempt to deny it. He planted his

feet wide. "The queen gave me no choice. No more than you had about coming to London."

"Aye," Aidan lashed out, "but I did not come here to butcher the citizens, steal their land, rape their women and raid their livestock."

"And that is not my purpose in Ireland." Richard cursed and flung his velvet hat to the ground. "I am being sent to keep the peace."

"Ah, that is rich," said Aidan. "Did you ever think, my young lordling, that if the Sassenach would stay out of Ireland, then we would be at peace?"

"If we were not there, the Irish would fight amongst themselves."

"Then give us that freedom, man!" Aidan roared. "Let us destroy ourselves at our own discretion, with no help from you." He flung out his arm in agitation. His fist hit a canvas-wrapped parcel, toppling it. There was a tearing sound, and the corner of a crate ripped through the parcel.

"God's teeth." Richard bent to pull aside the wrapping. A large portrait of a lady, now pierced by the wooden crate, stared up at the gray morning sky.

"I'm sorry," Aidan said brusquely. "'Twas an accident."

The woman in the picture was remarkable—dark and serene with misty eyes the color of winter rain. "Your betrothed?" he asked, picking up the ruined painting.

"My mother, Countess Wimberleigh. God knows when I shall see her again." Richard called out in a foreign tongue. The burly servant with the mustache hurried over and reached for the portrait.

"Wait a moment." Aidan held up a hand and frowned at the picture. The countess wore a rather plain gown of dove gray. Her one ornament, a brooch, looked out of place pinned to her bodice.

His heart lurched. The ornament was large and

unusual, cruciform in shape, decked with a huge red stone encircled by twelve matched pearls.

He swallowed past a sudden dry heat in his throat. "When was this painted?"

Richard shrugged irritably. "Sometime in the first year of my parents' marriage, about twenty-five years ago."

"Does your mother still wear that jewel?"

He frowned and shook his head. "I've never seen it." He exchanged words with the foreign servant who then carried off the portrait.

"I'll pay to have it repaired."

"Never mind," said Richard. "My lord, I'm sorry to part with you on these terms. I would that we could—"

"How did you come to have Russian servants?" Aidan's mind was starting to pull together the fragments of an amazing puzzle.

"My family has ties to the kingdom of Muscovy. The Muscovy Trading Company was begun by my grandfather Stephen, Lord Lynley. He and my grandmother still live in Wiltshire."

"Did she sing to you?"

Richard regarded him with a confused scowl. "Sing?"

"You know, ballads. Lullabies. In Russian."

"I don't know. Perhaps. I don't remember."

Aidan saw that he was rousing Richard's suspicions. He cut himself short and said, "I have no quarrel with you until you set foot on Irish soil. Then, it will be as if our brief friendship had never occurred."

If Richard replied, Aidan did not hear him. He had sudden pressing business at Whitehall with the queen's fool.

Pippa pretended to be totally absorbed in the game of chess she was playing with Rosaria, the Contessa Cerniglia. In reality, her attention was secretly trained on the travel-weary courier who claimed he had urgent news from Ireland.

The crowded room buzzed with activity. The courier, a man with long cheeks and sunken eyes and a clear tenor voice, pressed his hands on the petitioner's table in frustration. Pippa noticed that he was missing a finger on his left hand.

"What do you suppose his problem is?" asked the contessa.

Pippa smiled at her across the chessboard. "Who, my lady?"

The contessa's lips thinned. "You know very well who. You have been staring at him since he walked in. You have also been cheating at chess, but I like your company, so I'm letting it pass."

Pippa stared at her. No one—*no one*—had ever caught her cheating.

The contessa laughed softly. "I am the daughter of the Venetian ambassador," she reminded Pippa. "My father built his life around observing people, seeing what is in their minds by watching what they do, particularly with their hands and eyes. I learned all I know from him."

"Sorry about the cheating," said Pippa. "It is a habit with me."

The blond contessa gave her a brilliant smile. "Never mind. Are you interested in learning the news from Ireland?" She nodded toward the courier, who was still arguing with a palace official. Leicester and his stepson, Essex, went to join in the discussion.

"Certainly not."

"Of course you are." The contessa rose from the table. "The news might concern your lover."

"The O Donoghue Mór is not my—" Pippa clapped a

hand over her mouth, furious at herself for letting the contessa trick her into blurting out his name.

The cool, beautiful woman patted Pippa's arm. "I thought as much." She led Pippa through the packed room, exchanging polite snippets of greeting with the courtiers they passed. "Now, what about the other one— is he a brother?"

"No, Donal Og is Aidan's cousin."

"Donal Og." The contessa's mouth stretched into a smile. "Has he a wife?"

"No, he—" Pippa stopped walking. "You're smitten with Donal Og!"

"Smitten is too chaste a word, *cara*." The contessa winked and took her hand. "My feelings have progressed well past smitten." When they drew close to the petition table, she paused and took out her fan, fluttering it in front of her face.

Pippa held back. "They'll see us," she said. "They'll know we're trying to listen to them."

Rosaria smiled. "Here is a basic truth about men. When their minds are not on lusty matters, women are invisible to them. They will not even notice us."

It was true. The messenger spoke in low, agitated tones to Leicester and Essex and did not even pause for breath when Pippa and the contessa moved in close, pretending to have a whispered conversation behind their fans.

"…an emergency. The danger is barely under control," he was saying. "His kinsmen kidnapped six Englishmen while they were on maneuvers. I fear they mean to kill the hostages."

"Have the rebels made any specific demands?"

"None that I know of. I strongly suspect they will contact Lord Castleross and await his instructions. In fact, a letter to a priest or monk called Revelin was seized at the port of Dingle."

Pippa's blood froze.

"Then you know what we must do," said Essex.

"Don't crane your neck so," the contessa warned Pippa. "It is too obvious."

"We must make certain the O Donoghue Mór does not receive word from—"

"Pippa!" The contessa's harsh whisper failed to stop Pippa's sudden departure. She raced to the end of the hall and fled past the ever-present gentleman pensioners flanking the doorway. Beyond the hall lay a sunlit passageway with tall, slender windows and a soaring arched ceiling.

Courtiers and petitioners milled around the area. Robed barristers, minor noblemen and the occasional hard-eyed Puritan could be seen. She rushed past them all with only one thought in mind. She had to find Aidan and warn him.

When she was halfway down the corridor, she saw a large man striding toward her, his midnight hair flowing out behind him.

Aidan. It was as if her frantic thoughts had summoned him.

She lifted her skirts, heedless of the disapproving glares of the Puritans, and hurried on, skidding to a tottering halt when she reached him.

"My lord!" The sight of him was, as always, a shock to the senses. He possessed, in extravagant excess, every male charm conceived of by God in Her wisdom. Being away from him for a few days only made him that much more fascinating.

For a few seconds, she stared in rapture at his perfectly hewn Celtic features.

"Mistress Pippa." He took her hand and lifted it in formal greeting to his mouth. When his flame-blue eyes met hers, she saw her startled face reflected in their depths and remembered her purpose.

"My lord, I just found out—"

He touched a finger to her lips. Perhaps it was her imagination, but he seemed to be studying her intently, drinking in the sight of her. Could it be that he had missed her, too?

"*A storin,*" he said, "a most singular thing has occurred."

"*Seize him! Seize the rebel O Donoghue!*"

The call came from the arched doorway of the Presence Chamber.

Aidan's head snapped up. "What the—"

She grasped his thick, muscular arm and tugged with all her might. "Run!" she said desperately. "They mean to arrest you!"

Instead of fleeing as she begged him to do, he planted his feet and glared at the oncoming guards and pensioners. The captain of the guard bellowed his orders again.

"Seal the doors! Seize the rebel Irish lord."

Strong hands grabbed Pippa and dragged her away from Aidan. She screamed a curse. The roar of raised voices and thundering footfalls drowned her protest. Reverting to tactics she had learned from street fighters, she lashed out at those who detained her, kicking and elbowing, looking for something vulnerable to bite.

There were too many of them. This was the queen's chief residence, after all. It was more heavily guarded than the royal treasury. Firm hands subdued her. Furious, she stopped struggling long enough to look at Aidan.

He towered over the guards, but at least a dozen surrounded him, making escape impossible. He was like a great noble stag cornered by snapping curs.

His gaze found hers, and she felt her heart turn to ice. For the eyes of the O Donoghue Mór were filled with hatred and accusation.

Dear God. He thought she had betrayed him.

So this, thought Aidan grimly, was the great Tower of London.

He had been given a room in Beauchamp Tower where, years before, Guilford Dudley had suffered and pined for his Lady Jane before being led off to die. The room was hexagonal in shape, with walls of light-colored stone, narrow windows giving a view of the Thames on one side and Tower Green on the other.

Tower Green, where the heads of traitors were lopped off.

He paced like a caged lion. Three days and nights had passed, and no one save the warden and guards had come to ease his isolation. No one had told him the precise reason for his arrest.

Ah, but he knew.

He continued to pace, noting that the furnishings in the room, though sparse, were of good quality. The low bedstead had rails of carven oak, and the thick tabletop was covered by a chessboard. His noontime meal—untouched—sat upon a tray of silver.

He had all the amenities of a prisoner of rank. That was something, he supposed. But it was not enough.

He swore under his breath, went to the window, and braced his palms on the ledge. Fury boiled silently inside him. He did not know who made him angrier—Revelin of Innisfallen, for advising him to stay on in London, himself for heeding that advice, or Pippa for her part in his arrest. There, in the gallery of Whitehall, she had given him the Judas kiss. How quickly she had deserted him.

News from Ireland had arrived like an ill wind. The rebels had fired flaming arrows at the Browne residence in Killarney. Most of those involved were violent men of little honor and lesser sense.

His reply had been an express and urgent order to withdraw and await the chieftain's return. Obviously, Revelin had either not received the message or was ignoring it. The rebels had seized English hostages.

Panic clawed at Aidan's throat. He was afraid—but not for himself. The past few years had stripped him of all fear of dying.

Nay, he feared for the people of his district, what would become of them if the Sassenach host took it upon themselves to avenge the insult dealt by the rebels. Aidan had seen Sassenach justice at work in Ireland.

It took the form of wanton, wholesale slaughter.

Old women and babies were dragged from their cottages and gutted like pigs. Men were hunted in the forests and spitted on swords and pikes. Women were raped and left to die or to bear the children of the men who had brutalized them.

The barrier between the atrocities and a peaceable solution was thin and fragile. For now, there was a standoff. Six Englishmen were prisoners of the rebels. Aidan was likewise a prisoner of the Crown.

Nothing would happen until one side or the other lost its hostage.

Stricken cold by an idea, he turned away from the window. For many long moments he stood unmoving, staring at the table with its hearty meal of meat and wine laid out for him.

A wave of fatalism rolled over him. With glass-edged clarity he saw a way out.

Perhaps the most useful thing he could do for his people now was to die.

Diary of a Lady

We had a most singular visitor today—Rosaria, the Contessa Cerniglia. I found her to be delightful and unfettered in her conversation. I was early taught that women should press down their frank opinions and bold ideas; what a mercy my dear Oliver showed me otherwise!

Worldly (as most Venetians are), the contessa took a great fascination in the Russian retainers in Richard's service, and even found merriment in trying to read words written in that alphabet.

Ah, Richard! My son! The very thought of him mars my pleasure in recounting the contessa's visit.

For tomorrow, he takes ship to Ireland.

—Lark de Lacey,
Countess of Wimberleigh

Ten

Bits of litter, buffeted by an unseasonably chilly wind, rolled along the street in front of Pippa. She clutched her shawl tighter around her and lowered her head, hurrying on.

The queen's ladies, eager to train the newest royal plaything, had cautioned her not to stray from the palace without formal leave.

"Formal effing leave," she muttered, her words swallowed by the wind, "my pink backside."

"Come with us, sweetling," called a rough voice.

She saw a pair of wet-mouthed soldiers clutching flasks and ambling toward her. "We'll keep you warm."

In the weeks she had spent with Aidan, she had almost forgotten the ugly sensation of being threatened by brutes. But she would never forget how to dispense with them.

As she had dozens of times before, she bit the inside of her lip until she tasted blood. The routine was so familiar that she didn't even wince. She spat blood on the street in front of the soldiers. "Want to take your chances with me, lads?"

Cursing her, they stumbled off, cramming themselves through the doorway of the nearest tavern.

She nursed her cut lip with her tongue and quickened her pace. Her heart was pounding by the time she reached the street gate of Lumley House.

Please be here, she thought.

But no one greeted or challenged her at the gatehouse. She pushed through to the inner courtyard and went around to the kitchen garden behind the main house.

The entire place echoed with emptiness. Shivering, she leaned against the well sweep to catch her breath. Memories crept up and seized her unawares.

"No," she whispered, but the feelings raged like the wind, unstoppable, impossible to ignore. She had no idea memories could be so sad and so sweet all at once.

There was the pear tree where she had juggled for Aidan, easing the frown off his face and finally coaxing laughter from him. There was the arbor under which she had shown him the cut-and-foist technique of a seasoned thief and the eastern way of self-protection, taught to her by a tumbler from the Orient. At the top of the steps she had sat with Aidan and explained the intricacies of dicing while shafts of sunlight had bathed him in radiant splendor.

He had touched her that day, as he did so often, with gentle solicitude, his long fingers brushing back a curl of her hair and then lingering, for perhaps just a heartbeat too long, upon her cheek. He had taught her things as well, good things, valuable things, magical Gaelic words to describe the color of clouds at dawn and the feeling one gets while watching children at play. He had taught her that she did not always have to measure her value with the applause of strangers. And he had shown her that families could take many forms and that some of the strongest bonds were forged not by blood, but by the heart.

Tender leaves and blowing petals drifted down, littering the pathway. The herb garden had burst into bloom, and the pungent dry aroma of lavender and mint hung in the air.

She swallowed past a welling of grief in her throat. The house and garden stood still and silent, empty and desolate, as if her weeks with Aidan had never happened. As if the halls had not rung with laughter, with Pippa mimicking Donal Og's accent or singing an island ballad in Spanish with Iago.

They had been, for one brief, shining season, a family.

Dashing away a stinging tear, she went to the back wall of the garden and entered the adjacent priory of Crutched Friars. The only sign of life was a thin trickle of smoke from the glassworks.

She stood in the doorway of the foundry and waited for her eyes to adjust to the dimness. A lone artisan worked at the forge, heating molten glass into a glowing blob at the end of a steel rod. With several deft twists, he transformed the shapeless mass into a goblet, expertly using tongs to break it off when he was finished.

"Hello," said Pippa.

The goblet slipped and shattered on the packed earth floor. The area was already littered with broken glass.

The artisan let loose a stream of invective that impressed even Pippa.

"I'm sorry to startle you," she said.

He set aside his rod and yanked off his thick gloves. "It's not your fault," he said in disgust. "Actually it is, but you ought to tell me it's my punishment for working on the Sabbath."

She had forgotten it was Sunday. "I thought that was against the law."

He propped a hip on the worktable and spat on the floor. "I fell behind. The Earl of Bedford wanted his goblets yesterday."

The dull glow of the forge lit his face, and she saw that he was a mere boy, beardless and soft cheeked, a troubled frown puckering his brow.

"You're an apprentice?" she inquired.

He nodded.

"What happened to the guests at Lumley House?"

"All gone away, and good riddance, I trow."

"Do you know where they went?" She tried to show only casual interest. She had come dreading the worst—that Donal Og and Iago and Aidan's men had been rounded up and arrested or, Jesu forfend, put to death.

"They just sort of slipped away in the night," he said. "Odd, that." The youth smiled. "I think it were *her* idea."

"Her?"

"The foreign mort. Blond, she were. Big—dimples." He winked. "A mite bossy, but after she yammered at them for a while they all up and followed her. Never came back."

Pippa sagged with relief against the door frame. The contessa. Somehow she had warned Donal Og and Iago of impending danger.

Perhaps they were in hiding or on their way to Ireland. Once there, Donal Og would know what to do. He would free the English hostages and put down the rebellion. The queen would have no further need to detain Aidan in London Tower.

Pippa thanked the apprentice and left, taking Petty Wales Street south toward the river. Nearby loomed the Tower, handsome and imposing, pennons flying from each corner tower.

Aidan, she thought. The merest thought of him made her turn weak and warm.

The idea that he was in danger filled her with a fear that ripped like the thrust of a sword through her. She stood across from the grim edifice for a long time, staring and thinking while the evening closed around her and deepened into night.

After a while, she heard the Ceremony of the Keys being called out. A scarlet-coated and feather-bonneted warder appeared with a lantern and a massive escort. Bemused, Pippa crept through the shadows of Water Street, watching their progress. As each gate of the fortress was locked, a sentry called out, "Halt! Who comes there?"

"Queen Elizabeth's keys," the warder answered. "All's well." At the end of the ceremony, the men removed their massive hats and cried, "God preserve Queen Elizabeth!" A bugle signaled the end of the ceremony.

Pippa wanted to laugh at the determined formality of it all, but the thought of Aidan drove all mirth from her.

She had to find a way to get him out.

But first, she had to find a way to get herself in.

The queen was in a fine rage. The usual lavish nightly feast lay uneaten before her, and her attendants scurried to clean up the plate of comfits she had just swept to the floor.

Standing amid the queen's ladies, Pippa looked on goggle-eyed as Her Majesty darted up from the table and began to pace. She was spry despite the weight of her jeweled and embroidered court dress. She paused to glare at Sir Christopher Hatton, who stepped forward to offer her a cup of spiced wine.

"Begone, Sir Mutton," she snapped. "I need wise counsel, not strong drink."

He bowed from the waist and stepped back. Distinguished by steel-gray hair and long, elegant legs, Hatton was one of Elizabeth's most seasoned courtiers. Pippa suspected he was used to braving the storm of the queen's temper.

"The O Donoghue Mór means to shame me," wailed the queen. "How dare he?"

How dare he what? Pippa wanted to yell back. A Tower official had scurried in, and the moment the queen had gotten the report, Pippa had known it was something serious.

She pressed her hands together and squeezed her eyes shut. Please let this mean he has escaped, she thought with all her might. Please please please.

"He'll make me out to be more of a monster than Czar Ivan," Elizabeth bit out. "I ought to have him beheaded at once."

"Madam," William Cecil pointed out, "that would serve his purposes quite well."

"I know that, damn your feeble eyes." She glared at her ladies, who pretended, like well-trained parade horses, that nothing was amiss. "But the insolent foreigner has angered me enough to move me to murder."

Pippa gritted her teeth to keep from choking in horror.

Elizabeth swung around to glare at the constable of the Tower. "Tell me, sir. Did the O Donoghue Mór explain precisely why he has decided to starve himself?"

Pippa did not hear the mumbled reply. Starve himself! Had Aidan gone mad?

No, she realized with a sick lurch of her stomach. He knew precisely what he was doing. There was a terrible, cold logic to it. He meant to die in the custody of the English Crown.

If he did, Elizabeth would be shamed, disgraced, vilified in the eyes of the world even more viciously than she already was by her enemies.

"Make him eat," the queen snapped. "I won't have it said that I allowed an Irish lord to starve. I won't lose my one bargaining lever against the Kerry rebels. If you have to, tie him down and feed him by force."

The image made Pippa ill. "Ma'am!" She spoke before she lost her nerve. She sank to one knee in front of the dais.

"What is it?"

"With all due respect, perhaps there is a better way than forcing him."

"Ah." The exclamation dripped with sarcasm. "And I suppose you have just the answer. If you dare to suggest I set him free, then you shall find yourself in custody as well."

"I can persuade him to eat," Pippa said recklessly.

The queen's black eyes flashed in the candlelight. "Since you came to court you have done nothing unforgivably foolish. This would be a very bad time to start."

"I am asking you to let me try, Your Grace. If I fail, then punish me."

Silence lay over the gathering like a heavy cloak. The queen stood motionless, expressionless, an icon carved of stony power. "You think you can make the Irish chieftain eat," she said at last.

"Yes, ma'am." Pippa's face burned. Her wits lagged far behind her quick tongue tonight.

"Your success would mean a great deal to me," Elizabeth said with soft steeliness. "A great deal indeed. In fact, if you do as you promise, I would be inclined to grant you the favor we discussed this morning."

The floor pressed hard and cold against Pippa's bended knee. This morning, the queen had questioned her about her background and Pippa had confessed her earnest wish to find the parents who had abandoned her so long ago. A word from Elizabeth could summon every noble in the land, could send officials poring over census rolls and records. The possibility shone like a beacon in her mind.

"Oh, madam," Pippa said, rising as if buoyed by hope alone. "I could ask for no greater boon."

"You could," the queen said wryly, "but you're wise not to. Very well, visit the prisoner. Talk sense into his thick Irish head. And pray you, don't fail me, mistress."

With each successive meal, the fare looked better— more succulent, more plentiful, more delicious.

Or so it appeared to Aidan.

The current meal was dainty enough to grace the royal table. A large bowl of shining black olives, a delicate poached trout, cheese and smoked meat. The bread was nearly white and looked as soft as a cloud.

More tempting to his empty stomach than the food was the jar of deep red wine set beside a stoneware goblet. It took all the powers of his will to resist the wine. He imagined its harsh, hot bite and the numbing oblivion that would come over him, blotting out his frustration.

He cursed and went to the hard, narrow bed, flopping down to glare at the chipping plaster on the ceiling. Correspondence was so slow between London and distant Kerry on the far western peninsula of Iveragh. He wondered how long he would last.

A bitter smile thinned his mouth. What an unpleasant predicament for Queen Elizabeth, to have the death of the O Donoghue Mór on her hands. It might force her to unbend in her policies regarding Ireland.

A pity the cost might be his own life.

He heard the patter of footsteps and an incessant, familiar voice.

"…and don't give me any of that blather, for I've a paper right here that says I, Pippa Trueheart, have a warrant to visit him."

Aidan stood so quickly that he nearly bumped his head.

"Where?" demanded the nasal voice of Smead, the sentry. "Show me where it says that."

She laughed. "Ah, that's an old ruse, sir, to keep me from finding out that you don't know how to read."

"Of course I—good God!" Smead's voice rose an octave. "What are you doing with that knife?"

Something bumped against the cell door. Aidan would have paid in gold to see what was happening outside.

"Nothing," Pippa said, "yet. But what a pity if I should be so dismayed by your recalcitrance that my poor hand should slip."

"Now, look, mistress—"

"No, *you* look." Her voice had an edge to it Aidan did not recognize. "This is a very sharp blade, and it happens to be perilously close to your puny codpiece. Now, open that cell immediately."

"Jesu!" Smead squeaked. "Very well, but I shall report to the constable that you coerced me."

"Oh, that should make a pretty story. Coerced by a mere slip of a girl."

A key ground in the lock. The door swung open to reveal a white-faced Smead. Pippa had one dainty, slippered foot propped on the doorjamb. She yanked back her skirts to reveal a shapely leg with a small sheath fastened by a garter. Into this she slid the bone-handled knife she had stolen from Aidan the day they had met.

"Mistress?" Smead's gaze stayed riveted to her leg.

"What?"

"You cannot take a weapon in—"

"Smead?" She straightened and shook out her gown.

"Aye, mistress?"

"Kiss my backside, Smead." With that, she kicked the door shut and faced Aidan.

Neither spoke. They both stared. He drank in the sight of her curls escaping their coif, wide eyes, sweet angel face that haunted his dreams. He was in a delirium, he thought, as a greater hunger overtook him—hunger of the soul. "To God," he whispered, in spite of himself, "I have missed you."

A soft, involuntary sound came from her. Just for a moment, she looked as fragile as an ornament of spun glass, and he feared she would shatter.

Then she tossed her head and the artful change came over her. A cocky glint appeared in her eyes and she set her hands on her hips. "Is that so? Well, I haven't missed you."

By now he saw through her facade. He strolled toward her, past the shadows that hung in the corners of the cell. He touched her cheek, almost wincing at its soft purity.

"No, *a gradh,*" he whispered. "You do not want to miss me. That is different."

"I did not come here to debate with you," she snapped, pulling away. "I wish to make certain you know I had nothing to do with your arrest."

"I know that now." And in his heart, he did. She had no reason to wish him ill. "When I was first brought here, I thought the worst."

"I tried to warn you." She touched his sleeve, her fingers perched there like a shy bird. "If it gives you any comfort, I have news of your men."

His mouth dried. "Arrested?"

"Quite the opposite. The contessa helped them leave

London rather quietly. Only Donal Og and Iago remain, and they are in sanctuary aboard a Venetian galley."

He looked away, his eyes and throat burning. *"Cead mile buiochas,"* he whispered. "Thank God." He wanted no more innocent blood on his soul. Feeling as if a weight had been lifted from him, he said, "It is a blessed thing for you to come and tell me this."

"I owe you that and much more." She shivered. The meager brazier that heated the room stood near the bed. Since there was nowhere else to sit, he led her there, pressing gently on her shoulders until she sat on the thin, hard mattress.

Time froze in the oddest way. He felt himself being swept into an elaborate fantasy. He was not Irish, nor was she English. Nothing existed beyond the charmed circle formed by the two of them. They alone made up the entire universe.

He shook off the thought. Beyond this cell, the world awaited. And for each of them, for different reasons, the world was a dangerous place.

With sharp clarity he recalled his visit with young Richard de Lacey. The image of the lady in the portrait haunted him. How lovely she was, this Lady Lark, Countess of Wimberleigh, wearing a brooch of gold and pearls and rubies.

The days in prison had given him time to think. Perhaps the resemblance of the brooch was purely coincidental. Perhaps Lark had lost or sold the piece.

Or maybe, his mind kept whispering to him, *Pippa is kin to the Countess of Wimberleigh.*

He knew one thing for certain. He would say nothing yet. He did not want to raise her hopes only to have them dashed. Besides, he knew nothing of Lord and Lady Wimberleigh. If they were as haughty and intolerant as the other Sassenach nobles, they would not welcome a rollicking street performer like Pippa; indeed, they would surely not believe she belonged to them.

She had been rebuffed so many times in her life. He would not make her suffer yet another betrayal.

Unbeknownst to Pippa, Aidan had been in contact with another lady—Rosaria, the Contessa Cerniglia. Only to her had he confessed his suspicions about the connection between Pippa and the de Laceys. Long ago, he had copied the foreign symbols from the back of the brooch. Two days earlier, he had bribed a guard to deliver the message to the contessa. She had promised to make discreet inquiries.

"You look so far away," Pippa said, breaking in on his thoughts. "Where were you?"

He sat beside her and pulled her into his arms. "My sweet, I was closer to you than you can imagine."

She tucked her cheek against his shoulder. "You were thinking of me?"

"I was."

She pressed closer, her hand slipping into his. In a movement as natural as breathing, he bent his head and laid his lips carefully over hers, tasting her, feeling the softness of her mouth, his tongue seeking the moist heat of hers. She lifted herself against him as if to meld their bodies. Her hands tangled in his overgrown hair; her breasts pushed against his chest; her legs shifted, brushing his thighs with unknowing, scorching intimacy.

He pulled back before it was too late, and he tried not to see the joy and the yearning in her upturned face.

"It is so hard not to love you," she said with her customary stark honesty.

"You'll find it easier once you come to know me." His voice was gruff with frustration. Pippa was here, she was ready, she wanted him. His every instinct urged him to take her. And then, like a wall of stone, his sense of honor held him back.

He must not compromise her, not now, not when he was powerless to protect her from the vicious world. If she were to have a child—an Irishman's bastard—the queen would banish her in disgrace. She and the babe would be set out to starve.

She lifted her free hand to his stubbled face. "I do know you, Aidan. That is why I came. Can we—" She bit her lip. "We must talk about it."

"About what?"

"Do not pretend you don't know."

"The fast."

"Aye. You look pale and thin already. You must end it."

He thrust her away and stood to prowl through the confines of his cramped quarters, ignoring the now familiar dizziness that swept over him. "Did they send you to tell me that?"

"No." She looked delectable, her clothes and hair charmingly rumpled, her full mouth moistened by his kisses. "The next person they send to you will be a team of sentries who will force you to eat."

The idea chilled his blood. He did not doubt that the Tower officials would carry out the barbaric plan. Neither did he doubt his ability to fend off the attempt.

"Please eat," she whispered with a tremor in her voice.

The sight of her, so wide-eyed and concerned, took him apart inch by inch, each word a chisel to his will. "I can't," he said. "Don't beg me to compromise myself. They have taken everything from me except my convictions, and I'll die before I surrender that."

"You place a high value on your will," she said. "What of your people who need you?"

"I'll serve them better by dying."

"No!" She shot up from the bed and flung herself at him, pounding her fists on his chest. "Don't speak of dying. I won't let you die."

He caught her hands. Her tears came freely, streaming down her cheeks. "You must not die. I'll kill you if you die."

"An interesting thought," he said with black humor. "Here is the way these things work. I am a useful hostage for now. But what if the rebels in Kerry murder their English hostages? What if the English army retaliates and takes over my lands? What if the name of the O Donoghue Mór comes to mean nothing? The English will not need me. I'll die. Either quietly, comforted by a cup of poison, or with much ceremony, at the hand of an expert axman before a crowd of Londoners, so that I am an example to others."

"How can you speak so calmly of this?"

"Because my demise is not going to happen the way they planned it." He dragged in a deep breath. "It is going to happen the way *I* plan it, and the shame will be on the queen."

She absorbed his ultimatum like a woman bracing herself for a storm. Her head was slightly bent, shoulders hunched, arms wrapped protectively around her middle. Then she looked up, and the storm burst.

"You are the most idiotic, bull-witted, stubborn, white-livered embarrassment to manhood I have ever met."

He could not suppress a smile. "What sort of persuasion is that?"

"Is it working?"

"No."

"What if you were to be freed?" She went to the window and pressed her hands on the ledge. Daylight fell over her dainty features, and the sun glistened in the long sweep of her eyelashes.

"And who would be freeing me," he asked softly, "when they went to such trouble to lock me up?"

She turned and stared him in the eye, and although she was clean and wore beautiful clothes, she resembled the bundle of bold energy he had first spied on the steps of St. Paul's.

"I could do it," she stated.

"Break me out of the Tower of London."

"Yes."

"No one has escaped the Tower in this century."

"The century is not over yet. At least, I don't think it is."

If the proposition had been made by anyone other than Pippa, he would have discounted her for a fool. But she was the most resourceful person he had ever met.

"Very well," he said quietly, cautiously. "You get me out of here and I'll eat a whole roasted pig."

She grinned. "I thought you'd like that idea." She took his hand and tugged him over to the table. "Now," she said, picking up the soft loaf of bread. "Eat."

He pulled his hand from hers. "No."

Fear and anger blazed in her eyes. "You must. You'll need your strength."

"I have strength for another day or two. So if you mean to carry out your promise, you'd best make haste."

"But you have to eat now," she said. "You see—"

"No, I don't see," he roared, then remembered to lower his voice. "If I eat, and the escape fails, then I am set back on my plans, and I'll look like a weakling."

"It won't fail," she said through gritted teeth.

"So long as I am a prisoner of Mother England, I will not touch a bite of food. You had best act quickly, or you'll be dragging out a corpse."

* * *

"He'll wish he was dead before I finish with him," Pippa muttered under her breath as she crept along the slimy river wall of the Tower.

It was deep night, and she worked solely by touch and memory. Here was a jut of the wall; around the corner would be a shaft with an iron grate over it. She had seen workers using this little known portal to carry out garbage and muck from the stables.

She knew it to be a place of rats and filth, but she would have to bear the unpleasantness. The O Donoghue Mór wanted to escape, and he expected her to do the work.

The insufferable jack-dog.

She took a deep breath, pulled her cloak of filched rags around her and wedged herself into the portal. It was a close fit; the damp stone scraped her. At the end, she encountered an iron grate.

Her speech was larded with curses as she picked at the mortar. By the time she twisted one of the iron bars away and squeezed through the opening, her hands were raw and bleeding and she had run out of oaths.

Carrying the iron bar, she stole past Devereux Tower. A bellman called out the hour of nine. Pippa hurried. Soon the Ceremony of the Keys would begin.

Why couldn't Aidan have eaten? She would have looked like a heroine to the queen, Elizabeth would have summoned her nobles and Pippa's family would be found. In her heart she knew it was unlikely, yet it had given her the sweetness of hope.

But the stubborn Lord Castleross had no faith in her abilities. He refused to eat until he was a free man. She tried to feel angry at him, tried to curse his obstinance, but instead she felt sick with worry. What if he died?

Her triumph at court would mean nothing if Aidan was gone. If she lost him, there would be nothing left of her heart to share with a family even if she were to find them.

Pippa spied the first guard. Reeking of ale, he loitered in a circle of torchlight, whistling between his teeth. She edged closer. He stopped whistling and sniffed the air like a hound on the scent.

Damn. She should have ditched the cloak.

Before she could move, he blinked blearily at her. "You there!" he said. "What—"

"Evening, sir!" Before he could reply, she clasped his hand in both of hers and twisted. Bless the troupe of tumblers she had traveled with through Lincolnshire. They'd taught her how, with the proper momentum, she could land a large man flat on his back.

The guard's ale-sour breath left him in a rush. She clucked her tongue in sympathy. "Just keep silent and all will be well."

He wheezed as she secured a gag around his mouth and tied his hands to a gatepost. She roundly cursed Aidan O Donoghue. For his sake, she was putting her only chance in jeopardy. Still, in her heart she knew that all she truly wanted was for him to survive.

To that end, she thought of Mort and Dove, her accomplices waiting at the Galley Key. If indeed they were. She had surrendered a gold crown and promised two more if they were still there, acting as lookouts, when she and Aidan arrived.

She intended to see him off, wish him godspeed and then return to her new life at court.

So why did she feel so empty when she thought of going on without him?

The question did not matter. She could not let it matter. The guard growled something through the rags she had stuffed in his mouth. She snatched his shortsword from its sheath. "I'm afraid I'll be needing this," she whispered. "Your trousers as well."

He made a garbled sound of protest. She ignored him, slicing away the buttons that held his canions in place. They fell down around his ankles. With trembling hands she pulled them on, tied the drawstring snug, then plucked his coat from a peg on the door. Finally, she left him tied in the dark and went to take his post at Bloody Tower archway.

The long scarlet coat and huge bonnet engulfed her, but she would have to hope no one noticed. Swinging his candle lantern, the chief warder went from gate to gate, followed by a sergeant and three other guardsmen. She stood stiffly at attention, the way she had observed while formulating her plan.

"Halt!" she said in a deep voice. "Who comes there?"

"The keys," replied the warder.

Pippa could not remember what came next. "Keys? Whose keys?"

"Queen Elizabeth's keys." He delivered the reply in a bored voice.

"Advance the keys. All's well." She held out her hand, praying it would not tremble.

The warder hesitated. "Are you falling ill, Stokes?"

"Mayhap, sir." She scratched her throat.

When the keys were passed to her, she neatly substituted those she had pilfered from the pantler at Whitehall. After the ceremony, she marched off to the guardroom with the others. At the door, she stopped.

"Problem, Stokes?" someone asked.

She tugged down the brim of her hat. "I have to take a piss."

Her fellow guard took down a torch from a wall sconce. "You seem strange tonight, Stokes."

She snatched the torch from him. "Nay, what is strange is making prisoners of innocent men." With that, she tossed the torch onto the thatched roof and fled, praying for a miracle as the guards screamed in fear and rage.

She raced to Beauchamp Tower, bounded up the winding stairs and unlocked Aidan's cell.

"Don't think for a minute," she said to the darkened room, "that I have forgotten your promise about the pig."

He made one of those Celtic exclamations she so dearly loved, and then he hauled her in his arms, squeezing her so deliciously hard that the breath left her. He whispered something heartfelt and Gaelic.

"And what does that mean?" she asked tartly.

"It means you are a shining little miracle."

"Also an idiot," she said, pretending his words meant nothing. "A brainsick idiot."

Mortlock and Dove surprised her. Like a pair of watchdogs they stood at the Galley Key, waiting patiently; it had taken Pippa and Aidan most of the night to steal out of the Tower and make their way to the riverside. The flaming thatch on the guardroom had provided enough of a diversion to get them out onto Petty Wales Street, but they had narrowly escaped a party of guards by hiding in an abandoned well. Though she would never admit it, she had loved every minute of the adventure.

"So you showed up after all," Dove said. "Did you bring the rest of our pay?"

"You'll have it after I see that you've done as you promised," Pippa said.

Both Mort and Dove subjected Aidan to a long inspection. "So who's the toff, anyway? He's the same one what saved you from the pillory, eh?"

"And that's all you need to know." She was getting

nervous. These two had never been trustworthy, and she did not like the way they were eyeing the fine needlework of Aidan's shirt and the quality of his leather boots. He looked weary, his cheeks hollowed by his fast. While they had hidden in the well she had made him eat a loaf of bread she'd brought with her, but it would be days before he regained his strength.

"Did you get the boat?" she asked Mort and Dove.

Mortlock's eyes narrowed. "What's your hurry?"

Aidan took a step toward him. Despite his lack of food and sleep, he towered like a mountain over Mortlock. "I believe," Aidan said softly, "the lady asked you a question."

Mort's crooked nose twitched, a sign of fear Pippa recognized. "A lady, are we now?" he asked, his tone derisive even as he edged away from Aidan.

"Ooh!" said Dove, fluttering a make-believe fan.

She touched Aidan's sleeve. "Ignore them. They have always been obnoxious."

"Ob-nox-shus," Dove said, trying the word.

She tried not to let her irritation show, tried not to let her gaze stray to the middle of the broad river, where the Venetian galley lay at anchor, waiting. "A pity you failed to accomplish the simple task of securing a boat. I'll have to find a ferryman—"

"It's here." Mort jerked his thumb upriver. "In the boathouse yonder."

She paid them. They bit the coins and bobbed their heads but did not leave. "Look," she said, "I've nothing more to spare." She shrugged out of the voluminous guardsman's jacket and dropped it on the ground. "We're off, then," she said, and started toward the boathouse.

Muttering, Mort and Dove slunk off into the shadows. At the watersteps of the rickety structure, she turned to face Aidan. "You understand what you must do."

"Take the lighterboat to the Venetian galley." He pointed to the shadowy hulk at anchor in the deepest part of the river. A hint of dawn colored the smoky sky.

"The contessa assured me you'll have diplomatic sanctuary there. Once you're aboard, the English can't touch you." She could barely speak past the lump in her throat. "It is so hard to say goodbye."

He caught her against him. "I know, my sweet. If I live a thousand years, I should never forget you."

Weeping, she lifted her face and waited for his kiss. His lips brushed hers and then their mouths clung, breath and tears and hearts mingling until she almost cried out with the pain of it.

She broke away and stepped back. "Even though I do not love you," she whispered, "I shall miss you as I miss the sun in winter."

"Pippa—"

"Seize them!" shouted a voice from the gloom. "Seize the fugitives."

She glanced back at the Galley Key, and her heart plunged to her knees. In the blink of an eye, she realized her mistake. Mort and Dove were supposed to keep an eye out. Instead they'd taken the money and run.

Straight to the Tower guards.

Her curse echoed across the river. The pounding of footsteps came from the black maw of an alleyway in front of them.

"It appears your friends found a higher bidder," Aidan said in a disgusted voice. "Now what do we do?"

She grabbed his hand. "Run!"

Her stolen, overlarge boots made running clumsy. She stumbled along the quay, then clutched Aidan's arm while she shook off the boots and left them behind.

She was glad for the predawn darkness, for it concealed her smile of pure pleasure. There was little that she missed about her former life on the streets, but every now and then a good chase was exhilarating.

Few people—certainly not the night bellmen or Tower guards—knew the rabbit warren maze of London streets as well as Pippa did. She prayed Mort and Dove had not offered their services as guides. "Just stay hard by," she said to Aidan, ducking her head beneath a brick archway to enter the underworld of the East End.

It was gratifying to be running for her life with a man like Aidan. He was swift and strong despite his fast, and he didn't ask stupid questions. If they stayed ahead of their pursuers and kept to the shadows, they should have no trouble eluding the guards.

She ducked down a cramped alley, tearing off her baldric as she ran and tossing the belt into a sewage conduit. At the end of the alley, they emerged into a small market square awakening to the business day. The spire of St. Dunstan-in-the-East loomed against the lightening sky. Even at this early hour, traders had arrived with rickety carts and hastily set up booths. A deafening roar of music, laughter, and general hubbub filled the air.

"Ah, this is splendid," said Aidan. "We've come to the one place where they'll be sure to spy us."

"Ye of little faith," she scolded. "We'll just go back the way we came."

The moment she spoke, excited shouts issued from the alley. The soldiers had found the baldric.

A nasty thorn of worry pricked at Pippa. They needed to hide. She shoved her elbow at a side doorway of St. Dunstan's. It swung open to reveal a set of dank, sagging stairs.

"What do you hope to accomplish by trapping us in a spire?" Aidan demanded.

"Trust me," she replied. "They won't look here." The stairs groaned ominously beneath their weight. The smell of rot hung thick in the air. At a high landing, a platform gave access to the large, heavy bell on one end and a low opening in the stone spire on the other.

They burst outside and found themselves on a wall walk surrounding the steeple. The surface was perilously slanted. A low murmur burbled from a dovecote in one corner.

Across another corner, someone had pegged a few articles of clothing out to dry.

"Ah, luck," said Aidan, plucking down a plain jerkin. He pulled it over his shirt. The garment fit taut across his chest, so he left the lacings open. Just for a moment, Pippa stared at his chest and all thought fled.

He cracked a smile. "There's something for you here, too." He took down a threadbare brown skirt and held it out for her. She yanked the skirt on over her breeches and used a square of linen to tie over her hair.

"How do I look?"

"Like an angel. Any moment now, I expect you to sprout wings."

"Very funny."

He grazed her cheek with his knuckles. "I was not trying to be funny. I—"

"There they are!" exclaimed a voice far below. Four armed men ducked into the stairwell.

"I wish you'd been right about the wings," she said.

He did not answer, but untied one end of the clothesline and made a loop in the rope.

Bumps and thuds and curses sounded hollowly in the old stairwell.

"Hang on to me," Aidan said. "Put your arms around my neck."

Falling from a church roof in the arms of the
O Donoghue Mór, she decided, was as good a way as any
to die. She latched her arms around his strong neck,
reveling for a moment in the firmness of his flesh. Thank
God he had not starved himself to death after all.

Brandishing pikes and long-handled axes, the soldiers
emerged from the stairwell and stormed across the roof.
Three sharp prongs from a pikestaff drove toward them.
Aidan turned to shield her body with his own. She squeezed
her eyes shut and buried her face against his chest.

He took one step backward, then swung out in a wide
arc. They dropped so fast, her stomach seemed to rise to
her throat. The rope sang as it paid out, hissing across the
eaves of the building.

They stopped with jarring abruptness and swung helplessly, bumping against the wall of the church tower.

"Now what, Your Loftiness?" she asked in a voice that
was little more than a squeak of fright. She clung to him
harder, winding her legs around his waist and locking her
ankles. He mumbled something in Gaelic, and she peered
at his face. Dear God, he was dizzy with weakness from
fasting.

"I wonder how far it is to the street," he said.

She peeked at the alley below. Many feet below. Many
perilous, bone-crunching feet below.

"Too far to jump." She dared to look up. "Uh-oh."

"What is it?"

She stared speechless as the dawn light glinted off the
curved ax head of a soldier's halberd. It swung down
once, twice, thrice.

Pippa screamed. They plummeted, breaking apart, her
skirts billowing. Her mind emptied in anticipation of the
end. Instead, she struck something and stopped falling.
She heard a grunt from Aidan.

They had landed in some sort of canvas awning. Before she could catch her breath, an ominous ripping sound began and they were plunging downward again.

This time, they had not far to fall. They landed in a tangle of canvas upon something soft and rather strangely warm. She apprised the situation through her dazed senses. Her nostrils flared, and she choked. She and Aidan lay atop a pile of manure in a cart.

Aidan muttered in Irish and bounded out of the cart, pulling her after him while the carter looked on, amazed. The canvas awning had shielded them from the worst of the muck.

They rushed along through the cloth sellers' booths and peddlers' carts. Slowly, gradually, they caught their breath, and Pippa conquered her shaking knees. Somehow she found the presence of mind to steal a roll of cheese.

"Eat," she said. "It's not a whole roasted pig, but chew on that."

He devoured the cheese in three bites. Pippa began to breathe more easily. But when they started toward the east exit of the square, two soldiers came toward them.

Aidan gave a short, lusty laugh. Instead of setting upon the soldiers, he took Pippa in his arms and kissed her, long and hard. She made a little whimper of surprise and then simply gave herself to him.

He kissed her until the soldiers had passed, apparently discounting them as a pair of eager lovers. Then, just as abruptly as he had grabbed her, he let her go and started hurrying again.

She almost stumbled as she tried to keep up. He acted completely unaffected by a kiss that had all but singed her eyelashes, damn him.

Shouts rang from the steeple walk. The men there,

black crows against the gentle pink sky, gesticulated wildly to their compatriots.

Pippa and Aidan ran through Fowler Street and turned back down toward the Thames. When at last they reached the Galley Key, both were nearing the end of their strength.

The lighterboat was gone. Gray rivers of fog swirled around their knees as they called to the ship's master. A tender broke away from the long galley and rowed silently toward them.

She squinted at the two men in the tender. She did not recognize them. Still, the contessa had assured her that the crew of the Venetian ship could be trusted.

She shivered. "It is goodbye again, my lord. You should have taken my word for it in the first place."

One corner of his mouth lifted in a self-deprecating grin. "I needed a new set of clothing anyway. And of course—" he touched the tip of her nose "—it is fitting that our parting was as perilous as our meeting."

"Our parting," she whispered, despising the finality of it. "Ah, Aidan, I shall never forget you."

"A touching sentiment," said a melodious, accented voice. "You can tell her on the voyage." Out of the mist stepped the contessa, wrapped in rich black silk velvet. Behind her stood an escort of Venetian bodyguards. "You're late," she added. "The tide is up, and they were about to leave without you."

The tender bumped gently into place. Aidan hesitated. "A moment, Your Ladyship—"

"You don't have a moment, and neither does Pippa," snapped the contessa. "If you're caught now, I'll offer no more help. Now, get in, both of you."

Pippa gasped. "I'm not going to Ireland!"

"You must."

"My lady," she whispered past the tears that burned in her throat, "you don't know what you're asking. I have a place at court now, and the queen—"

"She's asking you," Aidan snapped, "to get in that boat before I hurl you in. The contessa is right. If you stay, you could be arrested for helping me escape."

"But—"

"Your role in the flight of the O Donoghue Mór will be found out," he declared. "Perhaps if the dodge had been quieter, we might have eluded attention. But you've been seen with me."

The contessa handed something to Aidan. He pushed Pippa toward the boat. "You would be treated not as a prisoner of noble rank, but as a common traitor. Do you know the punishment for that?"

The contessa made a slashing gesture across her throat.

Pippa felt cold inside. What a fool she had been. She had bought his freedom at the price of her dreams.

The contessa kissed both her cheeks and whispered, "Go with the O Donoghue Mór. It is better to run toward the future than cling to the past."

Pippa turned to Aidan. He stood poised with one foot braced on the quay and the other in the service boat, his large hand held out for hers, his face utterly inscrutable.

The rising sun set fire to the sky behind him, and for a moment he looked as splendid as a painting on a church wall. His black hair drifted, a long ripple on the breeze. His eyes were penetrating, yet impenetrable.

"Come with me, Pippa," he said at last. "I'll make it all right, I promise. Come with me to Ireland."

Part Two

It is sweet to dance to violins
When Love and Life are fair:
To dance to flutes, to dance to lutes
Is delicate and rare:
But it is not sweet with nimble feet
To dance upon the air!

—Oscar Wilde
The Ballad of Reading Gaol, st. 9

Diary of a Lady

It is only now, days later, that I am able to dry my tears and take pen in hand. Yea, I do grieve as any mother would, for my son has gone to war, but this is not the reason for my distress.

Oliver is like a madman, pacing the halls of Blackrose Priory and laying curses upon anyone who has the ill fortune to cross his path.

Neither of us can sleep at night; we have not been able to sleep since the message was delivered from London. Cruel trick or honest report; I know not which it is.

I know only that someone penned me a message, copying the inscription from the back of the Romanov brooch. That singular object was given to me by Oliver's stepmother, Juliana. I thought it had been lost forever.

The last time I saw the precious jewel, I had pinned it to the bodice of my beloved little daughter, just before I said farewell to her, not realizing I was never to see her again.

—Lark de Lacey,
Countess of Wimberleigh

Eleven

A idan sought shelter in an abandoned fortress by the sea. Dunloe Castle once housed the O Sullivan Mór, but he had died, like so many others, in Desmond's great war against the English.

The windy hall stood as bleak and empty as a plundered tomb. Aidan tried not to think about the slaughter that had occurred here as he awaited word of Ross Castle and thought about Pippa.

She had hated the voyage. She had spent the entire time in a cramped private berth, doubled over by seasickness and shivering with fright. He had expected her to perk up once she was on dry land, but she was more subdued than ever.

He went to a window and looked out, and his heart lifted. The rounded hills, greener than the green of England, wore sturdy necklaces of drystone tillage walls. Sheep and cattle grazed upon the verdant abundance, and cloud towers swept toward the heavens.

This was Ireland—a tragic beauty blithely unaware that she was doomed. The thought filled him with the sharp, sweet ache of loving something, knowing in his heart it was hopeless.

Hearing a footstep, he turned. Iago and Donal Og strode into the hall. "Has the news come yet?" asked his cousin.

"No." He returned to the table and poured heather beer into cups for each of them. "If O Mahoney doesn't return by daybreak, I'll send someone after him."

"Where is our guest?" Iago asked. "Is her sickness passed?"

"She went to walk out in the fields." Aidan pinched the bridge of his nose. "Would that I could ease her melancholy."

"Can you?" asked Donal Og.

"Yes and no." Aidan drew out the letter the contessa had pressed into his hand at their parting. "The symbols on the back of Pippa's brooch are from the Russian language. The contessa found someone to translate the words. 'Blood, vows and honor.'" He shivered, remembering Pippa's story of the dying Gypsy woman.

Donal Og stroked his beard. "Someone's motto?"

"It is the motto of a clan called Romanov, far across the seas. They are associated with a family we know well." He took a sip of ale. "The de Lacey family."

Iago and Donal Og exchanged a glance. "Richard de Lacey?"

Aidan set down his cup. "He could be her brother."

"Diablo!" whispered Iago. Donal Og gave a low whistle.

Aidan had worked it all out from the information gathered by the contessa. Years earlier, plague had stricken the de Lacey household, and Oliver de Lacey was not expected to live. His wife, fearing their only child would fall ill, too, had sent their tiny daughter on a voyage to the kingdom of Muscovy to stay with the kin of her grandmother.

"The ship was lost," Aidan told his listeners. "No survivors were found."

"You think there was a survivor," Donal Og said.

"And that her name is Pippa," Iago added.

He felt that odd lift of nervousness in his gut. "Philippa," he said. "The lost child was named Philippa."

Iago stroked his chin. "It is Pippa. It has to be."

"Imagine." Donal Og quaffed his ale in one swallow. "The ragamuffin's got noble blood. Have you told her yet?"

"No!" Aidan stood and prowled through the musty hall. "You're to say nothing. Nothing."

"But it's her family. Her heart's desire. Surely, coz, it's a grand and wanton cruelty to withhold the information."

"Call me cruel, then," he snapped. "I'll say nothing until I am absolutely certain."

"It all fits," Iago said. "She looks like Richard—the hair of gold, the brilliant smile, the lack of reverence for her betters—"

"You didn't notice that until I told you what I learned," Aidan pointed out. "I don't want her hurt. You say what insufferable snobs the English nobles were. The de Laceys accepted their loss more than two decades ago. What if they do not want the old wound reopened? What if they are ashamed that their daughter lived as a common street performer, a thief?"

Donal Og nodded, understanding dawning on his face. "What if they call her a pretender who stole that brooch?"

"Or what if," Iago chimed in, "they decide to accept her, only to learn she is an outlaw for helping the O Donoghue Mór escape London Tower?"

Aidan looked from one to the other. "Now you see why I hesitate."

Iago walked to the window and seated himself in the

embrasure, where weak sunlight trickled over him. "Ah, why do we bother so with this toilsome life?"

Donal Og snorted. "Is there another choice?"

Iago turned and gripped the edge of the embrasure. "Upon my soul, there is."

Donal Og made a heart-thumping gesture with his hand on his chest. "The islands in the great western sea of the Caribbees." He mimicked Iago's round-voweled accent and musical timbre. "Where the sun shines all day, where food falls from the trees, where the water is warm enough to swim in naked."

"It is all true, you large Irish ogre. Ah, I am the first to admit there are a few problems—"

"Slavery, disease, the Inquisition—"

"But a man can live free if he is smart enough. There are uninhabited islands by the thousands. A man can make what he wants of his life. With *whom* he wants."

"Ah, Serafina!" Donal Og pretended to swoon.

"No wonder you have no woman." Iago curled his lip in a sneer. "You have the mind of a jackass. No, that is an insult to the jackass. The mind of a brick of peat."

"A brick of peat *has* no mind," Donal Og roared.

"Precisely," said Iago.

As their conversation deteriorated into bickering, Aidan spied a movement on the slope leading down to the sea. A flash of gold, a flutter of brown skirts. For a moment he stood transfixed. The hills and the crashing sea were so vast. Pippa looked as vulnerable as an autumn leaf on the wind.

She found a sheep path leading down along a crumbling cliff. Below her, treacherous breakers bit at the shore. In one heart-seizing instant he remembered something else the contessa had told him about Oliver de Lacey.

In his youth, Wimberleigh had a reckless reputation. His moods swung from giddy to melancholy. Some—even his half brothers and sisters—swore he harbored an earnest wish to die.

Iago and Donal Og were too busy arguing to note how quickly Aidan left the hall.

A dark fascination with the sea drew Pippa. Now she felt strong enough to move close to the seething ocean, to witness the violence and drama of the battering waves.

She clambered down a path. The slope was pocked by large gray rocks around which grew clumps of grass and wildflowers. Ireland was surely the loveliest place she had ever seen. It was stark and wild and uncompromising—just like Aidan O Donoghue.

The path ended at a great cleft between two hills. Within the fissure, a fall of broken boulders and old driftwood tumbled into the roaring sea. She teetered on the edge, tasting the sharp salt air and feeling the wind rush over her like a great, sweeping, invisible caress. The boom of the waves exploding on the rocks below filled the air. Beads of spray touched her face and clung in her hair. Then, without warning, she was lost, swamped with memories. Uttering a low cry, she tumbled into the dream world inside her head.

Up and up and up she climbed, battling her way through the rushing water on each successive deck. She could no longer see Nurse nor hear her saying Hail Mary Hail Mary. The sailors were all gone. But for the dog, she was alone now.

She poked her head up through a square hatch and was out in the face-slapping rain with thunder shouting and a burning bolt of lightning turning night to day.

It stayed light only for an instant, but she saw the man

*in the striped shirt who had been shouting about batten-
ing hatches and shortening sail. He lay all tangled in
thick rope. His face was gray, his lips were black, and his
eyes were wide-open like the eyes of the stag head that
hung in Papa's hunting lodge.*

*She clung to a ladder while the dog scrabbled and
lurched on long, skinny legs. The boat began to tilt and
groan, riding up one side of a wave that was bigger than
a mountain. Higher and higher they went, like the forward
arc of her garden swing. The big boat hovered at the peak
and seemed to freeze there, waiting, before it fell over.*

*Down and down and down, barrels crashing every-
where, toppling one against the other like ninepins. The
lightning flashed again. In the distance a shape rose out
of the sea like a great rock or perhaps one of the towers
in the palace where her godmother lived.*

*She wished she could remember the name of her god-
mother, because she surely needed help now. But all she
could recall was that the lady had blazing red hair, mean
black eyes and a loud, bossy voice. Everyone called her
Your Majesty.*

*Then she lost all thought. A big wooden barrel broke
loose and rushed straight at her as if someone had hurled
it—*

The breath left her in a *whoosh* as she was flung to the
ground. She had no voice to scream as a hard body
covered her and pinned her against the grassy turf.

At last she regained her breath. "Jesus Christ on a
frigging crutch!" she yelled. "What do you think you're
doing?"

The O Donoghue Mór had his body pressed to hers.
She could feel his heart beating rapidly against her
chest. Somehow that pleased her. He had run all the way
to see her.

"Well?" she asked, sounding more annoyed than she felt. She was still slightly dazed by the— What was it? A vision? A waking dream? A true memory? Then the images faded and dispersed.

Aidan lifted himself by bracing his hands on the grass on each side of her. This was, she realized with a heated thrill, the time-honored pose of lovers. She had seen it depicted in a book of disgusting sonnets Dove had stolen from a St. Paul's bookseller.

The wind caught at Aidan's ebony hair, and sunlight glinted in the single beaded strand. Ah, he *was* Ireland, in all its pain and splendor; like the land, he was rugged and beautiful, untamed and untameable. She had the most indecent urge to run her fingers through his hair.

"Do you often attack unsuspecting females?" she asked. "Is this some Irish ritual?"

"I thought you were getting too close to the edge. I wanted to stop you before you fell."

"Or jumped?" she asked. "By my troth, Your Highness, why would I do such a thing as that?"

"You would not?"

"That is the act of a madwoman or a coward. Why would I want to die? Life is hard. Sometimes life hurts. But it's all so blessedly interesting that I should not like to miss any of it."

He chuckled and then laughed outright. There was something deliciously intimate about the way his body vibrated against hers. She pressed her fists into the grass to keep from winding her arms around his neck. Part of her longed to give in to impulse, but another part held back, resisting, wary.

"Are you going to remove yourself sometime between now and eventide?"

"I have not decided. You are very soft in certain places."

He placed his lips close to her ear. With a warm gust of breath, he said one of the sweetest things she had ever heard. "It is a rare thing indeed for a man to feel so perfectly comforted by a woman."

She forced herself to scowl. "I know what you are doing."

"Getting ready to kiss you?" His mouth hovered above hers.

Lord, but she wanted to draw his taste inside her. She used all of her willpower to say, "I don't think you should."

He lowered his mouth and then, quite deliberately leaving her hunger unsated, he turned his head to nuzzle her neck.

"Why not?" he whispered.

"You're trying to make me forget how vexed I am with you."

"Vexed? Why?"

She was stunned. "Because, you arrogant stuffed doublet, you gave me no choice. Do you think I *wanted* to come here? *Wanted* to be dragged along on that horrid ship for an endless sea voyage?" She scrambled out from under him and sat back on her heels.

"I thought you wanted to help me," he said. "As I helped you, once upon a time."

"That was once upon a time. All I wanted," she said, "was the chance to earn the queen's favor." To her shame, her voice cracked. "The queen was going to help me find my family. I broke you out of the damned Tower! All I wanted was for you to end your hunger strike, and you wouldn't give me that."

"I could not," he said. "I had to stay firm."

"You could have given in just so the queen would reward me."

"And if the escape had failed?"

She had no answer, so she scowled at him.

"Pippa," he said, "if it means that much to you, we can claim I forced you to come along as hostage."

"That," she said, "would not be so far from the truth."

"We could arrange for you to be rescued by the English."

The idea of being taken in by strangers was repellent to her, but she could not let him see the truth. She drew herself up and said. "Ha! You'll not be rid of me that easily, my lord."

Aidan saw that she was close to shattering. Pippa, sturdy survivor of the London underworld, was about to be driven to weeping by the only man who cared about her.

He wanted to touch her again, to gather her to his chest, but touching was dangerous. His blood was still on fire from their embrace. He might not be able to stop himself a second time.

"Tell me more of this reward, *a gradh*," he said, brushing a curl away from her temple.

"The queen made me an offer. If I persuaded you to eat, she'd help me. All you could think of was your fast, and your honor—your stupid, precious honor."

The lash of anger was sudden, unexpected. "You and the queen made a bargain? That's why you wanted me to eat?" As quickly as the fury had seized him, it fled. So she had made a bargain, using him as leverage. It was no worse than what he had done.

"Ah, Christ." He grabbed her and pulled her against his chest. "I didn't know."

"She was going to summon all the noblewomen of the realm, get an army of clerks to search the records." She clutched at the front of his shirt. "Nothing would have come of it. I know you're thinking that. But it was my only chance. And now it is gone."

"You should have explained it all," he said. "Nay, it would have made no difference. I would not have compromised myself even to give you your most cherished wish. The true cost would have been exacted from the people of this district."

She blew out a disgusted breath. "I wouldn't have been able to live with myself if something terrible happened here."

He ground his teeth together to keep himself silent. He knew in the very marrow of his bones that she was Philippa de Lacey.

Instead of telling her, he forced himself to think matters through. The lofty de Laceys might reject her, which would be more painful than never knowing.

"I'm sorry," he whispered into her hair. "Somehow I'll get you back to England. You'll be blameless, I swear it."

She pulled back to look up at him. "If all of your eloquent speeches were solid gold, I should be a wealthy woman indeed."

He stood and helped her to her feet. "I never promised I would be good for you."

The breeze tousled her curls, which by now had grown nearly to her shoulders. "You were good to me. Never doubt it."

He took her hand, and they started up the hill together. If someone had told him that one day his best friend in the world would be a Protestant Sassenach street waif, he would have laughed them out of his presence.

Yet the most unlikely of circumstances had come true.

At the top of the hill, O Mahoney met them. His face pinched and white, the scout sat upon a lathered Connemara-bred mount.

"What news?" Aidan asked. "Have you been to Ross Castle?"

"I have seen it." O Mahoney glanced at Pippa and switched to Gaelic. "Ill news. The ramparts are flying English colors."

By the time the party rode into Aidan's district, Pippa had ceased complaining. She was still terrified of riding on horseback, but all her protests fell on deaf ears.

The sharp sea air gave way to the rich green scents of woodland and pasture. The forest thickened, and in some places, branches and debris lay across the path.

"'Tis plashing," Donal Og explained, gesturing at a heap of broken trees. "The Irish damage the paths through the woods to slow the advance of the Sassenach."

She shivered. This war was real here, imminent. Not just some vague idea murmured about at court. The trees soared to the sky, the trunks like massive pillars, the leaves a translucent canopy. Velvet moss grew on the forest floor. Sunlight, filtered through the leafy awning, glowed with a verdant luminescence. A hush hung in the fecund air.

No wonder the Irish believed in enchantment. Only magic could have created a place so holy and silent. It was like standing in a cathedral; the star-shaped leaves, shot through by sunlight, were glass panes in the most glorious of windows.

"It was a fine, grand place to be a boy, long ago," Donal Og said, kneeing his mount to draw abreast of Pippa.

"This is where you and Aidan played?" She thought it extraordinary for a person to have ties to a particular spot on earth. That was an alien notion to her.

"Playing? Nay, it was all serious business. I was always the bigger lad, but he was the braver and the better thinker, though if you tell him I said so, I'll damn you for a liar."

"Your secret is safe with me." She pictured them, one dark, one fair, darting through greenwood groves or leaping across one of the many burbling springs or hiding in the cleft of a rock.

"No wonder London seemed so strange to you," she said. "This is a place apart. A wild, magical world."

"Like all magic, it has its perils." Donal Og clicked to his horse and trotted to the fore to fall in step with Aidan.

They had reached the edge of the forest. The shadowy woods opened out like a set of lofty doors flung wide. With a cry of wonder, Pippa shaded her eyes. The forested hills surrounded a misty blue-and-green valley. Lakes dotted the landscape, and here and there little rock-bound bits of tillage hugged the shores.

Very far away, on a jut of land pushing out into the largest of the lakes, stood a castle. The massive tower was built of light-colored stone, surrounded by lofty battlements near the top. Small, defensive windows pierced the walls and ramparts.

High atop the tower flapped the banner of England.

"That is Ross Castle," she said.

"Aye, it is." Aidan's voice sounded strained.

They rode the rest of the way in silence. Aidan's one hundred soldiers were already encamped on the shores of the middle lake, awaiting orders.

The main tower of the castle shone like alabaster, the foundations formed by a great upheaval of ancient rock. A narrow neck of land led to an imposing gate with an arching guardhouse. The iron teeth of the raised portcullis gave the menacing look of an evil grin.

A guard stepped out to challenge them. "Halt, while I summon the master."

Aidan barely glanced at the guard. He rode straight on through the arched gate while the Englishman spluttered and gesticulated wildly. "Attack!" he called. "Invasion! The barbaric hordes are upon us!"

Donal Og's fist swung down like a hammer and clobbered the guard on top of the head. The man staggered against a wooden rail, clung there briefly, then sank in a daze.

Two faces peered from a half door at the front of the stables. "Come along, then," Aidan called in an exasperated voice. "Since when do you fear the O Donoghue Mór in his own house?"

One lad shoved the other along in front of him, and they emerged from the stables. Aidan dismounted and tossed his reins to the taller boy, a skinny lad with flamered hair. "And how are things with you, Sorley Boy Curran?"

The boy hunched his shoulders and let the reins fall without catching them. "Begging your pardon, my lord, we've been told we must serve a different master now."

The other lad, like enough to Sorley Boy to be his brother, nodded fearfully. Pippa held her breath and watched Aidan, even though she wanted to shield her eyes from the expression on his face. She recognized it, the numb shock of betrayal. There was something especially poisonous when treachery came from children.

The boys would never know what it cost Aidan to smile at them and hold out the reins once again. He spoke in Gaelic. The lads exchanged a glance, replied to Aidan with relief in their voices, then set to putting up the horses.

"This way." Aidan led them to a stairway that spiraled

up the outside of the main keep. Aidan seemed a stranger to Pippa. His face was set and grim, his strides long and purposeful.

As they climbed the lofty tower, she could smell boiled cabbage and roasting meat, and in a few moments they found themselves in a huge hall with an arched ceiling made of plastered wicker. At one end of the gallery was a broad hearth and table where a host of enemy invaders sat eating their midday meal.

All four of them saw the face of the new master of Ross Castle. Pippa blinked at him in astonishment. "God's holy nightgown," she whispered.

Aidan made a dangerous sound in his throat, a combination of growl and Gaelic curse. The expression raised prickles on her arms. She could only wonder what it did to the folk in the hall.

The O Donoghue Mór strode to the high table. His huge hand shot out and lifted the usurper off his bench. "Enjoying your stay, my lord?" he asked in a voice Pippa had never heard before.

Even growing red-faced and goggle-eyed from lack of air, Richard de Lacey still managed to look ridiculously handsome.

"I…can…explain," he choked out.

Four English guards rushed forward.

Richard made a quelling gesture with his hands, and the guards subsided. Aidan loosened his hold a notch. "Talk," he barked.

"*I* shall explain," said a strong female voice.

A remarkable woman stepped down from the dais. She was dressed from neck to toe in unrelieved black, and she kept her head covered by a thick, heavy cloth.

The lack of adornment only made her beauty more apparent. It was like seeing the face of the moon in a cloudless night sky. She had perfect, smooth cheeks and expressive eyes, a bowed mouth and small white hands. A prayer-book pouch hung from her waist.

"Felicity," Aidan said in a cold voice, "be quick with your explanations, or dear Richard might expire from lack of air."

Felicity? Pippa looked to Donal Og and Iago for a hint, but both of them studiously avoided her eyes.

"I invited Lieutenant de Lacey to occupy Ross Castle," said the mysterious Felicity.

Aidan relinquished his hold on Richard, who sank to the bench and loosened his collar.

"Oh, that is fascinating," Pippa burst out, unable to contain her outrage. "By what right do you offer the home of the O Donoghue to strangers?"

The silence in the hall was absolute. Felicity stared at Pippa, regarding her with such false pity and false tolerance that Pippa wanted to choke her.

Felicity walked with measured paces to stand directly in front of Aidan. She held out her dainty porcelain hand. She stared up at him, although she directed her answer at Pippa.

And somehow, in some remote place in her mind, Pippa felt it coming, the thunderhead of emotion hurling like a storm toward her. She braced herself for agony beyond enduring, already knowing what she would hear.

"What right have I? By my right," said the poetically lovely Felicity, "as Aidan's wife."

From the Annals of Innisfallen

‑‑‑∾⟲⟳∾‑‑‑

The day Aidan O Donoghue agreed to wed Felicity Browne was a day like any other—with one exception.

It's true that the abbot frowns on superstition, but I, Revelin of Innisfallen, do swear on the heavenly bosom of my own sinless mother that I heard a fairy horn blow that fateful morn.

To God, Aidan felt he had no choice. Fortitude Browne, the father of Felicity, came up from trade and had what the Sassenach would call Ambitions. He wanted his daughter to marry a lord. Even an Irish lord would do.

Constable Browne required the marriage as part of the peace he made with Ronan. Of course Ronan refused, but Aidan saw a way to bring about peace in the district. Ah, but it was a fine rage that came on Ronan. He did, quite literally, have a "fit" of temper.

Aidan is convinced he slew his father by his own hand. Still, he wed her—a Protestant and Puritan to boot—just as he had promised.

She was beautiful in the flawless fashion of a marble

saint—holy, remote, untouchable. It was that quality, perhaps, that drew young Aidan. The challenge of her. The promise that beneath her porcelain Sassenach surface lay a loving heart.

It was the one time Aidan should have listened to his father. It was the one time the instincts of Ronan O Donoghue were right.

—Revelin of Innisfallen

Twelve

If Aidan could have slain a person with his eyes, he would have done so, and cheerfully. He hated Felicity with a virulence so sharp and toxic that he wondered how she could still be standing at this moment.

"What the devil are you doing here?" he murmured for her ears only. "You're supposed to be gone."

"Did you think, my lord, that Revelin's feeble annulment petition to Bishop O'Brien would drive me off?" Her hand in his felt cold as stone.

He pulled away and looked at Pippa. There she stood with her heart in her eyes, and in that instant he understood.

She loved him. No matter what she said, no matter how loudly she protested it, she loved him.

And now his betrayal had struck a fatal blow to her soul. He looked into her eyes and could see her love for him dying by inches.

"His wife," Pippa said in a small, clear voice. "You are the wife of the O Donoghue Mór."

Felicity's smile softened to perfect sympathy, and only Aidan could see the hard falseness in her expression.

"We have been married nigh on a year. And who might you be?"

"Nobody." Pippa took one step back, then another. "No one at all."

And with that, she turned and fled.

A curse wrenched from Aidan's throat as he followed her out of the hall and up another flight of the stone steps. Clearly unfamiliar with the layout of the castle, Pippa came to a cramped landing, hurled her shoulder against a low door and burst through it.

This led along the open-air battlement overlooking Lough Leane. She paused between two square-topped merlons.

He froze several feet away from her. For a moment a horrible terror seized him, the same fear he had felt when he had seen her on the sea cliffs, swaying as if in a dream world. She had only to thrust herself forward a few more inches, and she would plummet to her death hundreds of feet below in the rock-bound lake.

"Surely I'm not worth dying for," he said softly.

She looked at him with dazed hurt glazing her eyes and her face pinched and pale. "Never think it," she said.

He chanced a few steps forward and leaned against the wall. "See that island out there?"

He pointed, and she looked out across the blue glass surface of the lake. "Innisfallen?" she asked.

"Aye."

"I can see the roof of a church through the trees. Do you think your friend Revelin is still there, or do you suppose Richard de Lacey ousted the canons as well?" She spoke with perfect, understated acid.

"I imagine they are all still there. The place is of little strategic value."

"I will be interested to meet Revelin," she said. "To

meet the man who was your tutor, charged with turning you into a man of honor." She regarded him with piercing sympathy. "What a disappointment you must be to him."

"That," he said, hating himself, "is no doubt correct." He forced himself to look at her when all he wanted was to hang his head in shame. "Pippa, what shall I say to you? Shall I tell you I'm sorry? Tell you how she came to be my wife and why she is no wife to me at all?"

That, at least, sparked a flicker of interest. "Telling me all of those things explains nothing. Not why you deceived me. Not why you took me in and gave me gifts and treated me with more kindness than anyone ever treated me before. Not why you held me in your arms and kissed me, caressed me, made me—" She bit her lip and turned her face away.

"At least hear me out," he said.

Other than the weary sigh of the wind, he heard no sound. He held his breath until she looked back at him and asked, "Why?"

"Because I care about you, Pippa. God forgive me, I have from the very start."

The breeze corrugated the lake with shimmering ripples. She stared at him, her mouth agape. She looked as fragile and beautiful as a new-made flower, uncertain of her position or what to do next.

Finally, after a long, windy silence, she kicked her heels against the castle wall. "Why should I believe you?"

"You should not. You should be able to hear the truth in my voice and feel it when your very touch makes me burn, *a gradh*."

"Lust. That's what I see in you. Lust and deceit." She raked a hand through her wind-mussed hair. "I can't think of a single reason I should believe a word you utter."

"Don't believe words. Believe what you see and feel."

"I don't know what I feel," she said. "I wish I could rage at you and throw things, but I feel too numb for that." She looked at him over the top of the merlon. Her face was soft with suffering and bewilderment. "Why didn't you tell me?"

A shudder of self-disgust passed over him. "At first, there seemed no reason. You were a stranger who did not need to know my business. Later, I thought I would leave you at Queen Elizabeth's court, never to see you again. I did not even speak of Felicity to my friends, much less acquaintances I didn't expect to last."

He winced at the stark pain in her eyes. "But you lasted. You came to mean the world to me. I would have done anything not to hurt you, Pippa. I said nothing because I knew the day would come that I would have to leave you. Selfish as I am, I wanted to leave you with a fondness for me in your heart, and so I said nothing. By the time I realized you were coming to Ireland with me…" He hesitated and studied the broken-backed line of Macgillycuddy's Reeks in the distance, outlined by the marbled blue sky.

"After that, I just couldn't find the words. I hoped I would never have to speak of her to you. I had a letter from Revelin stating that an annulment would be granted. She was supposed to have gone back to her father. Even so, there is no excuse. I should have told you about her."

"Then tell me now."

He got up and then sank to one knee before her, holding out one hand. "Please come down."

She hesitated, and that brief distrust cut at him. He had lost her. The old Pippa would have leaped into his arms. At last she took his hand and stepped down.

"I wish we could be alone somewhere, far from the rest of the world," he said.

"You wish for the impossible. The world will never go away." She shivered and hugged herself. "Neither will your wife."

He stood, dropped her hand and gave a harsh laugh. "Aye, here she is, having surrendered my castle to the enemy." He propped a shoulder on the stone wall and listened for a moment to the wind off the treetops. "Still, that does not excuse my deception."

"She is the reason you never made love to me, isn't she?"

He nodded. "For the very worst of reasons, I pledged a vow to her. I am bound to keep that vow."

Pippa gave a self-deprecating smile. "At least that's a crumb for my vanity. Each time you stopped and put me aside, I thought something about me repelled you."

If she had not been so gravely earnest, he would have laughed. Instead he said, "Quite the opposite, *a stor.* There is nothing in the world I find more beautiful than you." He smiled. "Does that surprise you? Don't look so pale, love. From the first time I saw you performing at St. Paul's, I found you completely captivating. I even liked it when you sang in the bath. Ah, Pippa, you worked so hard to entertain me so I would keep you close. What you didn't know is that I wanted to keep you forever. But I could not." He slid a glance at the archway leading back into the keep.

"Why did you marry her?" Pippa asked.

"For the sake of my people." He gave a bitter laugh. "How noble that sounds. I wed Felicity in order to form a much needed alliance with the English constable in Killarney town. My father had been working feverishly to finish building Ross Castle. I was given a choice of offering for Felicity or suffering an attack on the stronghold."

"But that is not so unusual," she said with touching credulity. "Don't the gentry always marry for reasons of expedience?"

"That is the reason I told the world. The truth is, I wed Felicity in order to spite my father." There. After all this time, he admitted it. He felt again that hot stab of emotion brought on by thoughts of his father. He closed his eyes and let the wind rush over his face.

He remembered it all with razor-edged clarity: his father's snort of disbelief, followed by a bellow of outrage, and then the blows, two of them, open-handed slaps across the face, so hard that Aidan's head had snapped from side to side. These went unchallenged, and more blows followed, until Aidan had sunk to the floor and put up a hand to stanch the ooze of blood from his split lip.

Ronan O Donoghue would have murdered his son barehanded, Aidan was certain of it. As the older man hammered away, and as Aidan all but sat on his hands to keep from fighting back, the long buried truth had come out.

"You are no son of mine," Ronan had roared, "but a Sassenach mercenary's get, a bastard. Your faithless mother tricked me into believing I had sired you, but I finally beat the truth out of her."

The old sickness built in Aidan's throat. He pressed his back against the wall and inhaled through his teeth. He would never know for certain if his father had spoken truly that night. The rumors that Máire O Donoghue had died by her husband's hand seemed likely. Ronan had never sired another child, so perhaps his accusation was true also.

"Blood will tell," Ronan had bellowed. "I thought I could make a true warrior of you, but the moment I turn my back you crawl into the lap of the Sassenach."

The beating and bellowing had gone on. Hatred formed like a ball of ice in Aidan's chest. He would not let himself fight back, for his rage was too strong. He could not trust himself not to kill his father.

And then, after all, he did kill him. Ronan had stopped screaming midsentence, his arm raised for yet another blow. His purplish face contorted, his eyes bulged, and he pitched forward.

His heavy bulk had landed on Aidan. Slowly, on fire with agony from the barrage of blows, Aidan extracted himself and stood. He remembered looking at his father for what seemed like a long time. He remembered walking—not running—down the winding stone steps of the tower to find someone to send for the barber surgeon.

"Aidan?" Pippa's soft voice rescued him from the hellish memories. "Go on."

Aidan surprised himself. He told her. For the first time, he revealed to another person every hideous, humiliating detail of that night.

"My defiance was the ax that killed my father," he concluded. "He died while raging at me about Felicity. His death did cause me considerable guilt, so I finished building the castle according to his plans."

She listened without taking her eyes off him. She looked at him as if he had become a stranger. She was pale and still, yet rather than disgust or accusation, she regarded him with sympathy. "I thought people who had families were happy," she said at last.

Clasping his hands behind his back, he paced the wall walk. "Within hours of marrying Felicity, I knew I had made a mistake."

"Within hours?" She blushed. "You mean the wedding night."

He stopped walking. "I suspected something was

amiss when she barred me from the marriage bed. Just in case I misunderstood, she declared she would remain a virgin until I and all my subjects renounced the Catholic faith and embraced the new Reformed religion."

"She placed a high price on her virtue."

He smiled at Pippa's dark but ready humor. "It proved to be little incentive. Call me strange, but I find nothing attractive about smashing icons and cursing the pope." His smile vanished. "In every sense that counts, I have never been married at all. Yet I am consumed with guilt over my feelings for you."

She gave a soft moan and stepped back as if to resist going into his arms. "What do you intend to do now?"

His heart beat slowly, heavily. He allowed himself to smooth his hand lightly over her cheek. "When I married her, I had no idea it was possible to care for a woman the way I have come to care for you." He wanted to say he loved her, but he couldn't. Not now. Not when he had no idea what he could offer her.

She tilted her head so that his hand cradled her cheek, and he could feel the warmth of tears. It proved to be his undoing. He gathered her into his arms and pressed his lips to her hair.

"It is too late for us, isn't it?" she whispered.

"That is what common sense tells me. But my heart tells me we will find a way."

"Aidan—"

"We were never properly introduced," Felicity called from the arched opening of the stairwell. An icy sheen of hatred gleamed in her cornflower-blue eyes.

Aidan and Pippa broke apart to see her standing there. An odd turbulence seethed in Felicity's eyes. She had always been strange and fanatical. She appeared tense, as if she were a tautly coiled spring.

Pippa put her hands on her hips and faced Felicity unflinchingly. "You may call me Mistress Trueheart."

"Mistress?" Felicity hissed out the word. "Don't you mean leman, or perhaps *whore?*"

Pippa lay awake that night, fuming about Felicity. At Richard's insistence she had been given a private chamber as a guest of honor.

Deep down, she reluctantly admired Felicity. Being married to the O Donoghue Mór and staying chaste was an exercise in greater willpower than Pippa could ever hope to possess.

"He has but to crook his finger, and I come running," she muttered, punching her pillow. "At least the intolerant bitch has the courage of her convictions."

Meanwhile, Aidan was trying to negotiate a treaty with Richard. His men wanted war. Pippa had heard them arguing in the guardroom. They spoke in Irish, but she could glean some of what was said. She understood enough to know how desperately Aidan loved his country and his people.

"Felicity, you foolish, foolish woman," she whispered to the windy darkness. "You have no idea what you are missing."

If he put Felicity aside, Aidan reasoned, then the terms of surrender she had signed as Lady of Castleross would be null and void. There would be no agreement with the Sassenach. But he knew the power of the Browne clan. Their rage could set a torch to wholesale slaughter.

Standing at the window in an upper-story room he had occupied since boyhood, he felt a lifting of his heart. The battle would come to a head whether he kept Felicity or not, and according to Revelin, he had permission from

Rome to set her aside. He should send her to her father in Killarney.

The shame would slay her. But she was the one who had betrayed her marriage vows and barred him from her bed.

The thought of being free intoxicated him. Free to show Pippa what was in his heart. It was like a blessing from heaven. God, how he wanted her!

He would tell Felicity first thing in the morning. She might have driven Revelin away, but she would not deter Aidan from carrying out the annulment.

A latch clicked and the chamber door swished open. He turned, reaching for his shortsword.

A cloaked and hooded figure entered the room. "Stay your hand, my lord," said a soft, female voice. "Please, I beg you." She sank to her knees in a pool of pale moonlight.

"Felicity?" His hand relaxed. "What are you doing here?"

She dropped back the hood and opened the cloak to reveal that she was wearing naught but a translucent linen shift beneath.

He froze, transfixed. For the first time ever, he saw her unbound hair, sleek and rich as polished wood. He saw the dark tips of her generous breasts thrusting against the thin garment. He saw the ivory skin of her throat, with the pulse beating gently beneath the surface.

She raised her perfect face to his, and he saw the disquieting turbulence in her eyes, more pronounced than it had been earlier.

She took a deep breath. "I came here to do what I should have done the very night we were wed. I should have given myself to you then. But the Lord spoke to me and told me I must wait."

"I see. And now the Lord tells you it is all right to spread your legs for me?"

She flinched at his crudeness. "It was wrong for me to refuse you. I know that now. I realized it the moment I saw you tempted by the evils of lust for another woman."

"Nay, Felicity. You realized it the moment you knew I would set you aside and invalidate your treaty with the English."

Her expression remained serene, empty of emotion. He lauded her self-possession, though there was a quality about it that discomfited him.

"I think not at all of the treaty," she insisted. "Greater matters are at stake. Matters of the soul."

"Madam," he said, "you are a huge and constant liar."

"No!" She glided to her feet. The gown wafted against her as she rushed to him. Her figure was outlined in silver moonlight. "I want you, my lord, my love. I always have. Surely you know how hard it was to keep from begging you to take me. I am begging now, Aidan. I can give you children—"

"Felicity," he said softly, regretfully, "you will never get the chance." Before she could protest he went on. "Life is short, and life does not wait for us to decide when and how to live it."

He had a bleak, fleeting thought of how dazzled he had once been by her beauty, her purity. And by the idea that their union would also unite their two peoples. "We both made the mistake of trying to seize control of something that is out of our grasp."

She flung herself at him and covered his face with kisses. Taken by surprise, he stepped back. "Felicity, please. Don't make this worse than it already is."

"All will be well," she whispered huskily. "Aidan, you are my husband!"

She moved nearer, and to avoid her, he stepped through the doorway to the stone-railed balcony. The cold air of a clear night blew over him. She followed and clung to him, whimpering and kissing his mouth, his chin, wherever she could reach.

"You never understood," she said, her voice a chilling whisper in his ear, her grasping arms curving around behind him. She was clumsy yet insistent, and again he felt a pang of regret that any sweetness they might have shared had been doomed from the start.

"I did love you much, my lord," she said.

"Nay, Felicity, nor did I ever truly love you." Her arms still imprisoned him; he wished she would let go. "We must end this. Now. Tonight. Revelin has the papers all ready."

"I will not let you shame me!"

At first he felt nothing; then a searing, sharp pain stung him. He froze, too amazed to move. The bitch had stabbed him in the back. She raised her arm to stab him again.

He gave a wordless cry and thrust her away. The wound sent icy tingles of shock and agony down his back. She lifted the small knife and rushed at him.

He caught her by both wrists. Images skipped past his blurring vision, and he realized he was on the verge of falling unconscious. "Don't do this, Felicity. It's mad, do you hear me?"

She tried to thrust down with the knife, but he tightened his grip. "You're destroying yourself, woman, not me," he said through his teeth. With a little more pressure, he could snap her wrist, but he did not want to hurt her. "Just go back to your family. Blame it all on me. Tell them I'm an ogre, tell them I beat you or made you say the rosary. We can claim our barren state is my fault, we can say anything—"

"Never! You papist bastard!" The blade quivered in her hand.

He pressed his thumb into her pulse point, finding the nerve. She dropped the knife and went limp against him. Hot blood seeped down his back. He felt airy, without substance, as if he could float away. He needed to sit down, put his head between his knees, call for Iago to dress the wound.

But first he had to deal with Felicity. "It's over," he whispered. "The whole ugly farce is over. Let us end it now before we hurt each other any more."

She gazed up at him. "But I love you. And you love me."

He was certain she missed the irony of the words she had said to the man she'd just stabbed in the back. "I wanted you in order to anger my father and please yours," he explained. "You wanted me in order to further your Reformed crusade. We were wrong, both of us. It's over."

"No," she said, stepping back. She leaped up onto the stone railing. The wind caught at the hem of her cloak and tossed her beautiful long hair in a dark nimbus around her tormented face. "Not quite over, Aidan."

"God, Felicity!" He took a stumbling step forward. "What are you doing? Please come down." He heard himself repeating words he had said to Pippa just a short time ago. But Pippa had not been determined to destroy him no matter the cost to herself. Pippa's eyes had not shone with that silvery, manic light.

A grating sound came from somewhere above, the creak of hinges, perhaps. He ignored it and held out his hand. "I didn't mean any of it, darling," he cajoled. "I'll take you to bed tonight, make love to you, make you so happy."

"Your lies come too late." She grasped the front of her shift and rent it asunder so that her pale breasts spilled out. She raked a hand across her chest, scoring her flesh with ugly red stripes. "Your lies will not save either of us now. Your lies will damn you to hell. By morning, they will all know you killed me."

He lunged for her, but she was quicker, stepping back and then falling, falling, her hair and cloak billowing, her face a stark, white oval that disappeared into blackness.

Aidan clung to the railing and vomited. Sweat beaded his forehead as anger built in his chest. Even in death, she controlled him. By morning they would call him a murderer.

Unless he left now, in secret, and did not return until he had an army at his back.

Richard de Lacey handed Pippa a handkerchief. She dried her eyes and glanced up at him. "How many of these do you have?"

"Four more, I think."

She gave a long, miserable sniff. "I shall need more than that."

The sun had not shown its face. A dull rain drummed on the eaves of the small corner office where she sat with Richard and a woman named Shannon MacSweeney.

Shannon had come at dawn to see if the rumors that flew about Killarney were true. With her vivid red hair and tall, proud bearing, she resembled a flaming torch as she patted Pippa's shoulder and watched Richard with sharp green eyes.

"So she is dead for certain," Shannon said.

"She is."

"And did the O Donoghue attack her and fling her over the wall? That is what her father claims, and that is what her cousin, Valentine Browne, announced at the village well."

"Completely untrue," Richard said furiously. "I saw it all. I heard voices, and looked out my window, which is directly over the terrace. She stabbed Aidan, then leaped up on the rail, rending her gown to make it look as if he had attacked her." Richard's voice thickened with horror and grief. "He tried to get her to come down, but she jumped."

Pippa crushed the handkerchief to her eyes, wishing she could scrub away the image his words made. "Why did he flee?" she whispered. "That only makes him look guilty."

"He was right to flee," Shannon MacSweeney said. "He'd be hanged by sunset if he stayed."

"I would speak in his defense," Richard insisted.

Shannon gave a bitter laugh. "Do you think that would matter? Fortitude Browne is looking for any excuse to be rid of Aidan O Donoghue."

Filled with cold fury, the O Donoghue Mór swept down the Iveragh peninsula, mustering rebels from every hamlet and town. It was not hard to find violent, discontented men to follow him on his quest to take back Ross Castle. For a generation now, English rule had bowed their backs beneath greed and injustice. The recent hanging of rebels by Fortitude Browne in retaliation for Felicity's death had pushed them to the breaking point.

Willingly they took up arms, and within a month a formidable army was camped on the far shores of Lough Leane.

Pippa, who had spent most of the time at Innisfallen in the company of the canon Revelin, arrived by rowboat at sunset. She spied Iago working with a company of archers. Watching their arrows *thunk* into straw, man-shaped targets made it all chillingly real. They meant to kill every last Englishman.

"Where is Aidan?" she asked Iago.

Iago's eyes widened. "You should not be here."

"Just answer me, Iago."

He looked at Revelin, who had come with her. "She should not be here."

"Sure and who's going to stop her?" Revelin asked in his thick brogue. "Like a battering ram, she is, pounding away at a man's good sense until he all but begs her to do as she wills."

Grim humor flashed in Iago's smile. "I see you have gotten to know our Pippa."

"Well?" she demanded, speaking brusquely to cover her nervousness. "Where is he?"

Iago pointed. "Just there, at the edge of the woods, at the source of the spring." He touched her shoulder and regarded her with troubled brown eyes. "There's a shrine to his mother there. And *pequeña,* he has been at the poteen, I fear."

She tossed her head and struck out for the spring. "I've seen drunken men before." Yet anxiety pounded in her chest as she passed through the encampment. The soldiers were silent, their anticipation palpable, like invisible taut threads strung across the camp.

The past weeks had been a turbulent time for the whole district, the English crying foul in the death of Felicity Browne O Donoghue, the Irish passionately proclaiming Aidan's innocence, and Richard de Lacey himself, still entrenched at Ross Castle, strangely silent. No doubt preparing for war.

She climbed a short, muddy pathway to the spring. A

beautiful stone Celtic cross stood beside the burbling waters.

Aidan did not seem to hear her approach. He sat upon a large rock, his elbows resting on his knees, a deerskin flask dangling from his fingers, and his hair, longer than ever, falling forward in unkempt hanks.

Despite his haggard appearance, he still looked every inch the chieftain, fierce and strong and unconquered, yet oddly reluctant, as if he played a role for which he was ill suited.

"Aidan," she said softly.

He looked up at her. She saw the terrible rage and reckless defiance burning in the bluer-than-blue centers of his eyes. In that instant she understood, saw his torment as if he had laid it all out before her. He considered himself a dead man now. Getting himself killed in the siege would be a mere formality.

"Please," she said, stepping into the glade. "Please don't do this. Find another way, Aidan. I beg you."

"Find another way." His harsh, drink-roughened tone mocked her. "What would you suggest? Marrying a Sassenach to keep the peace? Or murdering one when she becomes a burden?"

She caught her breath to keep in the horror. "You blame yourself, don't you?" Her voice shook. "Revelin said you would."

"Revelin is seldom wrong."

The anguish she heard in his voice touched her. At his core, Aidan O Donoghue was a kind and decent man with too many responsibilities and too few choices. She dropped to her knees beside him and sat back on her heels.

She picked up the flask and touched it to her lips. It was still warm from his mouth, and she tilted it back and drank deeply, watching him from beneath her lashes. He stared back, looking skeptical. The strong drink lit a bonfire in her stomach, but she would not allow herself to gag or even flinch.

As calmly as she could, she set down the flask.

"Well?" he asked.

"That would put a plowhorse under."

He favored her with a quick, bitten-off laugh, and then the shadows fell over him again.

"It was not your fault," Pippa insisted. "Not your father's death, nor even Felicity's. Both were victims of their own hatred."

He stared at the carved stone cross. A Gaelic inscription was etched at the bottom.

"I wish to God I could believe you." He took a long, comfort-seeking pull on the flask and wiped his sleeve across his mouth. He looked debauched, hopeless, remote.

Pippa had never seen him like this, and she did not know how to reach him. He was so bitter and tense that she feared he would explode at any moment. "Your mother was called Máire," she said, her finger tracing the letters and whorls carved into the stone. "Is this her name here?"

"Aye."

"Tell me about her."

"Ah, another happy subject." He drank again, then flung the flask onto the grass. The sharp fumes of poteen made her eyes smart. "Supposedly she was unfaithful to my father, and I am half Sassenach. At least that is what my mother confessed while my father was beating her for the last time."

Shaken, she put her hand lightly, tentatively, on his forearm. His muscles were coiled. "A woman in torment will say anything. Revelin said that Ronan was a hateful and hated man."

She drew a deep breath for courage and finally said what she had come to say. "If you take these men to storm the castle, you will be acting just like him. Is that what you want? To become your father?"

He snatched his arm away and glared at her. "You don't know what you're talking about."

She wanted to shrink from his anger but forced herself to stay there, pinned by his glare. "I do, my lord. You told me yourself. Ronan O Donoghue offered up men's lives without regard to the widows and orphans they would leave behind. If you so desperately need something to feel guilty about, then feel guilty about that. Not about your father keeling over in a fit of pique or Felicity taking her own life."

He moved so quickly that she did not even have time to cry out. Grasping her by the shoulders, he hauled her to her feet. His fingers bit into her.

"Enough," he said through his teeth. "I'll hear no more. These affairs are none of your concern. Begone now, and leave me to do what I must do."

She stared down at his fingers. "You said you cared about me. Is this how you show it?"

He muttered something anguished and Irish, then let her go. It was all there in his face, the determination, the desolation, the cornered look of a man who had run out of choices. "Pippa—"

She wrenched herself away and fled.

He had decided to take the castle at dawn. By now, Richard de Lacey would have gotten word that an army was gathering, but there had been no time for reinforcements to arrive.

Ross Castle was reputed to be impregnable, and perhaps it was. But not to Aidan. He had personally overseen the design of its defenses. With luck, he and his men would cross the narrow causeway unchallenged and make it at least as far as the guardroom before engaging the enemy.

The fog-laden chill of dawn settled into his bones. He kept hearing Pippa's voice. *Is that what you want? To become your father?*

Hard questions. Things no one else dared to ask him. Things he dared not answer. Couldn't she see he had no choice?

He turned to the silent, waiting men behind him. Dressed in traditional tunics and fur, barefoot and crudely armed, they exuded an anger honed by generations of subjugation. They wanted this fight, Aidan reminded himself. They were ready. More than ready.

Iago and Donal Og caught his eye and nodded to signal their flanking troops.

"God be with us all, then," he said in clear Gaelic.

Donal Og winked. "And may we all get to heaven before the devil knows we're dead."

Nervous laughter rippled through the assembly. Aidan turned and led the way to the stronghold. He expected to see scouts melting from their lookout posts and slinking back to warn de Lacey, but in the forest they met with nothing more fierce than a badger and a flock of birds.

His hopes rose as they crossed the natural causeway formed by the peninsula projecting out into the lake. The Sassenach host did not lift a finger to stop them.

When he found the main gate unbarred, he felt the first prickle of apprehension. He turned to Donal Og and whispered, "It's a trap."

Donal Og nodded grimly. "Bound to be. Shall we go on?"

"Aye." Aidan went first, despite offers from some of the men. He wanted to prove himself different from his father.

They crossed the inner courtyard and entered the guard-room. The dim, unsteady light revealed six hulking shapes stationed at the windows and stairwells. He braced himself for a fight but quickly surmised that something was wrong.

He motioned for the men behind him to stop and entered the guardroom alone. Good Virgin Mary, were the guards dead?

A long, blubbering snore filled the air.

He nearly came out of his skin. When he realized what the situation was, he blew out a sigh of relief. "See that they're disarmed," he said to his men.

"My lord," someone said in an incredulous whisper, "they've already been disarmed."

"Their hands and feet are bound," Iago noted.

Beyond the guardroom, they climbed the stairs. At each separate landing, they found a sleeping Englishman. It was uncanny, as if the *sidhe* had cast a spell over the entire household.

By the time they had reached the great hall, Aidan had begun to believe victory was in his grasp.

But from the landing of the staircase, he heard voices and froze. He cocked his head to listen.

"All right, then," said a sweet, feminine voice, "what about this one?"

Revelin's distinctive silvery chuckle wafted on the foggy air. "Not quite, my dear. I believe you are surrounded."

"Oh, geld and splay you—" She broke off as Aidan stepped into the room, followed by Donal Og, Iago and the first troop of men. She stood and grinned at him, and it was the sweetest smile he had ever seen. "Welcome, Your Eminence," she said.

He strode to the table, where a *fidchell* gaming board had been set out. "What in God's name is going on here?"

Revelin stroked his long white beard. "Well, my lord, it looks as if the young lady is about to surrender her key pegs and lose the game."

"I mean *here*." Exasperated, he gestured at the men strewn about the room.

"Ah, them." Revelin dipped his head in a sage nod. "We drugged them."

"We did," Pippa confirmed. She pointed to a stack of shortswords and shields and stabbing daggers at the base of the dais. "We put their weapons here. Does that suit you?"

"We also sent the strongbox of Ross Castle to the coast for safekeeping." Shannon MacSweeney spoke from a corner of the room where she sat placidly doing needlework. "I had to tell them about the chest of gold, Aidan," said his childhood friend. "I hope you don't mind."

She stroked the golden hair of Richard de Lacey, who lay on a cushion beside her. "I hope he doesn't mind, either."

For a moment, Aidan could not speak. When he found his voice, he said, "You drugged them."

"That's right," Pippa said.

"A bit of Tristram's knot in the poteen," Revelin said. "Well, perhaps more than a bit." He went back to studying the *fidchell* board.

"And also in the porridge and ale," Pippa added. "And I'm quite afraid I added some to the wine and ale just for good measure. But you had better hurry up and defeat them or do whatever it is you do when you conquer a castle. Once they wake up, they are bound to be most unhappy fellows."

Aidan walked over to the table. He stood very still, looking across at her, drinking in the sight of her face, all soft in the morning mist. He stared at her for so long that she blushed.

"You really should make haste, my lord."

"I shall." For the first time in more than a month, he smiled. It felt good to smile. "There is one thing I must do first."

"What?"

"This." He slid his arms around her and leaned down to place a long, lush kiss on her startled mouth. Ah, he had forgotten what she meant to him.

But never, not for a moment, had he forgotten how much he loved her.

"If you mean to thank me in the same manner," Revelin said, "you'll find yourself highly unappreciated."

Aidan straightened, his eyes never leaving Pippa's face. "I'll save my kisses for her, if it's all the same to you."

The tension among the men dissolved into loud guffaws. Donal Og beat his chest like a warrior of yore. "Come, lads!" he bellowed. "Let us make short work of the prisoners before they awaken and make us sweat for our victory!"

Diary of a Lady

～⊙⊙～

We had a most perturbing report from Richard in Ireland. It seems he and his forces were compelled—by means he did not explain in his letters—to abandon Ross Castle and retreat to Killarney. Even more disconcerting is the news that he has fallen in love with an Irishwoman and means to marry her before the ban on Irish and English unions takes effect. Imagine! My Richard, a bridegroom.

I fear his duty to England will dim his joy. He has called for reinforcements, but Oliver says more men are unlikely to be sent, as the queen's forces are already taxed to their limit.

However, Oliver himself is quite capable of raising an army and a fleet of ships as well, for the Muscovy Company has grown unimaginably rich on the trading begun by Oliver's father.

Perhaps a voyage to Ireland would allow us to investigate the truth of the mysterious message we received that dredged up such a sweet, aching wealth of memories.

For now, I shall put aside my cares. The delightful

contessa is coming to Blackrose Priory for another visit. She is always full of the most deliciously shocking gossip.

—Lark de Lacey,
Countess of Wimberleigh

Thirteen

"Will you marry me?"

Aidan looked up from the document he was studying. The bewilderment on his face disheartened Pippa, but she forced herself to stand calmly in the middle of the counting office, waiting for his answer.

He gave her a soft, distracted smile, his eyes hazy with distant thoughts. "I'm sorry. I didn't hear you correctly. I thought you just asked me to marry you."

"I did."

His eyebrows shot up. "You did?"

"I did."

The eyebrows descended in a frown. "Oh." With his thumb, he curled the corner of the letter on the desk, then frowned and turned the document facedown.

An awkward silence stretched out between them while the afternoon sunlight, streaming through a narrow window, painted lazy patterns on the stone floor.

Fool, she called herself. All her life she had lived in dread of rejection, so much so that she had learned to shield herself from any kind of intimacy. Now here she was inviting the ultimate rebuff—from the one person who could wound her the most deeply.

It was too late to retract her question, so she took refuge in a cocky pose, with hands on hips and a challenging lift of her chin. "Well? Will you?"

"Will I marry you?" He tasted the question as if it were some exotic drink. How maddeningly attractive he looked this afternoon. Three weeks after signing terms of surrender with Richard de Lacey, the O Donoghue Mór seemed a new man, hale and assured, lord of his domain.

Richard and his army had withdrawn to the northern shores of Lough Leane, near Killarney. Aidan was home now, truly home for the first time since she had known him, and he looked at ease.

Also puzzled, as he sat with his elbows resting on the table, fingers forming a steeple. "Forgive me, but isn't it the usual way for the man to ask the woman?"

"I don't know anything about the usual way. I only know my way." She tossed her head as if his reply did not truly matter. "I know that marriage is a grave business, and for a chieftain to wed an outsider is unheard of, but—"

"How do you know these things?"

"Revelin told me."

"Ah. Revelin the all-wise. What else did he tell you?"

"That you would say yes." She was so embarrassed, she could barely choke out the words.

He rose slowly, with a predator's grace, and moved past the writing table. "Revelin misunderstands."

Through sheer force of will, she kept herself from melting of shame. She summoned a sparkling smile and winked at him, pretending the whole thing had been a joke. "Of course," she said briskly. "The whole idea is quite preposterous. You are absolutely right to refuse—"

"I adore you with all my heart," he said softly.

She let out an involuntary sigh. His declaration sent warmth rushing through her, raising a flush on her skin and lifting her hopes until breathing became painful.

"And I cannot marry you," he continued. "Not now. Perhaps not ever."

Her heart turned to stone in her chest. The old torment stormed through her, the all-too-familiar feeling of abandonment. It was the numbness that had come over her when she had stood on a windswept strand in England while they buried old Mab; it was the freezing sense of isolation she had experienced each time a troupe of players melted apart; it was the forced aloofness she cultivated even in the teeming yard of St. Paul's.

She thought she had prepared herself for the hurt, but she had underestimated its strength. If his words had been blows, they would have killed; they were that lethal.

Turning away, wanting to get out before he saw her pain, she managed to mumble, "I see." There would be no quick recovery for her this time, no blithe laughter to hide her tears.

He stood to bar her from leaving and reached for her hands. "Nay, my love, you do not see. Come here." He led her out a low doorway and up a short spiral of stairs, then through a tower door. They emerged onto the west section of the wall walk. It was a perfect day, the sun soft upon the treetops and the lake reflecting a clear blue sky.

"Look well upon the beauty," he said, standing behind her and speaking intimately into her ear. "Who knows when you shall see its like again? It is too lovely, too piercing, to last."

She was not sure if he meant this kingdom or the feelings between them. "Why do you say that?"

"Because we won't be left alone here, to live and love

and make bairns and do all the things ordinary people dream of doing."

Her hopes began to sink beneath the weight of his logic. "You mean Richard will return."

She felt his broad shoulders stiffen as if preparing to bear a great burden. "With reinforcements. And he won't stop at taking Ross Castle. He'll have to take me as well."

"No," she said. "Could you not just come to terms with him? Why should he need you as a prisoner?"

"If it were only Richard, I would not worry. For all that he's a Sassenach, he has acted with honor." Aidan turned her in his arms so that she faced him. "Felicity has a powerful family."

The mention of Aidan's late wife sent a dark chill rippling over Pippa's skin. She clung to his arms, feeling suddenly sick and dizzy. "Her father continues to insist you killed his daughter, doesn't he?"

Aidan nodded, and his thoughts strayed to the letter lying on his desk. "He will not rest until he sees me hanged."

The chill deepened to an icy sting. She wanted to clap her hands over her ears, to close her eyes, to make the feeling of dread go away.

But Aidan was right. It would not go away. A man had lost his daughter. How could he rest until he felt justice had been served?

"I still want to marry you," she whispered.

Aidan smiled sadly and touched his lips to her brow. "Perhaps today you do."

"I think I wanted to the first moment I saw you. So don't try to tell me this feeling will fade away."

He seemed to have to work to keep his embrace gentle; she sensed a strained tension in him. "If you have even a fraction of the desire I feel for you, then your wish is understandable."

"It is more than mere desire," she insisted. "It is like wanting to find my family, only stronger than that. One thing I have come to realize is that if I have you, I don't need them. It is probably impossible to find out the truth anyway."

"But if you were to learn who they are?" His voice sounded taut, the words forced.

"I might be curious about them. But I don't care anymore. I don't wish to know."

He closed his eyes, and a look of torment shadowed his face. Yet when he opened his eyes, he was smiling. "My sweet, entirely adorable colleen," he said, lowering his mouth to kiss her, "is there anything you won't say?"

"I think not." She shuddered as his tongue flicked out to taste her lips. "Not to you." His kiss deepened, and she felt the love and desire flowing so richly through her blood that she moaned with the urgent pleasure of it. She was shaking when he pulled back. "You know," she whispered, "I'm certain there are worse reasons to marry than rampant lust."

"I'm certain you're right," he said, some of the old laughter creeping into his voice. But then, as he studied her upturned face, he sobered. "Sweetheart, you need a reliable husband, not someone who is likely to end at the gibbet."

She clenched her hands into fists and struck his chest. "Don't talk like that!"

"But what if I were to be seized by Constable Browne?" he persisted. "What would you do then?"

She forced a laugh. "I suppose, my lord, I would be a rather wealthy widow."

He laughed, too, and bent his head again to kiss her. Just before their lips met, she fancied she saw a flash of crazed desperation in his eyes. But when his warm mouth covered hers, she forgot all about their macabre conversation.

I suppose, my lord, I would be a rather wealthy widow. Her words, though spoken in jest, clung in Aidan's mind like a burr in a horse's mane.

Late at night, when all the household lay at rest, he climbed to the topmost point of Ross Castle, where he could brace his foot on the wall and look out across the moonlit lake to the far mountains.

How simple life had been for his forebears, he reflected. Simple and brutal. A chieftain ruled the domain for as far as he could see.

Now the Sassenach had come, preserving the brutality, heightening it, creating complications for which Ireland was unprepared. The Irish would lose much of themselves in this war; Munster was in pieces, and even the great rebel Earl of Desmond had been driven into the misty mountains of Slieve Mish.

Aidan thought of the flurry of furious letters, warrants and proclamations he had received since making peace with Richard. He could not say how long he could keep the force of Constable Browne's fury at bay—a month? Half a year? He knew only that they would come for him; it was the way of the Sassenach.

So there it was. Felicity had won. She had defeated him. Except on one matter.

A soft, heartfelt smile unfurled on his lips as the night wind lifted his hair. She had not managed to destroy his love for Pippa.

His clenched fist came down hard on the top of the wall. He noticed a smear of blood but felt no pain, only a deep, quiet exultation as he came to his decision.

Aye, he would marry Pippa. He would steal joy from the jaws of despair. And secretly, without her knowledge, he would prepare her for a future without him.

I suppose, my lord, I would be a rather wealthy widow.

"And so you shall be, my beloved," he whispered to the quiet night. "So you shall be."

They were married by Revelin of Innisfallen. The canon beamed as he held out his book for Aidan's offering of silver for the Arrha; his voice rang with triumph as he blessed the knotwork wedding ring of the O Donoghue.

During the celebratory mass that followed, Pippa sat in wide-eyed awe. The sacred mysteries intrigued her. She wondered why the Reformers found such things as Latin prayers and songs, clouds of incense, and unshakable faith so threatening. The little windy chapel of Ross Castle hardly dripped with decadent riches, and Rome seemed several worlds away. The people gathered here exuded a simple piety that was bound to change the mind of any Reformer.

Or perhaps not any. To her dying day, Felicity Browne O Donoghue had dedicated herself to converting these people to the Reformed faith. More stubborn than their mistress, the people of Ross had resisted, driving her to unbearable frustration. What a foolish waste, Pippa thought. God was God, no matter what church a person worshipped in, no matter how prayers were offered.

Even as memories of Felicity chilled her, a small, evil exultation nudged into her mind. Pippa was here, wed to the man she adored, because Felicity had taken her own life.

Filled with guilt, Pippa stole a glance at Aidan. He knelt with his head bent. His raven hair fell forward, the single beaded strand catching a glow from the candle-light. His face looked strong and intense, curiously determined, and so beautiful it made her heart ache.

She was stricken by a terrible fear. What in God's name was she doing? She, a common street urchin, marrying an Irish chieftain. It was madness. *Madness.*

She must have made some subtle sound or movement of distress, for he closed his hand around hers and caught her eyes. *"Pax vobiscum,"* he said, echoing the words Revelin had just spoken.

She closed her eyes and swayed toward him. Aye, peace. It settled around her like a golden mantle, enveloping her, comforting, healing her. All her life, she had sought the peace of knowing she was loved. Aidan O Donoghue was giving that to her. The magnitude of his gift struck her, and a tear seeped out from beneath her eyelashes.

With a touch as light as a moth's wing, he brushed away the tear. She opened her eyes to see him looking at her with an intensity that stole her breath.

"Those had best be tears of happiness," he whispered.

"So you should hope, or it is going to be a very long night," she whispered back, trying to lighten the moment and resisting the urge to sniffle loudly. "I am now your wife. What more could I want?"

His smile held such promise that a wave of shivers slid over her. "That," he said, bending to secretly trace the shape of her ear with his tongue, "is something we will explore tonight."

The maids spoke in rapid Gaelic, but their broad winks and friendly tweaks and pats delivered a universal message of good-humored bawdiness. Pippa realized that even for the older married women, there was something inherently exciting about readying a new bride for her husband.

With much giggling and sighing, they stripped her naked and bathed her in warm spring water steeped in fragrant herbs. One girl explained, in a dense brogue, that morning dew had been added to the bathwater in order to keep her skin beautiful. Pippa luxuriated; baths were still a novelty to her and the gentle care of womenfolk even newer yet. Sibheal, the local midwife, had strong, capable, cosseting hands. With wry laughter, she told of assisting the birth of the O Donoghue Mór, pantomiming hilariously the prodigious size—in all aspects—of the future chieftain.

The merriment continued to surge and lull like a friendly breeze. When Sibheal helped her from the tub to dry her and comb her hair, Pippa sensed a soft shock of memory. Just for a moment, she felt cosseted in a way that evoked the faint bittersweetness of a distant dream. Was it the barely remembered touch of a mother? The sensation fled quickly, and Pippa smiled, but her heart pounded with the realization that she had almost recalled her mother.

The other two maids rubbed her with rose oil until her skin was soft and supple. They draped her in a gauzy garment of fine white linen. It fit loosely, sliding down over her collarbones.

Sibheal pulled it up at the neckline and clucked her tongue. "We need a jewel to fasten this."

"I have just the thing." Pippa fetched her bag, which looked worn and paltry in the clean, well-swept chamber. She took out the broken ornament of gold. "This will hold it."

Sibheal pinned up the shoulder of the tunic, and Pippa sent her a grateful smile. Though plundered of its jewels, the brooch was the only link she had with a past she did not know. Even so, she drew a measure of comfort from wearing it on her wedding night.

The women fussed with her hair a little more until it was a mass of springy curls crowned by fresh marigolds. Then, curtsying and backing toward the door, the two younger maids left.

Sibheal took her to a lofty private chamber high on the main keep above the great hall. A wreath of hawthorn adorned the door. The women had decked the bridal chamber with garlands of fragrant wildflowers. The bedstead was huge and luxuriant, a carved oaken headboard and great linen swags cloaking the interior in fragrant mystery. In the hangings and bedclothes, the women had tucked small offerings—bundles of herbs and dried petals—to bring luck and bounty to the newly wedded couple.

After Sibheal had left, Pippa stood in the middle of the room and simply stared. "Bedding is a serious matter," she said faintly.

"That it is, my dear." With his raiments flapping loose like broken wings, Revelin stepped into the room, followed by two barefoot acolytes who tripped over their robes as they peered at the bride.

She blushed but gave them a smile of pure happiness. Let them look their fill. Let them know what a woman looked like when her dreams were finally coming true. She was the wife of the O Donoghue Mór.

One of the lads circled the room, swinging a censer that gave forth intermittent puffs of richly perfumed incense; the other held a basin of holy water. Revelin took a green rowan branch, dipped it in the water and sprinkled the bed while calling down blessings. "Our help is in Thee, O Lord, who made heaven and earth. Bless this bed, that all lying in it may rest in Thy peace, and preserve and grow old and multiply in length of days, amen."

Then, looking sheepish, he turned to Pippa. "I suppose the rowan branch is a mite pagan."

She drew in a nervous breath. "I'll take all the blessings I can get."

Revelin came and stood before her, tall and straight, his white hair and beard giving him a lordly dignity even as the twinkle in his eyes belied the severe look. "I never had a daughter," he whispered, "but if I did, I would pray God she was like you."

She raised herself on tiptoe and kissed his cheek. "I never knew my father," she confessed, "but now I feel as if I do. Thank you, Revelin."

He laid the palm of his hand on her forehead and murmured something in Gaelic. Then he was gone, and she stood alone in the room.

Two candles burned in holders attached to the bedstead, and a few coals glowed in a brazier. Everything looked rich and golden. She felt pampered and delicate, a princess in a charmed tower, the air heavy with promise. All was just as she had dreamed it would be, except for one minor detail.

She had never imagined that she would be afraid.

She was afraid; that much he could see right away.

Aidan stood in the doorway of the tower chamber and drank in the sight of her. Or at least what he could see of her. With her back turned, her head slightly bent, she lingered near the window.

Garbed in gauzy white fabric and intriguing shadows, she looked as slim and straight as a beechwood sapling. Her hair spilled over her shoulders and neck, and a circlet of flowers rested on the springy mass.

"You left the feast early." His throat felt strained. "The harper dinned us for at least another hour." A small lie, that. He had not been in the hall, either, but closeted in his office with Donal Og and Revelin, working out the documents that would govern Pippa's future when he died. He would leave her with the Ross Castle treasure and a safe conduct to England, to Blackrose Priory in Hertfordshire, the home of Oliver and Lark de Lacey.

"Aidan?" She broke in on his musings, and he was grateful, for they were melancholy thoughts.

He had not anticipated being so aroused by her appearance, but he was. By now he should know that the unanticipated was commonplace where Pippa was concerned.

Her only reaction to the sound of his voice was a stiffening of her spine.

"It's all right, *a gradh*," he said, crossing the room to stand behind her. "You can turn around. It's only me, remember? Aidan."

She moved as if an opposing force held her back—slowly, painstakingly, until finally she was facing him. "Only you?" she asked. "As in, only the O Donoghue Mór, Lord of Castleross, descendant of kings? I must be out of my mind. I don't belong here."

Despite her challenging speech, he could not answer her right away. He was too busy staring. She was perfect. Too beautiful. It was not the remote perfection of a marble statue, but the vibrant appeal of a bride of the *sidhe*. She was warm and glowing, her lips full, the lower one vulnerable, her eyes wide and uncertain.

"My lord?" She folded her arms across her middle as if to shield herself. "Why do you look at me so?"

He sank down on one knee. "To God, you are lovely, lass. You look like a fairy maiden, all white and gold and pure as the rain."

She bit her lip and gazed at him with a worried look. "And that's supposed to put me at my ease?"

He laughed softly, coming to his feet. "I was being honest, my love. You have a curious effect on me. It's not often I burst out with dramatic poesies or tributes to beauty."

"Being considered a beauty is very new to me." A shy smile flirted about her mouth. "It didn't happen until I met you."

It was all he could do to hold his hands at his sides, to keep from devouring her with his eyes. "And now. May I touch you, my lady of Castleross, or are you going to make me suffer?"

Her smile widened, changing from wistful to impish. "You mean I have a choice?"

He nodded, wondering where he found the strength to endure his need. "By rights I should fling you on your back and have my way with you, regardless of your preferences. However, you bring out an honor I never knew I possessed."

"Really?"

"Truly. I will do nothing to hurt you. I will touch when you say touch and stop when you say stop."

She took a deep breath and moved toward the bed, halting in the pool of candlelight by the headboard. "Why would I say something so foolish as stop?"

He swallowed past a painful dryness in his throat. "It will be your prerogative. And my challenge."

Just then, one of the fat white candles on the headboard sputtered and flared higher, brightening the room. Her gown was, in a way, more enticing than total nudity. It clung to the tips of her breasts, and the light shone through, revealing the high, rounded shapes. The draping fell to her hips, where it clung once more, outlining the shadow of her womanhood.

A groan burst from him. "Pippa, for the love of God, tell me I can touch you! You're taking me apart."

She stepped toward him and pressed her small, warm palms to his chest. Her eyes widened when she detected the racing cadence of his heart.

"There is something so appealing about frankness," she said.

"I could not possibly hide my desire for you," he admitted. Ah, God, he was hard. Hot. Aching for her. Was this her idea of torture? "Well?" His voice rasped like a rusty hinge.

She kept her hands in place. The heat radiated from there, burning him. "I do not want you to touch me."

A groan of frustrated outrage ripped from him. "For Christ's sake, woman—"

"Touching is not enough," she continued with almost painful honesty. "I want more than that, more than touching. I want you around me, inside me, all through me. Do you understand?"

He could only nod. What good had he done, what marvel had he performed, that God had given him this woman?

He would be a fool to tempt his good fortune, so he left the question unanswered and slipped his arms around her. His embrace was deliberately restrained; he teased and enticed them both with what was to come. Slowly he traced his finger down the side of her cheek, ran it along her jaw, stopping under her chin to turn her mouth up for his kiss.

Like a flower in full bloom she was, her lips damp and ripe, unfolding for him, falling open to receive him. His mouth devoured her, drank from her, and she was the sweetest delight he had ever tasted.

He had kissed her before, aye, but always those kisses

had been marred by creeping guilt. This was the kiss of a new husband to his new wife, of a man who adored the woman in his arms.

She pressed herself against him, making a sound of startlement when she encountered the evidence of his need. He slid one hand down her back and cupped her closer still. After long moments, his mouth left hers to trail down her throat. She arched back to give more of herself to him; she hooked one leg around him. If not for their clothes, they would be fully joined.

"Ah," she whispered, "Aidan…"

"Are you all right? Am I… Is this uncomfortable?"

She straightened and dug her fingers into his hair. "I had no idea a man was—" She flushed and looked away.

He was intrigued now. He kissed her ear and whispered, "Was what? Go on with what you were saying."

"Well, of course I heard bawdy jokes about it, but I simply didn't realize your—his—you know—"

He chuckled softly, though given his present state, mirth was slightly excruciating. "You're not making yourself clear, my sweet."

She took a deep breath. "I was just startled to find that what I thought of as a rather benign body part could turn into such an interesting, uh, tool."

He pulled back, all but shaking with laughter. "Tool," he repeated.

She thrust up her chin. "I have heard it called more ridiculous names than that. Some men even christen theirs."

"We wouldn't want a total stranger making all our decisions for us."

Her embarrassment dissolved into giggles, which then relaxed into a dreamy, comforted smile, this one totally devoid of the fear he had sensed in her when he had first come into the room.

Thank God, he thought. He had banished her fear. Now there was room for nothing but pleasure. Even so, he knew her state of trust was fragile. It took all his restraint to move slowly.

He touched the ugly golden brooch at her shoulder. "May I?"

She nodded. "Of course."

Just for a moment, the meaning of the brooch stung him with guilt. He forced away the feeling and unclasped the pin. The garment slid, with a whisper of protest, to the floor. He felt a fresh blast of heat. "You may call me interesting," he said, "but that doesn't begin to describe what I see when I look at you."

"It must have been the bath. Or the oil of roses."

"Ah, love," he said, "it's you. Simply you." He was surprised to hear a catch in his voice. The truth was, she moved him—to something beyond need and passion. When he looked at her, standing quietly in the candlelight, he felt an emotion so pure and sweet that his soul trembled.

With unsteady hands he removed his shirt, then stood looking at her while she looked back, and the silence, thick with desire, hung between them.

"Now what?" she whispered after a time, her gaze traveling over his scars. "Why do you hesitate?"

"Because I don't know what to do with a woman like you." He cradled her cheek in his palm. "You conquered your fear of this night, but it seems mine is just beginning."

"You're afraid?"

"Aye." Her cheek felt like satin against his rough hand. "I want tonight to be perfect."

Her breath caught, and he was shocked to feel the heated dampness of a tear on his hand. "Don't you see?"

she whispered. "It's already perfect. I knew it when you said you'd never been with a woman you loved."

A groan tore from his throat as he slid his arms around her, reveling in the warm, silky feel of her unclad body and burying his face in her hair. "You make it all so simple, *a gradh.*" He pushed her gently back so that she reclined upon the bed, watching him through a golden haze of candleglow while he bent to remove his boots and trews.

Ah, she did make it simple. She, who had never belonged to anyone, now belonged in his heart. And he, who had never been loved, now looked into her eyes and saw that she adored him.

So why was he still afraid?

As he lay beside her and felt the glorious length of her curl against him, the answer flashed like a spark through his mind.

He knew the truth about her past; he knew the answers she craved. Yet he dared not give Pippa her heart's desire for fear of losing her sooner than he had to.

Then she draped her slim arms around his neck, and the spark died, and he knew only the need to bring her joy. And ah, she made it easy. Slim and supple and warm, she was like a tender sapling in springtime, drawn to him, basking in his touch as if he were the sun.

He braced himself on one elbow and settled his mouth over hers. His hand skimmed downward, circling her breasts and belly, outlining the curve of a hip and then the smoothness of her inner thigh. At his gentle pressure, her legs parted slightly, shyly, and he stifled a gasp at the excitement that singed him.

Something about her coaxed tenderness from him. Long after most men would have flung her down and plunged in, he loved her with his mouth and hands and endearments whispered in Gaelic. His tongue wrote love words on her skin, until she gasped with pleasure or cried out with a burst of joy.

"Ah, sweetheart," he said, "I want to touch you so deeply. But I don't want to hurt you."

"It's the wanting that hurts," she said, "not the touching."

He covered her with the whole hard length of his body. "How deliciously naive you are," he whispered, nipping at her earlobe. In Gaelic he added, "And I mean to take shameless advantage of that."

"But you are such a good teacher," she said, and then, also in Gaelic, "And I am a fast learner."

For a moment he was too stunned to react, and then he laughed softly into her ear. "Wench. How long have you spoken Gaelic?"

She lowered her head and licked a ridge of scars on his chest. Her mouth and tongue seared him, and he gasped with the pleasure of it. "I'll let you wonder."

"Then I'll leave you to wonder…" He lapsed back into Irish, and using terms she could not possibly know, he described in explicit, loving detail exactly what he wanted to do to her.

"I haven't a clue what you said," she admitted, her hands drifting down, lingering over his hips, "but I wish you would hurry."

"Nay, I'll not hurry. We have all night."

"But—"

"Hush. Trust me."

"I only meant—"

He pressed his fingers to her lips. "You talked all the way through our first kiss and nearly ruined it. And wasn't it so much better once you fell silent?"

Her mouth gaped beneath her fingers. "I cannot believe you remember our first kiss."

"How could I not? It changed my life."

With a choked cry, she flung her arms around his neck. "Mine, too. Ah, Aidan, I do love you so much."

He felt no surprise to hear her say it at last. He had known for a long time that she loved him, but he had also understood why she had resisted telling him. She feared abandonment. The fact that she would confess her love now could mean only one thing. She believed that he would never leave her. And he never would, not willingly.

But there were some things he could not control.

Pushing away the thought, he indulged his every urge to kiss and caress her, preparing her so thoroughly to receive his love that a flush swept her entire body. She lifted herself against him and rocked her hips in an unconscious, impatient rhythm.

Nearly mindless with desire, he knew he could not hold himself in check much longer. He tested her with a gentle, questing hand, loving the warm velvet smoothness of her, the flower-petal softness of her untried flesh, and the rush of damp heat that told him she was as ready as he.

He settled himself over her, stirred to near madness by the brush of her breasts against his chest and the wholly natural way her legs opened and then enclosed him as if their two bodies were parts designed to fit perfectly to form one whole. He lifted himself and paused, gazing down into a face that looked more beautiful to him than the sun, and then he kissed her softly, letting his tongue show her what their bodies would do. She whimpered and clasped him with her legs, drawing him closer. The need and the heat lit his soul with fire.

"More," she whispered between kisses, and then she sucked on his tongue, nearly causing him to lose control. "More," she murmured. "All of it. *Now*."

He drew closer still, yet hesitated, so reluctant to cause her pain that he nearly shook with the effort. He felt an almost blasphemous urge to worship her. Whatever he had expected of her, it was not this absolute and unquestioning generosity, nor this frank and compelling passion. Yet she gave him this and more with a selflessness that left him speechless with wonder. She had sparked a fire in the dark night of his soul, and every move he made, every touch and kiss, was designed to show her what she meant to him.

For a moment longer he held off, drawing back to look at her one last time in innocence.

Finally he buried himself in her giving warmth, and she cried out and surrounded him. When her maidenhead broke, her eyes opened wide, and her unsteady sigh was one not of pain, but of welcome, as if she understood that the moment bound their hearts forever.

He began moving with slow strokes that took him to the very limit of his control. She tilted herself with an instinct driven by love and desire, and his hand drifted down to help her, for he knew what she was reaching for even if she did not.

He touched her in a place that made her gasp and shudder, and then she dug her fingers into his back while long, silky spasms closed around him. Her abandon and pleasure would have coaxed a response from a stone, and Aidan, being flesh and blood, was far less resistant. He cupped her churning hips with his big hands and pressed himself home, indulging the need that had scalded him. His rush of pleasure was so intense and prolonged that it felt a bit as he imagined ascending to heaven would be—he saw naught but a blinding brilliance behind his eyes, and the entire universe seemed to shrink until it was encompassed by the small, passionate woman beneath him, who clasped him as if she would never let go.

He relaxed and settled over her and waited for his pulse and breathing to return to normal. Instead, he felt as hot and driven as ever.

"Ah," he said, nuzzling aside a sweat-damp lock of her hair so that he could whisper in her ear. "Are you all right, my love?"

"No," she said in a small, frightened voice.

He raised his head and stared down at her. "You're hurt? Do you need your maids, or—"

"Aidan, calm yourself." She brushed his cheek with a trembling hand. "All I need is you."

Worried that he had damaged her in some way, he lay beside her carefully and drew up the covers. He smoothed the wild, tumbled hair from her face to find that her cheeks were wet with tears, her eyes wide and haunted.

"My love, talk to me, please."

She gave him a wobbly smile. "I never thought I would hear you beg me to speak."

"I love to hear you talk. I always have. I even like your singing."

She sighed. "You are so good to me. So good. Please don't let my tears upset you. It's all so overwhelming. I'm not sad and I don't hurt. It's just that I never realized, never imagined, how sweet it could be for a man and woman to make love."

He pressed his lips to her temple. "You give me much relief."

She tangled her fingers in his long hair. "If I had known it would be like this, I would have worked harder to seduce you long ago."

"Ah. Then we shall have to make up for lost time."

"I agree completely, Your Eminence."

Ah, she was a joy to him in this dark time. Thus far, he had succeeded in avoiding thoughts of the future. What he had done was best for her. She would understand that when the time came.

She stroked him boldly with her hand, and his instantaneous reaction took his breath away.

"Again?" His whisper was a harsh, disbelieving rasp. "Now?"

"Yes," she said. "Show me that the first time was not a mischance, Aidan. Show me that it will always be like this for us."

"But it won't, *a stor.*"

Her face fell. "It won't?"

"Nay." His hand coasted down the length of her body, discovering softness, dampness, readiness. "I shall find as many ways to love you as there are stars in the sky."

And while the harper played in the hall below, Aidan blew out the candles and made good on his promise.

From the Annals of Innisfallen

—◦⟨◦⟩◦—

And may the Almighty King of Heaven strike me entirely cold and eternally dead if I have done wrong.

I have known Aidan O Donoghue since the moment he took his first living breath, holding him in my grateful hands and weeping like a maiden aunt while the birth blood still clung to him.

When I dared, when Ronan O Donoghue was looking the other way, I gave the lad the father's love Ronan denied him. Never has it been my wont to question this, but I have always felt responsible for the boy's happiness.

Some would say I overstep my bounds, that I should sit back with a distant chronicler's eye and let the events of his life unfold. Ah, meddlesome knave that I am, I lost my objectivity decades ago.

So they are married. So they will snatch a little joy from the hard troubles that await them. Is that such a bad and wicked crime?

—Revelin of Innisfallen

Fourteen

Pippa became superstitious about counting the days or even the hours of her life with Aidan at Ross Castle. Some apprehensive, small part of her said not to tempt fate by examining her contentment too closely or questioning her worthiness of it.

She refused to look to the future, to dwell on the fact that Richard de Lacey's forces had withdrawn to Killarney town, obviously to regroup and await reinforcements.

Like a dreamer borne on a cloud, she drifted through each day, singing until the other residents cringed. She learned, with clumsy earnestness, her duties as Lady of Castleross.

Hands that could juggle anything from pears to dead fish could not seem to master the intricacies of spinning and sewing. Finally Sibheal took pity on her and told her the household would be better served if she would simply supervise the work. Preferably from a great distance.

The comments were made in high good humor, and Pippa flung her arms wide while Sibheal and the others laughed in relief.

Aidan found them thus one morning after breakfast.

His booted steps rang ominously on the stone floor of the hall. "What is this?" he shouted.

The women froze and gaped at him. Without warning, he grabbed Pippa around the waist. "I never thought to hear ladies' laughter in my hall ever again," he said.

The women dissolved into giggles and whispers. Pippa's heart seemed to fill her chest, expanding with rampant happiness.

"My lord, Sibheal was just commenting on my skill at spinning."

"If it is anything like your skill at singing, she has my sympathy."

Forcing herself to scowl, she pushed away from him. "You're a bad and cruel husband, Aidan O Donoghue," she said, imitating his brogue.

"Am I, now?" His brows lifted over eyes bluer than Lough Leane. "That is a sad pity, then, my lady, for I suppose it means I cannot show you your surprise."

She clutched the front of his tunic. "Surprise! Ah, what a quick, sharp tongue I have. I am your adoring wife, and you are the grandest of husbands."

He thumbed his nose at her flattery. The maids who understood English all but fell off their stools with mirth. Aidan caught her against him. "See them smile on us, my love. Now that you are here, it is like the spring again after a long, bleak winter."

His words touched her like a caress. Her mirth disappeared, for she understood that his winter was his marriage to Felicity. "Come, my lord." She drew him toward the steps leading out of the hall. "You promised me a surprise."

"So I did," he said.

His presence was like an invisible buoy beneath her, lifting her up and sweeping her along, filling her with a warmth she had never felt before.

She did not know it was possible to feel all the things she was feeling. It was like discovering a new color in a rainbow or seeing a falling star—unanticipated, utterly thrilling.

As they crossed the bawn together, waving to Sorley Boy Curran and his brother, she squeezed his hand and said, "In sooth I don't need surprises, Aidan. I can think of nothing that could make me happier than I am now—Oh!"

She stopped and stared. There, in front of the stone and thatch stables, stood a boy holding the reins of a horse, saddled and ready to ride.

"It's a mare from Connemara, my love," said Aidan. "She is yours."

Pippa took a step toward the horse. She was magnificent, dun colored with shadowy black furnishings.

"Well?" he asked with endearing eagerness. "What think you?"

"She is the most beautiful horse I've ever seen. But you know what a poor rider I am."

"Not a poor rider." He walked her to the horse and placed his hands at her waist. "Just inexperienced."

Before she knew what was happening, he lifted her up and placed her in the lady's saddle. After she had hooked her leg around the bow, the seat felt as comfortable as a chair in a dining hall.

As always, the great height took her aback, and she clutched at the mare's mane. A groom brought out another horse, and Aidan mounted and smiled across at her. "Shelagh was bred and trained to be a lady's mount. I think you'll be pleased."

"Where are we going?"

He didn't answer, but the brief, smoldering look he gave her provided a hint. He had an uncanny ability to speak through his eyes alone; she could look at him and hear him telling her without words that she was beautiful, that he desired to please her and that she made him happy.

Only occasionally did she notice secretive shadows in his eyes, and she dared not speak of them. For the first time in her life, she was truly happy, and though she knew it was selfish, she wanted nothing to disrupt the delicate balance of their lives.

She refused to see the English forces camped outside Killarney, refused to acknowledge the worried looks Revelin had shot her last time she had visited him at Innisfallen.

With a guilty start, she thought of the letter that had been delivered from Dublin the day before. O Mahoney had looked so grave and hopeless when he had handed it to her, explaining that the lord deputy had learned that a thief was diverting Crown revenues from Kerry. No doubt they would hold Aidan responsible for that as well.

She would worry about that later, she vowed. But not now. Not when he was gazing at her with such sweet promise in his eyes. She wanted their idyll to last forever.

No, admitted a little voice inside her head. *It is not as simple as that.* She wanted an answer to the one question she was afraid to ask: Did Aidan truly love her?

Part of her had to believe that he did, for she felt protected and cherished when she was with him. But another part, a small, cold, dark place inside her, whispered doubts through her mind. What did she know of love? No one had ever loved her; how could she possibly know what it was?

That same evil whisper planted another doubt. All her life, she had been abandoned by every friend she had found. How could she be certain Aidan was different?

She couldn't.

Let the marriage bond be enough for now, she scolded herself. Let it be enough.

They rode across the causeway and along the shores of Lough Leane. It was high summer, and the woods were canopied and carpeted by leaf and moss and fern and lichen in a vivid, glowing green. The rich, earthy smell of the forest filled the air. The lake was as blue and deep as a sapphire jewel.

"So much beauty," she said. "It almost overwhelms the senses."

"Aye," he said, and he was looking not at the lake, but at her.

They headed up a twisting, sloping path, and after a while it seemed they were the only people on earth, so remote were they. She heard the *churr* of a pheasant and a rustle of leaves as some small animal scuttled for cover, but other than the thump of hooves and the occasional snort of a horse, the forest was silent.

They followed a stream over a bed of rocks, and after a time she detected a low, distant roar. Intrigued, she craned her neck to look ahead. Aidan reined his horse and motioned for her to ride on.

The change was so dramatic that it took her breath away. On either side of the path, trees clad in emerald moss soared like pillars. The high branches formed a vault overhead, where sunlight filtered through and filled the air with hazy warmth. Then, farther up the path, the branches opened up to the summer sky, and she saw a surging cataract. It sprang from a great cleft in the mountain and hurled outward with such force that the stream was pure white, spraying and tumbling down from the heights. On the rocks below, a fine mist filled the air and made rainbows in the great bars of sunlight.

"This is Torc Falls," he said, dismounting and then helping her down. "Some will tell you it's a place of powerful magic."

As her feet touched the loamy mat of leaves and moss, she smiled up at him. "I do not doubt that in the least."

He chuckled as he tethered the horses to a branch, where they could browse in the tender shoots beside the roaring stream. "A Sassenach who believes in Irish magic?"

"Absolutely." She ran and hugged him, loving the solid feel of him against her. He was her gentle protector, everything she had always thought a man should be and everything she had never dared to dream a husband could be.

She lifted her face to his. "Is this not powerful magic?"

"It is." He kissed her tenderly, his big hands holding her as if she were a treasure. "And aye, my lady, you have become my favorite form of enchantment."

"Aidan!" She lifted herself on tiptoe to kiss him. "I do love you beyond words."

"Ah. I've never seen you lack for words. And aren't you the saucy wench who said she did not love me?"

She sniffed. "If that is what you prefer, then no. I do not love you." She pushed her hands inside his mantle and splayed them across his chest. "Is that clear, my lord?"

He took in a sharp breath. "Aye, that it is. You have a very powerful way of not loving me."

"Wait till you see what I can do when I *do* love you."

She removed his cloak and then her own, spreading them on the springy ground in a golden green haze of sunlight. "Come here, and I'll show you more."

Intoxicated by the rarefied air, she felt brazen and unfettered, as free as a bird soaring from a cliff. Item by item, she removed his clothes, laughing at his astonishment and then soliciting his help in disrobing.

There was something pagan and delightful and, aye, magical about standing naked in the open forest, with sunlight and mist swirling about them. She had an uncanny feeling of rightness, as if heathen powers had ordained their union, as if the very elements themselves sanctioned their love.

They stood facing each other, and she could see that he, too, felt the extraordinary invisible forces pulsing around them. Perhaps aeons ago, when the world was young, two different lovers had come together in this silent, mist-filled sanctuary.

"Aidan," she said, the single word heavy with emotion. She put her hands upon his chest and feathered her fingers over the thick, long-healed scars there. "You have never told me about these."

He lifted one side of his mouth in a half smile. "I thought Iago would. He tells you everything else."

"He has the same pattern of scars."

"It's part of a manhood rite performed by the people of his mother's tribe. I was at a very impressionable age when I first met him. I found his scars most interesting."

She brushed her fingers over him and felt a surge of wanting. "I think I understand."

Low laughter rumbled from him. "To make a long story short, my own scars are the result of a boring sea voyage, a large flask of poteen and an excess of male pride."

She took a step closer. "It must have hurt terribly."

"Not half so much as the hiding my father gave me when he saw what I had done."

He spoke lightly, but she heard the undertone of resentment in his voice.

"You're much like me," she said. "You were abandoned, too, in a way."

"Only the one who abandoned me stayed near, so that I felt his displeasure every day of my life."

"It is a wonder we even know how to love," she said.

"You make it easy."

She leaned forward and pressed her lips to the ridge of scars that ran along the broadest part of his chest. She flicked her tongue out, and he gasped and went rigid. The idea that her touch could hold him filled her with a heady sense of mastery. The feeling of liberation drove her to boldness, and she swirled her hands around and over him, her caress an eloquent statement of her love. Lower she went, eliciting a delicious gasp from him as her hands and then her lips found him. Unfettered by timidity, she loved him with a boldness she had never thought herself capable of. She carried on until he loosed a hoarse sound—a cry of pleasure, a cry for mercy. He pulled her up and kissed her hungrily, and then they lay back upon the spread-out cloaks and she impaled herself upon him. She found the rhythm he had taught her, and while his hands traced her breasts and shoulders, she lifted and rode, controlling the pace until at last it controlled her, possessed her, and she could do no more than ride the crest.

She poured her love out to him, and she was like the great cataract surging from the heart of the mountain, exploding outward and splintering into a rainbow-hued mist.

When he pulsed into her moments later, she collapsed onto his chest and lay still, listening to the thud of his heart and feeling dazed.

Finally, with the gentleness she had loved about him from the start, he brought her to lie beside him, cradling her in the circle of his arms.

"You are," he said at last, "quite remarkable."

She gave a shaky laugh. "I am acting by instinct alone. Thank God you are a patient man." She smiled as latent pulses of pleasure coursed softly through her. She felt the warmth and passion all through her, at its deepest where her heart was. Out of her dazed contentment came a stunning thought, and she lifted her head to look at him.

"I wonder if we have made a baby yet."

His reaction was unexpected. Although he still held her in his arms, he seemed to withdraw ever so slightly. "I suppose we won't know that for some weeks."

She kissed his jaw. "I used to long for a child," she said. "I always told myself if I had a babe of my own, I would never, ever abandon him. I would love him and lavish attention on him and hold him so close to my heart that he would never fear I'd leave him."

"Ah, Pippa." He stroked her cheek. "And do you still feel that longing?"

"Well." She turned over and cupped her chin in her hands. "It is not so much a longing anymore. It is an expectation." A flush crept up her throat. "After all, we are both quite healthy, and we've been—that is, each night—"

"And day," he reminded her.

"Aye, we have most faithfully done our duty—" She stopped and broke into peals of laughter. "You know exactly what I mean, Aidan O Donoghue, so I'll not continue that awkward speech. We will have babies, and they'll grow up strong and happy—"

She broke off again. The change in him was so subtle that she almost missed it, but she saw a somberness come over him. His eyes darkened to the color of the lake in shadow.

A chill shot through her. "Aidan?"

"Aye, beloved?"

"You don't think this can last, do you?"

He fell still and studied her for long moments. Torc Falls crashed ceaselessly into the silence that hung between them. At last he pushed himself up with the heels of his hands. "We had best be getting back." Very tenderly, he helped her don her clothing, then put on his trews.

She sat back on her heels and clutched his hand. "It is worse for you to ignore my question, Aidan. You're frightening me."

He sat down, facing her directly. Shirtless, his chest marked, his hair flowing back over his shoulders, he looked like a savage god, the lord of the grove, who had the power to change the seasons.

As she gazed into his deep, sad eyes, she understood at last.

"Damn you," she whispered.

"Pippa—"

She wrenched her hands from his grip. "You've been deceiving me. *Again.*"

"Ah, beloved, I—"

"You never spoke to me of your worries. And I, fool that I am, never let myself ask. You made me believe everything would be all right."

Her tirade elicited a weary smile from him. "Is that not what a husband should do? Pippa, listen. You are so spritely and clever. Always with you I feel clumsy and inept. My heart tells me to protect you. Is that so wrong?"

"Yes. It is when something is eating away at you inside. You cannot keep things from me. When I wed you, it was to share your sorrows as well as your joys. Anything less is not fair to me. Anything less relegates me to the status of a child—an ignorant, spoiled child."

He rested his hands atop her shoulders. "So what shall

I do, Pippa? What is it that you want to hear from me?" A tempest stormed in his eyes. "You want to share my fears, is that what you want?"

His passion took her aback. She felt a niggling of fear, but she looked him in the eye and said, "Yes."

"I tried to explain this when you first said you wanted to marry. Our victory in reclaiming Ross Castle is only temporary. The Sassenach will return to take it back. Fortitude Browne holds me responsible for Felicity's death, and who is to say I am without guilt?"

"The woman took her own life," Pippa said desperately.

"Because of me. That is not something I can shrug off. Nor will Constable Browne."

"You can't be sure. Perhaps—"

"Ah, deny it, then," he said. "You asked. You insisted on knowing."

She turned away, feeling as if she had been struck.

He stood and finished dressing. When they were both ready, he lifted her onto her horse. By that time, all the anger had left him.

And all the magic had left the grove.

He gave her a rueful smile. "Do you see why I kept my fears in?"

She kissed him. "Aye, but you shouldn't have. This news doesn't mar my love for you. It deepens it. Can you understand that?"

He brought her hand to his lips and kissed it. "Then we'll speak no more of it."

One morning in early autumn, the news arrived with a cruel swiftness that took Aidan like a blow to the stomach. Donal Og arrived with the tidings.

Aidan was with Pippa in the counting office, showing

her ways to reckon the winter stores. Though she knew it not, he foresaw a day when she would have to carry on without him, and he wanted her well prepared. Each day she grew more precious to him and more beautiful to his eyes. There was an aura about her, a glow; she was like a rare jewel with the light behind it, sparkling and gorgeous to behold.

Aye, that glow. That had been missing when he had first met her. He considered it a small miracle that his love had put it there.

He went cold inside when Donal Og approached. His cousin took long, loose strides, looking ever the giant of legend, his shoulders stiff and hunched.

Aidan bent to kiss his wife and then stepped outside into the guardroom. He and Donal Og stopped and stared at one another. It was painful for Aidan to read defeat in his cousin's face.

"What news from Killarney?" he asked, bracing himself.

Donal Og leaned back against a wall. "It's not good. Fortitude Browne has slapped a heavy fine on all the cottagers. A punitive act due to the insurrection last spring. And he has banned mass for seven weeks."

Aidan swore. "The jack-dog. Faith is the only thing those people have left."

Donal Og glanced inside the counting office. Pippa sat at the exchequer's table, her head bent, absorbed in Aidan's ledgers and counting rods. He jerked his head toward a path that led out of the keep to the shores of the lake.

"So it gets worse," Aidan said once they were outside.

Donal Og, the largest, strongest, most fearless man in Kerry, sank to the ground and buried his face in his hands. "'Tis over, Aidan. No matter how hard we struggle, they will break us. There are too many of them."

Aidan's heart pounded. He had never seen his cousin so full of grim fatalism. "I think you'd best start at the beginning. What do they plan?"

"To crush us like ants beneath their boots. The reinforcements have arrived. It's a fleet of eight ships, Aidan. And more soldiers marched in from the Pale."

"Coupled with the forces of Richard de Lacey, that gives them an army at least five times the size of our own," said Aidan.

Donal Og picked up a rock, stood and flung it so far into the lake that Aidan did not see it drop. "It's clear they want a surrender without resistance."

Aidan stood listening to the roar of blood in his ears. His world was crumbling; he could lose Pippa. When he thought of never again hearing the sound of her laughter, seeing the morning sun on her face, holding her while she slept, he felt like a man on the verge of dying. "Surrender without resistance." He raised grim eyes to Donal Og. "This is a bit of a change for the Sassenach, is it not?"

Donal Og nodded. "In the past they took high delight in putting the Irish to the sword. What do you suppose this new offer of mercy means?"

"I fear it's as you said. It is over. The Sassenach will come whether we fight or surrender. The dilemma now is to hope for terms that treat the people as men, not slaves." Unbidden, an image of Richard de Lacey flashed in his mind. He was Sassenach, aye, but he possessed a core of humanity that was rare in an Englishman living in Ireland.

More hopeful than that was the news that Richard had taken an Irish wife. Shannon MacSweeney was a sturdy, stubborn woman; Aidan believed her fully capable of conquering the heart of her English husband.

He almost smiled, thinking of little Gaelic-speaking de Lacey children.

After a time, Iago found Donal Og and Aidan at the lakeshore. "There are some days," he said dangerously, "that I am tempted to get into a curragh and strike out for the horizon."

Aidan tried to smile. "That is quite a thought, my friend. To simply set sail and let the wind take us where it will."

Iago winked. "I would hope for San Juan. My Serafina still waits for me."

Donal Og snorted. "After all these years?"

Iago glared at him. "The heart does not count the years."

"That depends on what the lady has in mind."

"What news?" Aidan broke in impatiently.

Iago sobered. "A herald from the new English forces has arrived and waits in the hall."

Aidan did not stay to hear more. Filled with an icy calm, he hurried back to the keep.

A lone woman waited within. He stopped and stared at her in shock. She turned to him slowly, her face as serene as that of a goddess in a Florentine painting.

"My lady." He bowed over her extended hand. "It is an honor to welcome you."

The Contessa Cerniglia heaved a resigned sigh. "I know this is unusual, but I wanted to be the one to tell you. Is Pippa here?"

"Aye, my wife is in the counting office."

The contessa smiled. "Now there is news. I'd wager she is radiant."

He glanced at the parchment scroll she held in both hands. "For now." He led her to a chair and gave her a cup of mead.

She began to speak, and nothing she said surprised him. The English required total surrender. Whether he resisted or not, Ross Castle would fall to English hands and he would be forced to either leave or govern as an English vassal.

"So my only real choices," he said, "are to fight back or capitulate."

"Both will end the same," she said with true sympathy. "And if you surrender, there will be no loss of life."

None but my own, he thought. He said, "How can I trust the promises of the Sassenach?"

She took a long drink of her mead, then carefully set aside her goblet. "Because of the man who leads the English forces."

"Oh? And who is that? Surely not the rouged poppet Essex?"

"No. It is the Earl of Wimberleigh, Oliver de Lacey."

When Pippa was sound asleep that night, Aidan slipped away from the bed they shared. In silence, in the dark, he donned his tunic and trews, then carried his boots until he was outside. In the bailey, a wolfhound growled at him; he silenced the dog with a low, reassuring word.

He passed the cool, bleak hours the way he had passed many a troubled night. He took a boat and rowed himself to Innisfallen.

In the sanctuary of the chapel there, while the wind sang through the tall, narrow windows, he fell to his knees and tried to pray.

But instead of entreaties to the Almighty, his mind seethed with the news the contessa had brought.

Pippa still did not know, and the contessa had agreed that it was not her place to tell her. That decision, that agony, was for Aidan and Aidan alone.

The fact that Oliver de Lacey had come—and that he had brought his wife—confirmed what Aidan had suspected upon seeing the portrait of Lark. He had been waiting for the moment ever since sending them the message that their daughter lived.

Philippa de Lacey's parents had come for her.

But it was up to him to decide the terms of surrender.

Ah, surrender. Such an ordinary-sounding word. And now it encompassed his duties not only as the O Donoghue Mór, but as the husband of Lady Philippa de Lacey.

He reviewed what he and the contessa had learned. The family were of an ancient, respected line. Judging by the terms offered, Lord Oliver was more fair-minded than his peers. According to the contessa, the lord's wife was utterly beloved of all those who knew her.

"Ah, Christ." He brought his fists crashing down on the altar rail.

"An eloquent prayer, to be sure," said a wry voice.

Aidan stood and looked back toward the nave of the sanctuary. The gray predawn light picked out a tall, slim figure. "Don't you ever sleep, Revelin?"

"I'd not like to miss anything."

"It's my guess that you've missed nothing."

Revelin nodded, his long beard brushing his chest. "When I learned the name of the man leading the reinforcements, I knew he was the last missing piece to the puzzle. Have you decided what you'll do?"

Aidan glanced at the shadowy cross above the altar. He was glad he had confided in Revelin. "Almost."

"Ask yourself this," Revelin said. "What can the de Laceys give her that you cannot?"

"The security she has never known." The words came quickly, as if they had been waiting to be spoken. "They could spoil and cosset her. If she were free of me, she might one day find some proper English lord who would offer her the solidity of a settled life rather than sweeping her along on impossible adventures."

"So you're saying you can't stay at Ross Castle?"

"And be the pet spaniel of the Sassenach, performing for scraps?" With a sense of icy certainty, Aidan realized that every day Pippa stayed with him would sink her deeper into peril.

Revelin hesitated, then cleared his throat. "At least it would be a way to keep Philippa."

Aidan clenched his jaw. He had to force the words out. "Why would she even want me then?"

Revelin touched his shoulder. "Sometimes the most courageous thing is to know when to surrender, when to let go."

He threw off the comforting hand. He stalked past Revelin and rowed with savage strokes back to Ross Castle. Taking the stairs two and three at a time, he climbed to the highest parapet and burst out onto the walkway just as dawn was breaking.

This castle was the glory of the clan O Donoghue. It should represent the very pinnacle of his achievement.

How he despised it. He had from the start, when it had only been a minor peel house on the shores of Lough Leane. His father had been determined to turn it into a monument of defiance.

"You left me a legacy of hate," Aidan said between his teeth. He stepped up between two merlons and gazed outward from a dizzying height.

The dawn was bloodred. The bellies of the clouds beyond the mountains were heavy and swollen with a coming storm. But for now, the morning was clear and crimson. Already he could see the corrosive power of the

English landlords. Fields that used to roll on forever were becoming enclosed into neat, cold parcels. Churches stood empty except for the wind howling through them. Sacred images had been smashed, priests put to the sword or exiled to sea-scarred islands. Smallholdings and crofts disappeared like dust on a breeze.

For a moment the landscape parted like a curtain, and he saw the perfect oval face of Felicity as clearly as if she stood before him. She had died, and no one had paid the price.

How had she felt, falling all that way to her death?

Aidan imagined it was the way he felt now—wild, out of control, flung toward a destiny so certain it seemed almost preordained.

He took a last long look at the red dawn, and in his heart he knew there could be only one choice.

Pippa smiled in her sleep as Aidan's arms went around her. With her eyes still closed, she took a deep breath. The scent of the lake winds lingered in his hair.

She blinked herself awake and saw that it was barely dawn. "Where have you been?" she asked.

"Out on the parapet. Looking. Thinking." He reached past the bed hanging and handed her a cup of cold water. She drank deeply and gratefully.

There was no reason she should have felt it, but she sensed an edge of desperation. She put down her cup and hugged him, pressing her cheek to the warm hollow of his chest.

"I love you, Aidan," she whispered.

He plunged his fingers into her hair and turned her face up to his, kissing her thoroughly and hard. Within moments they were making love with a fervor that filled her with a strange sense of panic and joy.

He was not tender with her; she did not want him to be. He was intense and restless, like the waves pounding on the rocks at the shore. His love was a storm of raw emotion, and she wanted it, all of it, no holding back, no shielding her from its ruthless power.

There was a harsh beauty to his lovemaking. He turned her this way and that, his mouth and hands finding places of agonizing sensitivity. His excitement seemed to fill the entire room. The sky through the open window was on fire, and he was on fire, and his touch set her on fire.

He stroked her, and his mouth and tongue seared her until she cried out, first begging him to stop and in the next breath imploring him to go on.

When at last he mounted her, the sun had risen fully and the light glowed behind him, outlining his untamed, long hair and the raw desperation on his face.

"Now, yes, now," she said, lifting herself against him and sweeping their bodies together, completely engulfed by the maelstrom of his passion.

They clashed and separated, clashed and separated, loving enemies locked in loving battle, one that had no outcome save total surrender for both. He bent his head and kissed her neck, then kissed lower, harder, his teeth biting her. Some remote, observant part of her looked on in surprise. It was as if he wanted to brand her with the stamp of his passion. As if he wanted to mark her with an image that would never fade.

And ah, she wanted it, the rough pleasure, and she told him so with a harsh whisper in her ear. She crested higher and higher like a feather on the wind, and each time she thought he could not take her farther, he did, sweeping her so far she was afraid to look down, so high she was afraid the fall would kill her.

And then it didn't matter. She looked into his eyes and saw a flame of devotion that would never die, and her fear dissolved.

She cried out his name and flung her soul to the wind.

The fall was long and fast, and it ended with a strange crimson darkness that only later she discovered was created by her tightly closed eyes.

"Ah, Aidan." Her own voice sounded alien.

"Aye, beloved?" His did, too.

"I thought after all the times we've made love, you had shown me everything."

"And now?" A smile lightened his tone.

"I was wrong. It is new every time you make love to me. But particularly just now."

He kissed her, carefully settling his mouth on hers, gentle now and tender. "Did it disturb you?"

"No." Yet she could not deny a slowly awakening sense that something between them had changed. "I love you. Part of my love for you has to do with times like this. But—"

"What is it?" His gaze pierced her.

"It's silly. Never mind."

"Just tell me."

She hesitated, struggling to deny the thought. Finally she forced herself to speak. "You made love to me as if it were the last time."

Diary of a Lady

Ireland is more beautiful than I had ever imagined a place to be. The reports we heard in London concerned only the burned fields, the painted, shrieking warriors, the starving populace driven to violence.

Perhaps it was good fortune alone, for we saw only blue and green vistas, towering cliffs, sapphire lakes and emerald mountains. Ireland is a place where the unexpected comes true, so I suppose this is as good a place as any to face what I must face now.

Though Oliver pleaded with me to stay back in England and wait for word from him, I insisted on coming. The contessa was good company during the voyage, and she did her best to prepare me for the events to come.

Aye, she did her best.

But can a mother ever truly be prepared to meet, face-to-face, the daughter she had given up for dead twenty-two years before?

—Lark de Lacey,
Countess of Wimberleigh

Fifteen

"There is no easy way to tell you this," Aidan said. After breakfast, he had brought her to the most beautiful spot encompassed by Ross Castle. It was a lakeshore garden, wild with cattails and reeds, ducks and terns darting in and out of the marshes.

She looked up at him with the sweet, lazy smile of a woman who had been well and thoroughly loved and had, without regret, been awakened by a kiss before dawn.

A woman who had no idea she had been deceived.

"What is it, my love?" She bent and plucked a flower and tucked it behind her ear.

He hesitated, giving himself one last look at her while she still loved him. After he spoke, she would never regard him with such adoration again. It was like knowing he was seeing her for the last time. The total, open trust and acceptance would be gone in a few moments, so for now he gave in to selfishness, taking time to bask and indulge in her affection.

As he watched her watching him, he reflected that there was a sort of magnificence about their doomed love. A majestic, sweeping scope to it. Their passion was too huge and all-consuming to last as long as his dreams.

"Aidan?" She tilted her bright head to one side. "Why do you look at me so?"

"I have news," he said. "It concerns your family."

She sent him a melting smile. "You are my family."

"I mean the family you have been seeking."

An odd distress flickered in her eyes. He realized it was denial. "You are all I want or need," she said.

"Nay, it was your search for yourself that led you to me. Long ago, you asked me to help you find out just what occurred, how you happened to be lost at such a vulnerable age."

She paled. "What have you learned?"

He became very aware of the cool shadows, the blue scent of the lake and the way the morning light gilded her.

"I believe you are Lady Philippa de Lacey," he said. "Daughter of Oliver and Lark de Lacey, the Earl and Countess of Wimberleigh."

She made absolutely no movement. After several moments passed, he feared she had not heard.

Then finally she spoke in a dull, quiet voice. "Philippa de Lacey."

"Aye, my love."

"My parents are the Earl and Countess of Wimberleigh."

"Aye."

"And Richard?"

"Your younger brother." Now that he knew the truth, he wondered how he had failed to see the resemblance earlier. In looks, Richard de Lacey was a model of golden perfection, with an angelic smile and laughing eyes and a deep, unexpected cleverness. Donal Og was right. Pippa—or Philippa, as he should think of her now—was Richard's female equivalent.

"How did you find this out?"

"It started with the brooch you have. After you first showed it to me, I made a copy of the markings on the back. With the help of the contessa, I learned they were letters in the Cyrillic alphabet. The words are Russian. They mean 'blood, vows and honor.' It is a family motto."

He raked a hand through his hair. So much time had passed since that revelation.

Her breath caught. "That's a lie!"

"The words are the same as those spoken to you by the Gypsy woman."

"How did you decide it's a motto of the de Lacey family?" she inquired, her voice growing stronger.

"I saw a similar brooch in a portrait of the Lady Lark. It was painted twenty-five years ago. It had the ruby and twelve pearls, just as you told me." He wanted to pace but forced himself to stand still and continue. "The contessa learned that Lord and Lady Wimberleigh lost a daughter—their first child—in a storm at sea. They gave her up for dead."

"When did you find this out?"

"The day I was arrested and taken to the Tower."

"You've known since then." Her voice lifted in wonder. "How perfectly evil of you not to tell me." She pressed both hands to her stomach as if to quiet its churning.

"Pippa—"

"Of course you couldn't tell me," she went on, speaking in deadened tones. "Just as you couldn't tell me about your wife. You needed me to help you escape the Tower of London. You had to keep me in a helpless state of slavish devotion so I would do your bidding."

Her words, though spoken quietly, lashed out at him. He accepted their sting, absorbed it like the burn of a hot brand. "I deserved that. But truly, I was concerned for you. I wanted to be certain, so you would not raise false hopes. I wanted to be sure the de Laceys would accept you, not accuse you of being a fraud. And by the time we got here, I saw no point in telling you. For all I knew, you would never have the chance to meet your mother and father."

"Because after I helped you escape, I became an outlaw who can never return to England."

"True," he said.

"You made me an outlaw."

"True again. Pippa—"

"No!" For the first time, she shouted at him. "I want no more excuses. You found the answer to my dreams, and you didn't tell me."

"I'm sorry, beloved. I wanted to shield you from hurt."

A bitter laugh escaped her. "I find that odd, for I have never suffered such hurt as I have since meeting you. Tell me, why have you decided, all of a sudden, to reveal this to me now?"

It was almost too dramatic that, just as she spoke, a cloud obscured the sun and plunged the morning into a yellow-gray haze.

"They want to see you," he said. He had to trust that Lark and Oliver were as kind and loving as the contessa claimed. "They are in Killarney, waiting to meet you."

She shuddered. "My parents have come for me."

"Aye, my love."

"They gave me up for dead, and now they want to see me. To see if I am worthy of them. To see if my blood is blue enough."

He took a step forward, reaching to comfort her. His hands touched her shoulders. She pulled away, making an agonized sound in her throat.

His prediction that the revelation would destroy her love for him had come true. There was only one thing left to do to sever the ties completely.

"I think you should go to them."

Her head snapped up, and she gasped. Aye, that was the killing blow. The coup de grâce. Her love for him was dying before his eyes.

"Sweetheart," he said softly, "Oliver de Lacey has brought an army large enough to put all of Kerry to the sword. I am forced to come to terms with him."

"Am I part of those terms?"

"He would not be so crass as to state it."

Of course, she would know as well as Aidan did that it was one of the unspoken demands.

"Would you do something for me?" she asked in a small, cold voice.

"Yes, my love?"

She flinched at the endearment. "Would you please leave me be? Would you please today get out of my sight?"

He understood all too well what she needed. Her manner and countenance brought to mind a battle-shocked warrior, so emotionally devastated that thinking and feeling were dulled to sensation or constructive thought.

He watched her for a moment longer. She looked the same, yet not the same. She was his beloved golden Pippa, but something was different. The spark that lit her soul had died. She looked hollow, empty. A cold, beautiful vessel.

"Goodbye, my love," he said, and turned and walked away.

"I'm beginning to believe there's no such thing as dying of a broken heart."

It was much later that day, and Pippa had rowed herself to Innisfallen to seek sanity and wisdom from Revelin.

He handed her a linen cloth to wipe her eyes and blow her nose. More than a dozen such handkerchiefs lay at her feet in the garden in front of the island sanctuary.

"Why do you say that, my child?" he asked.

"I have tried several times to die of a broken heart, and each time, I just have to live with it."

"Then no doubt you were not meant to perish," he said. "You were meant to heal and go on."

"Ah. How noble that sounds. How simple."

"The words are simple. Not the deed." A strong breeze blew back his cowl to reveal the snow-white fringe of his tonsure.

She forced a weak smile. "You're good to me. I have no right to expect you to make up my mind for me. I suppose there is no decision. I must go to the de Laceys." Speaking the words aloud sent a shiver coursing through her.

"By the sound of it, they won't reject you."

Fresh heat came to her eyes, and she blinked back another onslaught of tears. "I don't suppose they will, since they came so far and brought an army with them. It is Aidan who cast me off," she added bitterly.

"Do you think he wanted to, lass?"

"He made it so neither of us has a choice."

"There is a choice to be made," the old canon said. "The choice of whether or not to trust. You have to be the one to make it."

He left her alone then, in the garden beneath the gray sky, breathing the heavy air. Very deliberately, aware of every movement, she got up and walked to the rocky shore of Innisfallen. She stepped into the light rowboat and cast off the rope, then sat back and closed her hands around the oars.

She did not row but drifted, lost in thought. She was in no hurry to go anywhere. Her gaze touched the bag containing all her belongings. She had dragged it along through all the years of her life, along all the miles she had traveled, filling it with objects that had meaning only to her. With a shaking hand, she took out the ruined brooch and pinned it to her shoulder.

How often she had imagined this day. The day she would meet her family. How different it had been in her imagination. Her heart skipped a beat, and she took a deep breath.

Steady. Think of things one at a time. Think of Richard.

The family connection explained much about him— why he appealed to her, why she was so comfortable with his servants, why she had understood a warning in Russian about a falling candle, why she seemed to know his house on the Thames.

A wave of wonder hit her as she realized the red-haired lady from her dreamy memories, her godmother, was Queen Elizabeth herself.

And Richard de Lacey, the most beautiful creature in the world, was her brother.

A pity he was the enemy, she thought with a sting of regret. Or was he? If she went to the de Laceys in Killarney town, would she be joining the English cause? Would she be any better than the Sassenach, the outsider come to invade the district?

Nay, she would always be like this boat, churning aimlessly, swept up by a storm of happenstance. Perhaps, she thought with a glimmer of hope, something good could come of this. She could appeal to the powerful de Laceys, possibly win sympathy for the Irish. She seized the oars and began to row, thinking harder.

The de Laceys were strangers to her. She had only other people's evidence that she was Philippa de Lacey. She could never know the truth for certain until she felt it in her heart.

Fat droplets of rain pelted her and pocked the surface of the lake. At first she felt no fear, only annoyance at being caught in the chilly rain. The weather, she thought bleakly, seemed somehow tied to the state of her heart. The weeks following her marriage to Aidan had been the golden days of high summer, days of sailing clouds and bountiful sunshine, nights of moonlit splendor in his arms.

Then the wind picked up, raising whitecaps on the surface of the water. She shrank from remembrances of how they had loved one another—deeply, with complete sureness…or so she had thought. In sooth their love had been built on his lies. She had been blissfully oblivious, a wanderer in the sunshine, unaware of a gathering storm in the distance. Ignorant of the destruction it could wreak.

A spear of lightning cleaved the sky, briefly illuminating the majestic, cloud-draped heights of Macgillycuddy's Reeks. The rain came faster, harder, in dense, icy sheets that blew her sideways and caused the boat to list.

"No. Oh God, no!" Her teeth chattered; she clenched them and prayed through them. "Please God, no…Hail Mary…"

She plunged into the chaos inside her head.

Hail Mary… Nurse's words pounded through her, even though Nurse was gone, sucked under the rushing river of seawater belowdecks. The dog kept barking and whimpering and staggering, but he was the only one left alive, so she clung to his soggy neck.

The ship bobbed, a little cork spilling this way and that. But after a while came a great cracking sound like the time the oak tree had fallen in Grandfather Stephen's garden.

When the lightning flashed again, she could see why the boat had stopped. A great sharp rock, tall as a church spire, had punched a hole in the hull. She clung to a fat, wet rope until another big wave came. When the next lightning struck, she could see another wave rising like a mountain of black glass.

The ship was lifted up and then plunged under. A whole army of stout barrels broke loose, rolling toward her along the crazily slanting deck. Something—the wind? a wave?—picked her up and hurled her into the sea. She flew through cold black space, and the water smacked her hard when she hit it....

A scream gathered in Pippa's chest as lakewater swamped the boat. She could barely make out the misty shoreline. The boat sat lower and lower in the water, finally tilting out of control before it began to sink.

She stopped screaming, for above the storm she heard the faint, hoarse yelp of a dog. Then the wind roared in her ears and she slid into the cold water, clinging only to a single oar as the boat was sucked out of sight.

She felt a twinge of regret, for the de Laceys had come a long way to see her. Then she felt nothing at all. The water closed over her, and beneath the surface she could not hear the storm. Beneath the surface it was quiet as a crypt.

At the height of the storm, two horsemen met at an abandoned shepherd's hut in the hills overlooking the lake. Aidan dismounted and led his horse into the dim shelter while Fortitude Browne, the lord constable of Killarney, did the same.

Aidan had come alone, even though he knew full well a troop of rain-drenched English soldiers waited below the hill. Browne was a man of great caution when it came to his own safety.

Aidan had disbanded his army and sent them into the hills, for that was one of Browne's first demands.

For a few moments they stood facing each other, not speaking, letting the cold rain drip down their faces. Even in the faint light of the storm-darkened evening, Aidan could see the hatred in Browne's lean, ascetic face. He had thin lips and high cheekbones, a cruel set to his jaw and hard eyes. Browne kept his hand on his sword, but Aidan did not fear he'd use it. Not here. Not now.

"You'll not believe this from me," Aidan said, "but I am sorry Felicity died."

"You should have thought of that when you murdered her."

Aidan had expected the fierce accusation. "Nay, sir, I did not, but my guilt runs deep. Felicity would be alive today if we had never met, never married."

Browne made a strangled sound in his throat and turned away, bracing his arm on the sagging lintel of the doorway and glaring out at the lashing storm. "You wanted to marry that beggarwoman. That is why you pushed Felicity to her death."

Aidan took a breath between his clenched teeth. "My lord, we both knew she lost her reason. She took her own life. There was a witness, an Englishman like yourself."

A light mist of steam rose from the sod walls of the hut. "Perhaps," Aidan went on, "I am responsible for failing to see her madness."

"You *drove* her mad, you murderer! The state of her mind is your fault!"

Aidan felt no anger, only a great weariness. "Did you

ever think of the state of her mind when you were forcing Felicity to kneel on stones or recite scripture through sleepless nights?"

Silence. The rain came so hard that it almost obscured the lake. Pippa hated storms, and now that Aidan had learned about her past, he understood why. He was glad she had gone to Innisfallen while the weather was still fair. As he himself had done, she sought solace on the lake island. Revelin would give her warmth and shelter; he would counsel her to go to the de Laceys.

Clenching his jaw against the searing pain of losing her, Aidan waited for Browne to speak again.

The older man turned back, running a hand through his thick, wet hair. "Do not sully my daughter's name by speaking it aloud. According to the letter you sent with the Venetian woman, you are prepared to accept my terms."

Aidan sent him a humorless smile. "I would not go so far as to call your demands for my surrender *terms*."

"You deserve to be drawn and quartered, made to die by inches." Browne's voice shook, and Aidan felt a stab of sympathy. The man had lost a daughter, after all. She had been beautiful, unearthly and rare with her pale, perfect skin; in her lucid moments, before she had begun to hate Aidan, she had been pleasant and mild.

"So long as you agree to uphold your side of this devil's bargain," Aidan said, "I will come along as your prisoner."

"Excellent." Browne went to the door and waved his arm. Four men approached, shoving Aidan up against the sod wall and clamping cold iron manacles around his wrists and ankles.

Browne led his horse out into the driving rain. He

smiled. "I shall take great pleasure in sending the O Donoghue Mór to hell."

A subtle scent hung in the air. Pippa shuddered, amazed and frightened by a dream so vivid that it would include smells.

It was a scent that her every instinct recognized and responded to, for it was the sweet, unique scent of her mother.

Her mother.

Had she drowned? Was she in heaven? Philippa dragged her eyes open to banish the dream. She wasn't dreaming, but lying in a strange bed. How had she gotten here?

She blinked in the candlelight and noted, just in passing, the rich yet unfamiliar bed hangings.

Then she turned her head on the pillow and saw the woman.

Mama.

Her heart knew at last she had come home.

Seized by horror and joy and dread and relief, Philippa pushed herself up and drew her knees to her chest. She stared, and the small, dark-haired woman stared back.

Candlelight flickered at the edge of Philippa's vision. She caught her breath and closed her eyes, and from out of the darkness surged a memory so clear, it might have happened only yesterday.

Mama clasped her to her breast, and Philippa inhaled the nice laundry-and-sunshine scent of her.

"Goodbye, my little darling," Mama whispered in a curious, broken voice. "I want you to take this with you to remind you of your mama and papa while you're away."

Mama pinned the gold-and-ruby brooch to the front of Philippa's best smock. Then she removed the little knife that fit inside it. "I'll keep this part. It's safer that way, Philippa—"

"Philippa," the woman said.

Her eyes flew open. "I am Philippa," she said in a soft, wondering voice. "Your daughter."

"Yes. Oh, yes, my darling, yes." The dark-haired Englishwoman wrapped her arms around Philippa. The scent of laundry and sunshine was as evocative now as it had been more than a score of years ago. It was the smell of comfort, of love, of Mama.

But between them gaped decades of estrangement. Philippa broke away. Lark de Lacey seemed to sense her need to adjust and let her go.

A moment later, a man stepped into the room. Lark went to meet him, taking his hand and bringing him to the bedside. At first Philippa thought it was Richard, but then she saw that this man was older, though golden and handsome as no other man she had ever seen.

Papa.

She sat perfectly still, while they stood unmoving, staring at her as she stared back. A storm of feelings swept over her: shock, confusion, disbelief, rage, helplessness and a terrible impotence.

But no love.

When she looked at them, she simply saw two handsome strangers with tears coursing down their cheeks.

Finally she found her voice. "You are Lark and Oliver de Lacey, the Earl and Countess of Wimberleigh."

"We are." Lord Oliver's eyes were blue. Not the deep flame-blue of Aidan's, but a lighter color, shining with tears as he took her hand and pressed it to his heart. Then he gave her his special kiss: cheek, cheek, lips and nose, always in that order. And her heart began to remember the gentle touch of this man.

"Welcome home, Philippa, my darling daughter."

"He's been condemned to die?" Donal Og asked the contessa in a low whisper. He had ridden fast and hard from Ross Castle, and the smells of rain and wind clung to his clothing and abundant blond hair.

She regarded him silently, solemnly, unable to speak until she conquered the lump in her throat. She did at last, swallowing with effort, and took his big hand in hers. "I tried my best. Wimberleigh tried. Fortitude Browne refuses to retract his accusations against Aidan."

Donal Og ripped his hand from hers and drove his fist into his palm. She winced at the force of the blow. The lamp hanging from a hook in the stables lit him strangely, making him appear even larger and more forbidding than usual. She had arranged to meet him here, in secret, near the Killarney residence of Oliver de Lacey.

"All my cousin ever wanted," Donal Og said slowly, "was to be left in peace. His father would not permit that. Nor would Felicity. Even now that they are dead, they grip him in a stranglehold."

Her heart wept for him, wept for them all. "My love, I am so sorry."

He grasped her shoulders, pulling her against him. "I must go to Aidan, break him free of his confinement—"

"No!" she broke in. "Ah, Donal Og, I feared you would try this. It is the one sure way to get both yourself and Aidan killed. He won't go with you, and you will be caught."

"I'll force him to go with me. I'm bigger than he, always have been."

"You are bigger than everyone. But think with your brains, not your brawn. If you spirit Aidan away, Fortitude Browne will water all of Kerry with innocent blood."

Donal Og clenched his jaw savagely and glared at the roof. "God, ah, God, kill me now so I do not have to see this through to the end."

She pressed a shaking hand to his cheek. "Find your strength, beloved. You will need it." A wave of frustration broke over the contessa. She had used all her skills, all her charm, all her considerable powers of duplicity, to convince the constable to show mercy. "All I could wrest from Fortitude Browne," she confessed, "was his assurance that no one else would be put to the sword."

He paced the floor. "I should put *him* to the sword. Consign him to hell with his crazy daughter."

"Stay the impulse. Fortitude Browne is crooked; we simply need proof." And we need it, she thought urgently, before he carries out his sentence against Aidan. "I will write again to the lord deputy in Dublin."

Donal Og released his breath in a deflated hiss. He opened his arms and gave her a weary smile. "Come here, my sweet."

She went willingly, finding comfort in the embrace of a man unlike any other she had ever known.

"What is to become of us?" he whispered into her hair. "Shall I disappear like a wounded wolf in the wilds of Connaught, where even the Sassenach fears to go?"

"I have a better idea. Wimberleigh has outfitted one of his ships for you and all the others who wish to leave. It's provisioned for six months, and an expert crew will take you anywhere you choose."

He chuckled. "Iago will be pleased to hear that. He'll have us bound away for the West Indies before the week is out."

"Is that such a horrible fate?"

He held her tightly. "It is if it means leaving you, my sweet."

From the dregs of despair, she summoned a ray of hope. "Is there some law that says I cannot come with you?"

He stared down at her, thunderstruck and finally, cautiously, joyful. "You would do that? You would follow me into exile?"

"I would follow you to the ends of the earth if need be," the contessa said.

"Ah, sweet Rosaria. That is probably where I shall take you," said Donal Og.

In the morning Pippa rose and dressed after a surprisingly sound sleep. As she washed and dressed, she pondered the extraordinary events of the day before.

Her muscles ached from battling the storm, and her mind was filled with all that had happened. According to Oliver, an English patrol had spied her fighting her way to the shore. Alerted by the hounds, one man had dived in just as she'd gone under. She had been half drowned, unconscious. They had brought her directly to the manor house.

After seeing her parents, she had taken a little broth and wine, then fallen into a deep sleep.

The hall of the Killarney house was lofty and sun washed. The aftermath of the storm left the surrounding gardens glistening and green. She was not surprised to see a tall, long-coated hound cavorting in an orchard. A borzoya. Papa raised them. And now she remembered that the handsomest of each litter was called Pavlo.

All three of them—Oliver and Lark and Richard—shot to their feet when Philippa entered the room. Her gaze took them in with a slow, troubled sweep.

"Will you break your fast with us?" Lark asked.

"I'm not hungry." Philippa heard impatience in her voice, so she tempered it with a forced smile. "Thank you." With cold hands she unpinned the brooch and pushed it across the table toward Lark. "I'm told this was once yours."

With an unsteady hand, Lark took out a small, sharp dagger with a jeweled hilt and slid it neatly into the sheath formed by the brooch. "Before me, it belonged to the Lady Juliana, your grandmother."

Philippa nodded. "She used to sing to me. I remember snatches of a Russian song."

Lark moved to hand back the brooch, but Philippa shook her head. "There was a time when that pin was the only thing I treasured. The only thing that belonged to me. The only thing I belonged to."

Richard asked, "Were the jewels stolen from it?"

"I sold them. To survive."

He reddened and looked down at his hands. Oliver made an anguished sound in his throat. "Philippa. My daughter. God, when I think how you have suffered, I despise myself. Somehow I should have sensed you were alive. Should have scoured all of England to find you."

Her throat felt tight, yet she remained distant from these three lovely, well-fed, well-bred people. "You know nothing about me," she said. "Nothing about the pain I suffered, nothing of the loneliness that ached inside me for so many years."

"We ached, too, Philippa," Lark said softly. "More than you know. We grieved for the daughter we thought we had lost."

Philippa hardened her heart. Long habit made her resist loving them. "Circumstances, it seemed, were not kind to any of us."

"We were deprived of each other's love," Oliver said, "but a miracle brought us together again."

"Not a miracle," Philippa said. "Aidan O Donoghue."
It hurt just to speak his name. "My husband."

Her pronouncement caused Lark's face to pale and
Oliver's to redden. Richard raked a hand through his
glossy golden hair. "So you married him."

"An Irish rebel lord," said Oliver.

"A Catholic," said Lark.

"A man!" Philippa slapped her hands down on the
table. "You speak to me of love simply as something that
exists between us due to blood ties. That is not love. That
is kinship. Love is something that is earned by constancy
and caring and attention and devotion, the very things
Aidan—not you—gave me."

"Philippa," Lark began, "we would have—"

"But you did not." She felt no anger, just exasperation.
"It was no one's fault. The point is, Aidan loved me when
I was dead to you. He loved me when I was at my most
unlovable. When I was poor and crude and homeless and
hungry. When I cared about nothing save who my next
gull was going to be."

Lark wept, making no sound, the tears falling from
eyes so like Philippa's that it was like looking in a mirror.

"I'm sorry for your grief," Philippa said. "No one is
to blame. I love my husband." Aye, that was true. The
shock of learning about the de Laceys had made her lash
out at Aidan, but she knew she had never stopped loving
him. "Nothing you can say will change that."

Richard cleared his throat. "Then why were you on the
lake, fleeing toward Killarney?"

His question made her blood run cold. She touched her
throat and began to pace. She trembled inside, wondering if she had destroyed Aidan's love by leaving him
with such bitter words.

Finally she faced her parents and brother. "He told me of your summons."

"It was a summons of the heart," Oliver said. "I wanted to see my daughter." He smiled. That smile brought back all the magic of her earliest years. For a moment he was no stranger, but her loving Papa who made her laugh. He formed shadow puppets on the nursery wall at night. He showed her how to hide her porridge from Mama when she didn't want to eat it. He gave the most special good-night kisses in the world—cheek, cheek, lips and nose, always in that order.

"I haven't yet told you," Oliver said, "how beautiful you look to me."

The words tugged her heart in one direction, but thoughts of Aidan pulled her in the other. "Perhaps," she said, "we will have plenty of time to visit one another in the future, but I must get back to Aidan. Your troops have threatened his people. I intend to stand at his side and fight—"

"My sweet," Oliver said, coming around the table and holding out his hands for her, "I can't let you go back to him."

"Don't touch me!" She snatched his dagger from its sheath.

He held out his hands, palms up in supplication and surrender. "Philippa, you misinterpret me. We have no objection to your marriage to Aidan O Donoghue, no more than we object to Richard's marriage to Shannon, hasty though it was. I admire your loyalty to the Irish."

"Then why do you try to keep me from Aidan?" She set down the dagger. "I'm going to Ross Castle within the hour."

"Philippa," said her mother, "he isn't there. He isn't at Ross Castle."

Dread pulsed at her temples. "What do you mean? What has happened? Have you killed him?"

It was Richard who spoke. He sank to one knee before her. "Philippa, the Browne family believes Aidan murdered his wife. Everyone knows Felicity was mad. She took her own life, but her father is demanding retribution. Fortitude sent Aidan an ultimatum. He was ordered to surrender Ross Castle to me and himself to Constable Browne."

She lifted her chin. "Aidan would never capitulate to Fortitude Browne."

Oliver clenched his jaw, then spoke with obvious distaste. "The constable promised to burn out one Irish family a day until the O Donoghue Mór surrendered."

"Can't you do something?" she asked her father. "You're a lord, a noble. Intervene, restrain Mr. Browne—"

Oliver pressed his hands on the table and took a deep breath. "I have tried. I was up all night writing letters, sending riders to Cork and Dublin and London, but I have no authority here. In Browne's district, I have little more influence than a common soldier."

Looking heartsick, Richard rose to his feet. "The O Donoghue Mór knows he is outnumbered, low on provisions, facing a starving winter."

"What are you saying?" Philippa asked in a harsh voice she did not recognize.

Oliver clasped her hands in his. "My sweet, he had no choice. Last night he disbanded his army and surrendered to Fortitude Browne."

She wrenched her hands from his and fled to a window seat, wishing she could curl up into a ball and make the world go away. "He knew," she said, whispering to herself, beginning to shake. "He knew this would happen."

Yesterday morning, she had almost guessed. He had loved her as if it were the last time.

She felt Lark's hand on her shoulder. "God," Philippa said, "oh God, he wanted me to leave in anger, wanted me to come to you. He had it all planned. Why didn't I see it?"

"He didn't want you to guess," Lark said.

Philippa looked up. *Make it better, Mama.* But no one could make this hurt go away. "What happens now?" she asked. "Will they send him to trial at Dublin Castle?"

Lark and Oliver exchanged a glance.

"Don't lie," Philippa said. "I'll never forgive you if you lie."

It was Oliver who told her what she had dreaded in her heart all along.

"They're going to hang him."

The ominous pulsebeat of a drum broke the morning quiet. The air held a chill as Aidan walked along the *boreen* toward the scaffold on a hill a mile distant.

In deference to his rank, his hands and feet were unfettered, and he wore his deep blue mantle to ward off the early autumn cold. His hair blew long and loose over his shoulders.

A troop of twelve soldiers surrounded him: three in front, three in the rear, three on each side. Constable Browne rode in grave, black-clad Puritan dignity in the fore. There was no real danger of his trying to escape. With sharp, well-honed cruelty, Browne had ensured his cooperation.

Irish people lined the roadway, slowing the pace of the death march. Their weeping was loud and unabashed and filled with a uniquely Celtic mix of curses and blessings.

The sound of his grieving people was curiously affecting. He tried to feel nothing, but they made it so hard. He had done his best for them.

At least he would not have to face Pippa today. More than ever, he was certain he had made the right choice—forfeiting her love and driving her into the bosom of her family.

"God bless you, my lord!" The cries came from all quarters, each side of the road, in front and behind, even above, for a group of defiant youngsters had climbed the trees to call to him and to hurl beechnuts at the soldiers.

"And a blessing on all of you as well." His voice rang strong and clear, and despite a bone-deep weariness he held himself tall. He had not slept the night before, had spent the entire time hammering out the terms of surrender.

Ross Castle and all its dominions were to fall under the jurisdiction of Richard de Lacey. Iago and Donal Og and the O Donoghue hundred were to be granted clemency and sent into exile. Iago swore he would find paradise. Donal Og challenged him to do so.

Fortitude Browne had agreed to all this readily enough. What he truly wanted was the death of the O Donoghue Mór.

And that was what he would get.

They were yet a quarter mile or so from the scaffold on a lonely hill high above Lough Leane when he heard the sound of galloping hooves.

He looked over the heads of his escort and saw a lone rider coursing toward him down a green hill. He knew of only one person who sat a horse and rode with such reckless clumsiness.

Pippa.

Ah, Christ, why had she come?

She barreled headlong through the crowd of onlookers. Fortitude reined his tall horse. "See here now—"

"Bugger off," she said, plowing her mount boldly across the *boreen* and forcing the soldiers to halt. She dismounted in an awkward billow of skirts and pushed past the escort.

How lovely she looked, flushed and golden as a ripe peach, her eyes moist, her lips parted. She stopped before Aidan, choked out a wordless cry and flung her arms around his neck.

All the love he had ever felt for her came flooding back, rising through him like a fountain of sunshine. He kissed her and tasted her and called himself seven times a fool for loving her so much.

"Your trick didn't work," she whispered against his mouth. "You tried to destroy our love. So losing you would not hurt me."

As she spoke, the soldiers stopped, shuffling their feet and staring at the amazing spectacle. But Aidan forgot them, just as Pippa had seemed to.

"You should have known better than that, Aidan. I will love you till the end of time."

Heat built in his throat, and his eyes smarted. He cupped her cheek in his palm and pressed her head to his chest. "What a selfish brute I am," he said. "To hold you in my arms. One last time." Yet he did not want her to see him die, to see the cart kicked out from beneath his feet, to see the noose tighten and his body jerk and his feet dancing helplessly in the empty air.

"Say farewell to me here and now. I beg you, don't finish this journey with me."

She pulled back and stared up at him. "How can you do this? How can you choose death rather than running for your life?"

He gestured at the crowd of Irish people. "If I fled, they would pay the price."

He could read on her face the words she would not speak: *Then let them pay!* And some small, selfish part of him agreed with her.

But he felt oddly invigorated now, holding the woman he loved. He even managed to smile.

"Beloved," he said, "it's too late for us. Ironic, isn't it? When first we met it was too early. Now it is too late."

She drew in a long, tremulous breath. "I begged my father and brother to intervene on your behalf."

"It is useless. Do not hold the de Laceys responsible for this. They have no authority to stop Constable Browne."

"So you have given up on everything. On Ross Castle. On us. On life. I won't let you!"

He skimmed his knuckles down her flushed cheek and nearly winced at the sweetness of touching her. "Not on us, beloved. Never on us. My faith has undergone many tests, but here's something I believe with all my heart. Love never dies. I'll never find a love so perfect as ours in this world or the next."

"Oh God!" She turned her head and pressed her lips desperately to his palm.

"I will be with you always," he said. "That is my pledge. That is my promise. I'll be in the warm breeze when it caresses your face. In the first scent of springtime, in the song of the meadowlark, in the flutter you get in your heart when you feel joy or sorrow." His hand slid down to cup her chin. Bending, he laid his lips over hers solemnly, silently, while in the background his people sobbed.

"Do you trust me, Pippa?"

She stared at him, looking as if the slightest movement

would cause her to shatter. Yet deep in her eyes, deeper than the grief, deeper than the despair, he saw the strength of her love burning like a bright, steady flame.

"Thank you," he whispered, knowing she would understand his gratitude. "Thank you for that."

It was her last gift to him. A pure, shining love that would carry him across whatever time and space was doomed to separate them.

Fortitude Browne barked an order. Gently but firmly, a soldier drew Pippa out of the way. For a moment, wild panic flared in her eyes, but Aidan steadied her with his gaze.

"Let go, my darling, my beloved," he whispered. He drank in a last image of her—wide eyes, soft lips, wind-tossed curls. Hand outstretched toward him. He wanted to take her hand, wished it could pull him into a magic, invisible world, but he made himself say again. "Let go."

She stepped back out of the way. The soldiers reprised their formation around him. To the steady thump of a drum, the O Donoghue Mór was led off to die.

From the Annals of Innisfallen

———◦◦———

How does a man tell of a life that is ended before the best part has begun?

I, Revelin of Innisfallen, find it impossible to pluck the words from my grieving, sad brain this day.

Likewise I find it impossible to pray, a grave problem for a man who has devoted his life to study and prayer. But what good is faith when injustice triumphs in this evil world? What good is prayer when the Vast Almighty is eternally deaf to my pleas on behalf of the best man I've ever known?

I had hoped the letter from Dublin and my efforts—and those of the contessa—to act upon it would bear fruit, but alas, it is too late.

It is time for me to go now, to be with the O Donoghue Mór in his most desperate hour.

And may the Almighty—deaf or not—have mercy upon the soul of my lord Aidan.

—Revelin of Innisfallen

Sixteen

"It's called a *what?*" Donal Og demanded, looking at the object Iago had drawn on the ship's deck with a bit of charcoal.

"A pineapple," Iago said. *"Anana."* He looked with exaggerated patience at the contessa. "Señora, you should tell your husband to pay closer attention. There are many new things for him to see in the islands of the Caribbean. He will be lost without my guidance."

The contessa sent an adoring smile to Donal Og. "My husband had a long night. Give him time. We are only one day out of Ireland. We have weeks of sailing ahead of us."

Iago shook his head in mock desolation. "Woe betide us all," he said. "This ship will sink 'neath the weight of all your sappy sentiment."

"This ship is unsinkable," the contessa said with a superior sniff, watching a pair of dolphins leap near the high bow. "It is a barque of the Muscovy Company Line. Lord Oliver assured me it is completely seaworthy and provisioned for up to six months."

"It will take us less than six weeks to reach San Juan

if the winds stay as fair as they are today. Ah, San Juan! Amigos, a new life awaits us!" Iago threw out his arms to encompass the gallowglass and crew and all those from the castle who had chosen to sail with them into exile.

The heavy tread of boots on wooden planks rang down the decks. Everyone looked toward the lofty stern-castle quarters.

There, gripping the gilded rail, his black hair flying on the trade winds, stood the O Donoghue Mór.

Huzzahs went aloft like signal flags. Aidan smiled, but it was an empty smile, one he did not feel in his heart. His heart was grieving for the woman he had left behind.

With mystifying abruptness, his captors had marched him not to the scaffold on the hill, but to a well-provisioned ship docked in Dingle Bay.

The deliverance had been arranged, he had learned, by Oliver de Lacey. Aidan would never know what pressure Wimberleigh had brought to bear, but the lord protector in Dublin had learned the name of the man who had been diverting Crown revenues for his own use. Only moments before Aidan's sentence was to be carried out, soldiers had raced in from Dublin with the lord deputy's decree. Fortitude Browne was sent in disgrace back to England.

It proved to be a bittersweet triumph. Though Browne was gone, so was Aidan's domain. He could never reclaim Ross Castle, for another Irish-hating constable would take Browne's place. Aidan was alive, yet without Pippa, a part of him was cold and dead. He knew he would never see her again. Doubtless her father did not consider an exiled Irish chieftain to be a suitable husband. Aidan did not blame him. A daughter like Philippa was to be cherished and kept close, not sent adventuring to an unknown land.

Did she realize he had been spared, or had her family deemed it best to let her think he had died? He pictured her, couched in the splendor provided by her father's riches, wistful with memories of him. He wondered how long he would last in her heart. A year? Two? She was young yet; perhaps she would learn to love another. But surely—please God—not with the wild, all-consuming love she had shared with Aidan.

The very thought tore into his heart, and he winced with the pain of it. Yet he did not wish her ill. One day, when the pain dulled to a persistent ache, he would allow himself to picture her with another man, a conventional Englishman who would offer her a safe, quiet affection for years to come. A man she could trust never to leave her.

But could she forget the incandescent passion that had lit their world for one magical summer season?

"Sail ho!" A boy shouted the alert from the topmast. "Fine on the port bow!"

All hands rushed to the rails. Sailors scrambled up the ratlines. Two colored flags flapped from the sterncastle of the approaching ship.

"They're signaling us to come about," the ship's master said. "They want to reconnoiter."

Aidan's instincts took fire with apprehension, but he deferred to the captain.

"It's a law of the sea," the wind-battered Englishman declared, and orders were whistled down the deck. "We must parlay with them. God help us all."

Aidan stayed where he was, gripping the rail on the high deck while the two ships drew closer. He braced himself for the worst. Somehow, Browne had found a way to haul him back to the gibbet.

Then he blinked in the bright glare of the autumn sun,

thinking his eyes deceived him. A woman stood on the midships deck of the other vessel, waving her arms while the sunlight shone down on wild curls the color of beaten gold.

"Pippa!" His shout rolled like thunder across the water. It seemed an eternity before the two vessels drew close enough.

He paced and swore, certain the moment would never arrive. Even when the ships came within boarding distance, time seemed to crawl.

"Patience, my lord," said Iago. "It takes time to steady the ships for a boarding plank."

"By God, I don't have time." He seized a rope that hung from a yardarm. Despite protests from all quarters of the ship, he tied on a grappling hook and sent it swinging toward the other ship. The hook caught on the third try, and without the slightest hesitation he looped a pulley over the rope and swung across.

He smacked against the midships rail, bounced off and hit the archers' screen. Heedless of his bruises, he scrambled over and landed on his feet in front of Pippa.

Her eyes sparkled like the brightest stars. "I can't believe you're here," she said.

He gave a whoop of pure joy and captured her in his arms. They kissed long and so lustily that it took a firm, fatherly clearing of the throat to interrupt them.

Aidan pulled back to face a grinning older man who stood with his arm around a petite woman. Lark de Lacey wore Pippa's brooch pinned at her shoulder.

"You are Lord and Lady Wimberleigh," he said. "My thanks. I owe you my life."

"For our daughter, that was not enough. She would give us no peace until we brought her to join you on this wild adventure."

"That is true," she said, tucking herself against his chest. "I can't imagine why any of you thought I would be content to sit and embroider handkerchiefs while you sailed the world." She pressed a hand to Aidan's broad chest. "I was born to go adventuring with him." She glanced at the companion ship, where all the men and the contessa had gathered at the rail.

Taking a deep breath, she broke away from Aidan and kissed her mother and father. All three of them wept and pretended not to notice. "Give Richard my love, and embrace my other brothers and the sister I've yet to meet," said Philippa.

"With the Muscovy fleet at our disposal," Oliver said, "I'll bring them for many visits." Shamelessly, he wiped his face with his sleeve.

Lark touched the ugly gold brooch. "Are you sure you don't want this as a keepsake?"

Pippa smiled up at Aidan. "I don't need it, Mama. Not now. I have all that I need."

"I could have it reset with jewels and bring it to the Indies."

"Mama, I would welcome a visit from you," Pippa said. "But as for the brooch, keep it for your grandchildren."

Aidan's chest ached with hope. "We'll see to it that you have plenty of those."

"Then take our love, and nothing more," Oliver said.

"That is all we need," said Pippa.

Aidan caught the pulley and swept her up in his embrace. Her arms went around his neck, clinging as he stepped to the rail. With a laugh of pure exultation, he leaped. They were suspended for a moment over seething open water. Then, on a great gust of wind, they swung across to the other ship and landed with a lurch on deck.

"You're carrying me," she said breathlessly.

"Aye."

"I can't believe you're carrying me."

"Again," he reminded her.

"Yes, again," she said, and laughed.

From the Annals
of Innisfallen

❧❧❧

Sure and it's a high blessing entirely to clap my poor old eyes on such a thing as Lord Richard has brought me this day, two years after he came on as master of Ross Castle.

It's a sheaf of letters and sketches from an island in a sea called Caribbee. It was delivered by Lord and Lady Wimberleigh, who have just returned from a visit to the islands to see their first grandbabe.

Imagine a place so littered with green islands that men of purpose can simply land on one and claim it as their own! That is exactly what Aidan O Donoghue and his merry adventurers did. Iago was their guide; they provisioned at San Juan—Iago had a bride waiting for him there, heaven be praised!—and set off on their own. They founded a great plantation where they grow enormous, tall cane that yields sugar, of all things. I'd never have believed it, except Wimberleigh's ship was fair crammed with sugar syrup when it arrived.

In addition to the blessing of a fat, black-haired baby boy, my Lady Philippa is increasing again. She and the contessa are both due to be delivered in the same month, and may the Great Almighty protect them and the bairns.

The O Donoghue Mór says I'm not to call him the O Donoghue Mór any longer and that I'm to stop chronicling his life. He tells me that all this constant, unremitting bliss makes for very boring reading these days.

And so I close this thick tome, built with laughter and tears, on a life well lived, on a triumph of the heart. I shall write no more of Aidan O Donoghue because he asked it.

But I shall think of him often, aye, and that is a thrice-made promise. I shall ever think of him as the O Donoghue Mór, last of the great chieftains, the twilight lord.

—Revelin of Innisfallen

* * * * *

Dear Reader,

Something old is new again. I'm very proud to bring you a brand-new edition of the Tudor Rose trilogy, first published about fifteen years ago.

These books were researched and written when the information superhighway was a mere goat track. But the themes and story lines are timeless, exemplifying the things that have always been important to me, both as a reader and a writer: fiercely honest emotion, ordinary people experiencing extraordinary challenges, passion and adventure, and of course, a satisfying ending.

In addition to being revised, the books have been given a new lease on life with fresh titles. Book One, originally titled *Circle in the Water* and now called *At the King's Command,* was the winner of a Holt Medallion. Book Two, originally called *Vows Made in Wine,* is now *The Maiden's Hand,* and was a finalist for a RITA® Award. Book Three, also a RITA® Award finalist, was titled *Dancing on Air* and is now *At the Queen's Summons.*

It is with pleasure that I invite you to step back in time, into a vanished world of court intrigue, where sovereigns ruled by the scaffold, and men and women dared to risk everything for love.

Susan Wiggs

2009

#1 *New York Times* bestselling author

SUSAN WIGGS

portrays the intrigue and majesty of
King Henry VIII's court in her classic Tudor Rose trilogy.

| August 2009 | September 2009 | October 2009 |

SAVE $1.00

on the purchase price of one book in Susan Wiggs's Tudor Rose trilogy.

Offer valid from July 28, 2009, to October 31, 2009. Redeemable at participating retail outlets. Limit one coupon per purchase. Valid in the U.S. and Canada only.

52608735

5 65373 00076 2   (8100)0 11613

MSWWHISTRI09CPN

SUSAN WIGGS

32617	FIRESIDE	___ $7.99 U.S.	___ $7.99 CAN.
32571	SUMMER BY THE SEA	___ $7.99 U.S.	___ $7.99 CAN.
32510	THE HORSEMASTER'S DAUGHTER	___ $7.99 U.S.	___ $7.99 CAN.
32504	THE CHARM SCHOOL	___ $7.99 U.S.	___ $7.99 CAN.
32493	SNOWFALL AT WILLOW LAKE	___ $7.99 U.S.	___ $9.50 CAN.
32475	DOCKSIDE	___ $7.99 U.S.	___ $9.50 CAN.
32414	THE WINTER LODGE	___ $7.99 U.S.	___ $9.50 CAN.
32325	SUMMER AT WILLOW LAKE	___ $7.99 U.S.	___ $9.50 CAN.
32147	THE OCEAN BETWEEN US	___ $7.50 U.S.	___ $8.99 CAN.
32019	HOME BEFORE DARK	___ $6.99 U.S.	___ $8.50 CAN.
32190	LAKESIDE COTTAGE	___ $7.50 U.S.	___ $8.99 CAN.
32286	TABLE FOR FIVE	___ $7.99 U.S.	___ $9.50 CAN.
66938	ENCHANTED AFTERNOON	___ $6.99 U.S.	___ $8.50 CAN.
66710	A SUMMER AFFAIR	___ $6.99 U.S.	___ $8.50 CAN.

(limited quantities available)

TOTAL AMOUNT	$ _____
POSTAGE & HANDLING	$ _____
($1.00 for 1 book, 50¢ for each additional)	
APPLICABLE TAXES*	$ _____
TOTAL PAYABLE	$ _____

(check or money order—please do not send cash)

To order, complete this form and send it, along with a check or money order for the total above, payable to MIRA Books, to: **In the U.S.:** 3010 Walden Avenue, P.O. Box 9077, Buffalo, NY 14269-9077; **In Canada:** P.O. Box 636, Fort Erie, Ontario, L2A 5X3.

Name: _____
Address: _____ City: _____
State/Prov.: _____ Zip/Postal Code: _____
Account Number (if applicable): _____

075 CSAS

*New York residents remit applicable sales taxes.
*Canadian residents remit applicable GST and provincial taxes.

MIRA®

www.MIRABooks.com

MSW0809BL